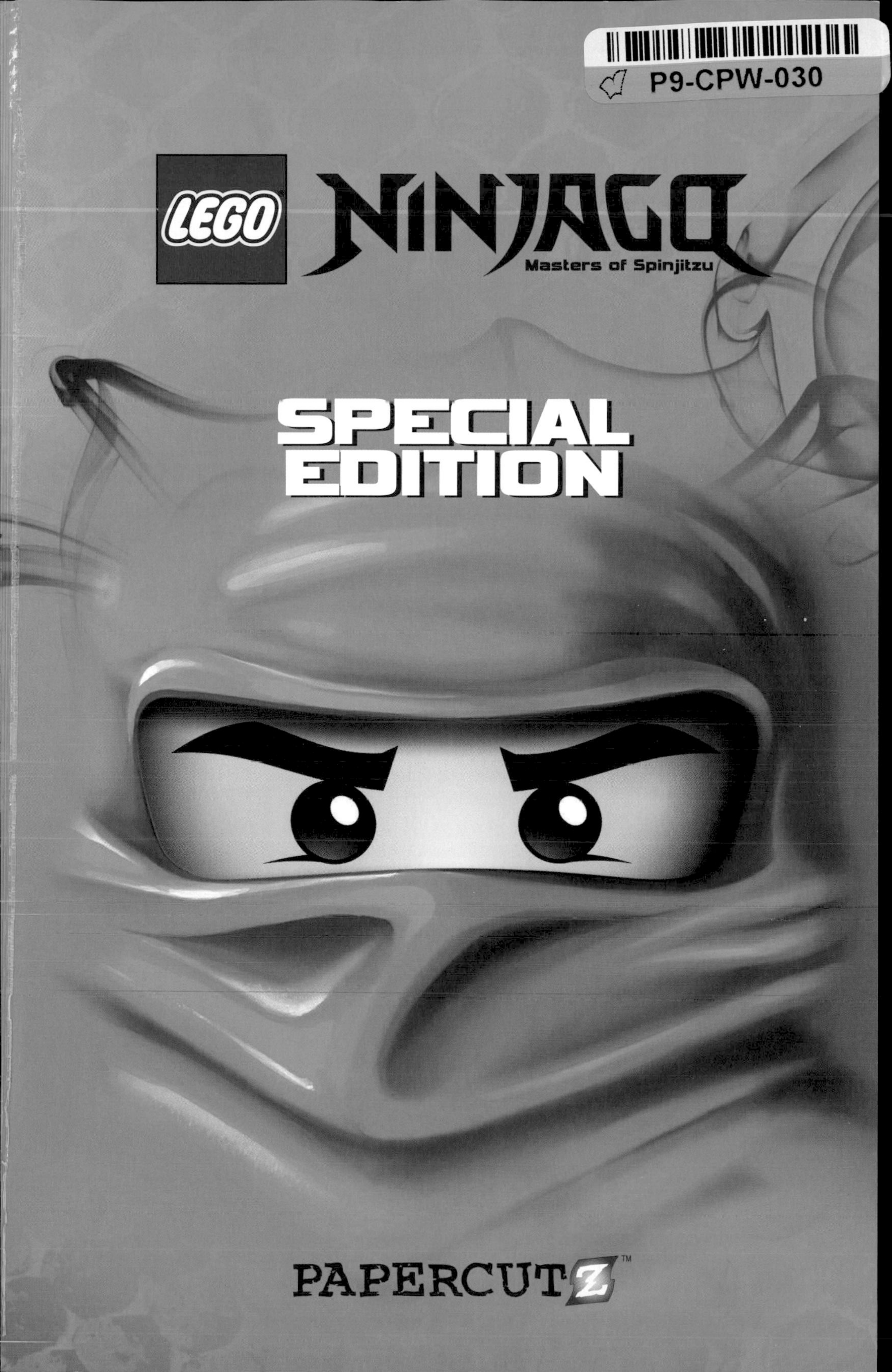
LEGO
NINJAGO
Masters of Spinjitzu
SPECIAL EDITION
PAPERCUTZ™

LEGO® GRAPHIC NOVELS AVAILABLE FROM PAPERCUTZ™

ALL-NEW! FULL-COLOR GRAPHIC NOVEL!
LEGO NINJAGO
Masters of Spinjitzu
"THE CHALLENGE OF SAMUKAI"
GREG FARSHTEY
PAULO HENRIQUE
PAPERCUTZ

LEGO NINJAGO #1

ALL-NEW! FULL-COLOR GRAPHIC NOVEL!
LEGO NINJAGO
Masters of Spinjitzu
"MASK OF THE SENSEI"
GREG FARSHTEY
PAULO HENRIQUE
PAPERCUTZ

LEGO NINJAGO #2

ALL-NEW! FULL-COLOR GRAPHIC NOVEL!
LEGO NINJAGO
"RISE OF THE SERPENTINE"
GREG FARSHTEY
PAUL LEE
PAPERCUTZ

LEGO NINJAGO #3

ALL-NEW! FULL-COLOR GRAPHIC NOVEL!
LEGO NINJAGO
Masters of Spinjitzu
"TOMB OF THE FANGPYRE"
GREG FARSHTEY
JOLYON YATES
PAPERCUTZ

LEGO NINJAGO #4

ALL-NEW! FULL-COLOR GRAPHIC NOVEL!
LEGO NINJAGO
Masters of Spinjitzu
"KINGDOM OF THE SNAKES"
GREG FARSHTEY
JOLYON YATES
PAPERCUTZ

LEGO NINJAGO #5

ALL-NEW! FULL-COLOR GRAPHIC NOVEL!
LEGO NINJAGO
Masters of Spinjitzu
"WARRIORS OF STONE"
GREG FARSHTEY
JOLYON YATES
PAPERCUTZ

LEGO NINJAGO #6

Coming Soon!

ALL-NEW! FULL-COLOR GRAPHIC NOVEL!
LEGO NINJAGO
Masters of Spinjitzu
STONE COLD
GREG FARSHTEY • JOLYON YATES
PAPERCUTZ

LEGO NINJAGO #7

SPECIAL EDITION
LEGO NINJAGO
Masters of Spinjitzu
IT ALL BEGINS HERE--
WITH "THE CHALLENGE OF SAMURAI" AND "THE MASK OF THE SENSEI"
GREG FARSHTEY
PAULO HENRIQUE
PAPERCUTZ

LEGO NINJAGO SPECIAL EDITION #1
(Features stories from NINJAGO #1 and #2.)

ALL-NEW! FULL-COLOR GRAPHIC NOVEL!
LEGO NINJAGO
Masters of Spinjitzu
"DESTINY OF DOOM"
GREG FARSHTEY
JOLYON YATES
PAPERCUTZ

LEGO NINJAGO #8

LEGO® NINJAGO graphic novels are available in paperback and hardcover at booksellers everywhere.

LEGO® NINJAGO #1-8 are $6.99 in paperback, and $10.99 in hardcover. LEGO NINJAGO SPECIAL EDITION #1 is $10.99 in paperback only. You can also order online at www.papercutz.com. Or call 1-800-886-1223, Monday through Friday, 9 – 5 EST. MC, Visa, and AmEx accepted. To order by mail, please add $4.00 for postage and handling for first book ordered, $1.00 for each additional book and make check payable to NBM Publishing.
Send to: Papercutz, 160 Broadway, Suite 700, East Wing, New York, NY 10038.

LEGO NINJAGO graphic novels are also available digitally wherever e-books are sold.

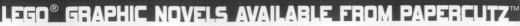

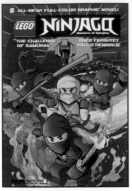

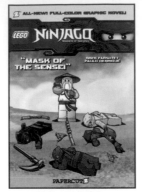

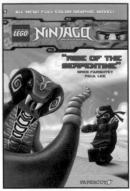

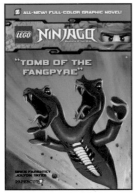

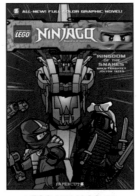

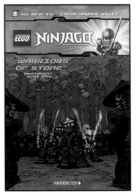

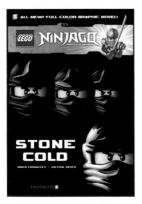

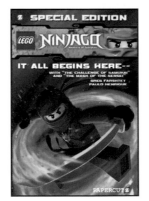

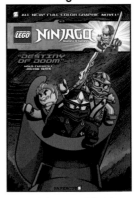

LEGO NINJAGO
Masters of Spinjitzu

SPECIAL EDITION #2
"RISE OF THE SERPENTINE" AND "TOMB OF THE FANGPYRE"

Greg Farshtey • Writer

Paul Lee, with Space Goat and Paulo Henrique; Jolyon Yates • Artists

Laurie E. Smith and JayJay Jackson • Colorists

PAPERCUT︎Z™
New York

LEGO ® NINJAGO Masters of Spinjitzu
SPECIAL EDITION # 2

"Rise of the Serpentine"
GREG FARSHTEY – Writer
PAUL LEE
with SPACE GOAT and
PAULO HENRIQUE – Artists
LAURIE E. SMITH – Colorist
CHRIS CHUCKRY – Color Assist
BRYAN SENKA and
TOM ORZECHOWSKI – Letterers

"Tomb of the Fangpyre"
GREG FARSHTEY – Writer
JOLYON YATES – Artist
JAYJAY JACKSON – Colorist
BRYAN SENKA – Letterer

MICHAEL PETRANEK – Production
BETH SCORZATO – Production Coordinator
MICHAEL PETRANEK – Associate Editor
JIM SALICRUP
Editor-in-Chief

ISBN: 978-1-59707-698-2

Printed in the USA
June 2013 by Lifetouch Printing
5126 Forest Hills Ct
Loves Park, IL 61111

Papercutz books may be purchased for business or promotional use. For information on bulk purchases please contact Macmillan Corporate and Premium Sales Department at (800) 221-7945 x5442.

Distributed by Macmillan

First Printing

FSC
www.fsc.org
MIX
Paper from responsible sources
FSC® C112431

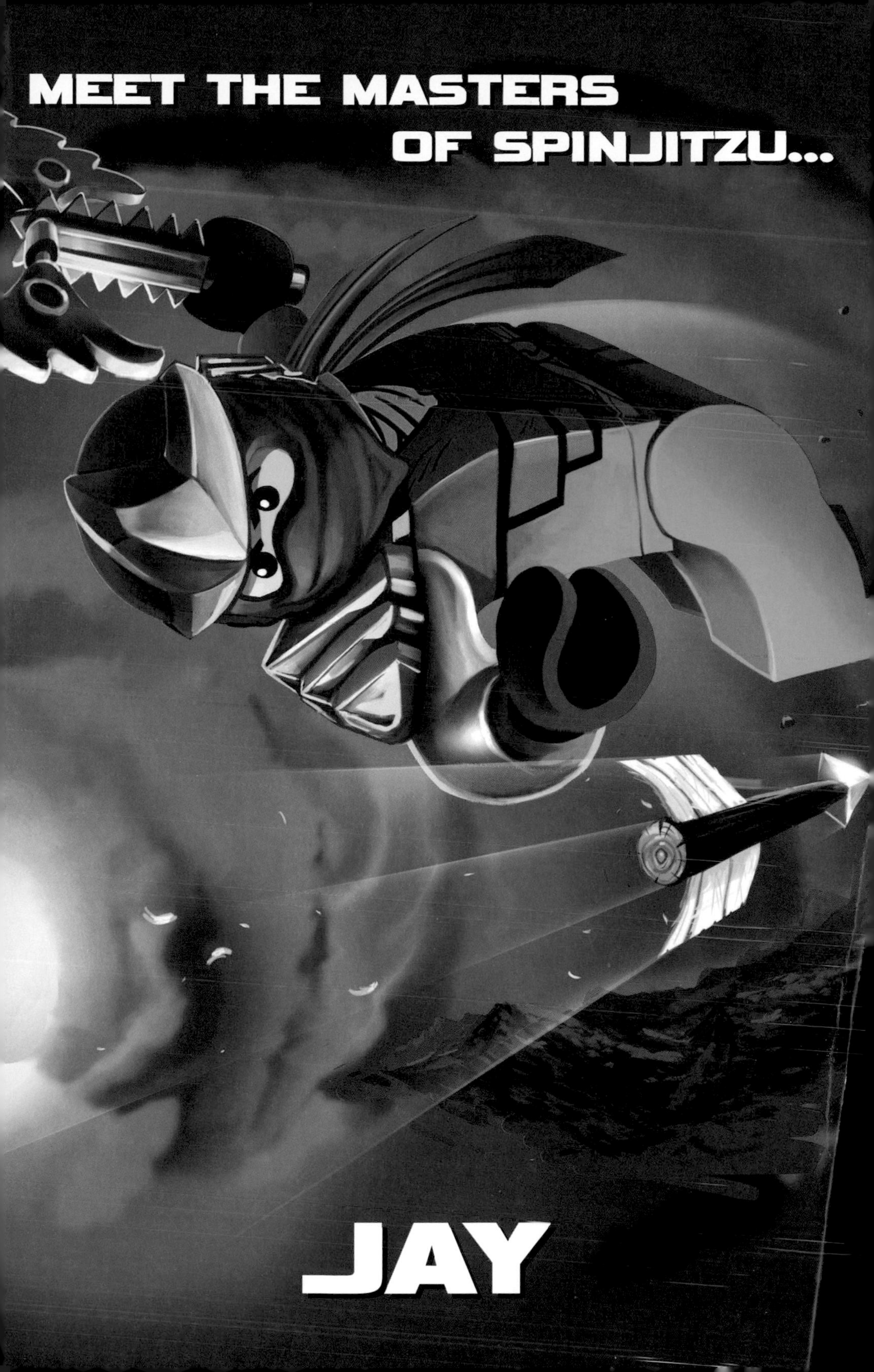
MEET THE MASTERS
OF SPINJITZU...
JAY

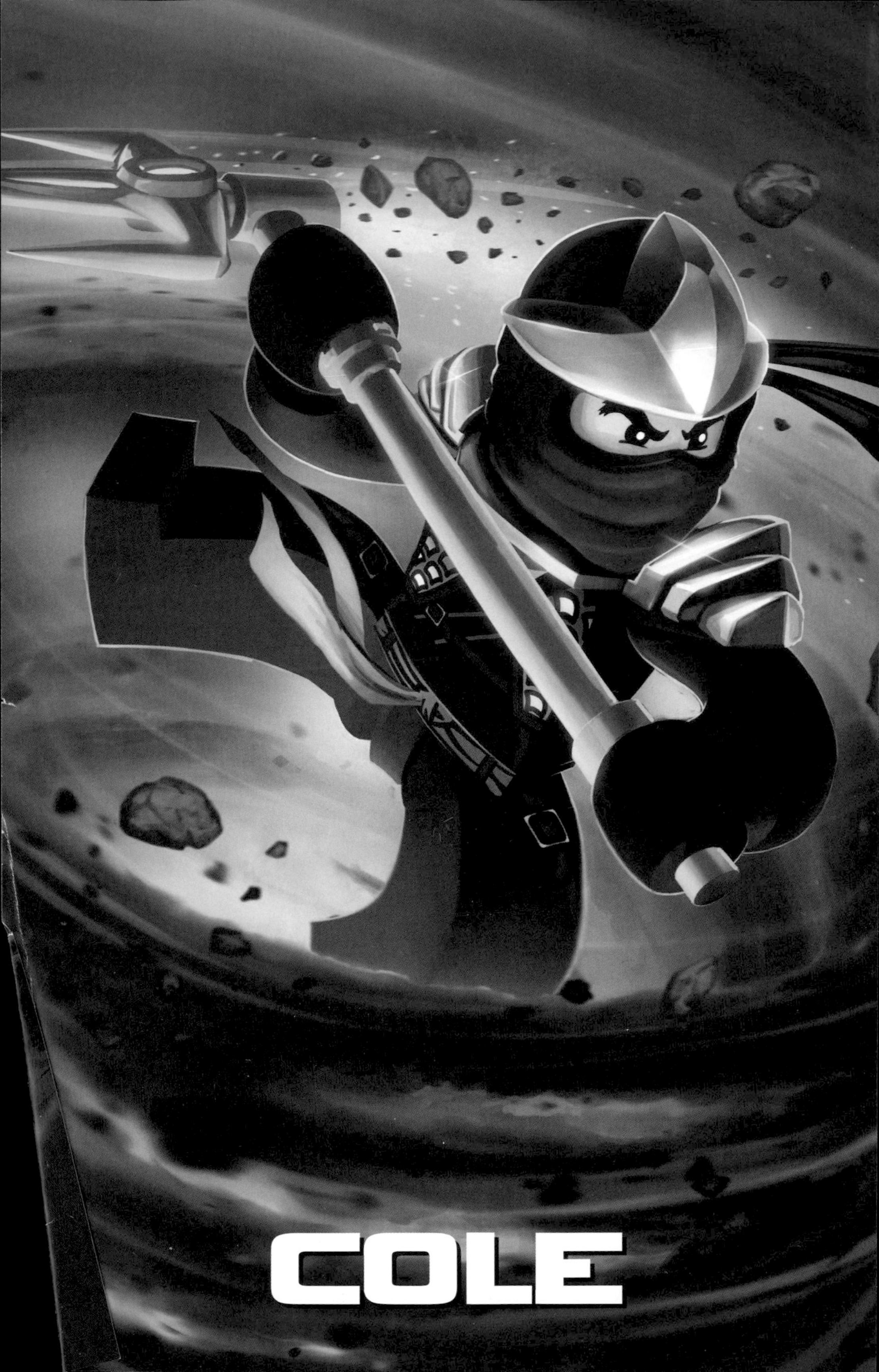

COLE

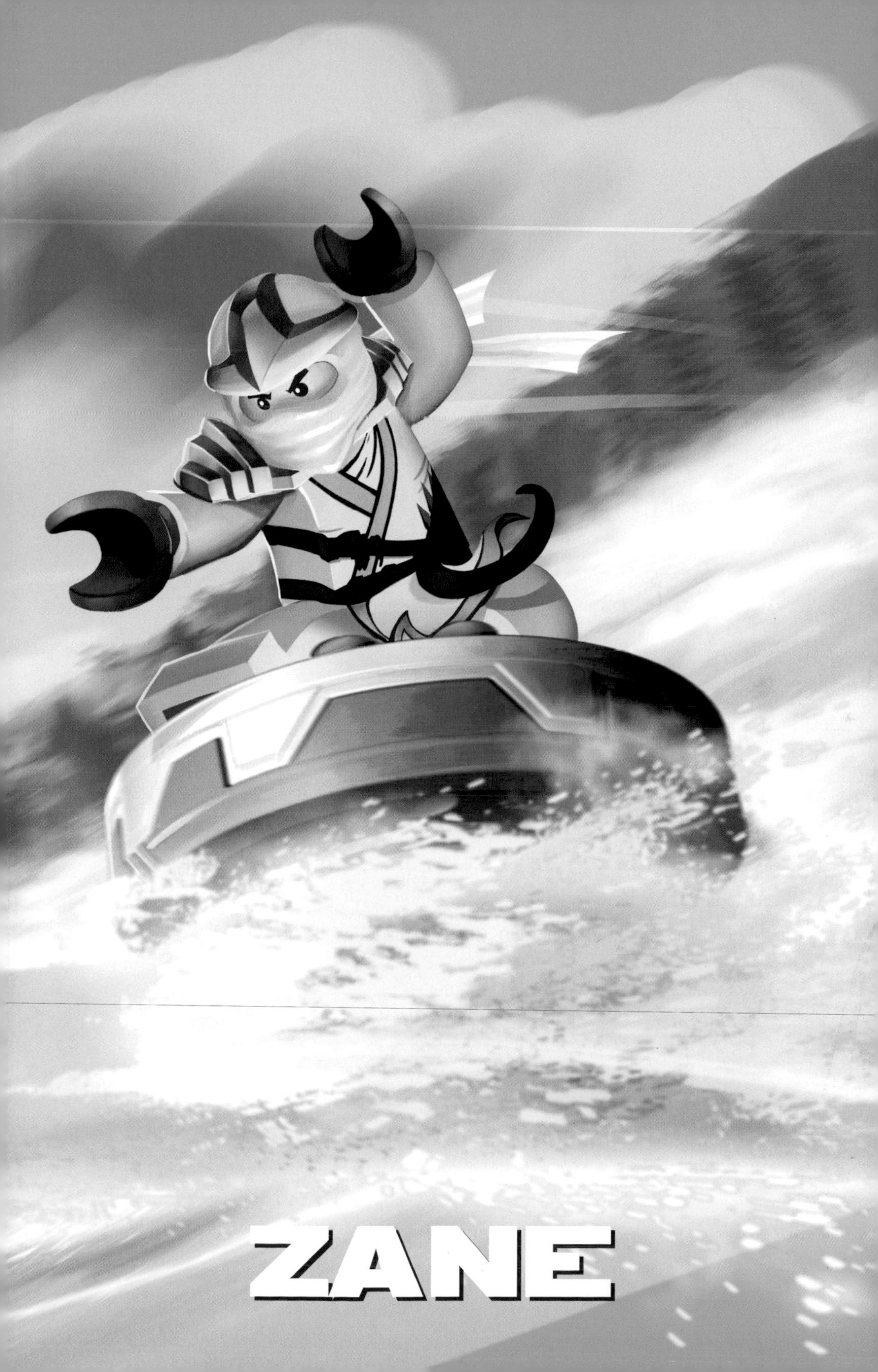
ZANE

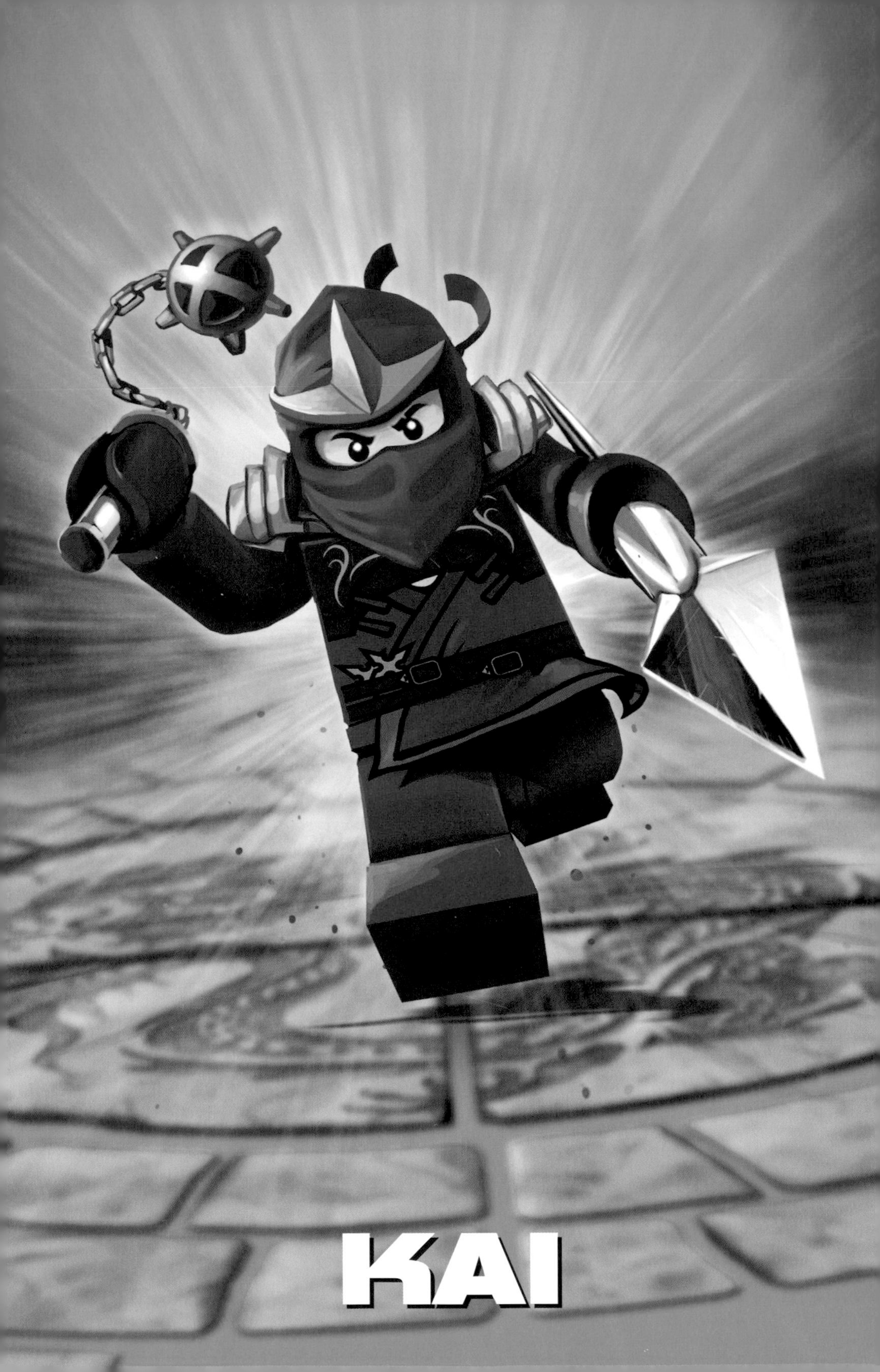

KAI

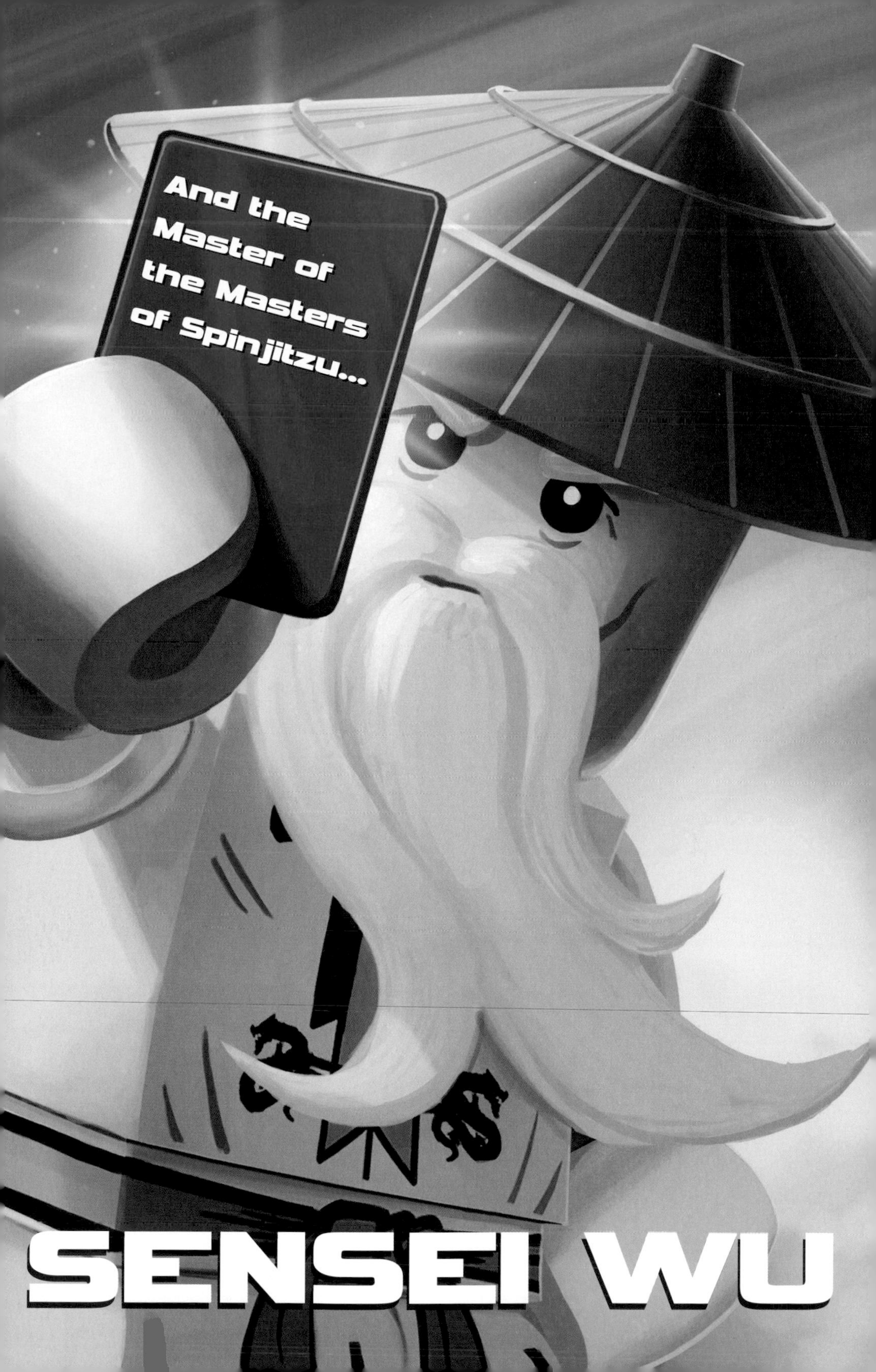
And the Master of the Masters of Spinjitzu...
SENSEI WU

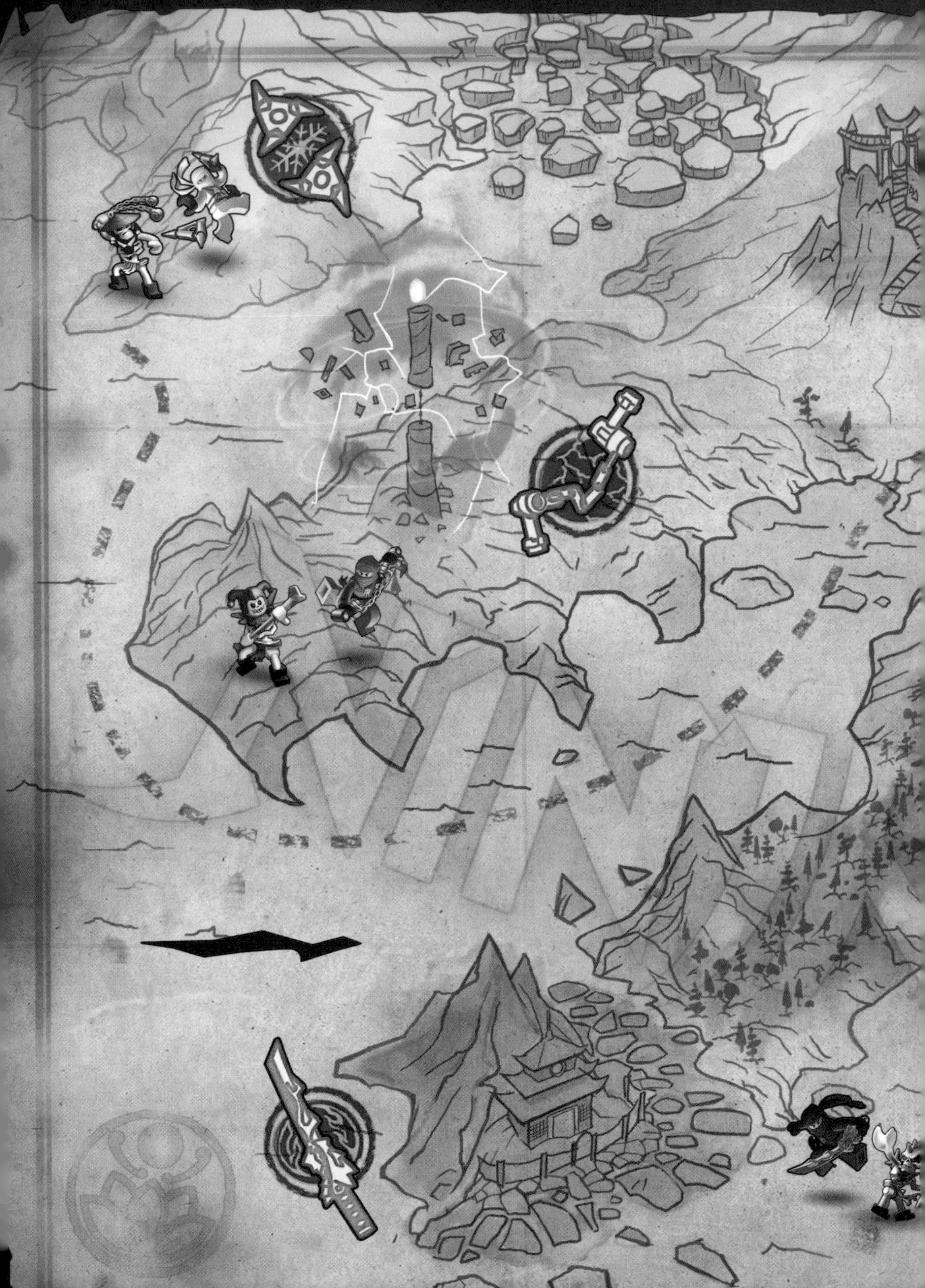

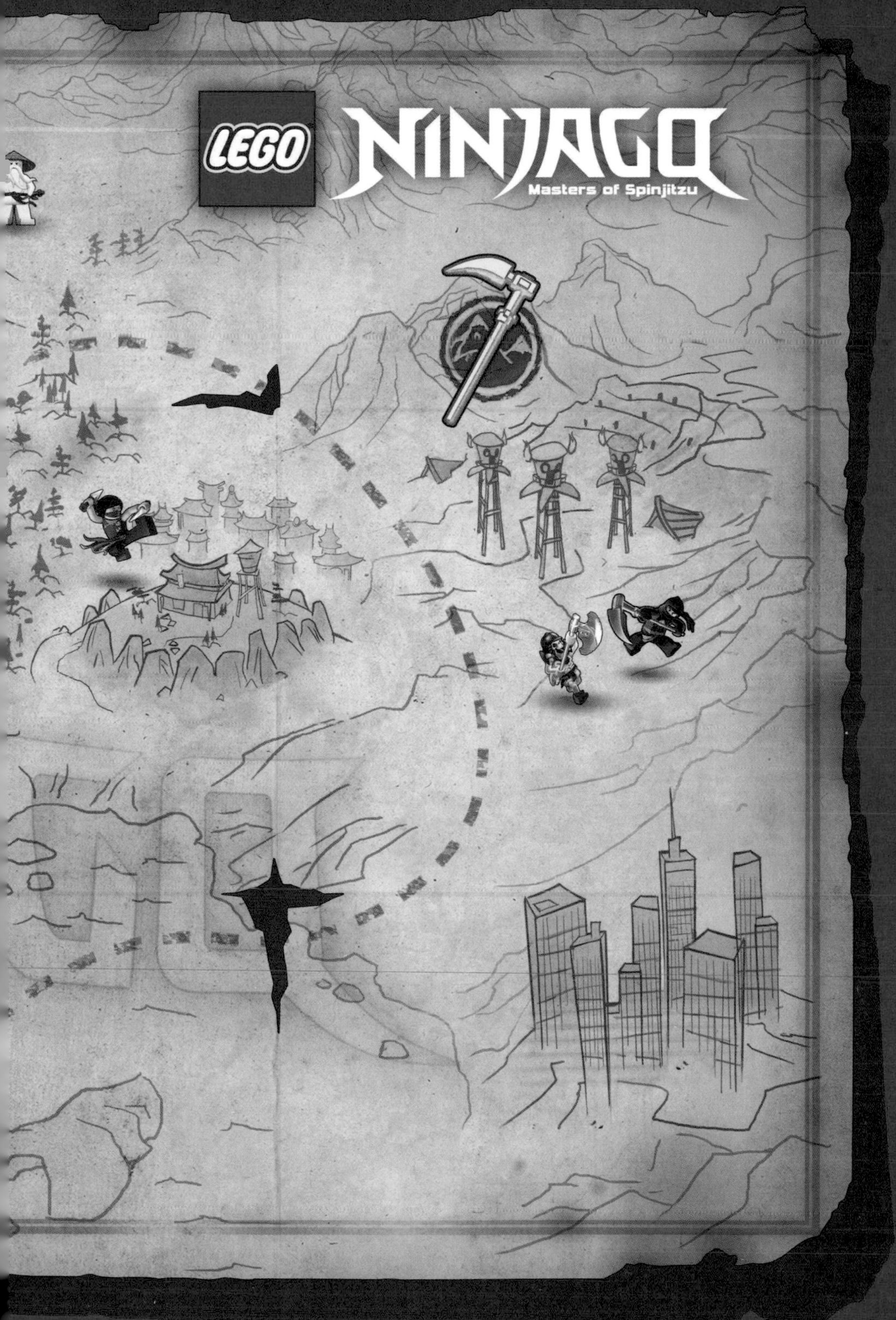
LEGO
NINJAGO
Masters of Spinjitzu

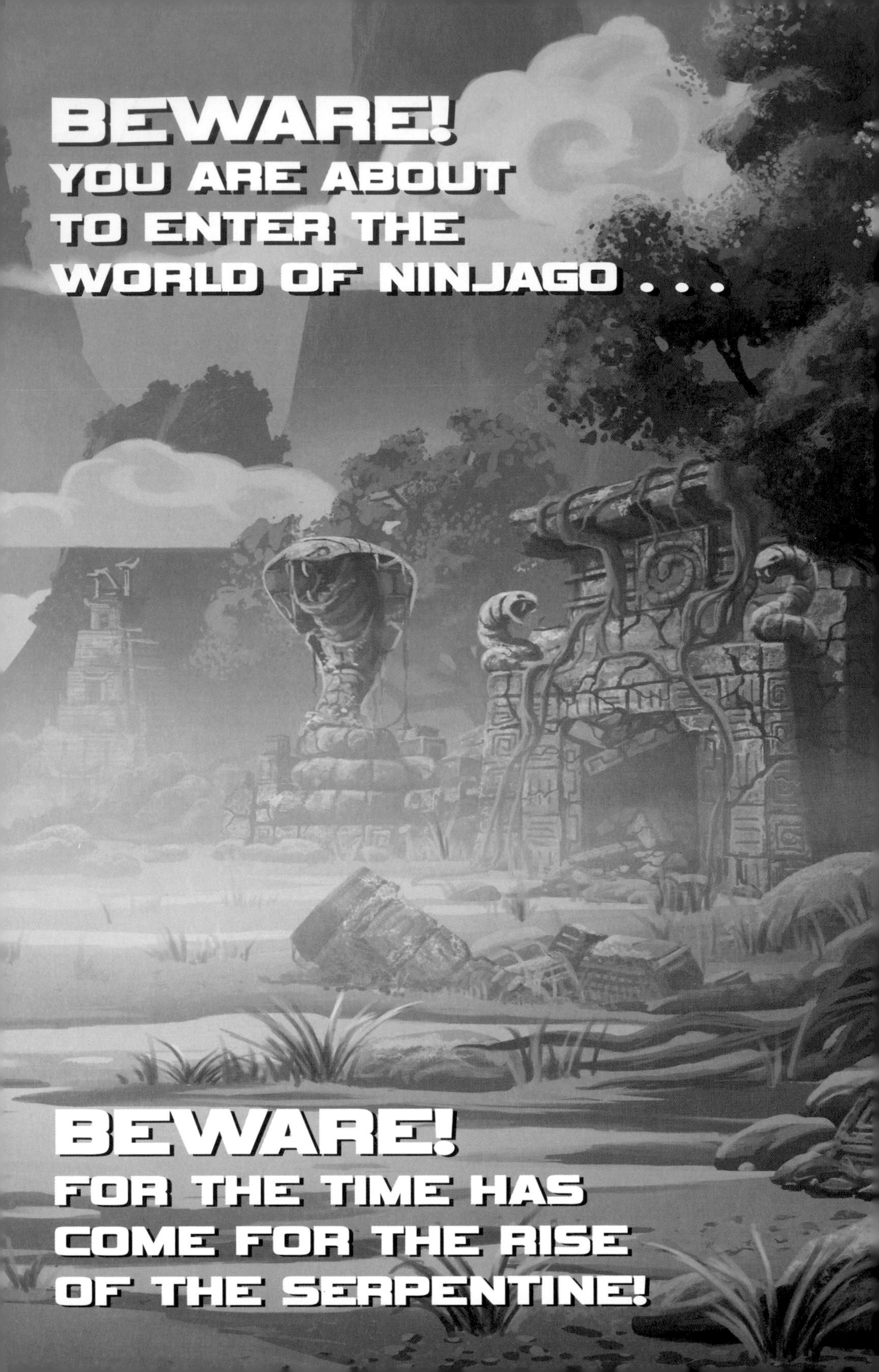

BEWARE!

YOU ARE ABOUT TO ENTER THE WORLD OF NINJAGO . . .

BEWARE!

FOR THE TIME HAS COME FOR THE RISE OF THE SERPENTINE!

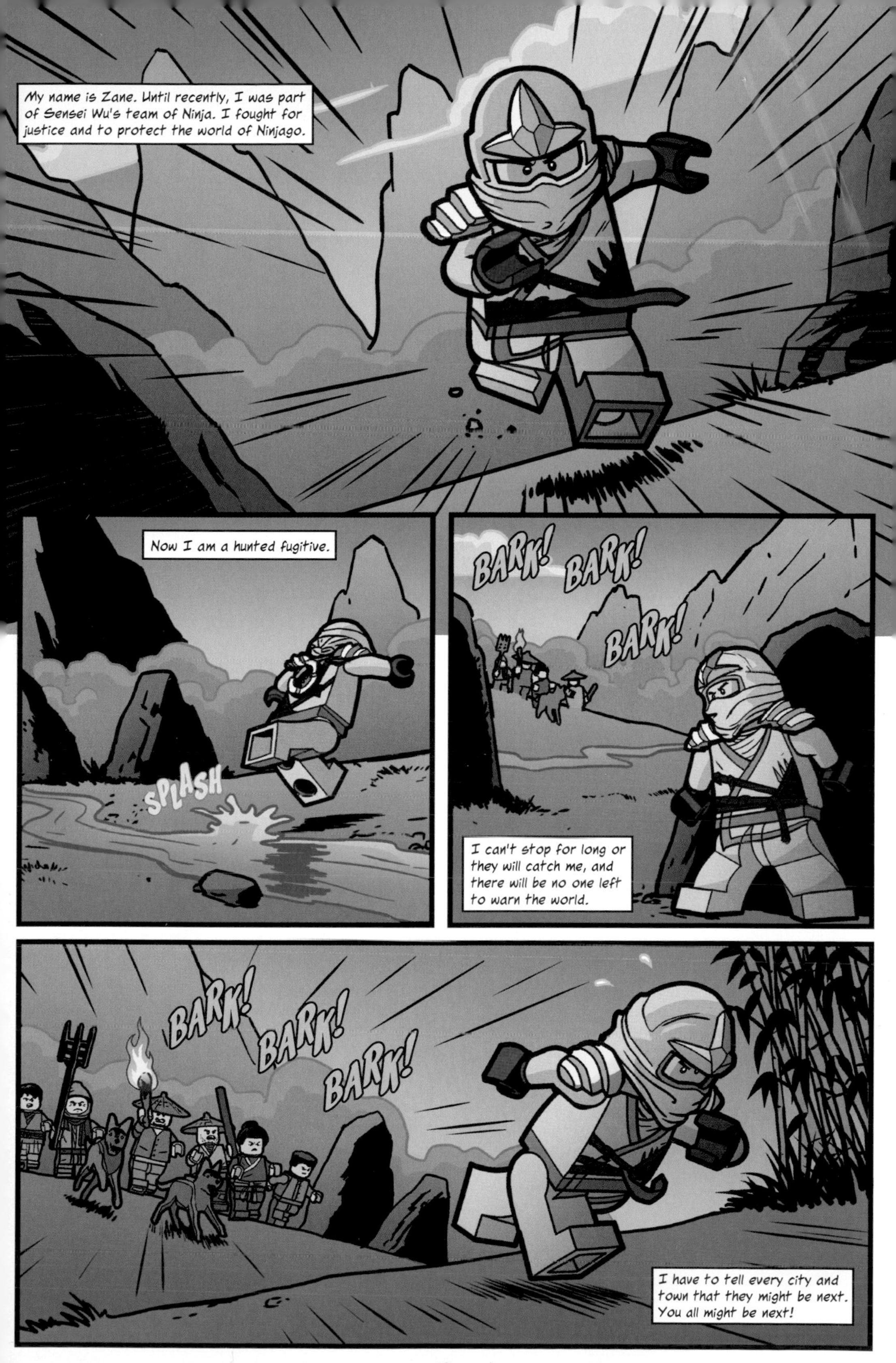
My name is Zane. Until recently, I was part of Sensei Wu's team of Ninja. I fought for justice and to protect the world of Ninjago.
Now I am a hunted fugitive.
SPLASH
BARK! BARK!
BARK!
I can't stop for long or they will catch me, and there will be no one left to warn the world.
BARK!
BARK!
BARK!
I have to tell every city and town that they might be next. You all might be next!

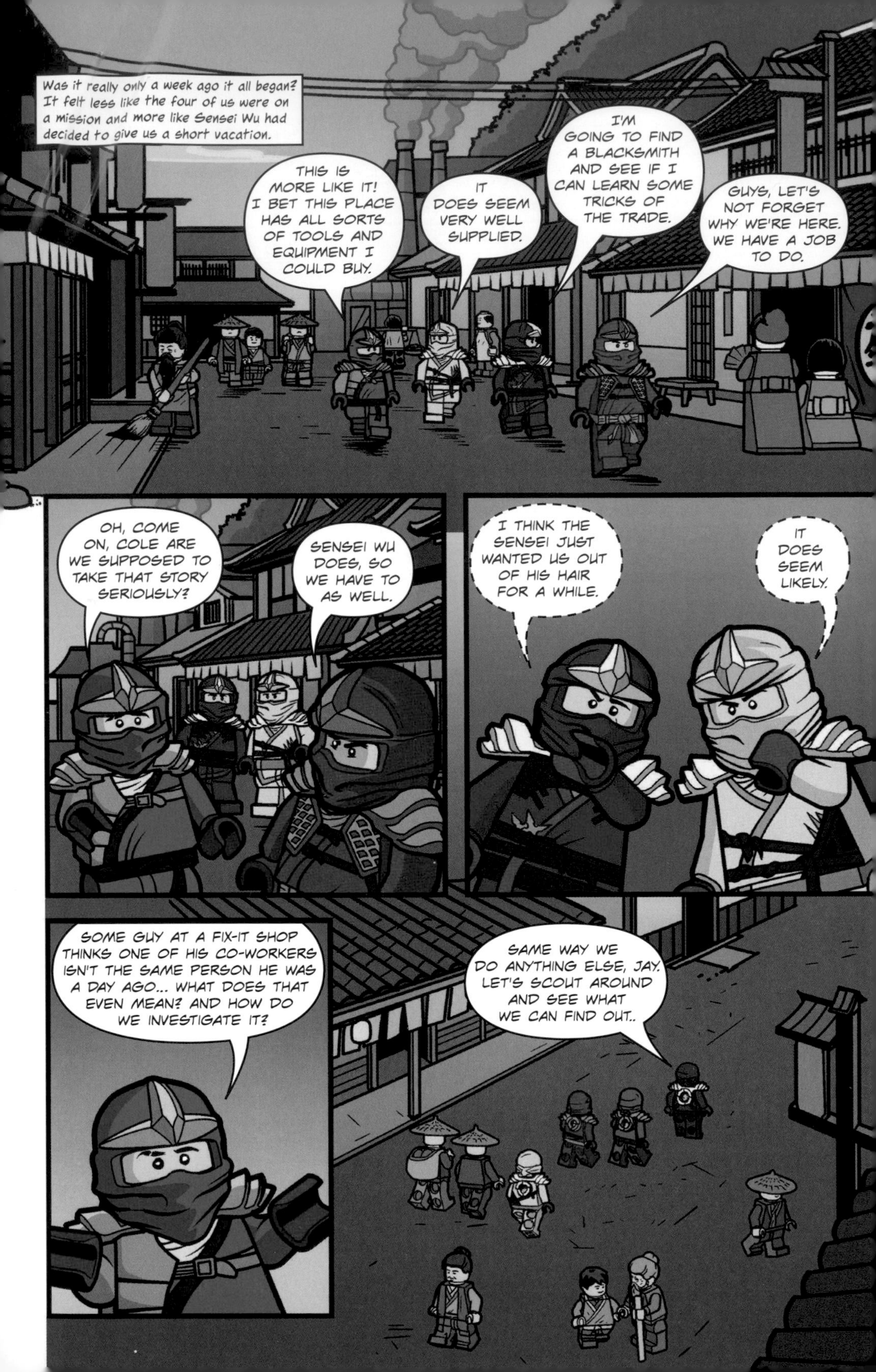
Was it really only a week ago it all began? It felt less like the four of us were on a mission and more like Sensei Wu had decided to give us a short vacation.
THIS IS MORE LIKE IT! I BET THIS PLACE HAS ALL SORTS OF TOOLS AND EQUIPMENT I COULD BUY.
IT DOES SEEM VERY WELL SUPPLIED.
I'M GOING TO FIND A BLACKSMITH AND SEE IF I CAN LEARN SOME TRICKS OF THE TRADE.
GUYS, LET'S NOT FORGET WHY WE'RE HERE. WE HAVE A JOB TO DO.
OH, COME ON, COLE ARE WE SUPPOSED TO TAKE THAT STORY SERIOUSLY?
SENSEI WU DOES, SO WE HAVE TO AS WELL.
I THINK THE SENSEI JUST WANTED US OUT OF HIS HAIR FOR A WHILE.
IT DOES SEEM LIKELY.
SOME GUY AT A FIX-IT SHOP THINKS ONE OF HIS CO-WORKERS ISN'T THE SAME PERSON HE WAS A DAY AGO... WHAT DOES THAT EVEN MEAN? AND HOW DO WE INVESTIGATE IT?
SAME WAY WE DO ANYTHING ELSE, JAY. LET'S SCOUT AROUND AND SEE WHAT WE CAN FIND OUT..

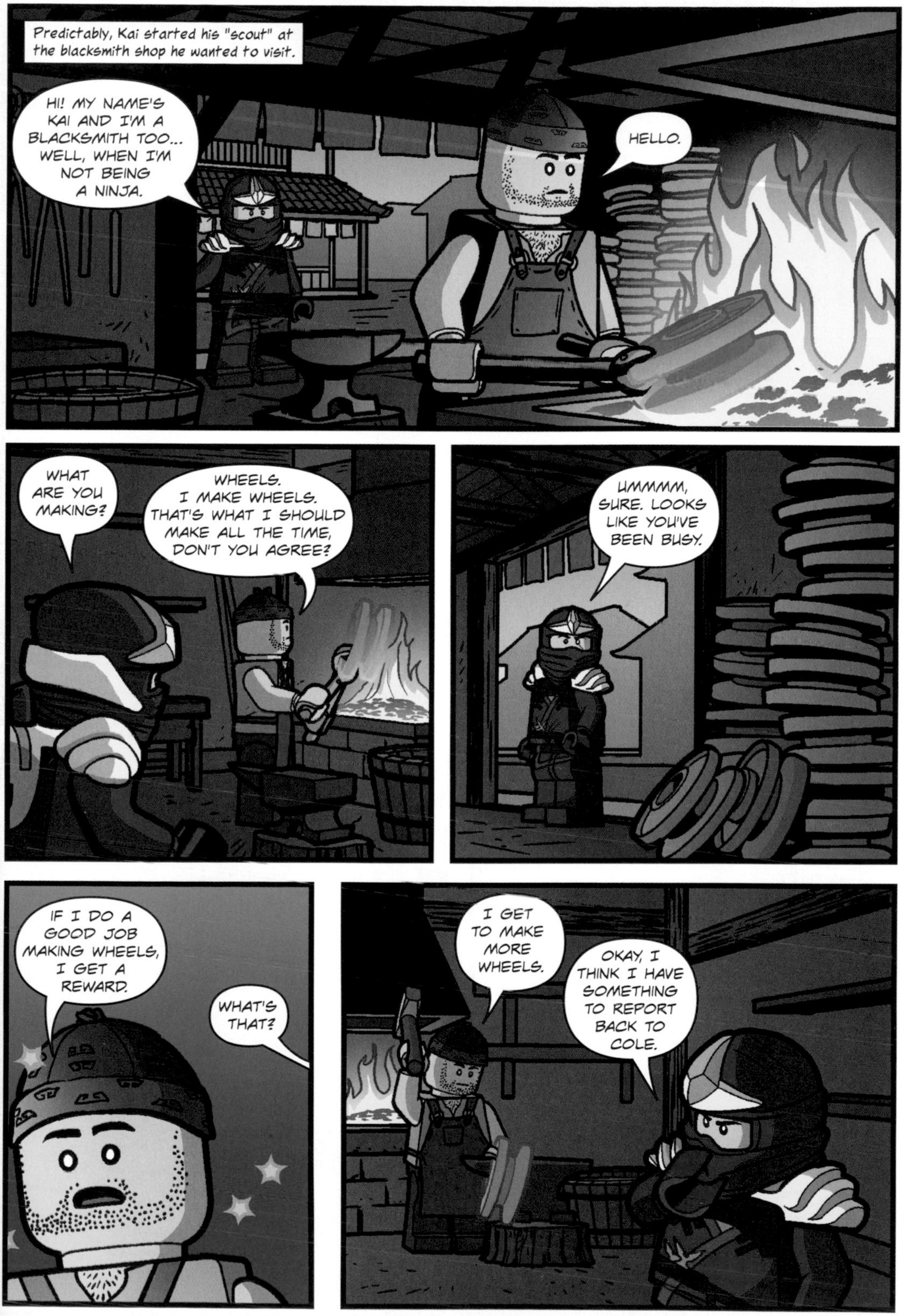
Predictably, Kai started his "scout" at the blacksmith shop he wanted to visit.
HI! MY NAME'S KAI AND I'M A BLACKSMITH TOO... WELL, WHEN I'M NOT BEING A NINJA.
HELLO.
WHAT ARE YOU MAKING?
WHEELS. I MAKE WHEELS. THAT'S WHAT I SHOULD MAKE ALL THE TIME, DON'T YOU AGREE?
UMMMM, SURE. LOOKS LIKE YOU'VE BEEN BUSY.
IF I DO A GOOD JOB MAKING WHEELS, I GET A REWARD.
WHAT'S THAT?
I GET TO MAKE MORE WHEELS.
OKAY, I THINK I HAVE SOMETHING TO REPORT BACK TO COLE.

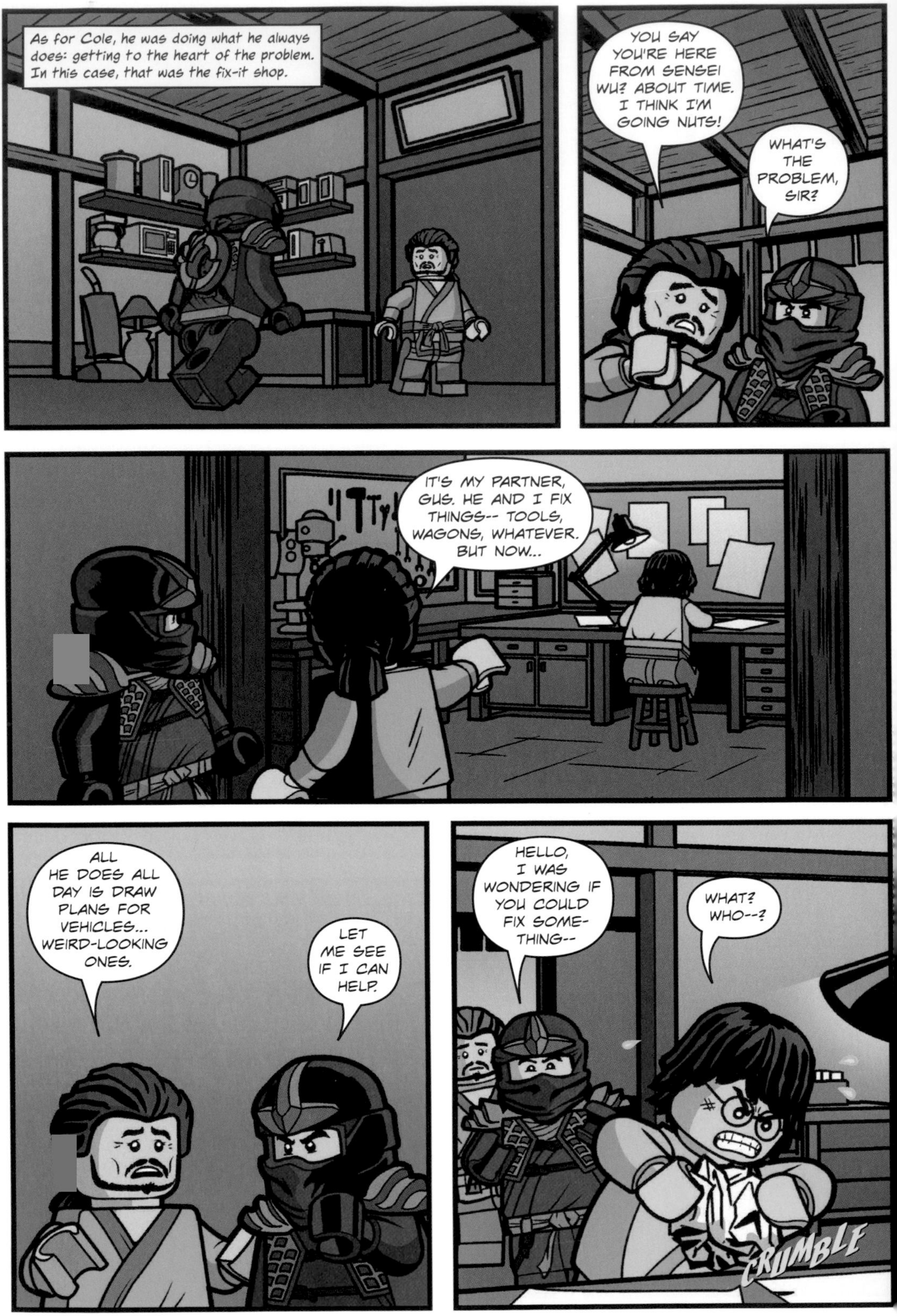

As for Cole, he was doing what he always does: getting to the heart of the problem. In this case, that was the fix-it shop.
YOU SAY YOU'RE HERE FROM SENSEI WU? ABOUT TIME. I THINK I'M GOING NUTS!
WHAT'S THE PROBLEM, SIR?
IT'S MY PARTNER, GUS. HE AND I FIX THINGS-- TOOLS, WAGONS, WHATEVER. BUT NOW...
ALL HE DOES ALL DAY IS DRAW PLANS FOR VEHICLES... WEIRD-LOOKING ONES.
LET ME SEE IF I CAN HELP.
HELLO, I WAS WONDERING IF YOU COULD FIX SOME-THING--
WHAT? WHO--?
CRUMBLE

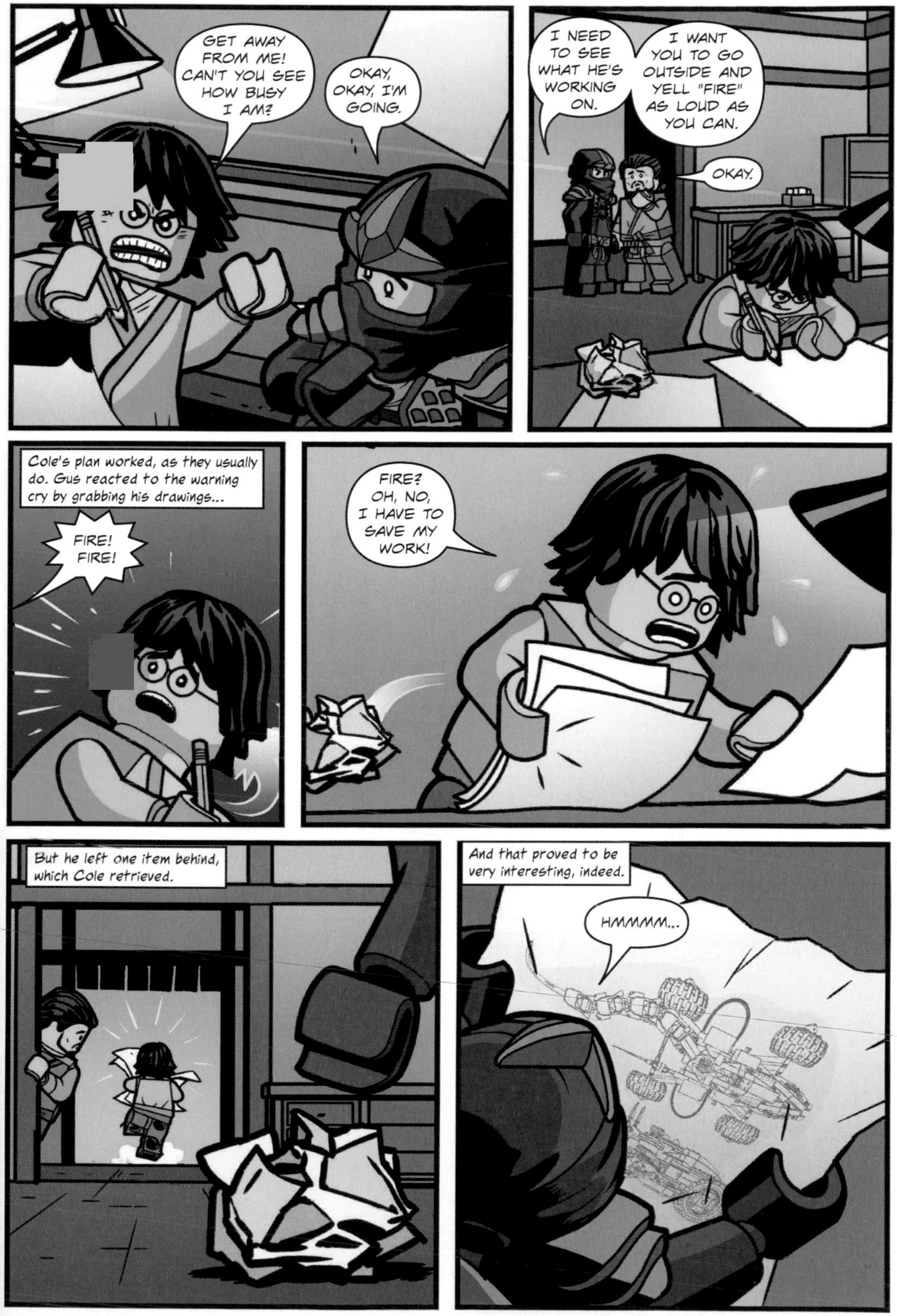
GET AWAY FROM ME! CAN'T YOU SEE HOW BUSY I AM?
OKAY, OKAY, I'M GOING.
I NEED TO SEE WHAT HE'S WORKING ON.
I WANT YOU TO GO OUTSIDE AND YELL "FIRE" AS LOUD AS YOU CAN.
OKAY.
Cole's plan worked, as they usually do. Gus reacted to the warning cry by grabbing his drawings...
FIRE! FIRE!
FIRE? OH, NO, I HAVE TO SAVE MY WORK!
But he left one item behind, which Cole retrieved.
And that proved to be very interesting, indeed.
HMMMM...

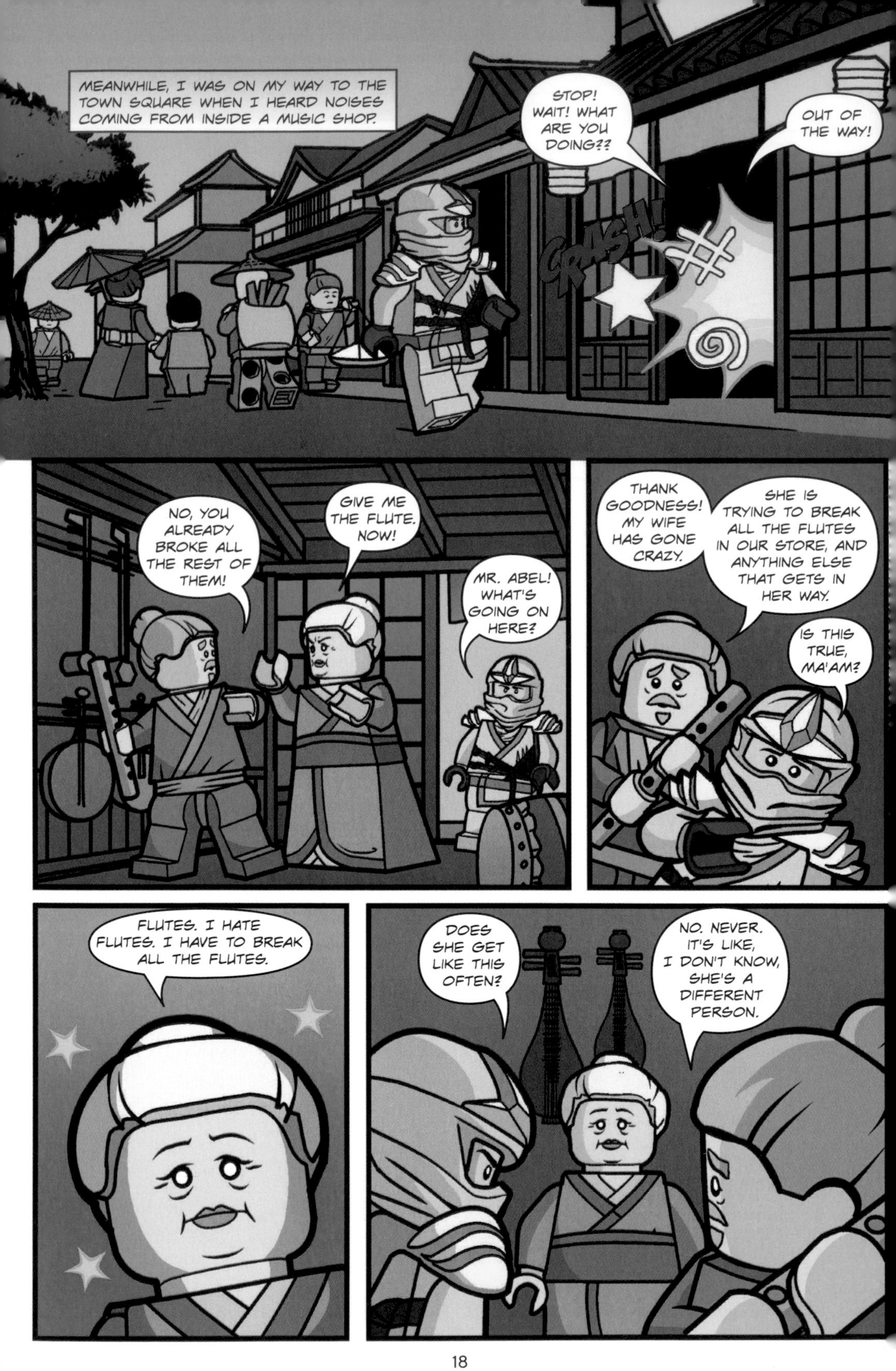
MEANWHILE, I WAS ON MY WAY TO THE TOWN SQUARE WHEN I HEARD NOISES COMING FROM INSIDE A MUSIC SHOP.
STOP! WAIT! WHAT ARE YOU DOING??
OUT OF THE WAY!
CRASH!
NO, YOU ALREADY BROKE ALL THE REST OF THEM!
GIVE ME THE FLUTE. NOW!
MR. ABEL! WHAT'S GOING ON HERE?
THANK GOODNESS! MY WIFE HAS GONE CRAZY.
SHE IS TRYING TO BREAK ALL THE FLUTES IN OUR STORE, AND ANYTHING ELSE THAT GETS IN HER WAY.
IS THIS TRUE, MA'AM?
FLUTES. I HATE FLUTES. I HAVE TO BREAK ALL THE FLUTES.
DOES SHE GET LIKE THIS OFTEN?
NO. NEVER. IT'S LIKE, I DON'T KNOW, SHE'S A DIFFERENT PERSON.

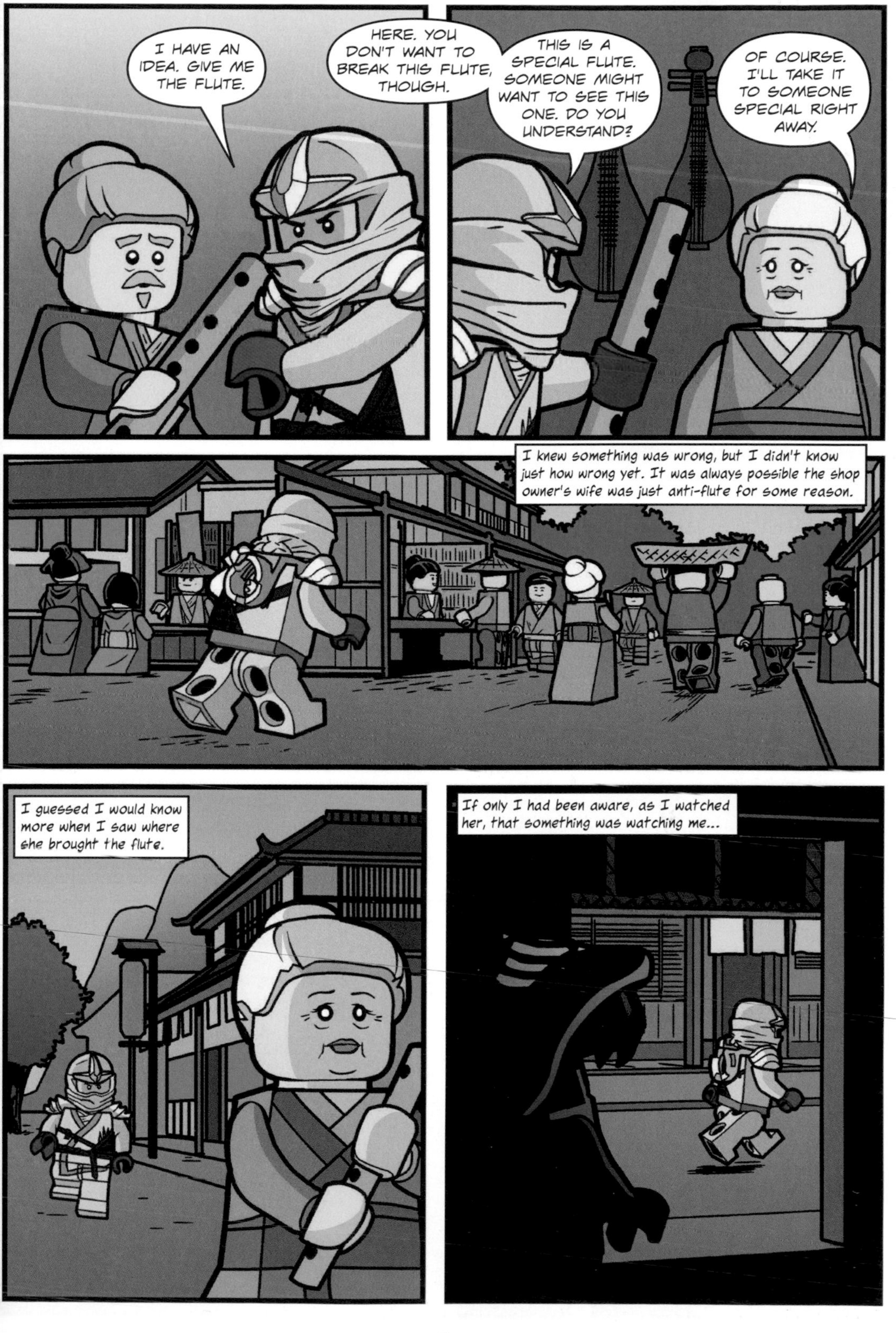
I HAVE AN IDEA. GIVE ME THE FLUTE.
HERE. YOU DON'T WANT TO BREAK THIS FLUTE, THOUGH.
THIS IS A SPECIAL FLUTE. SOMEONE MIGHT WANT TO SEE THIS ONE. DO YOU UNDERSTAND?
OF COURSE. I'LL TAKE IT TO SOMEONE SPECIAL RIGHT AWAY.
I knew something was wrong, but I didn't know just how wrong yet. It was always possible the shop owner's wife was just anti-flute for some reason.
I guessed I would know more when I saw where she brought the flute.
If only I had been aware, as I watched her, that something was watching me...

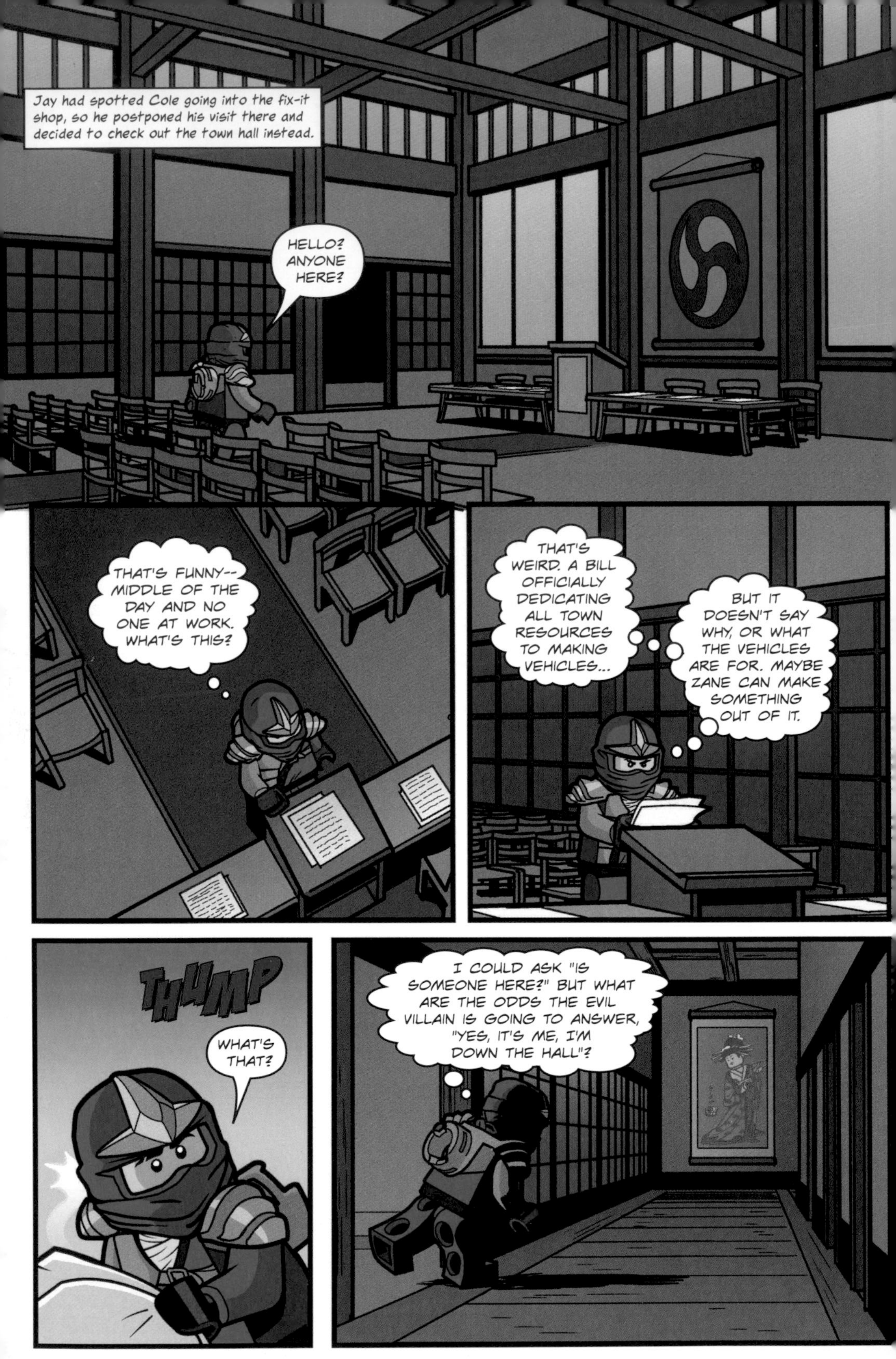
Jay had spotted Cole going into the fix-it shop, so he postponed his visit there and decided to check out the town hall instead.
HELLO? ANYONE HERE?
THAT'S FUNNY-- MIDDLE OF THE DAY AND NO ONE AT WORK. WHAT'S THIS?
THAT'S WEIRD. A BILL OFFICIALLY DEDICATING ALL TOWN RESOURCES TO MAKING VEHICLES...
BUT IT DOESN'T SAY WHY, OR WHAT THE VEHICLES ARE FOR. MAYBE ZANE CAN MAKE SOMETHING OUT OF IT.
THUMP
WHAT'S THAT?
I COULD ASK "IS SOMEONE HERE?" BUT WHAT ARE THE ODDS THE EVIL VILLAIN IS GOING TO ANSWER, "YES, IT'S ME, I'M DOWN THE HALL"?

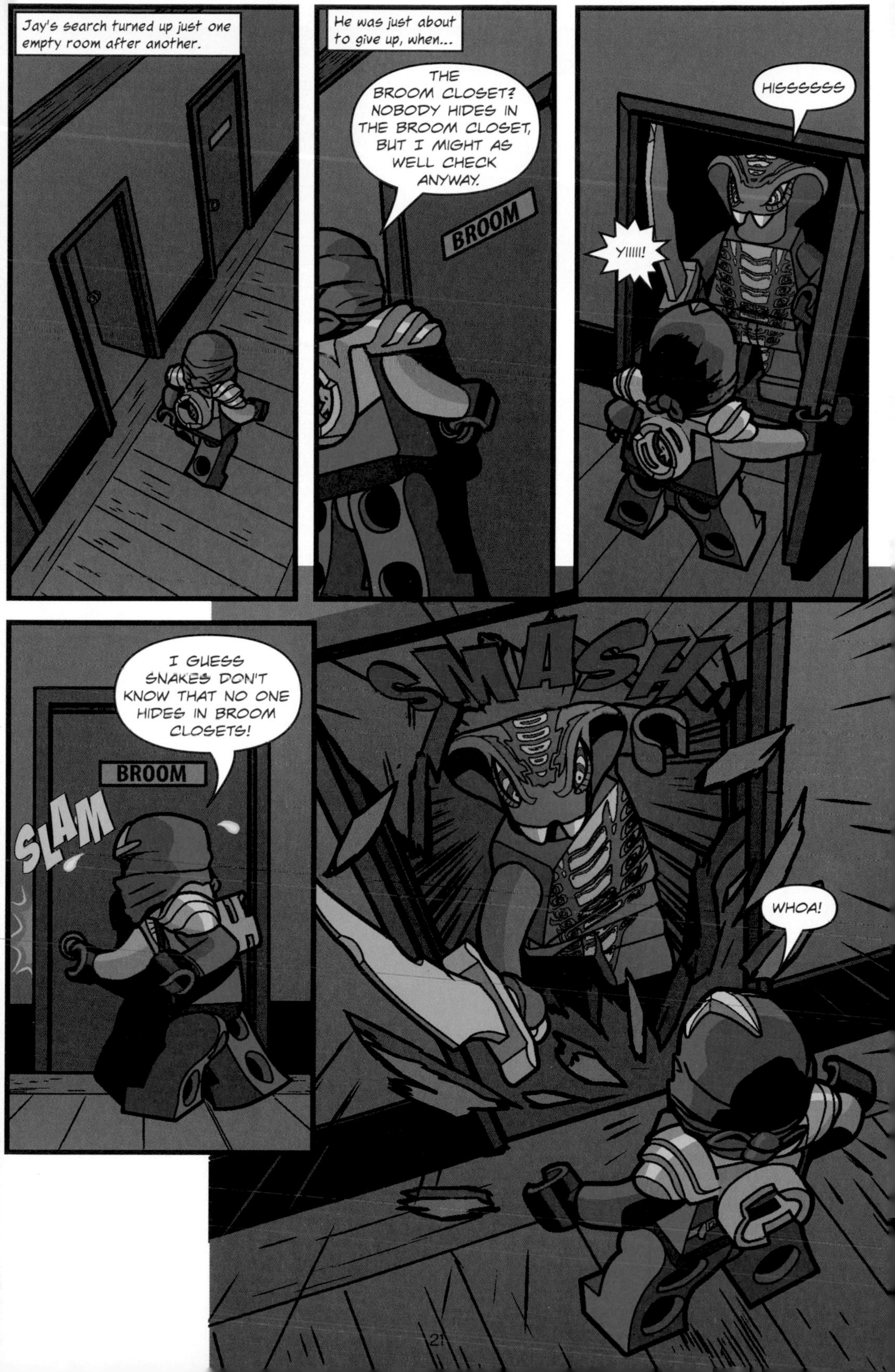
Jay's search turned up just one empty room after another.
He was just about to give up, when...
THE BROOM CLOSET? NOBODY HIDES IN THE BROOM CLOSET, BUT I MIGHT AS WELL CHECK ANYWAY.
BROOM
HISSSSSS
YIIIII!
BROOM
SLAM
I GUESS SNAKES DON'T KNOW THAT NO ONE HIDES IN BROOM CLOSETS!
SMASH
WHOA!

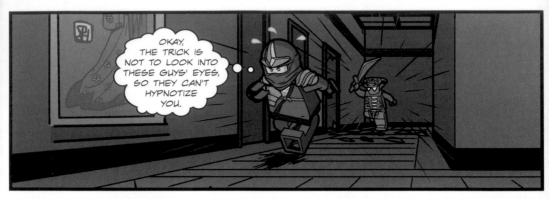

OKAY, THE TRICK IS NOT TO LOOK INTO THESE GUYS' EYES, SO THEY CAN'T HYPNOTIZE YOU.

HISSSSSS!

THAT TAKES CARE OF THAT PROBLEM! NOW TO WARN THE OTHERS.

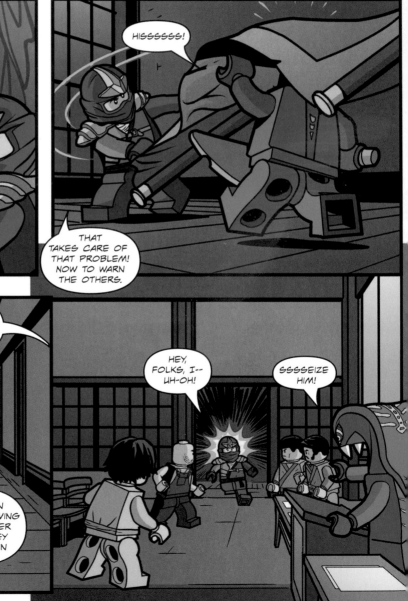

THE MEETING WILL COME TO ORDER.

SOUNDS LIKE THE TOWN LEADERS ARE HAVING A CHAT. I BETTER TELL THEM THEY HAVE SNAKES IN THE HOUSE.

HEY, FOLKS, I-- UH-OH!

SSSSEIZE HIM!

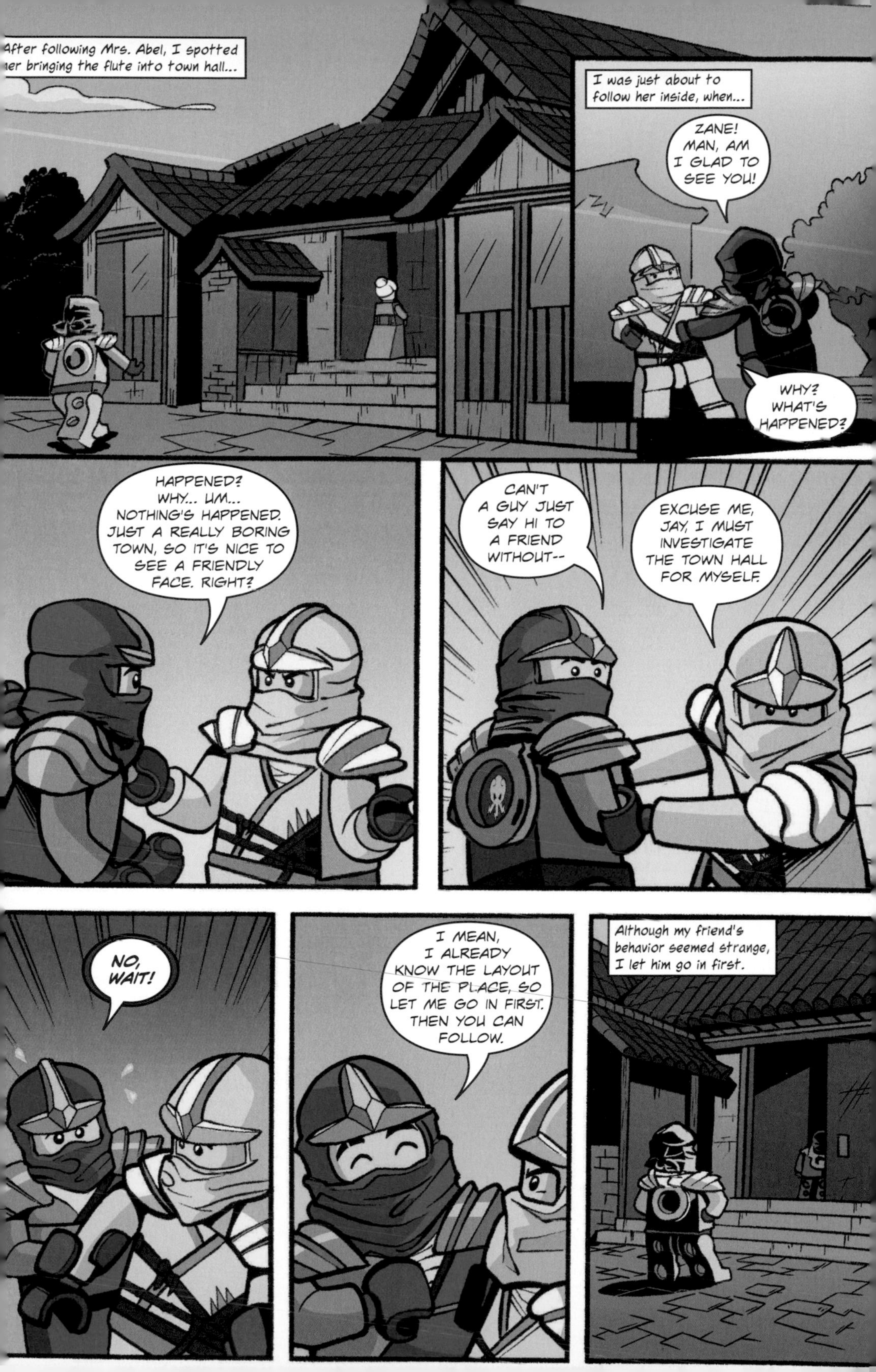
After following Mrs. Abel, I spotted her bringing the flute into town hall...
I was just about to follow her inside, when...
ZANE! MAN, AM I GLAD TO SEE YOU!
WHY? WHAT'S HAPPENED?
HAPPENED? WHY... UM... NOTHING'S HAPPENED. JUST A REALLY BORING TOWN, SO IT'S NICE TO SEE A FRIENDLY FACE. RIGHT?
CAN'T A GUY JUST SAY HI TO A FRIEND WITHOUT--
EXCUSE ME, JAY, I MUST INVESTIGATE THE TOWN HALL FOR MYSELF.
NO, WAIT!
I MEAN, I ALREADY KNOW THE LAYOUT OF THE PLACE, SO LET ME GO IN FIRST. THEN YOU CAN FOLLOW.
Although my friend's behavior seemed strange, I let him go in first.

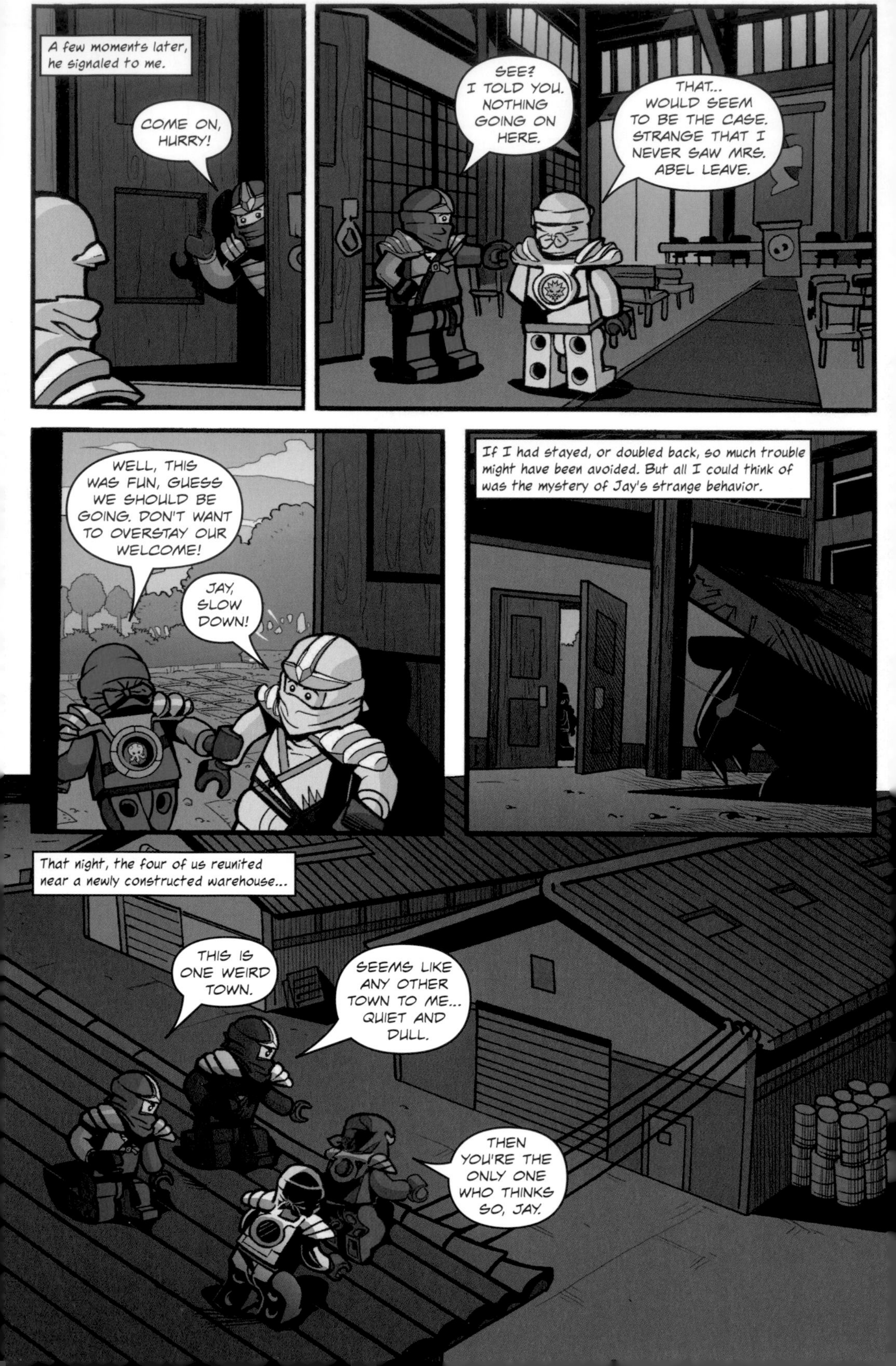
A few moments later, he signaled to me.
COME ON, HURRY!
SEE? I TOLD YOU. NOTHING GOING ON HERE.
THAT... WOULD SEEM TO BE THE CASE. STRANGE THAT I NEVER SAW MRS. ABEL LEAVE.
WELL, THIS WAS FUN, GUESS WE SHOULD BE GOING. DON'T WANT TO OVERSTAY OUR WELCOME!
JAY, SLOW DOWN!
If I had stayed, or doubled back, so much trouble might have been avoided. But all I could think of was the mystery of Jay's strange behavior.
That night, the four of us reunited near a newly constructed warehouse...
THIS IS ONE WEIRD TOWN.
SEEMS LIKE ANY OTHER TOWN TO ME... QUIET AND DULL.
THEN YOU'RE THE ONLY ONE WHO THINKS SO, JAY.

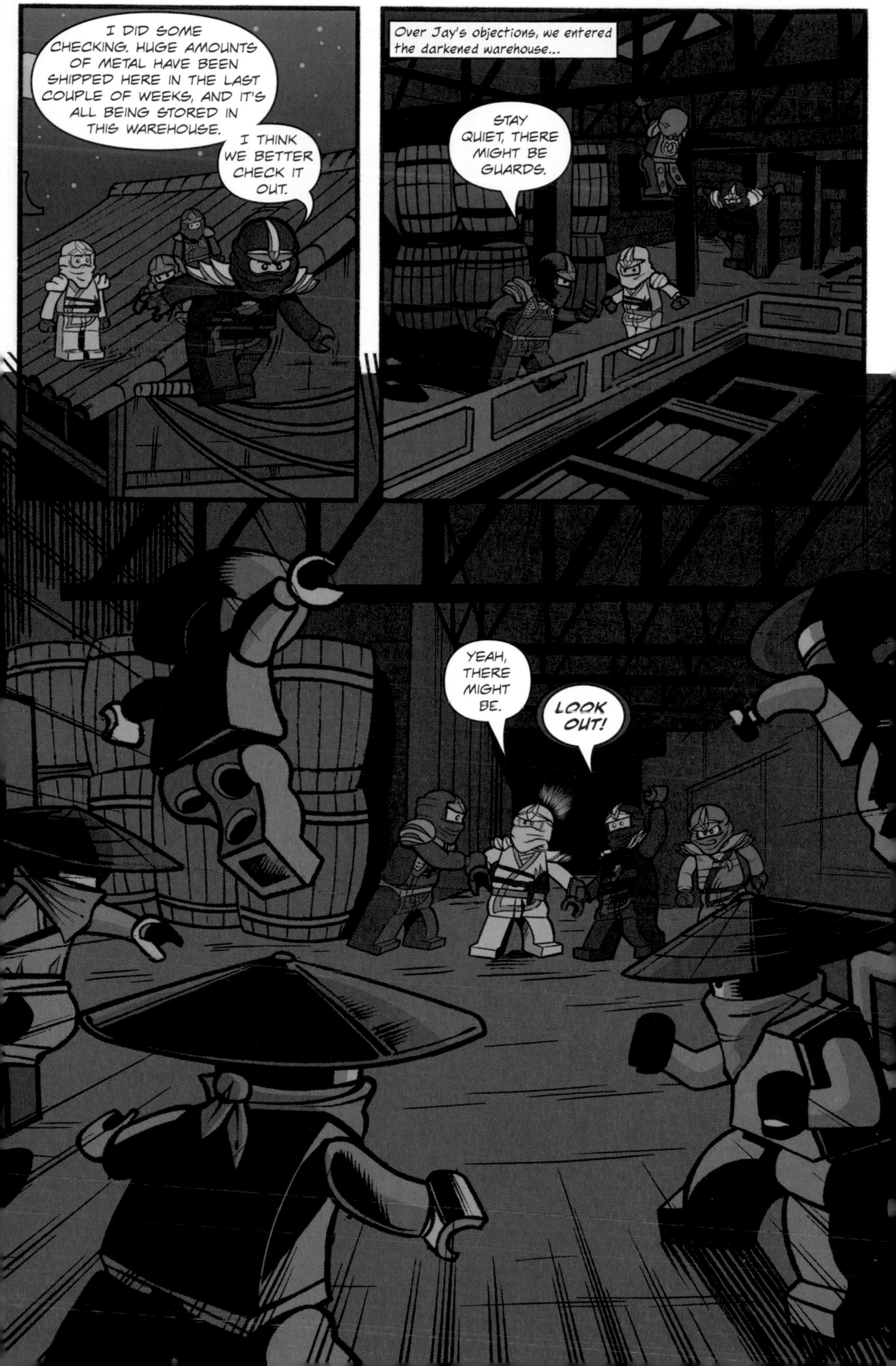
I DID SOME CHECKING. HUGE AMOUNTS OF METAL HAVE BEEN SHIPPED HERE IN THE LAST COUPLE OF WEEKS, AND IT'S ALL BEING STORED IN THIS WAREHOUSE.
I THINK WE BETTER CHECK IT OUT.
Over Jay's objections, we entered the darkened warehouse...
STAY QUIET, THERE MIGHT BE GUARDS.
YEAH, THERE MIGHT BE.
LOOK OUT!

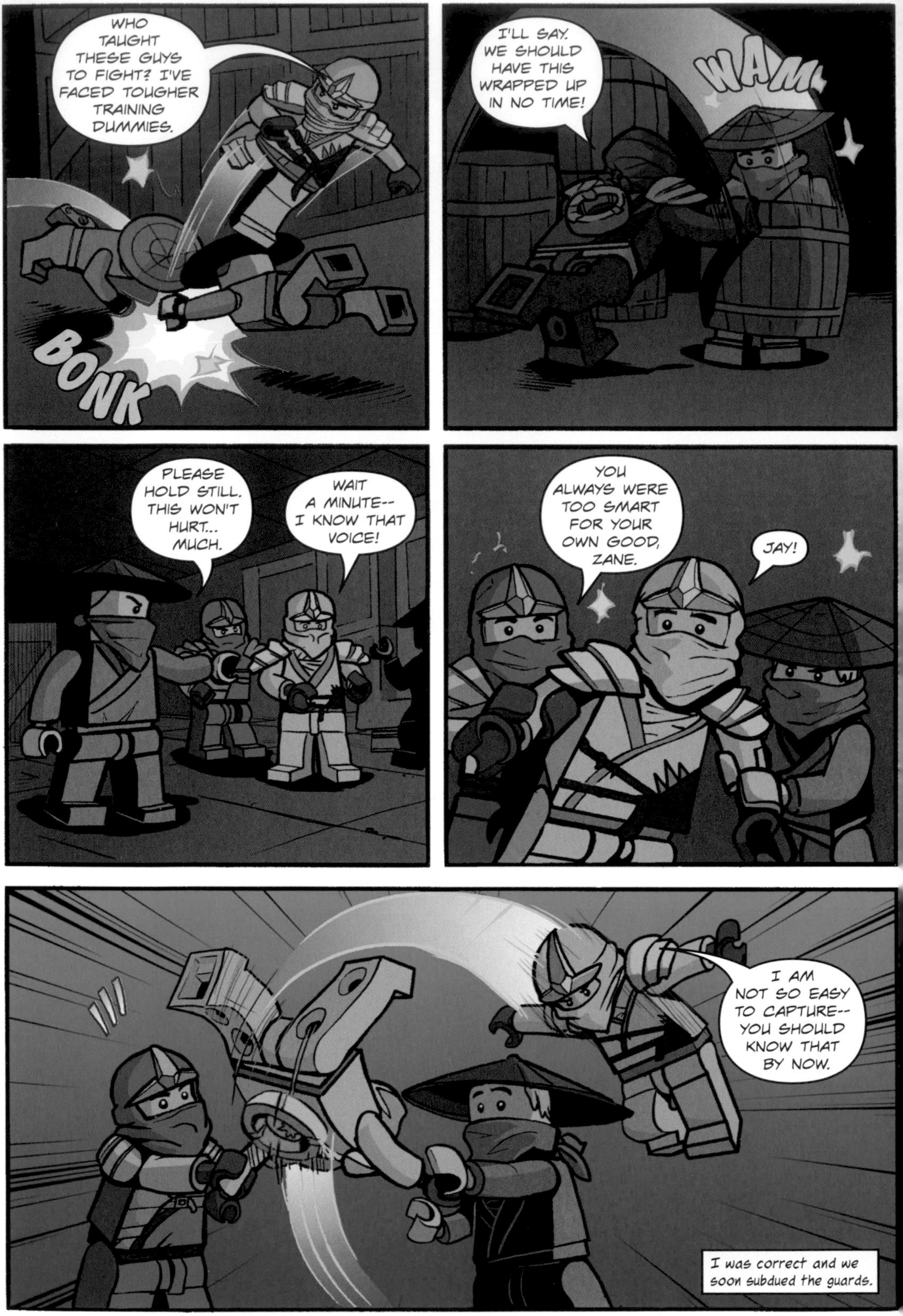
WHO TAUGHT THESE GUYS TO FIGHT? I'VE FACED TOUGHER TRAINING DUMMIES.
BONK
I'LL SAY. WE SHOULD HAVE THIS WRAPPED UP IN NO TIME!
WAM
PLEASE HOLD STILL. THIS WON'T HURT... MUCH.
WAIT A MINUTE-- I KNOW THAT VOICE!
YOU ALWAYS WERE TOO SMART FOR YOUR OWN GOOD, ZANE.
JAY!
I AM NOT SO EASY TO CAPTURE-- YOU SHOULD KNOW THAT BY NOW.
I was correct and we soon subdued the guards.

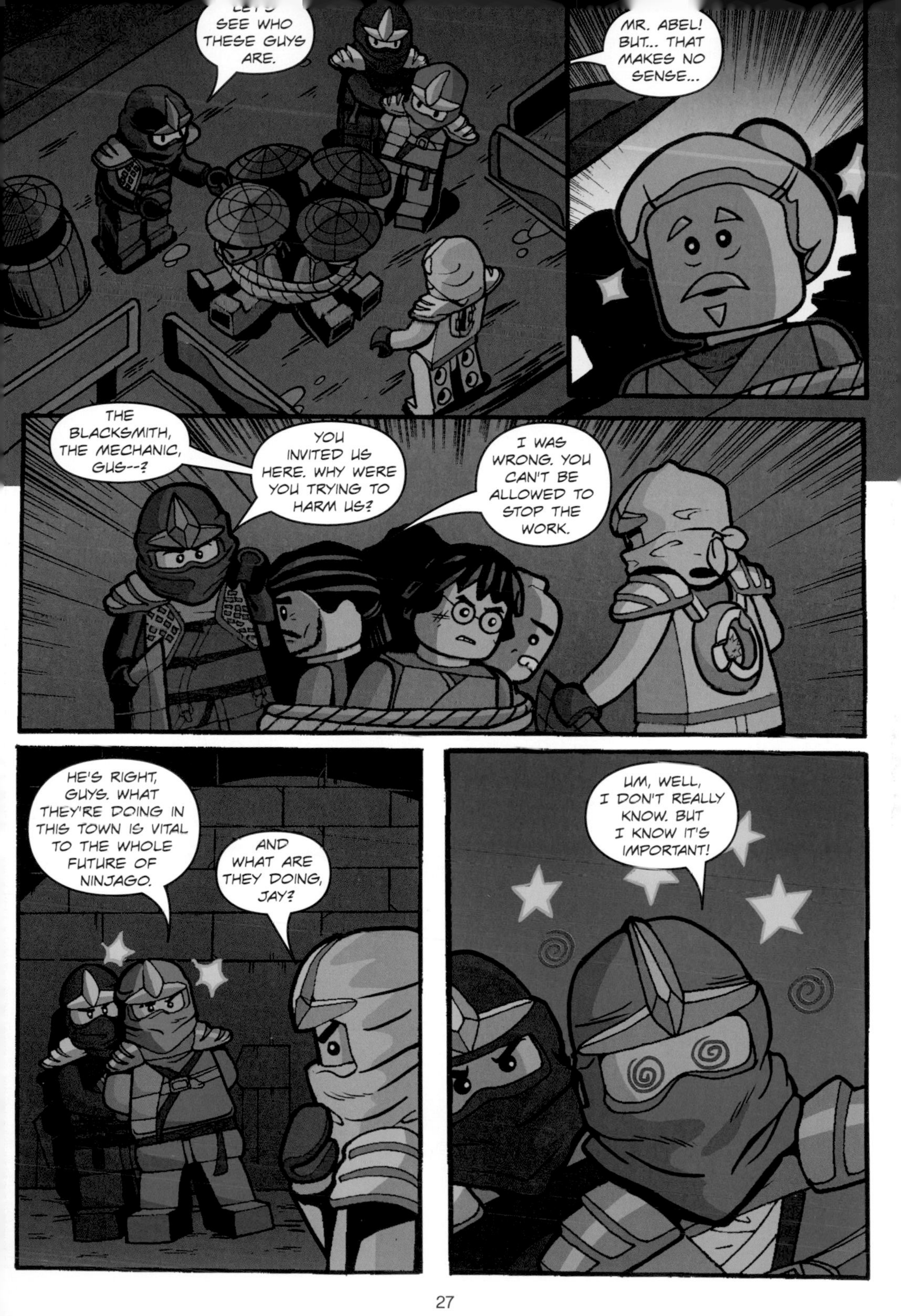
LET'S SEE WHO THESE GUYS ARE.
MR. ABEL! BUT... THAT MAKES NO SENSE...
THE BLACKSMITH, THE MECHANIC, GUS--?
YOU INVITED US HERE. WHY WERE YOU TRYING TO HARM US?
I WAS WRONG. YOU CAN'T BE ALLOWED TO STOP THE WORK.
HE'S RIGHT, GUYS. WHAT THEY'RE DOING IN THIS TOWN IS VITAL TO THE WHOLE FUTURE OF NINJAGO.
AND WHAT ARE THEY DOING, JAY?
UM, WELL, I DON'T REALLY KNOW. BUT I KNOW IT'S IMPORTANT!

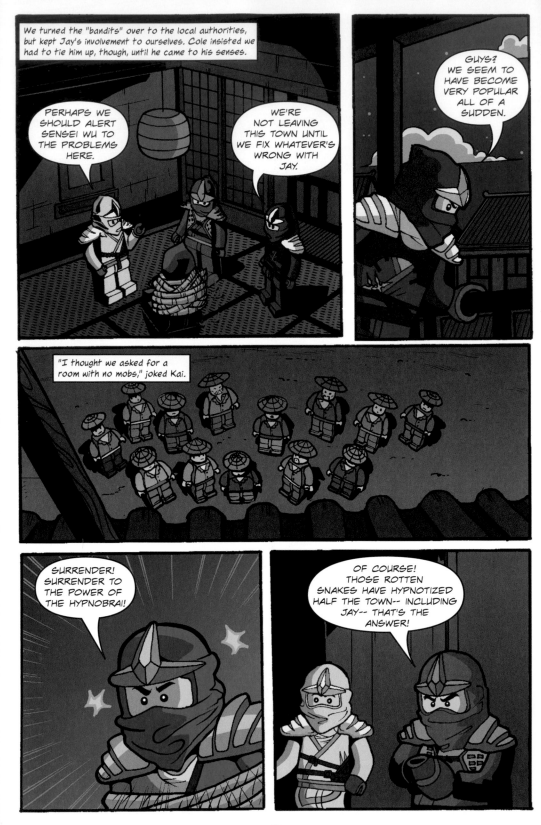

We turned the "bandits" over to the local authorities, but kept Jay's involvement to ourselves. Cole insisted we had to tie him up, though, until he came to his senses.

PERHAPS WE SHOULD ALERT SENSEI WU TO THE PROBLEMS HERE.

WE'RE NOT LEAVING THIS TOWN UNTIL WE FIX WHATEVER'S WRONG WITH JAY.

GUYS? WE SEEM TO HAVE BECOME VERY POPULAR ALL OF A SUDDEN.

"I thought we asked for a room with no mobs," joked Kai.

SURRENDER! SURRENDER TO THE POWER OF THE HYPNOBRAI!

OF COURSE! THOSE ROTTEN SNAKES HAVE HYPNOTIZED HALF THE TOWN-- INCLUDING JAY-- THAT'S THE ANSWER!

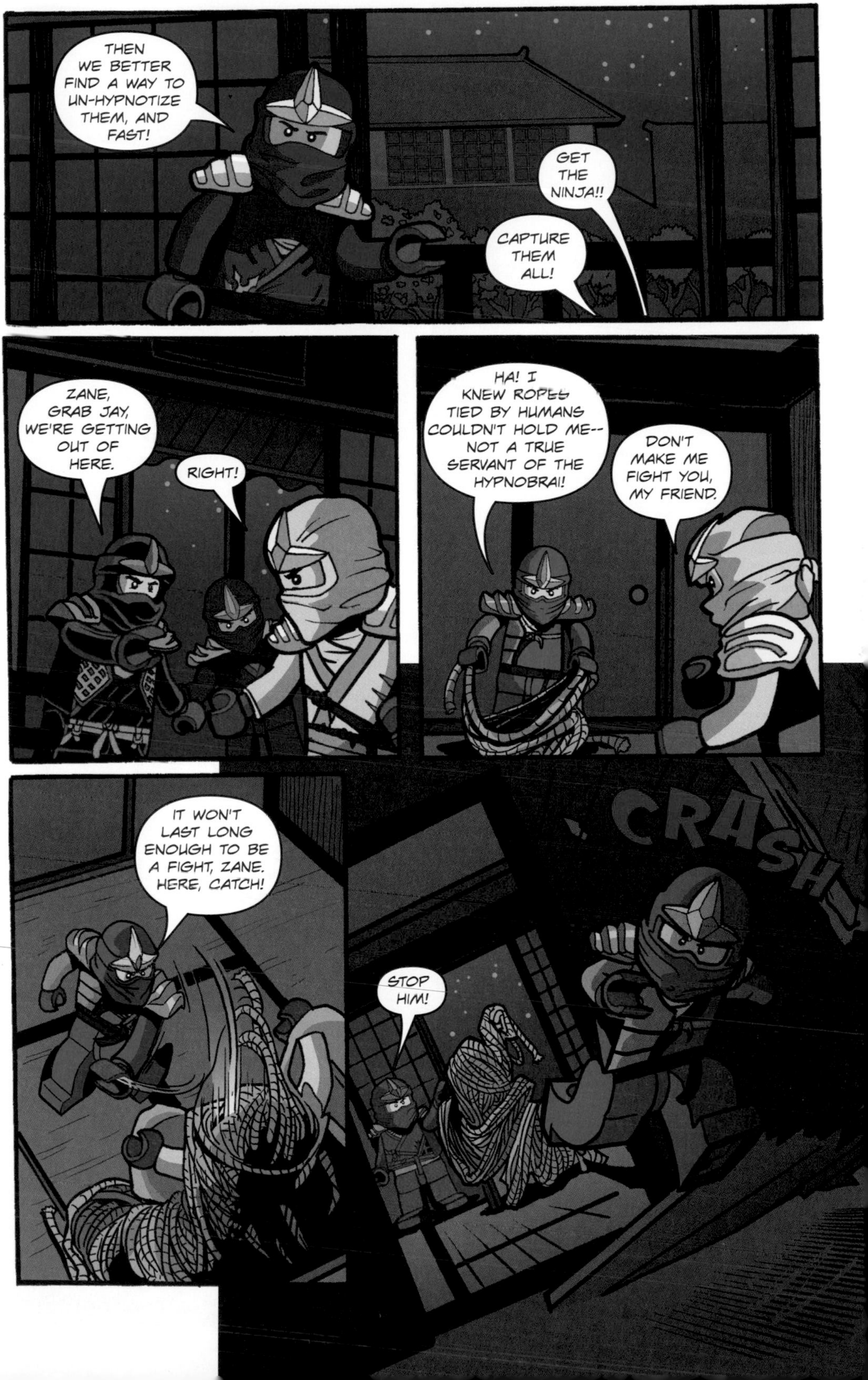
THEN WE BETTER FIND A WAY TO UN-HYPNOTIZE THEM, AND FAST!
GET THE NINJA!!
CAPTURE THEM ALL!
ZANE, GRAB JAY, WE'RE GETTING OUT OF HERE.
RIGHT!
HA! I KNEW ROPES TIED BY HUMANS COULDN'T HOLD ME-- NOT A TRUE SERVANT OF THE HYPNOBRAI!
DON'T MAKE ME FIGHT YOU, MY FRIEND.
IT WON'T LAST LONG ENOUGH TO BE A FIGHT, ZANE. HERE, CATCH!
CRASH
STOP HIM!

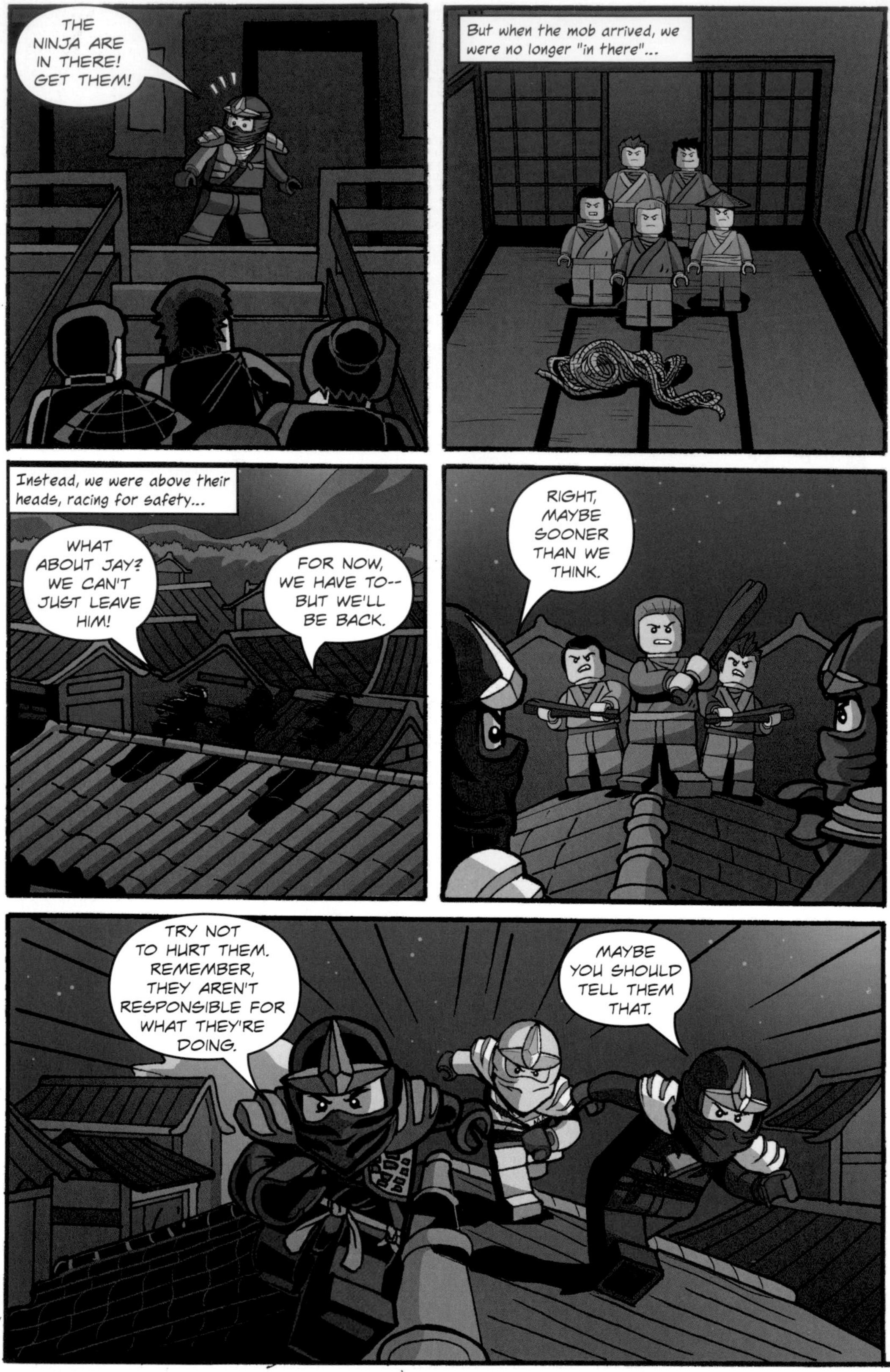
THE NINJA ARE IN THERE! GET THEM!
But when the mob arrived, we were no longer "in there"...
Instead, we were above their heads, racing for safety...
WHAT ABOUT JAY? WE CAN'T JUST LEAVE HIM!
FOR NOW, WE HAVE TO-- BUT WE'LL BE BACK.
RIGHT, MAYBE SOONER THAN WE THINK.
TRY NOT TO HURT THEM. REMEMBER, THEY AREN'T RESPONSIBLE FOR WHAT THEY'RE DOING.
MAYBE YOU SHOULD TELL THEM THAT.

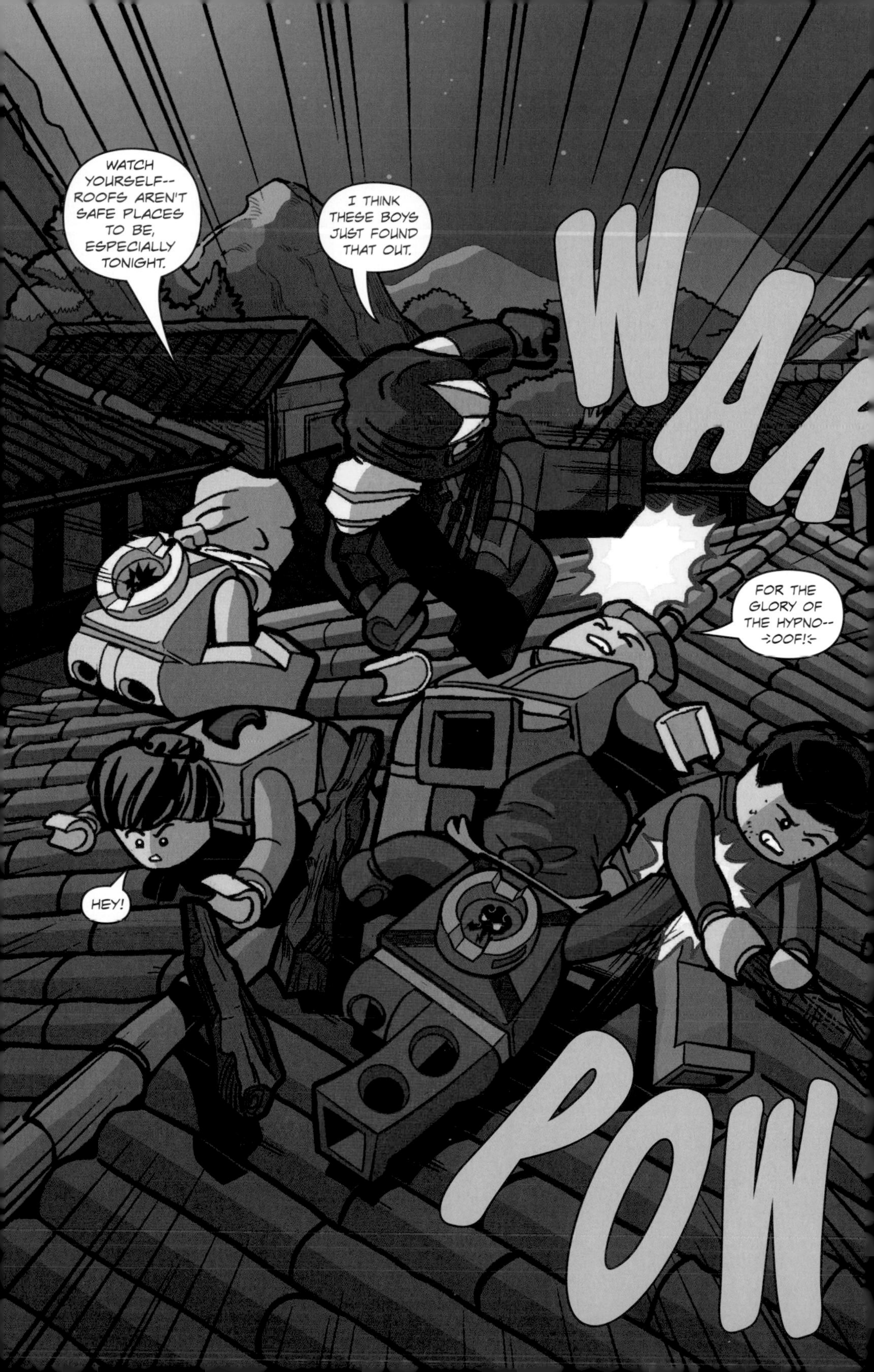
WATCH YOURSELF-- ROOFS AREN'T SAFE PLACES TO BE, ESPECIALLY TONIGHT.
I THINK THESE BOYS JUST FOUND THAT OUT.
WAR
FOR THE GLORY OF THE HYPNO-- OOF!
HEY!
POW

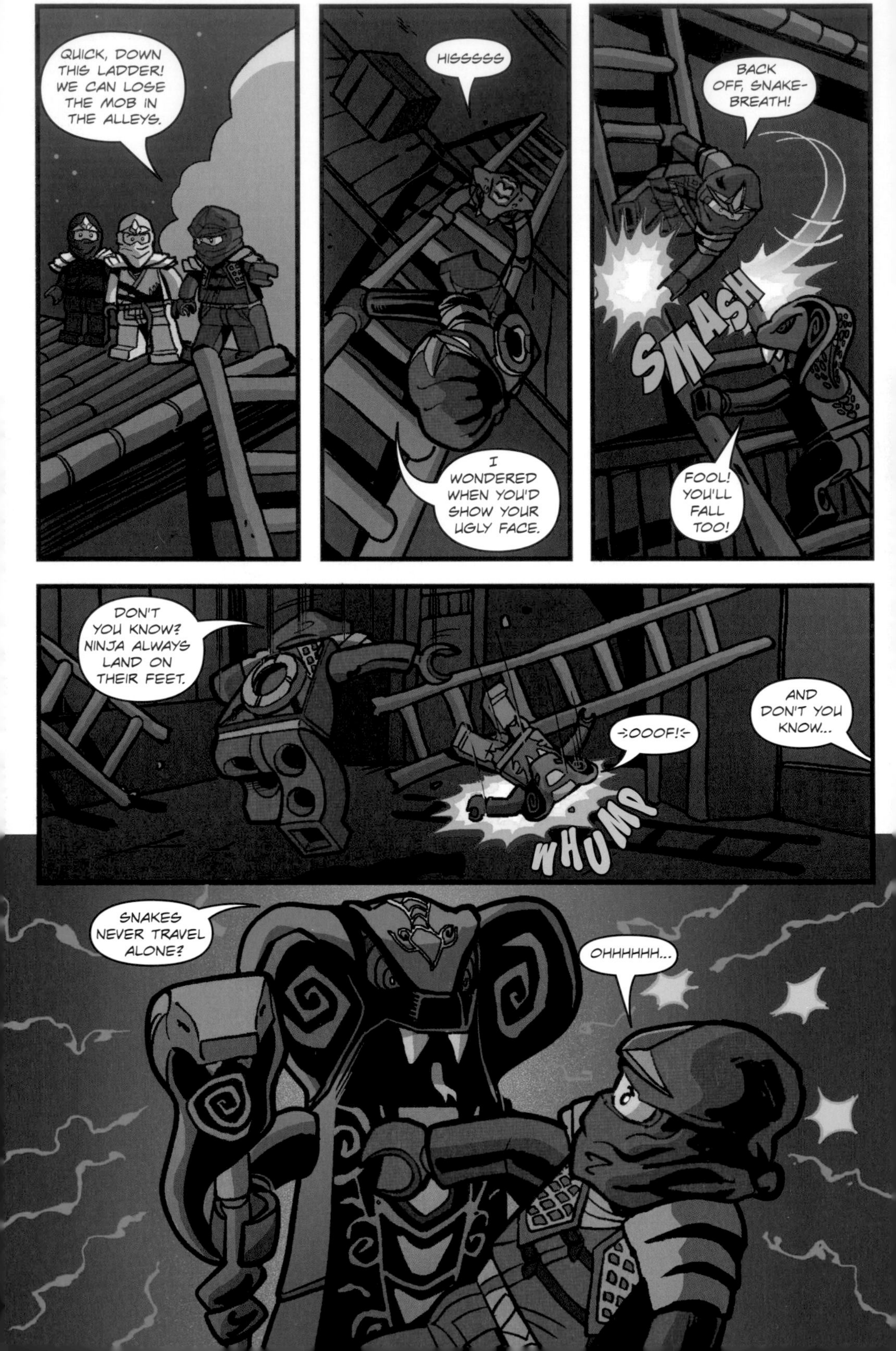
QUICK, DOWN THIS LADDER! WE CAN LOSE THE MOB IN THE ALLEYS.
HISSSSS
I WONDERED WHEN YOU'D SHOW YOUR UGLY FACE.
BACK OFF, SNAKE-BREATH!
SMASH
FOOL! YOU'LL FALL TOO!
DON'T YOU KNOW? NINJA ALWAYS LAND ON THEIR FEET.
OOOF!
WHUMP
AND DON'T YOU KNOW...
SNAKES NEVER TRAVEL ALONE?
OHHHHHH...

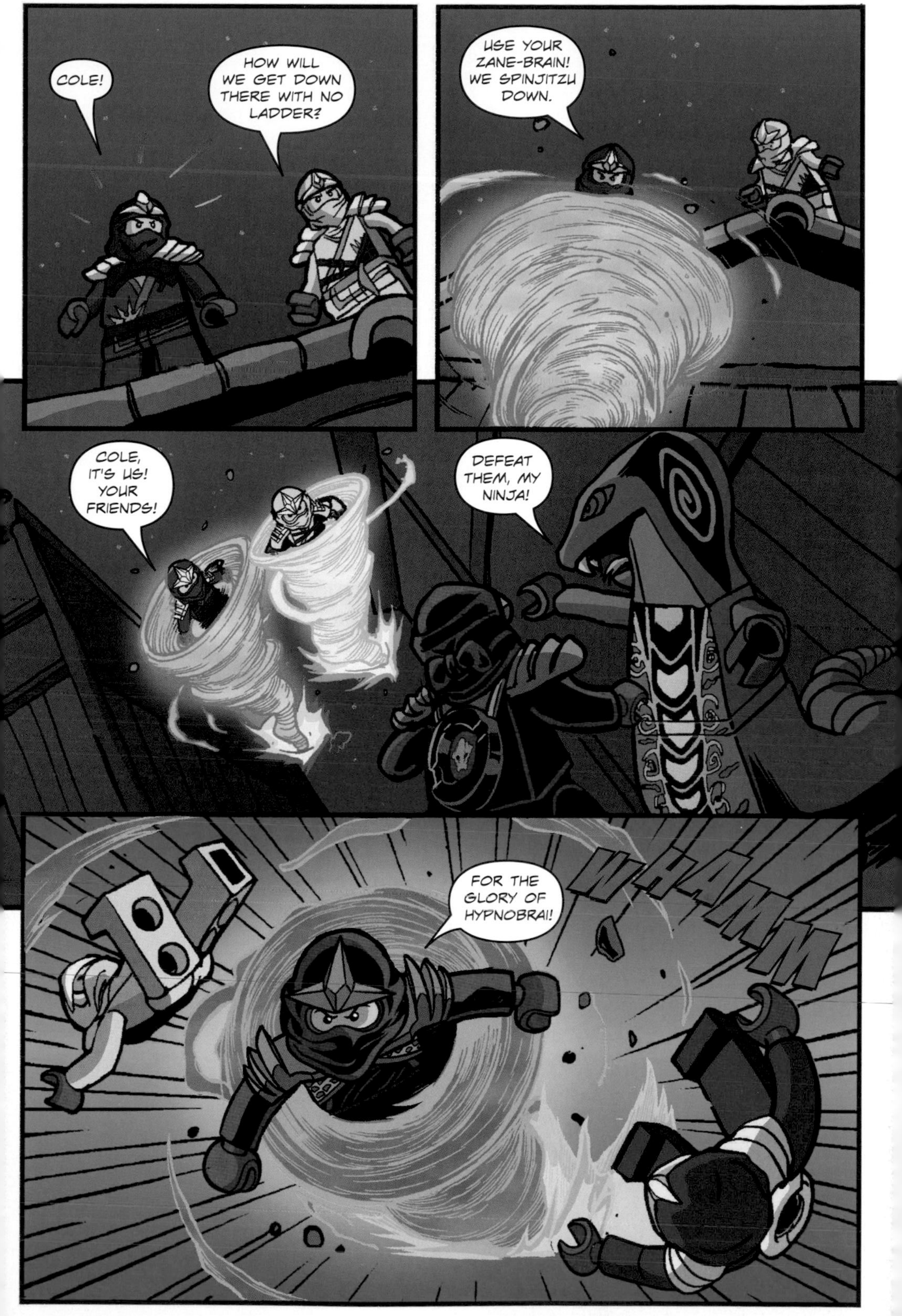
COLE!
HOW WILL WE GET DOWN THERE WITH NO LADDER?
USE YOUR ZANE-BRAIN! WE SPINJITZU DOWN.
COLE, IT'S US! YOUR FRIENDS!
DEFEAT THEM, MY NINJA!
FOR THE GLORY OF HYPNOBRAI!
WHAMM

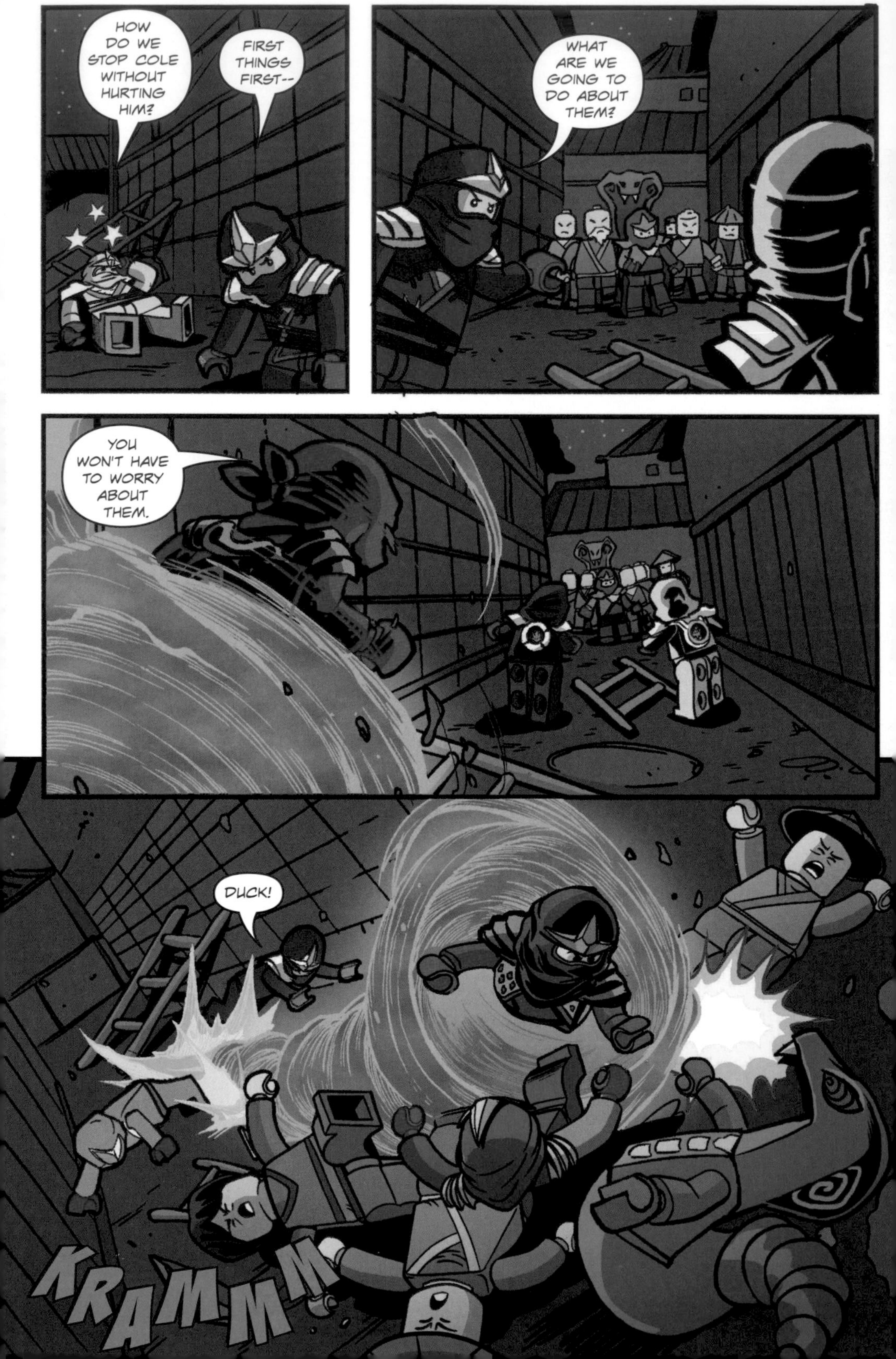
HOW DO WE STOP COLE WITHOUT HURTING HIM?
FIRST THINGS FIRST--
WHAT ARE WE GOING TO DO ABOUT THEM?
YOU WON'T HAVE TO WORRY ABOUT THEM.
DUCK!
KRAMMM

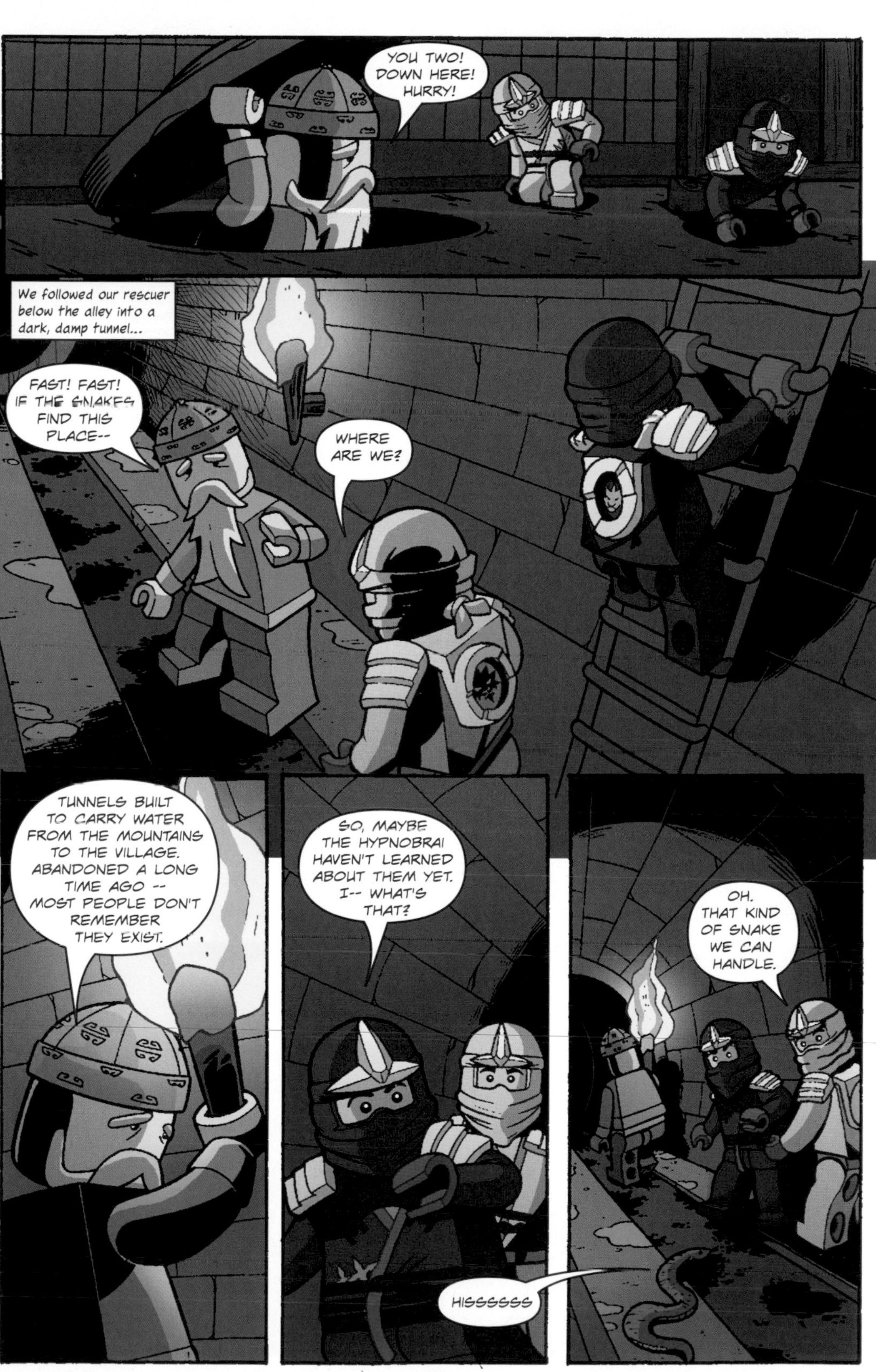
YOU TWO! DOWN HERE! HURRY!
We followed our rescuer below the alley into a dark, damp tunnel...
FAST! FAST! IF THE SNAKES FIND THIS PLACE--
WHERE ARE WE?
TUNNELS BUILT TO CARRY WATER FROM THE MOUNTAINS TO THE VILLAGE. ABANDONED A LONG TIME AGO -- MOST PEOPLE DON'T REMEMBER THEY EXIST.
SO, MAYBE THE HYPNOBRAI HAVEN'T LEARNED ABOUT THEM YET. I-- WHAT'S THAT?
HISSSSSS
OH. THAT KIND OF SNAKE WE CAN HANDLE.

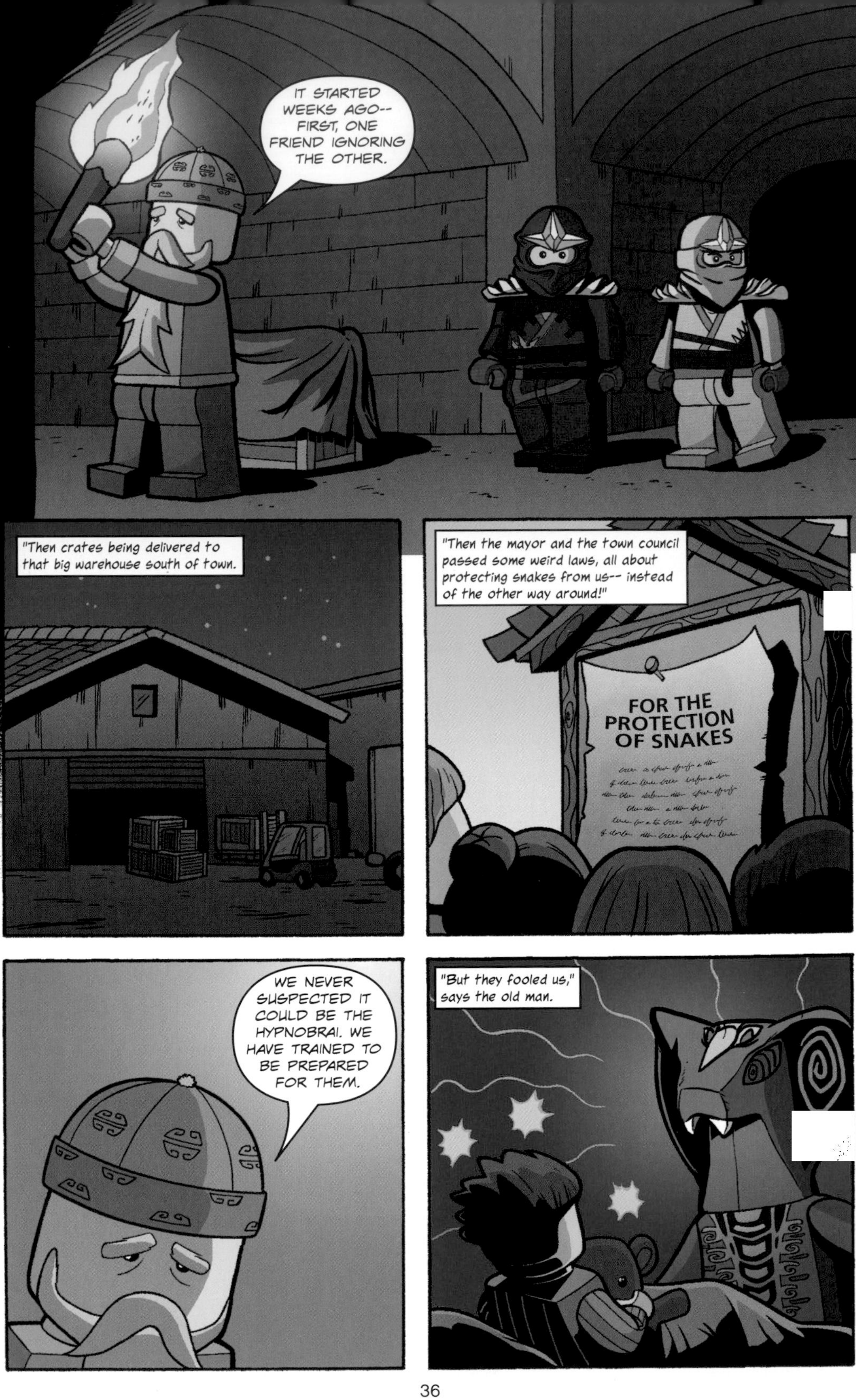
IT STARTED WEEKS AGO-- FIRST, ONE FRIEND IGNORING THE OTHER.
"Then crates being delivered to that big warehouse south of town.
"Then the mayor and the town council passed some weird laws, all about protecting snakes from us-- instead of the other way around!"
FOR THE PROTECTION OF SNAKES
WE NEVER SUSPECTED IT COULD BE THE HYPNOBRAI. WE HAVE TRAINED TO BE PREPARED FOR THEM.
"But they fooled us," says the old man.

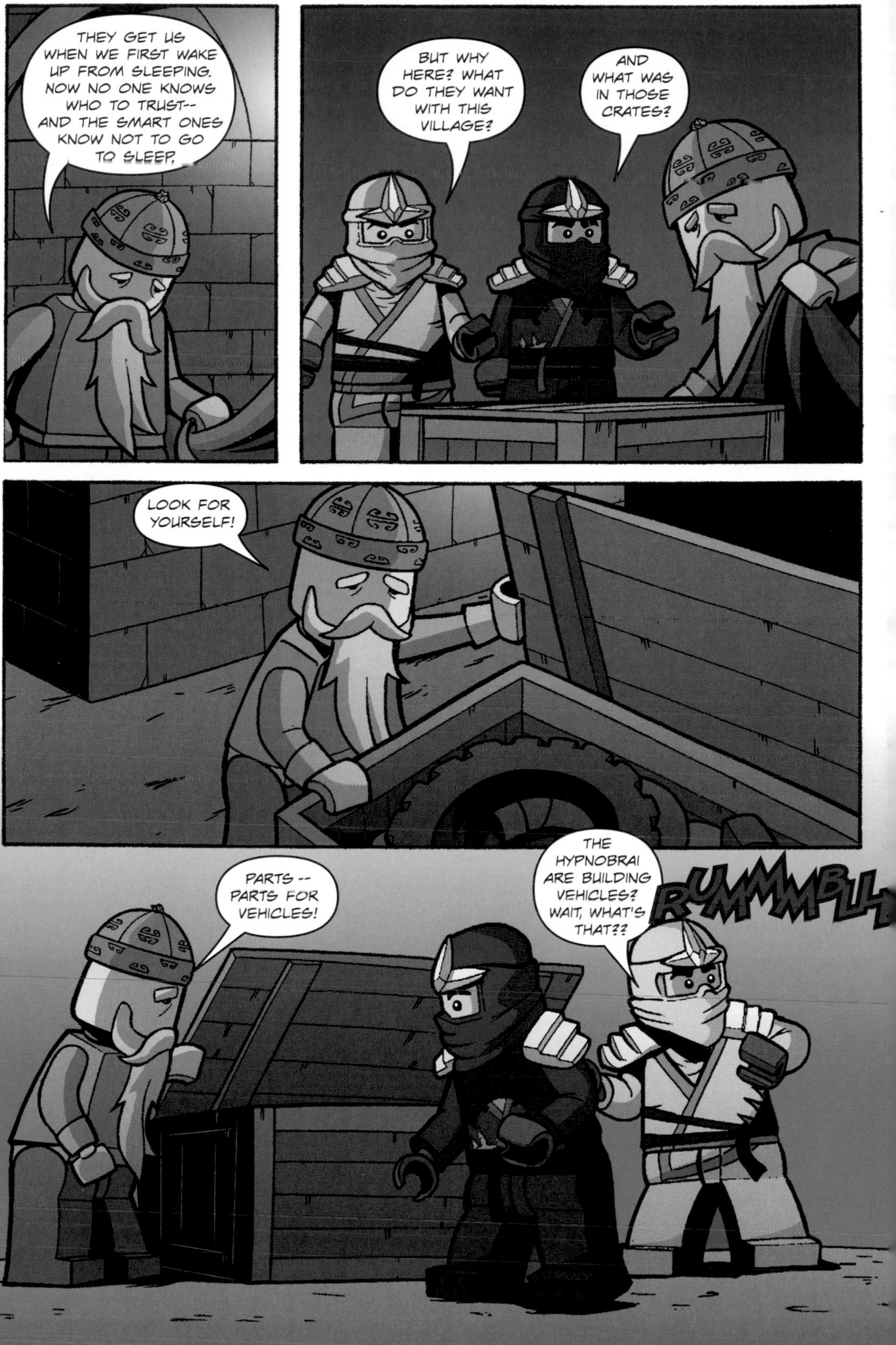

THEY GET US WHEN WE FIRST WAKE UP FROM SLEEPING. NOW NO ONE KNOWS WHO TO TRUST-- AND THE SMART ONES KNOW NOT TO GO TO SLEEP.
BUT WHY HERE? WHAT DO THEY WANT WITH THIS VILLAGE?
AND WHAT WAS IN THOSE CRATES?
LOOK FOR YOURSELF!
PARTS -- PARTS FOR VEHICLES!
THE HYPNOBRAI ARE BUILDING VEHICLES? WAIT, WHAT'S THAT??

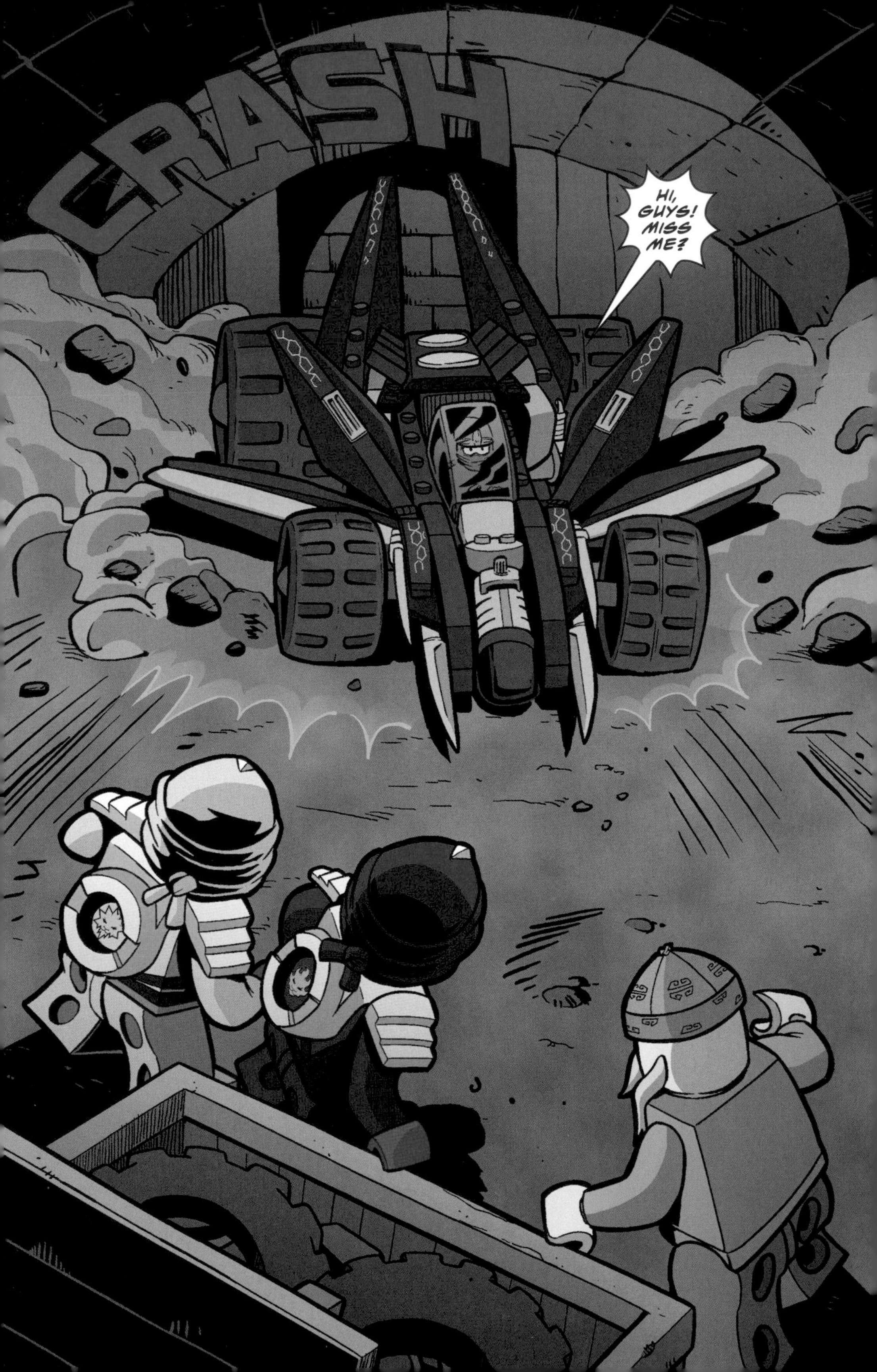
CRASH
HI, GUYS! MISS ME?

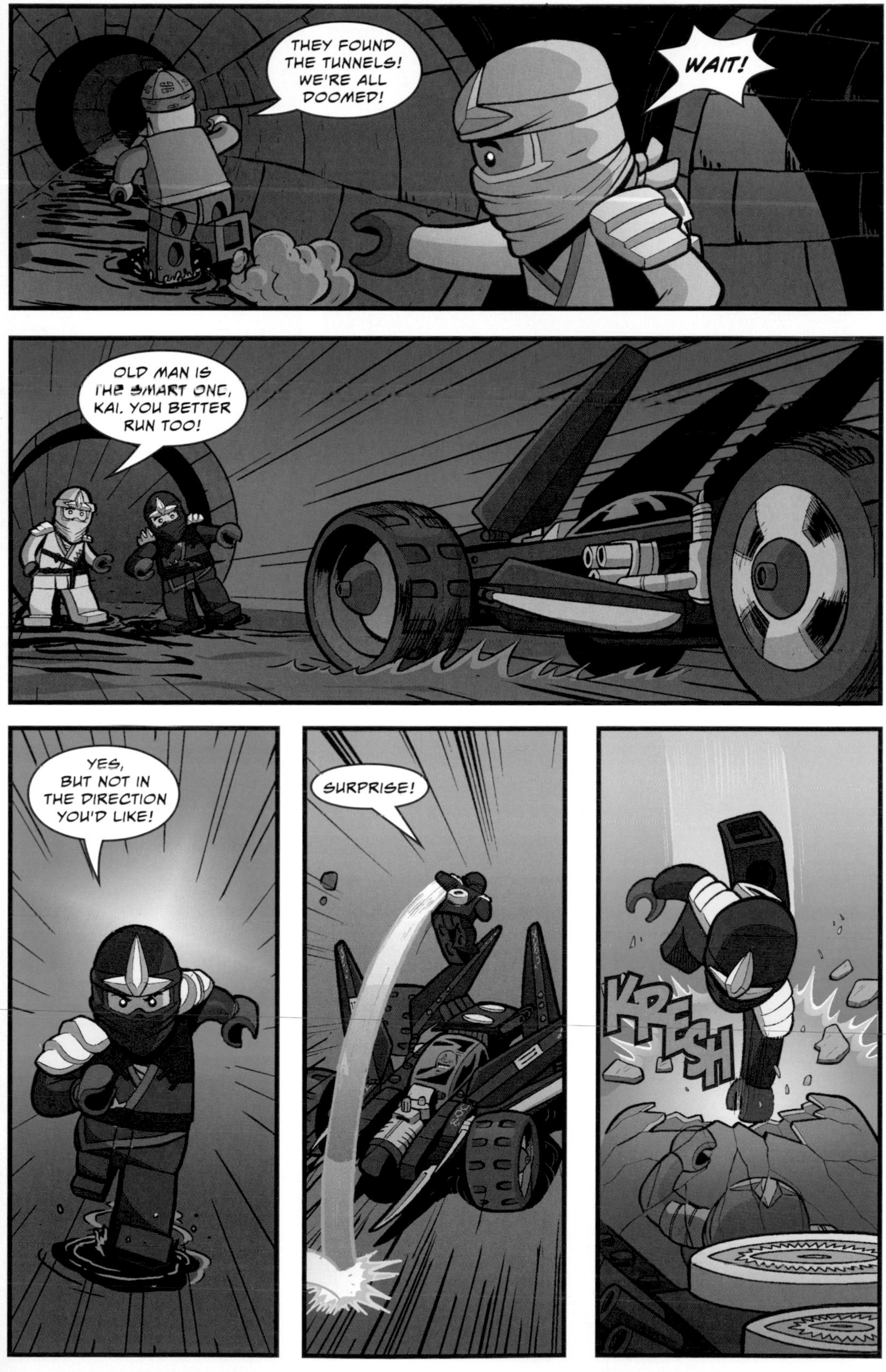
THEY FOUND THE TUNNELS! WE'RE ALL DOOMED!
WAIT!
OLD MAN IS THE SMART ONE, KAI. YOU BETTER RUN TOO!
YES, BUT NOT IN THE DIRECTION YOU'D LIKE!
SURPRISE!
KRESH

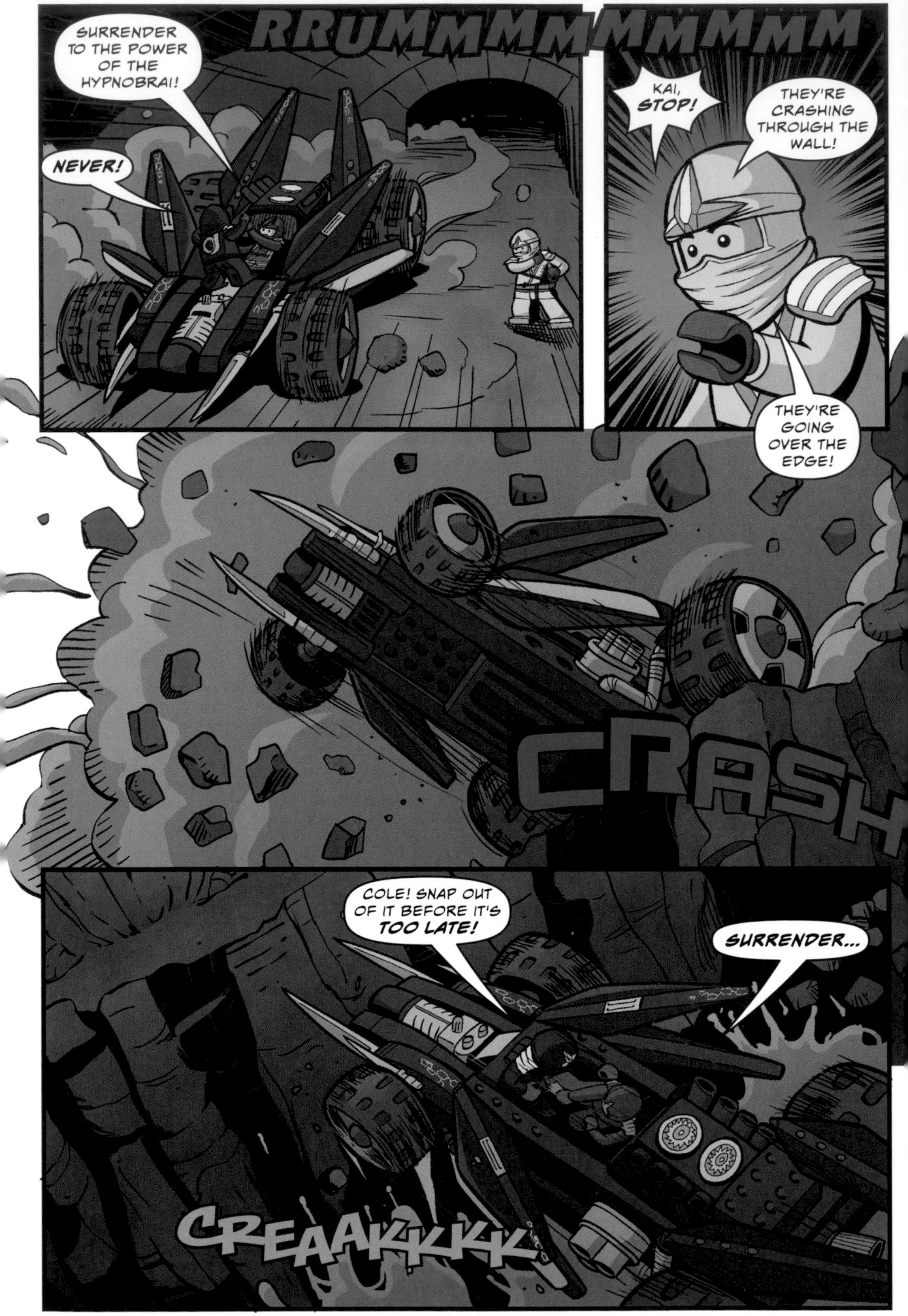
RRUMMMMMMMMM
SURRENDER TO THE POWER OF THE HYPNOBRAI!
NEVER!
KAI, STOP!
THEY'RE CRASHING THROUGH THE WALL!
THEY'RE GOING OVER THE EDGE!
CRASH
COLE! SNAP OUT OF IT BEFORE IT'S TOO LATE!
SURRENDER...
CREAAKKKK

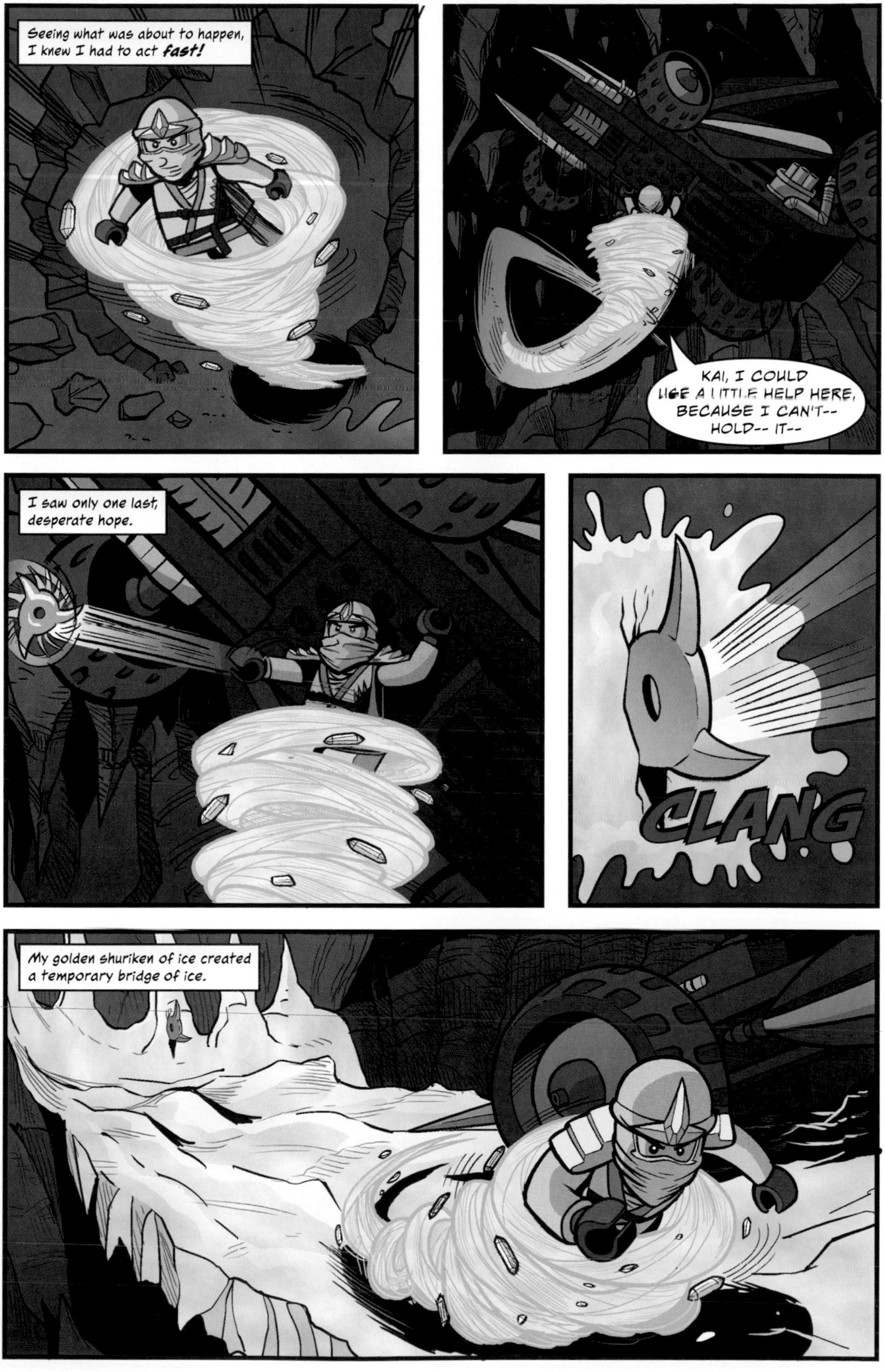
Seeing what was about to happen, I knew I had to act ***fast!***
KAI, I COULD USE A LITTLE HELP HERE, BECAUSE I CAN'T-- HOLD-- IT--
I saw only one last, desperate hope.
CLANG
My golden shuriken of ice created a temporary bridge of ice.

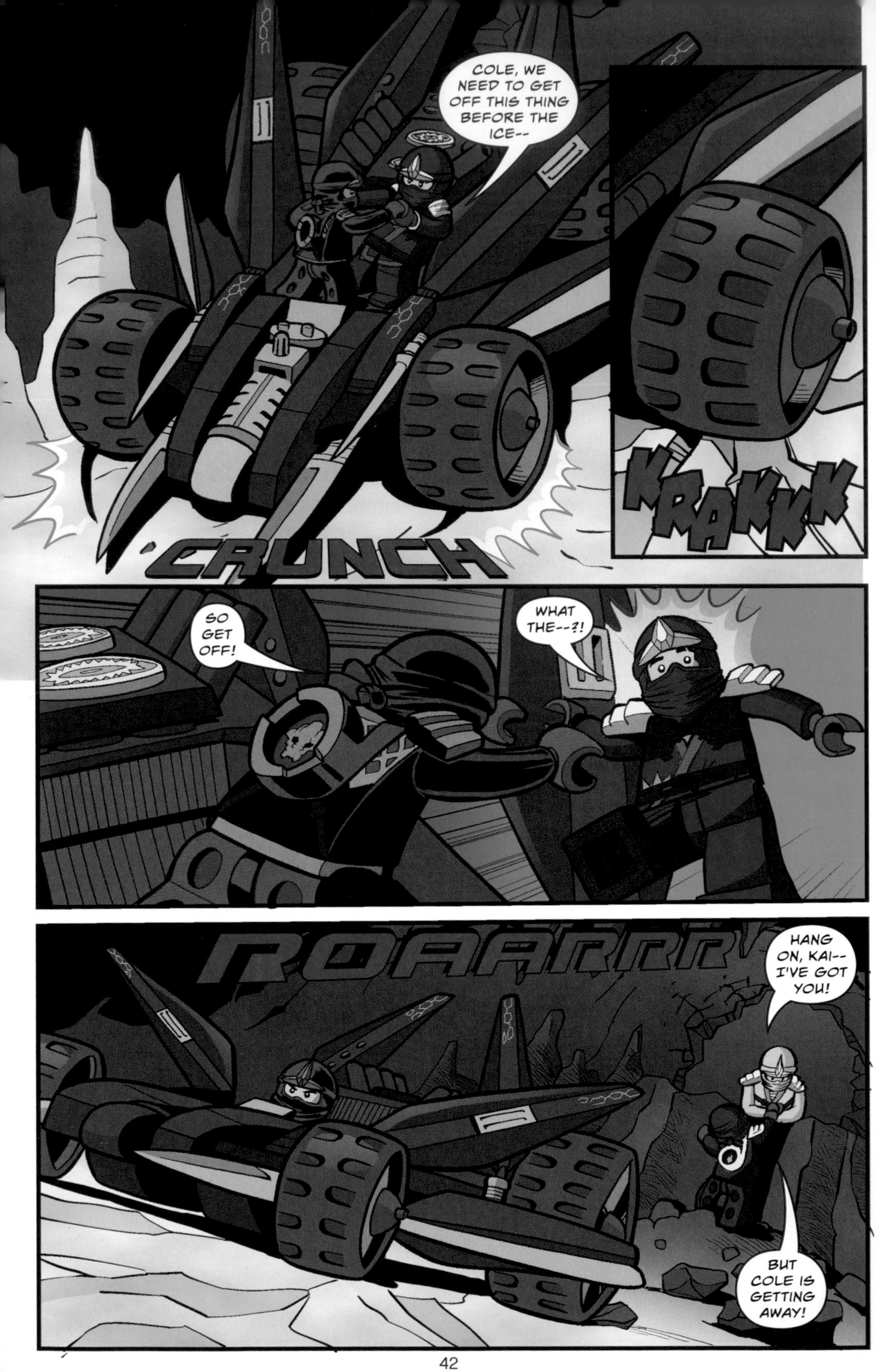
COLE, WE NEED TO GET OFF THIS THING BEFORE THE ICE--
KRAKKK
CRUNCH
SO GET OFF!
WHAT THE--?!
ROAARRR
HANG ON, KAI-- I'VE GOT YOU!
BUT COLE IS GETTING AWAY!

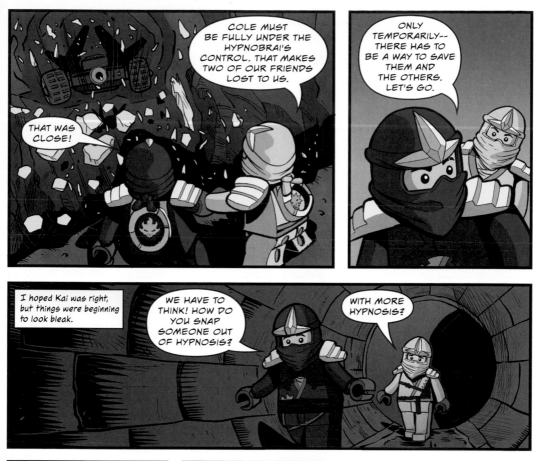

COLE MUST BE FULLY UNDER THE HYPNOBRAI'S CONTROL. THAT MAKES TWO OF OUR FRIENDS LOST TO US.

THAT WAS CLOSE!

ONLY TEMPORARILY-- THERE HAS TO BE A WAY TO SAVE THEM AND THE OTHERS. LET'S GO.

I hoped Kai was right, but things were beginning to look bleak.

WE HAVE TO THINK! HOW DO YOU SNAP SOMEONE OUT OF HYPNOSIS?

WITH MORE HYPNOSIS?

HOW ARE YOU GOING TO HYPNOTIZE DOZENS, MAYBE HUNDREDS OF PEOPLE, ONE AT A TIME? NO, THERE HAS TO BE SOMETHING ELSE.

PERHAPS... A SUDDEN BRIGHT LIGHT... OR A LOUD NOISE WOULD DO IT?

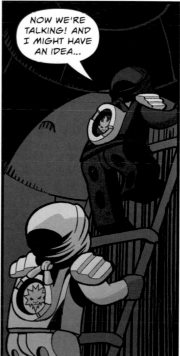

NOW WE'RE TALKING! AND I MIGHT HAVE AN IDEA...

Kai did not share his plan, insisting that we head for the warehouse the old man had mentioned. We stayed in the shadows, for obvious reasons...

Somehow, we made it to the roof of the warehouse unseen...

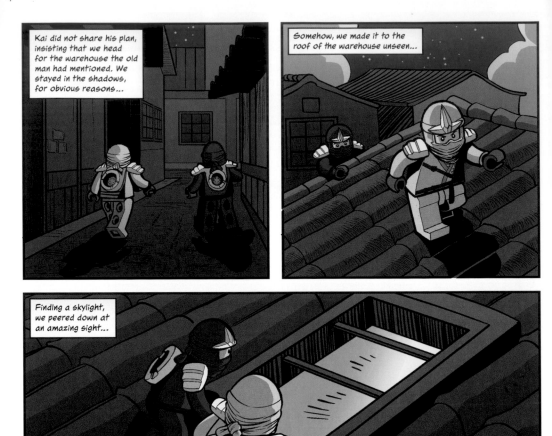

Finding a skylight, we peered down at an amazing sight...

The warehouse had been converted into a vehicle factory for the Hypnobrai!

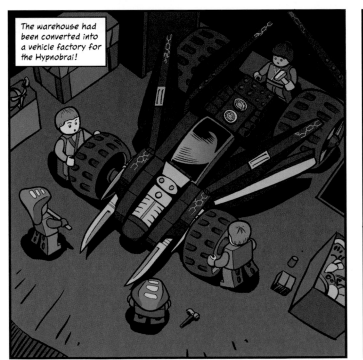

DO WE ATTACK?

NO, TOO MANY OF THEM... EVEN FOR ME. WE WAIT!

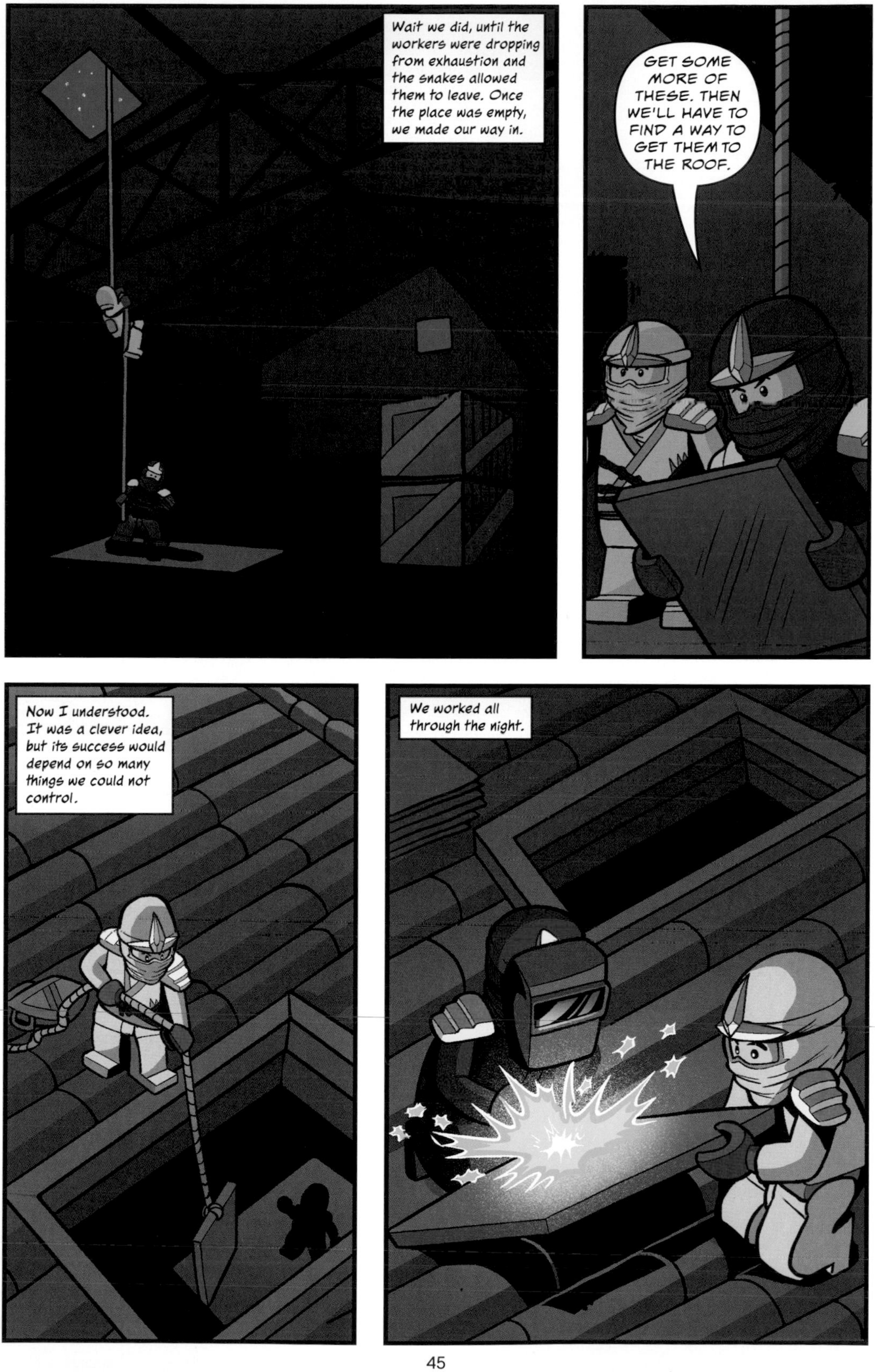
Wait we did, until the workers were dropping from exhaustion and the snakes allowed them to leave. Once the place was empty, we made our way in.
GET SOME MORE OF THESE. THEN WE'LL HAVE TO FIND A WAY TO GET THEM TO THE ROOF.
Now I understood. It was a clever idea, but its success would depend on so many things we could not control.
We worked all through the night.

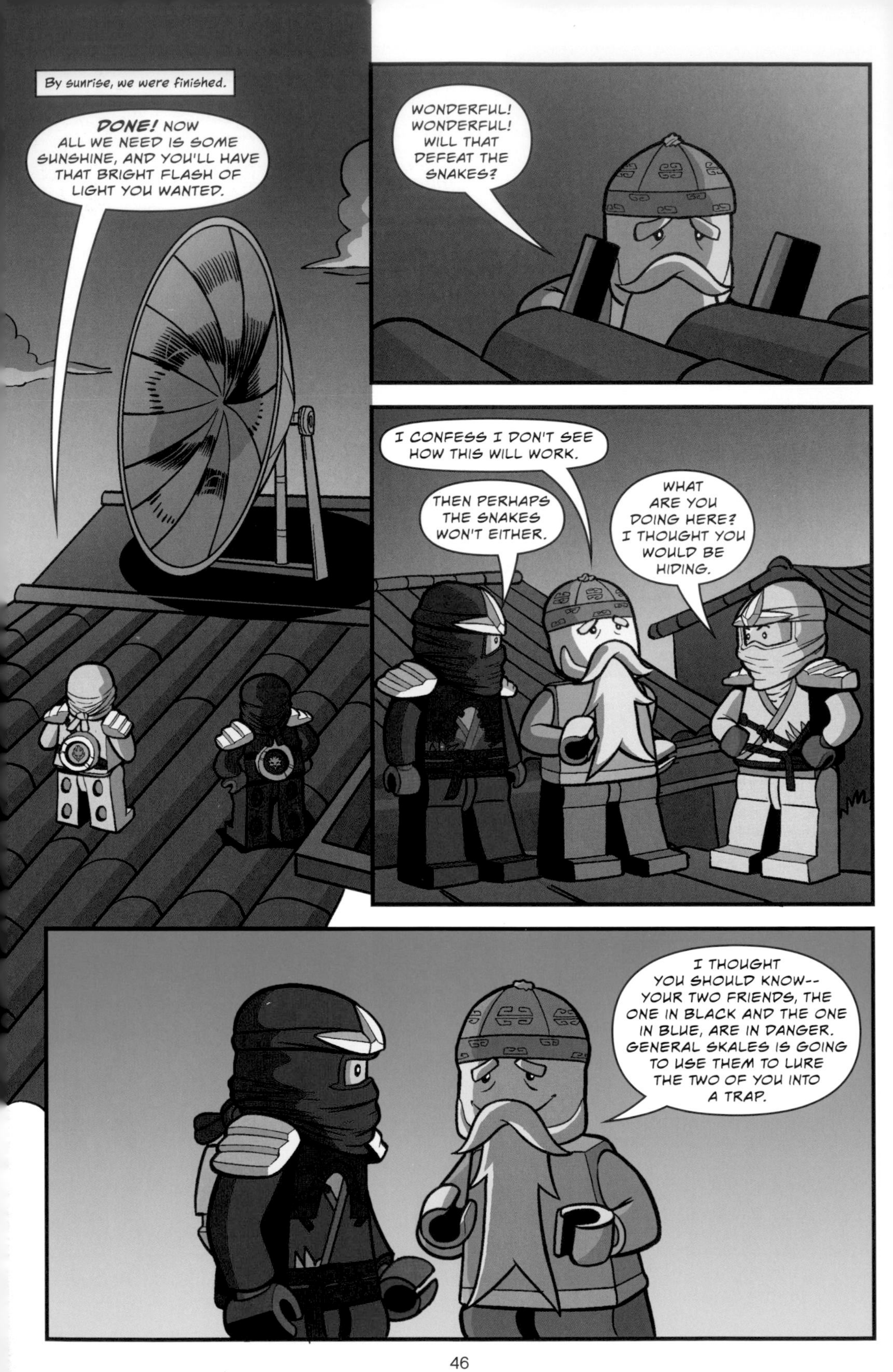
By sunrise, we were finished.
DONE! NOW ALL WE NEED IS SOME SUNSHINE, AND YOU'LL HAVE THAT BRIGHT FLASH OF LIGHT YOU WANTED.
WONDERFUL! WONDERFUL! WILL THAT DEFEAT THE SNAKES?
I CONFESS I DON'T SEE HOW THIS WILL WORK.
THEN PERHAPS THE SNAKES WON'T EITHER.
WHAT ARE YOU DOING HERE? I THOUGHT YOU WOULD BE HIDING.
I THOUGHT YOU SHOULD KNOW-- YOUR TWO FRIENDS, THE ONE IN BLACK AND THE ONE IN BLUE, ARE IN DANGER. GENERAL SKALES IS GOING TO USE THEM TO LURE THE TWO OF YOU INTO A TRAP.

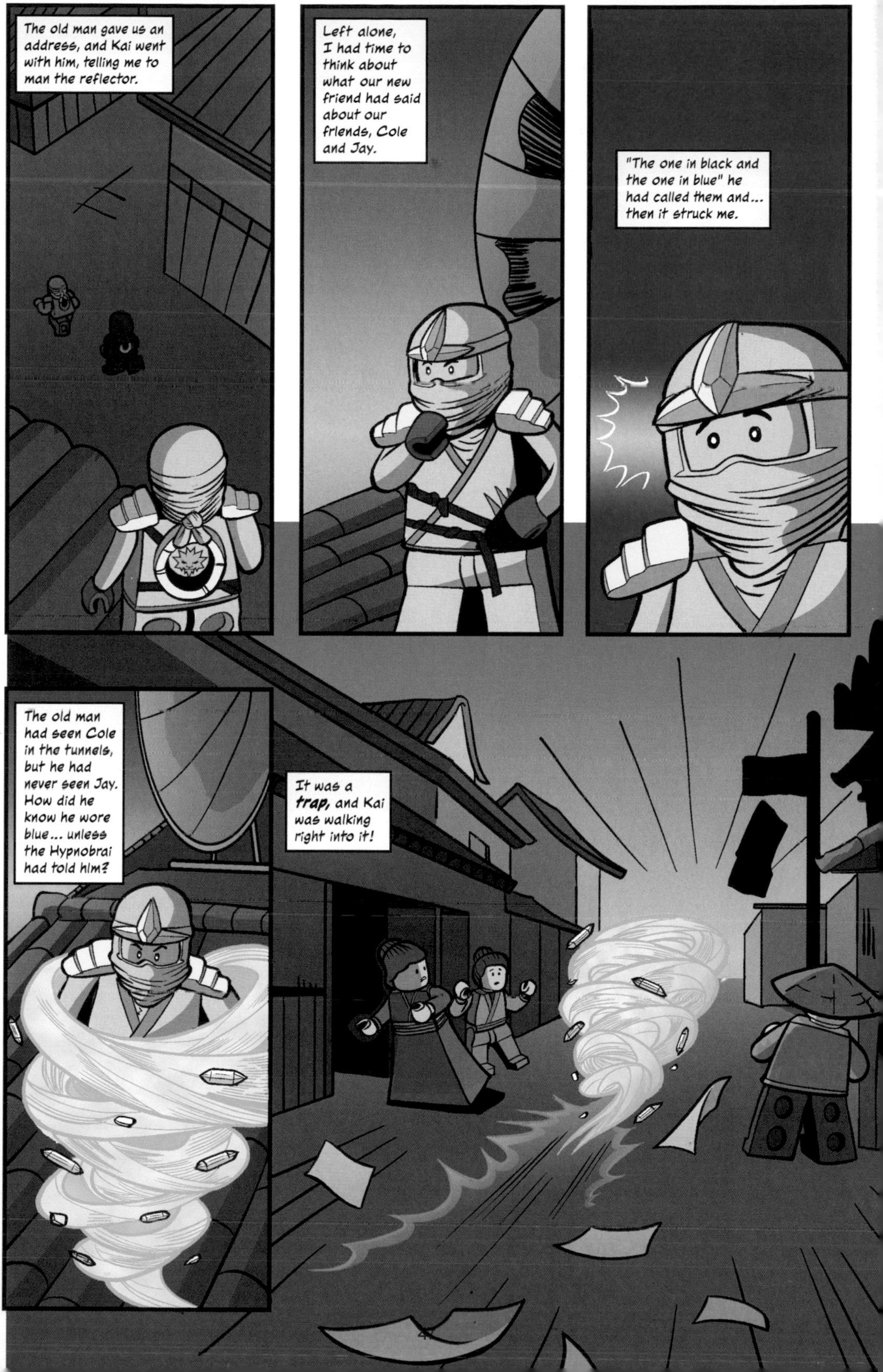
The old man gave us an address, and Kai went with him, telling me to man the reflector.
Left alone, I had time to think about what our new friend had said about our friends, Cole and Jay.
"The one in black and the one in blue" he had called them and... then it struck me.
The old man had seen Cole in the tunnels, but he had never seen Jay. How did he know he wore blue... unless the Hypnobrai had told him?
It was a ***trap,*** and Kai was walking right into it!

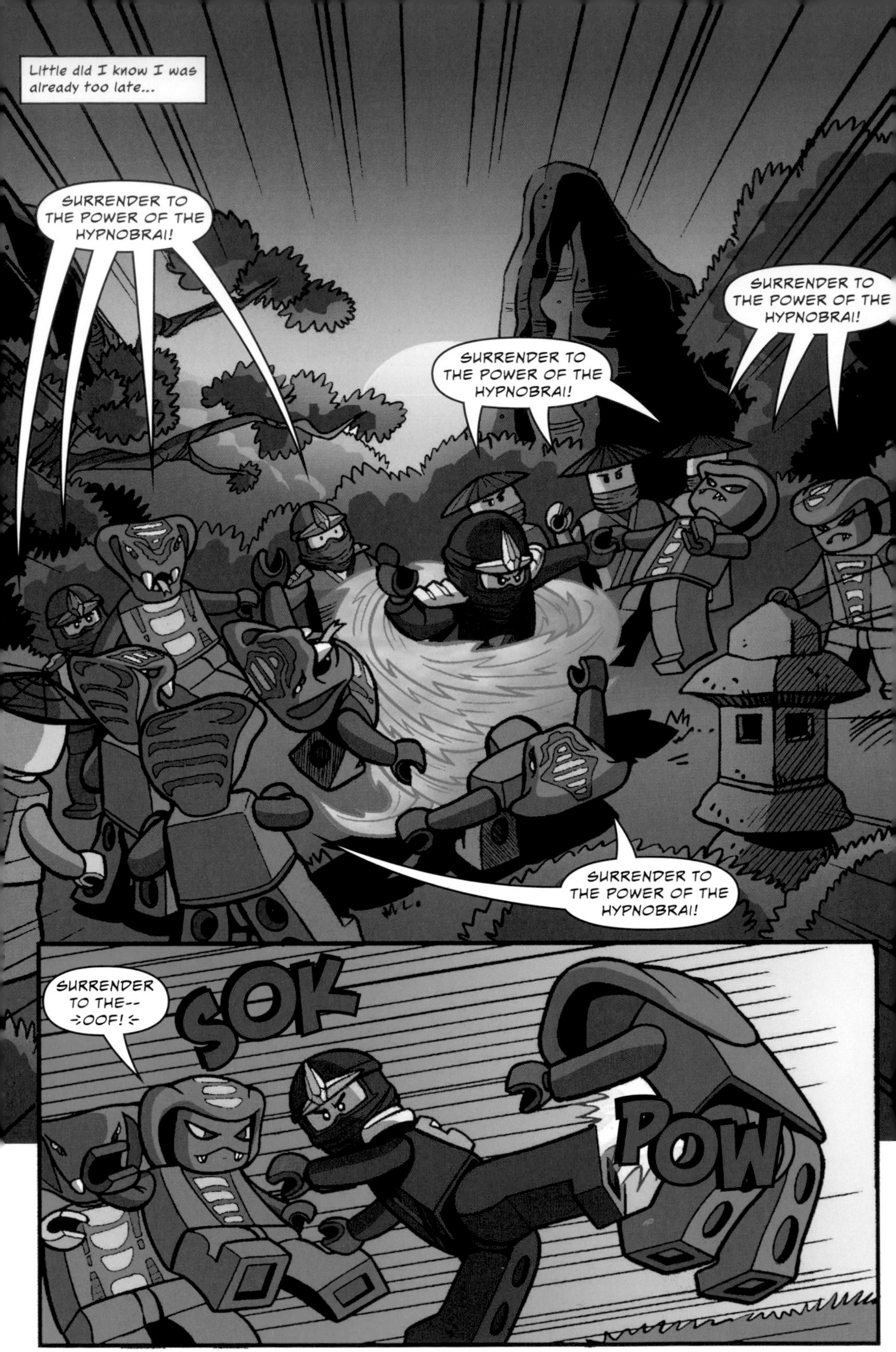
Little did I know I was already too late...
SURRENDER TO THE POWER OF THE HYPNOBRAI!
SURRENDER TO THE POWER OF THE HYPNOBRAI!
SURRENDER TO THE POWER OF THE HYPNOBRAI!
SURRENDER TO THE POWER OF THE HYPNOBRAI!
SURRENDER TO THE-- OOF!
SOK
POW

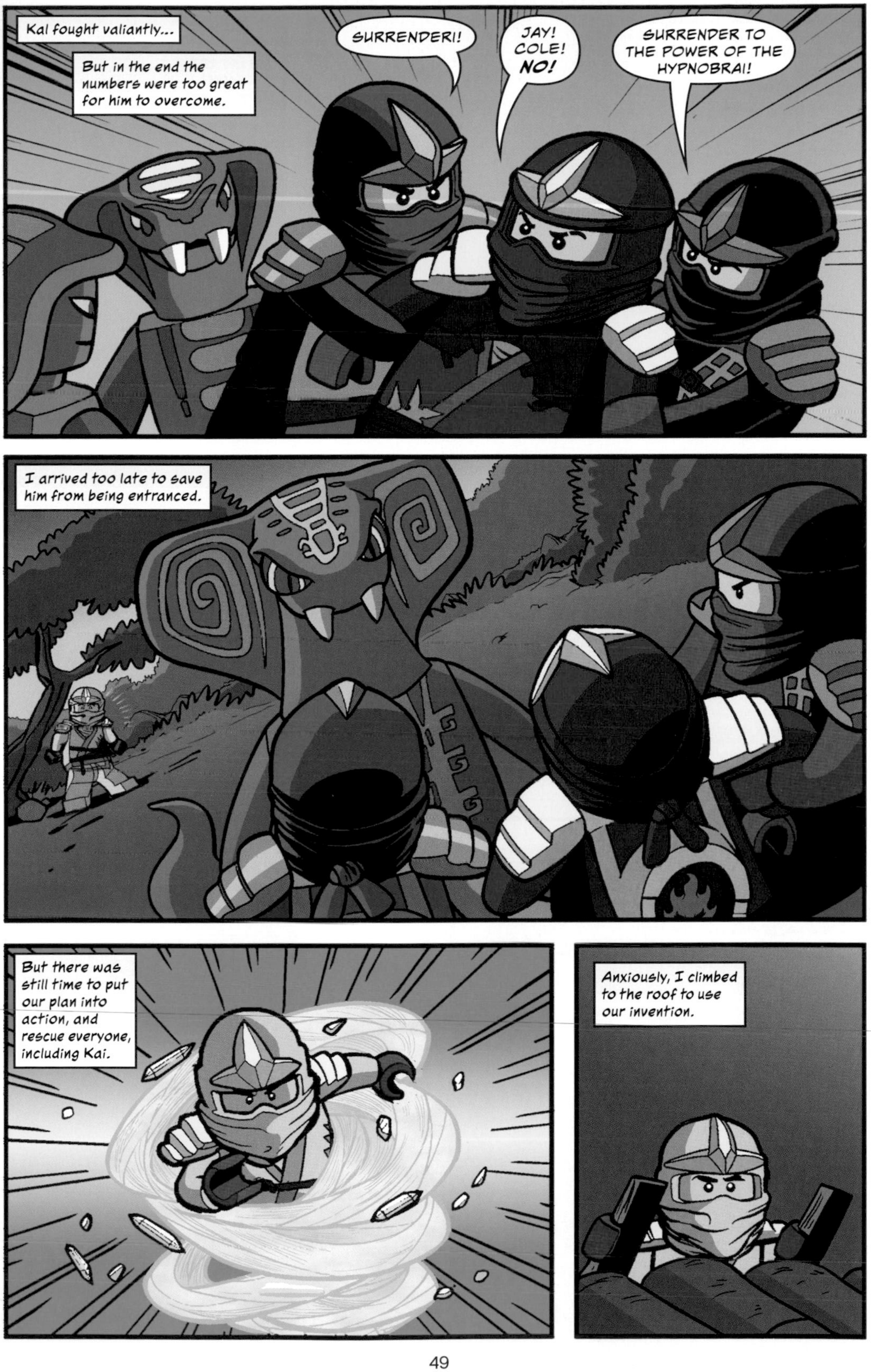
Kal fought valiantly...
But in the end the numbers were too great for him to overcome.
SURRENDER!
JAY! COLE! NO!
SURRENDER TO THE POWER OF THE HYPNOBRAI!
I arrived too late to save him from being entranced.
But there was still time to put our plan into action, and rescue everyone, including Kai.
Anxiously, I climbed to the roof to use our invention.

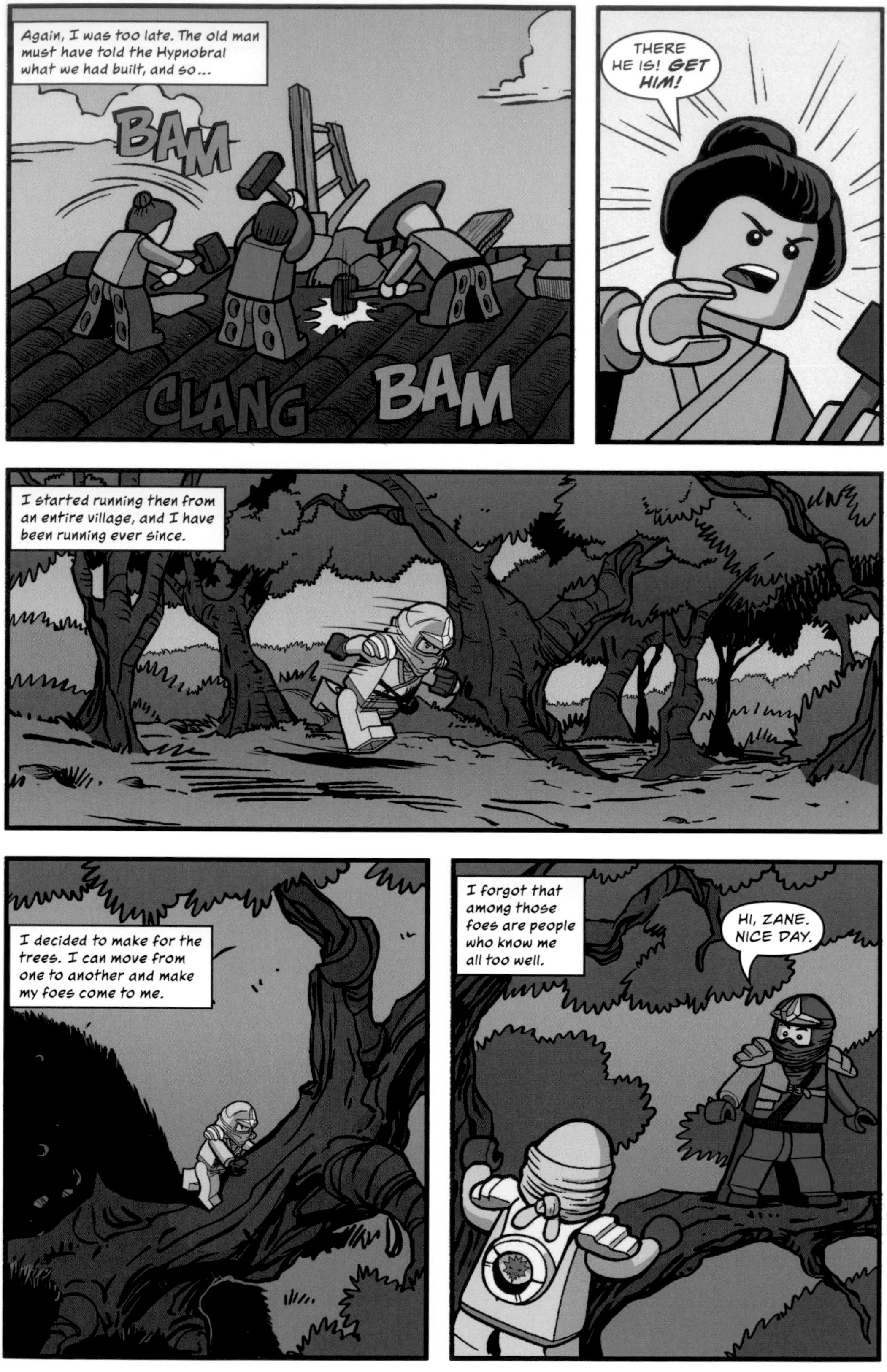

Again, I was too late. The old man must have told the Hypnobrai what we had built, and so...
BAM
CLANG
BAM
THERE HE IS! GET HIM!
I started running then from an entire village, and I have been running ever since.
I decided to make for the trees. I can move from one to another and make my foes come to me.
I forgot that among those foes are people who know me all too well.
HI, ZANE. NICE DAY.

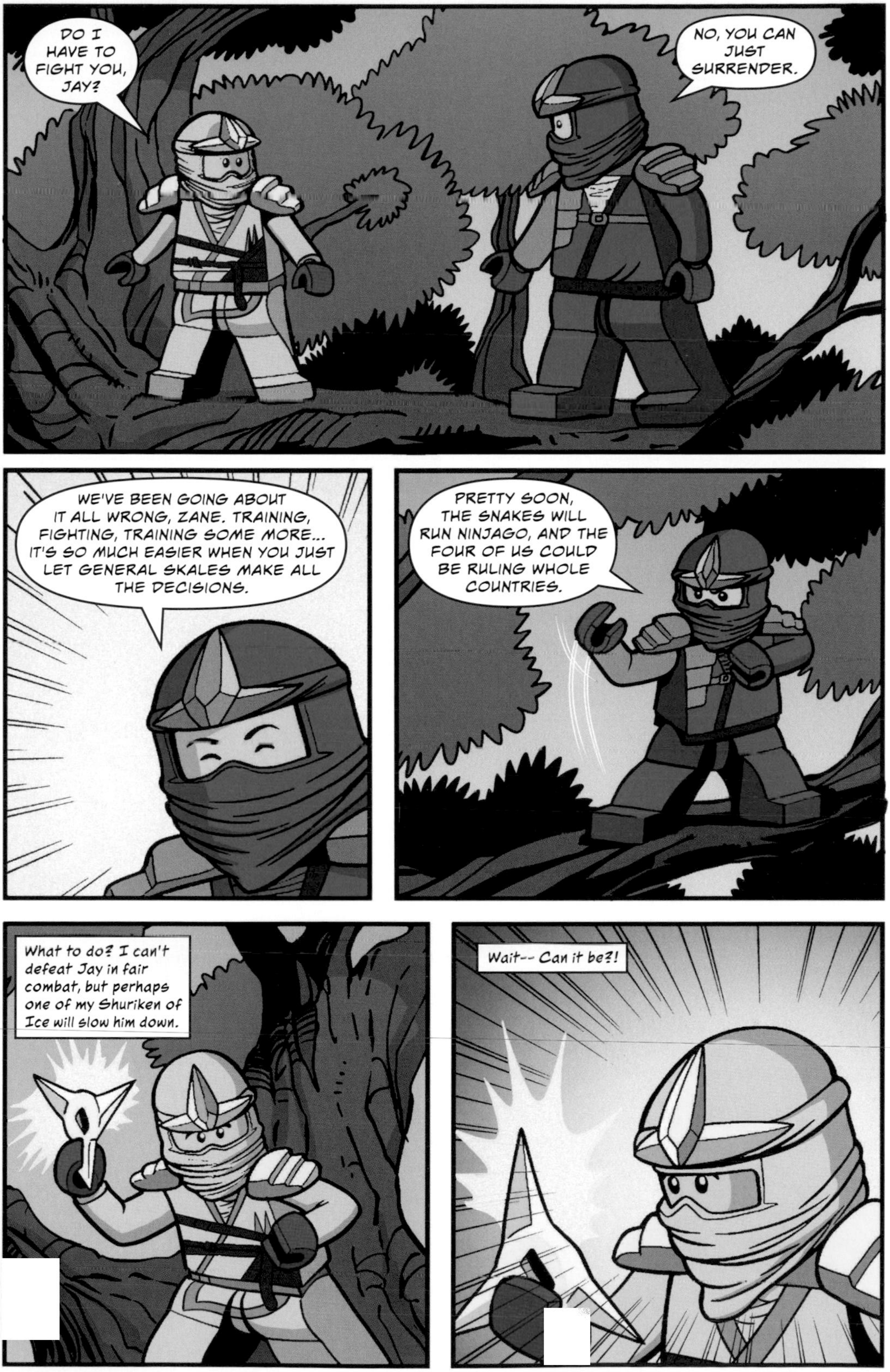

DO I HAVE TO FIGHT YOU, JAY?
NO, YOU CAN JUST SURRENDER.
WE'VE BEEN GOING ABOUT IT ALL WRONG, ZANE. TRAINING, FIGHTING, TRAINING SOME MORE... IT'S SO MUCH EASIER WHEN YOU JUST LET GENERAL SKALES MAKE ALL THE DECISIONS.
PRETTY SOON, THE SNAKES WILL RUN NINJAGO, AND THE FOUR OF US COULD BE RULING WHOLE COUNTRIES.
What to do? I can't defeat Jay in fair combat, but perhaps one of my Shuriken of Ice will slow him down.
Wait-- Can it be?!

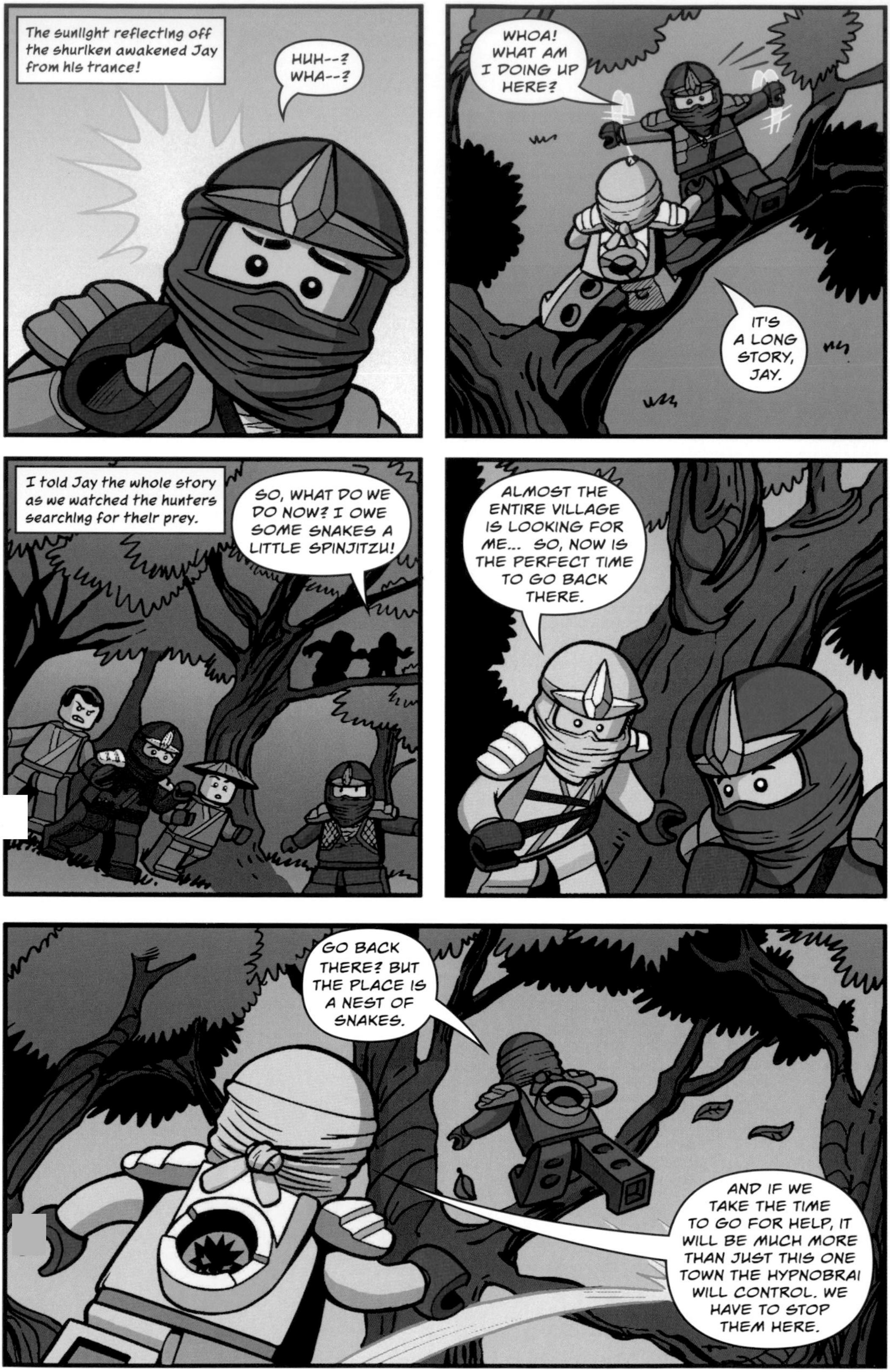

The sunlight reflecting off the shuriken awakened Jay from his trance!
HUH--? WHA--?
WHOA! WHAT AM I DOING UP HERE?
IT'S A LONG STORY, JAY.
I told Jay the whole story as we watched the hunters searching for their prey.
SO, WHAT DO WE DO NOW? I OWE SOME SNAKES A LITTLE SPINJITZU!
ALMOST THE ENTIRE VILLAGE IS LOOKING FOR ME... SO, NOW IS THE PERFECT TIME TO GO BACK THERE.
GO BACK THERE? BUT THE PLACE IS A NEST OF SNAKES.
AND IF WE TAKE THE TIME TO GO FOR HELP, IT WILL BE MUCH MORE THAN JUST THIS ONE TOWN THE HYPNOBRAI WILL CONTROL. WE HAVE TO STOP THEM HERE.

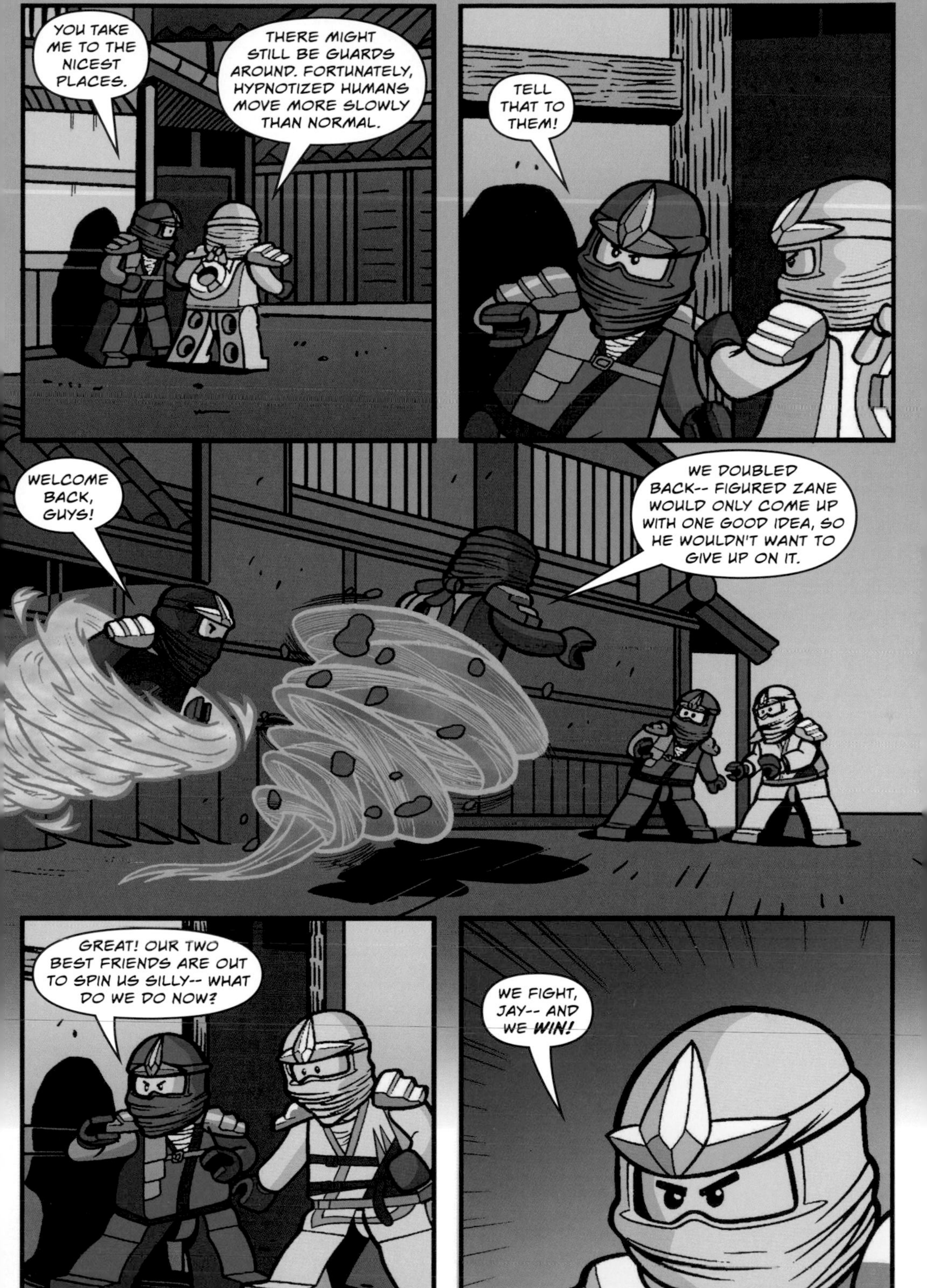
YOU TAKE ME TO THE NICEST PLACES.
THERE MIGHT STILL BE GUARDS AROUND. FORTUNATELY, HYPNOTIZED HUMANS MOVE MORE SLOWLY THAN NORMAL.
TELL THAT TO THEM!
WELCOME BACK, GUYS!
WE DOUBLED BACK-- FIGURED ZANE WOULD ONLY COME UP WITH ONE GOOD IDEA, SO HE WOULDN'T WANT TO GIVE UP ON IT.
GREAT! OUR TWO BEST FRIENDS ARE OUT TO SPIN US SILLY-- WHAT DO WE DO NOW?
WE FIGHT, JAY-- AND WE **WIN!**

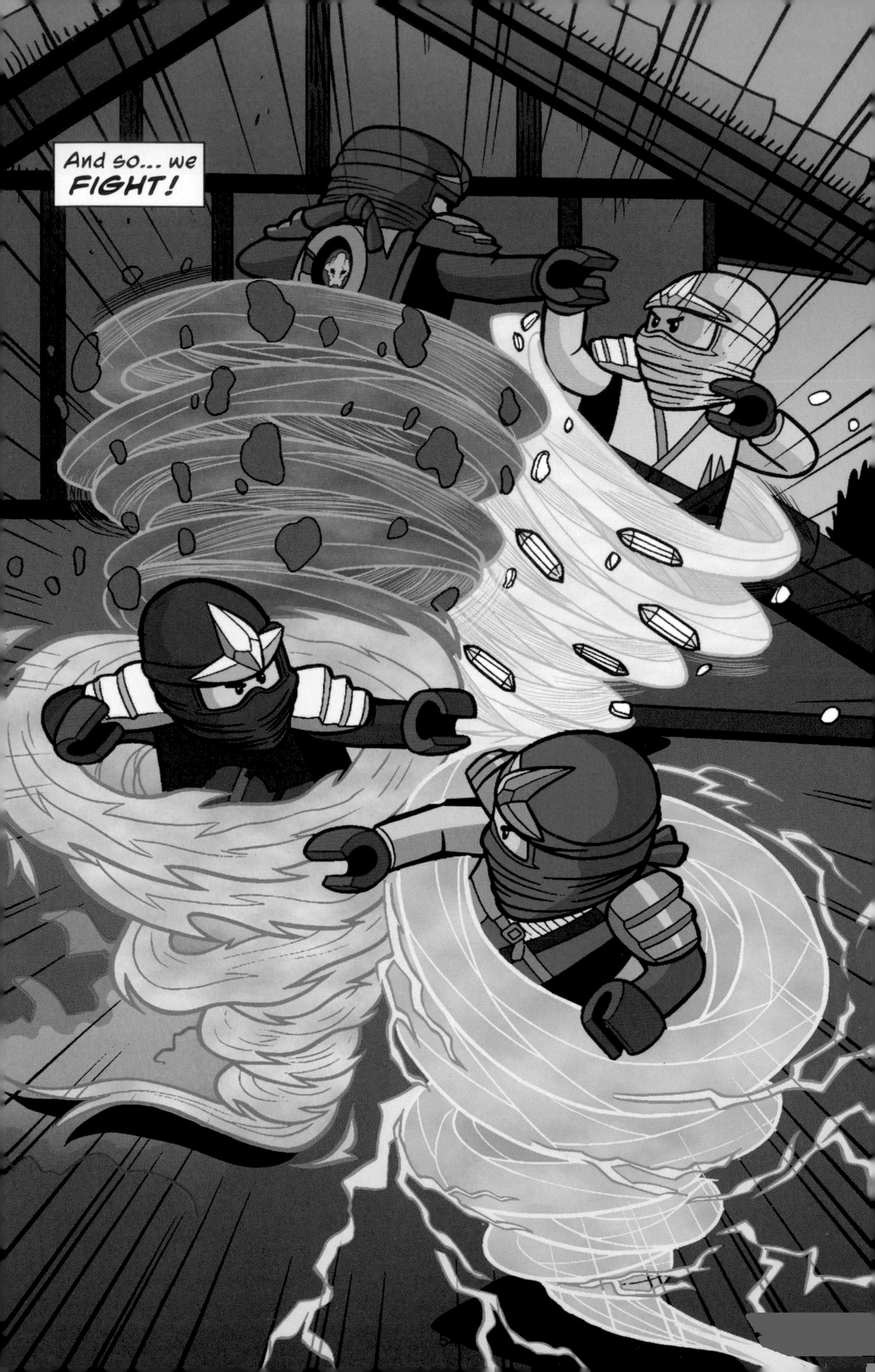
And so... we FIGHT!

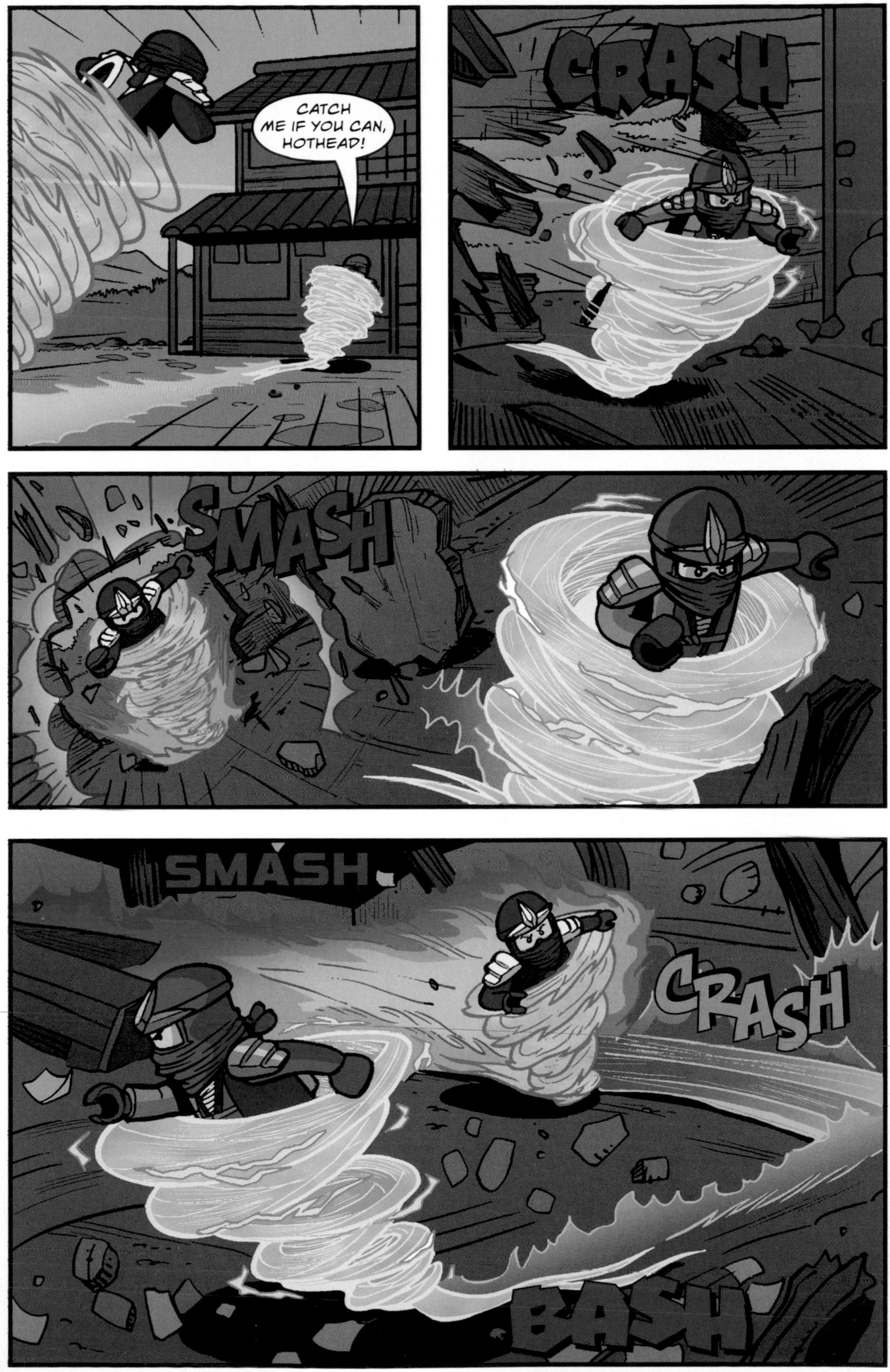
CATCH ME IF YOU CAN, HOTHEAD!
CRASH
SMASH
SMASH
CRASH
BASH

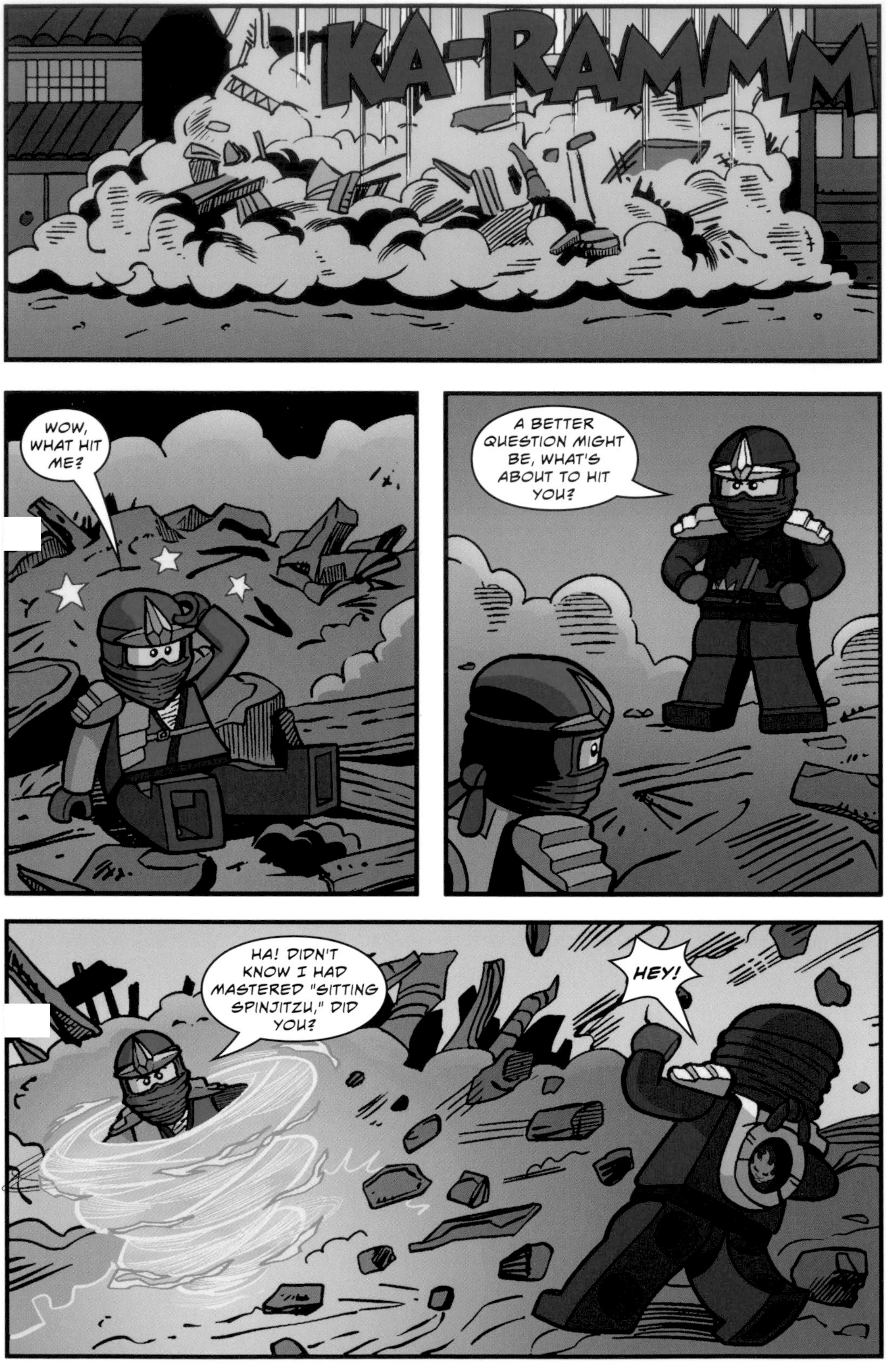
KA-RAMMM
WOW, WHAT HIT ME?
A BETTER QUESTION MIGHT BE, WHAT'S ABOUT TO HIT YOU?
HA! DIDN'T KNOW I HAD MASTERED "SITTING SPINJITZU," DID YOU?
HEY!

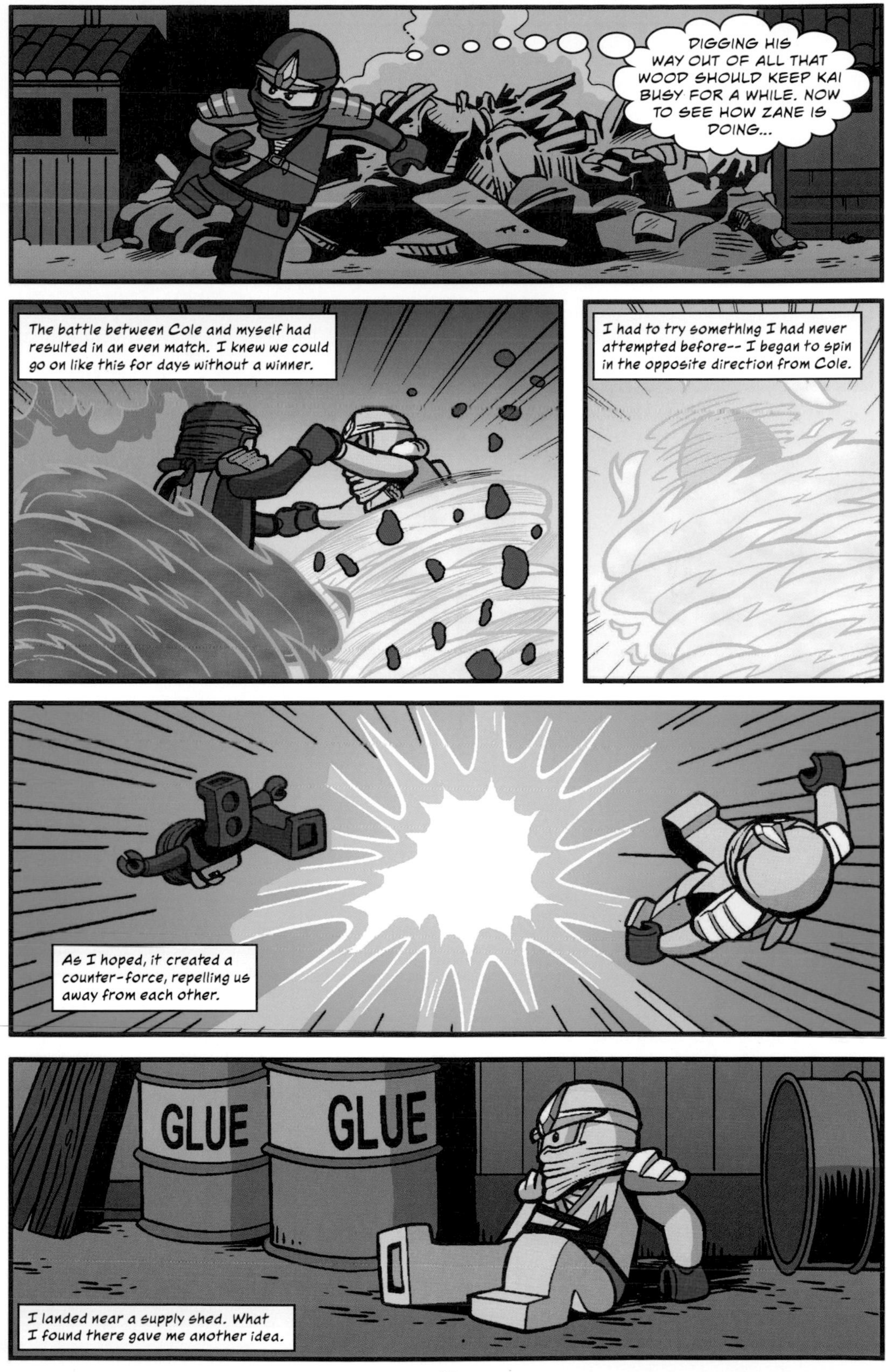
DIGGING HIS WAY OUT OF ALL THAT WOOD SHOULD KEEP KAI BUSY FOR A WHILE. NOW TO SEE HOW ZANE IS DOING...
The battle between Cole and myself had resulted in an even match. I knew we could go on like this for days without a winner.
I had to try something I had never attempted before-- I began to spin in the opposite direction from Cole.
As I hoped, it created a counter-force, repelling us away from each other.
GLUE
GLUE
I landed near a supply shed. What I found there gave me another idea.

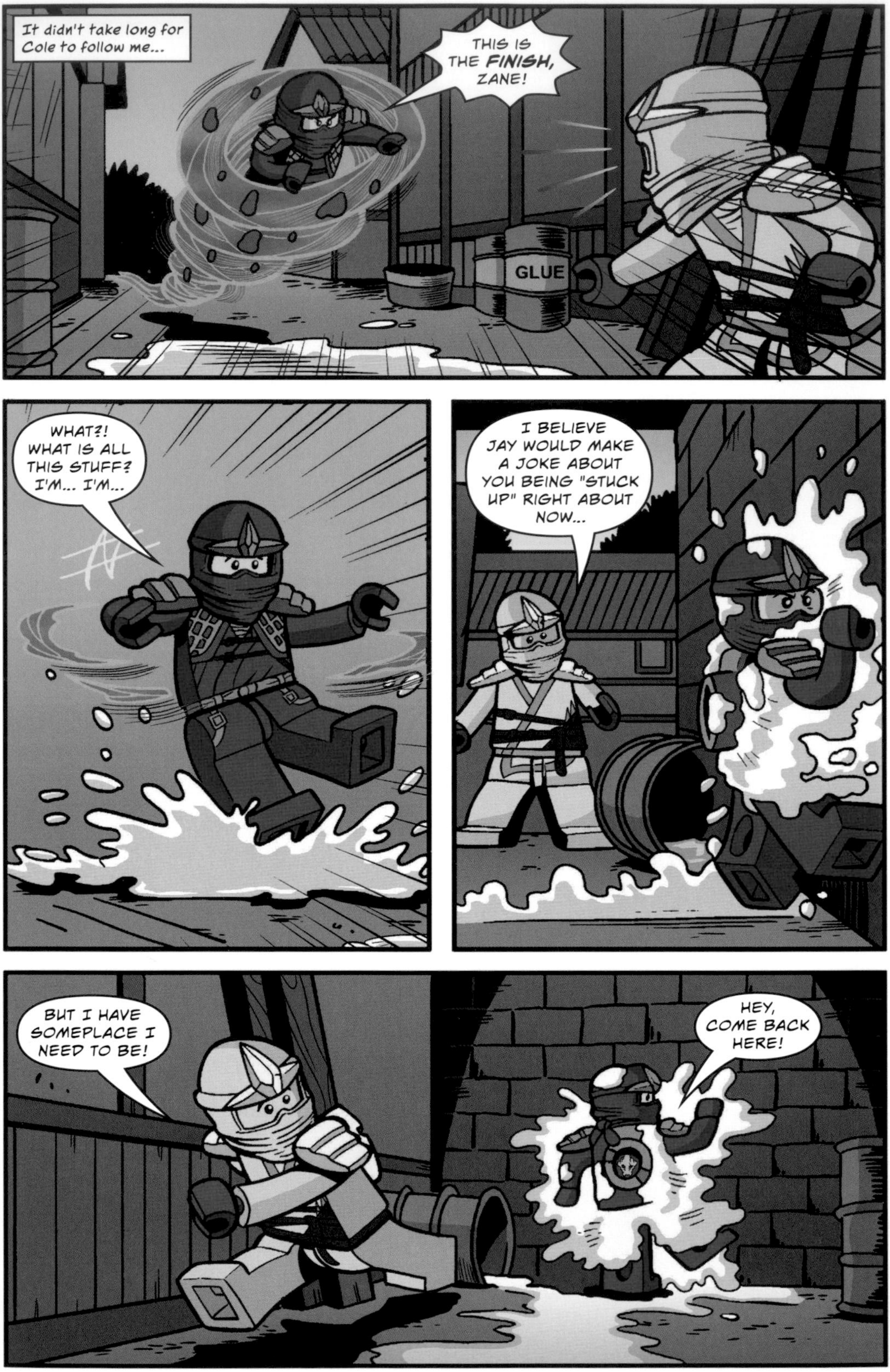

It didn't take long for Cole to follow me...
THIS IS THE FINISH, ZANE!
GLUE
WHAT?! WHAT IS ALL THIS STUFF? I'M... I'M...
I BELIEVE JAY WOULD MAKE A JOKE ABOUT YOU BEING "STUCK UP" RIGHT ABOUT NOW...
BUT I HAVE SOMEPLACE I NEED TO BE!
HEY, COME BACK HERE!

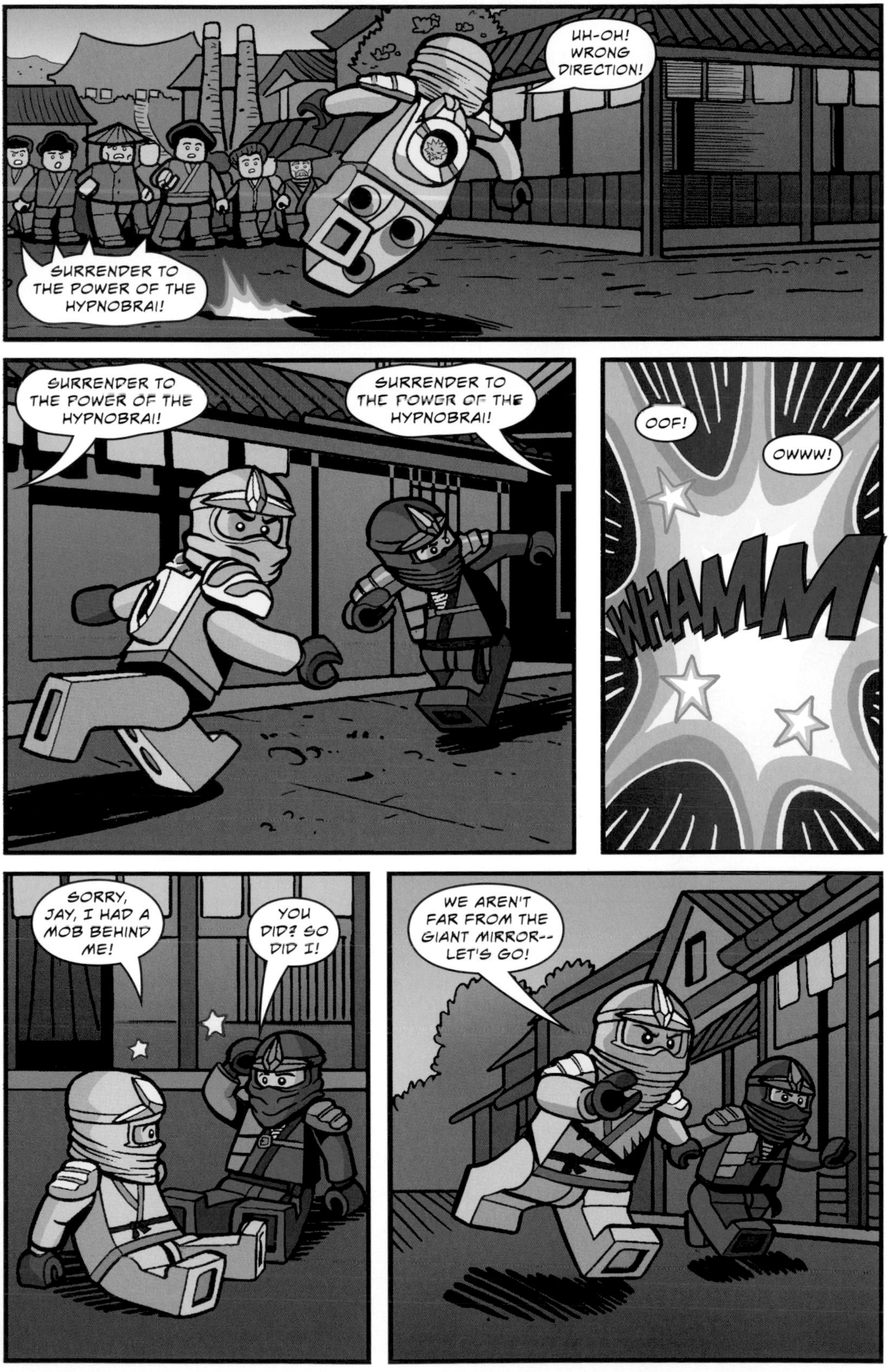
UH-OH! WRONG DIRECTION!
SURRENDER TO THE POWER OF THE HYPNOBRAI!
SURRENDER TO THE POWER OF THE HYPNOBRAI!
SURRENDER TO THE POWER OF THE HYPNOBRAI!
OOF!
OWWW!
WHAMM
SORRY, JAY, I HAD A MOB BEHIND ME!
YOU DID? SO DID I!
WE AREN'T FAR FROM THE GIANT MIRROR-- LET'S GO!

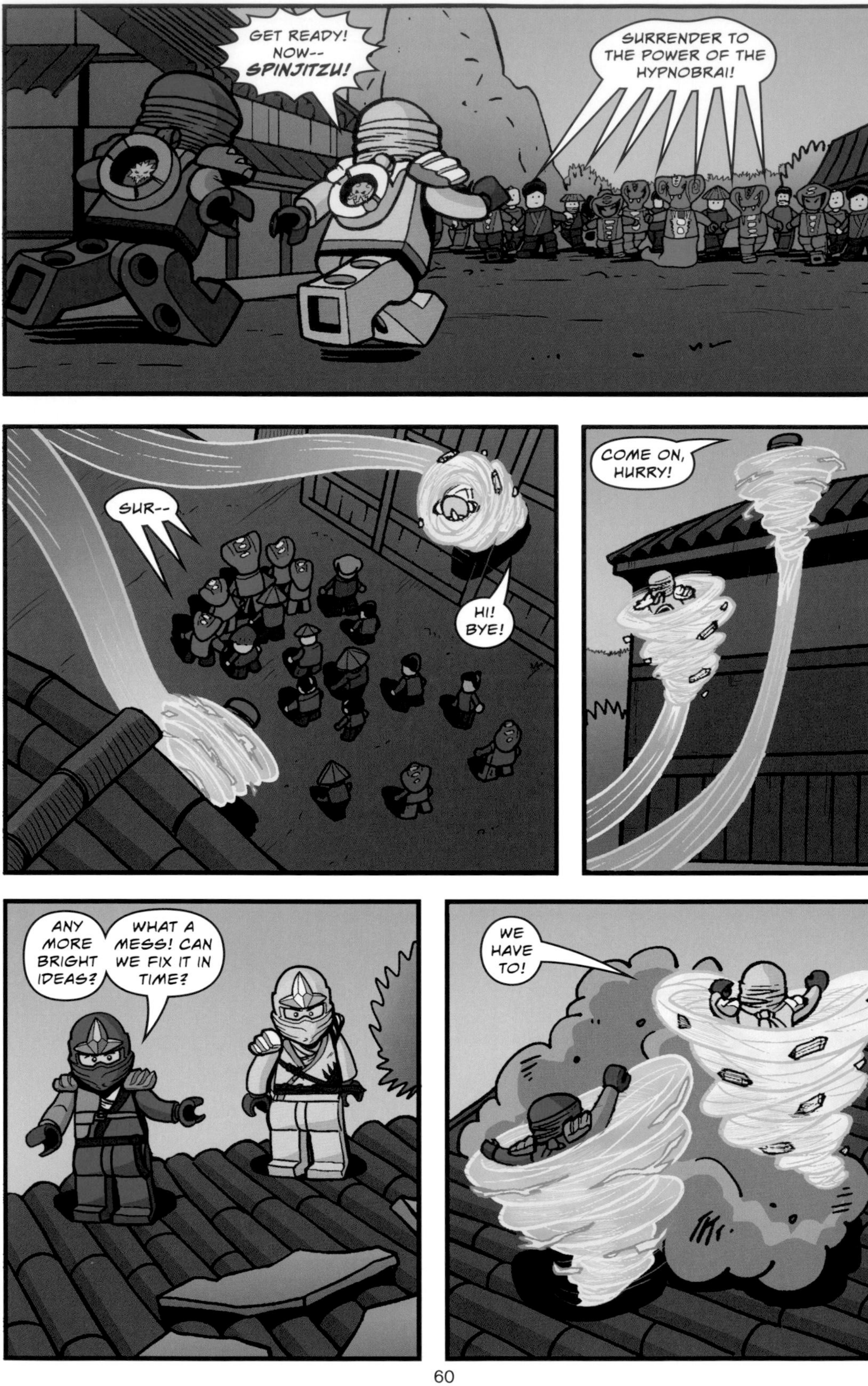
GET READY! NOW-- SPINJITZU!
SURRENDER TO THE POWER OF THE HYPNOBRAI!
SUR--
HI! BYE!
COME ON, HURRY!
ANY MORE BRIGHT IDEAS?
WHAT A MESS! CAN WE FIX IT IN TIME?
WE HAVE TO!

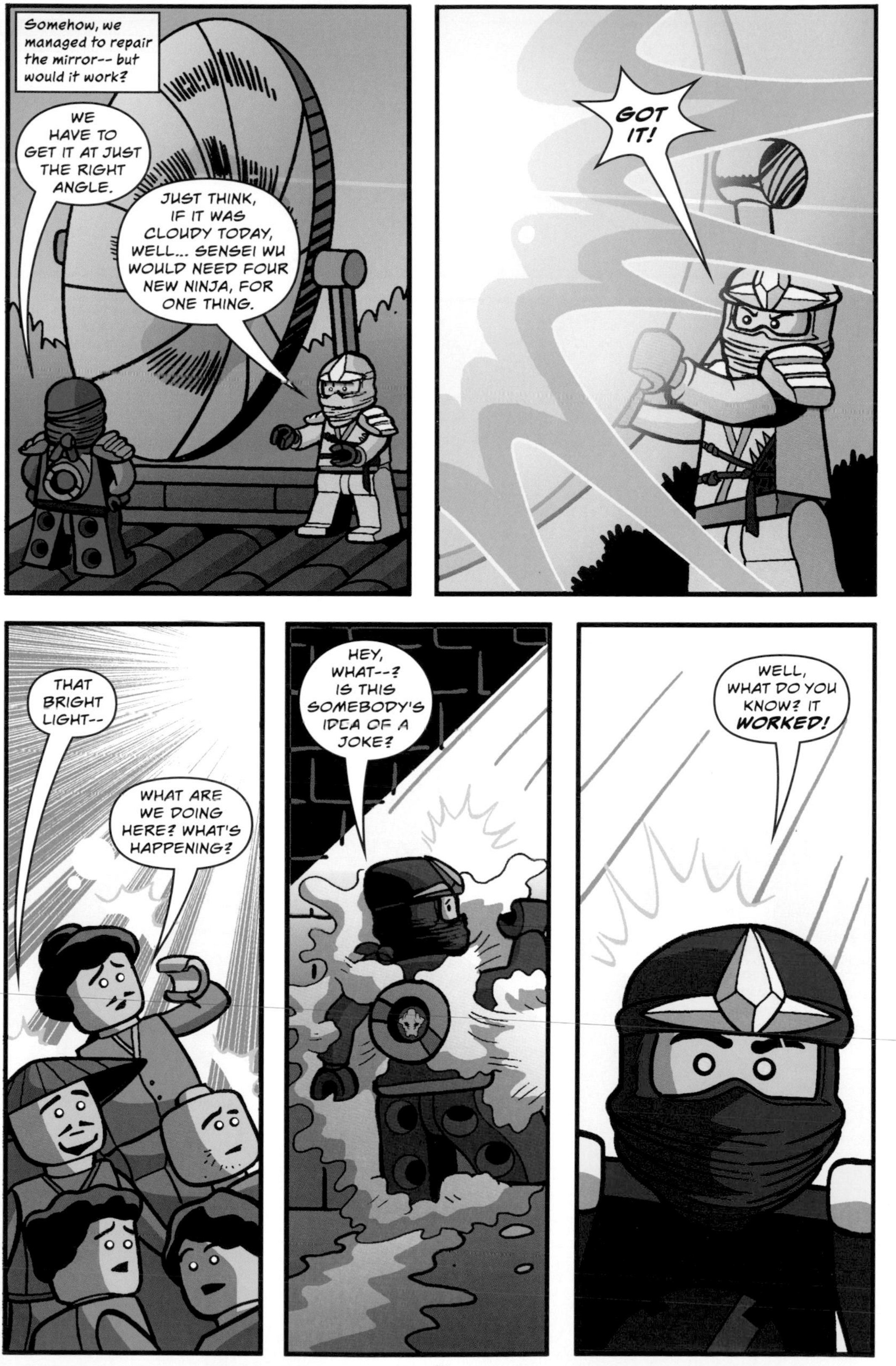

Somehow, we managed to repair the mirror-- but would it work?
WE HAVE TO GET IT AT JUST THE RIGHT ANGLE.
JUST THINK, IF IT WAS CLOUDY TODAY, WELL... SENSEI WU WOULD NEED FOUR NEW NINJA, FOR ONE THING.
GOT IT!
THAT BRIGHT LIGHT--
WHAT ARE WE DOING HERE? WHAT'S HAPPENING?
HEY, WHAT--? IS THIS SOMEBODY'S IDEA OF A JOKE?
WELL, WHAT DO YOU KNOW? IT WORKED!

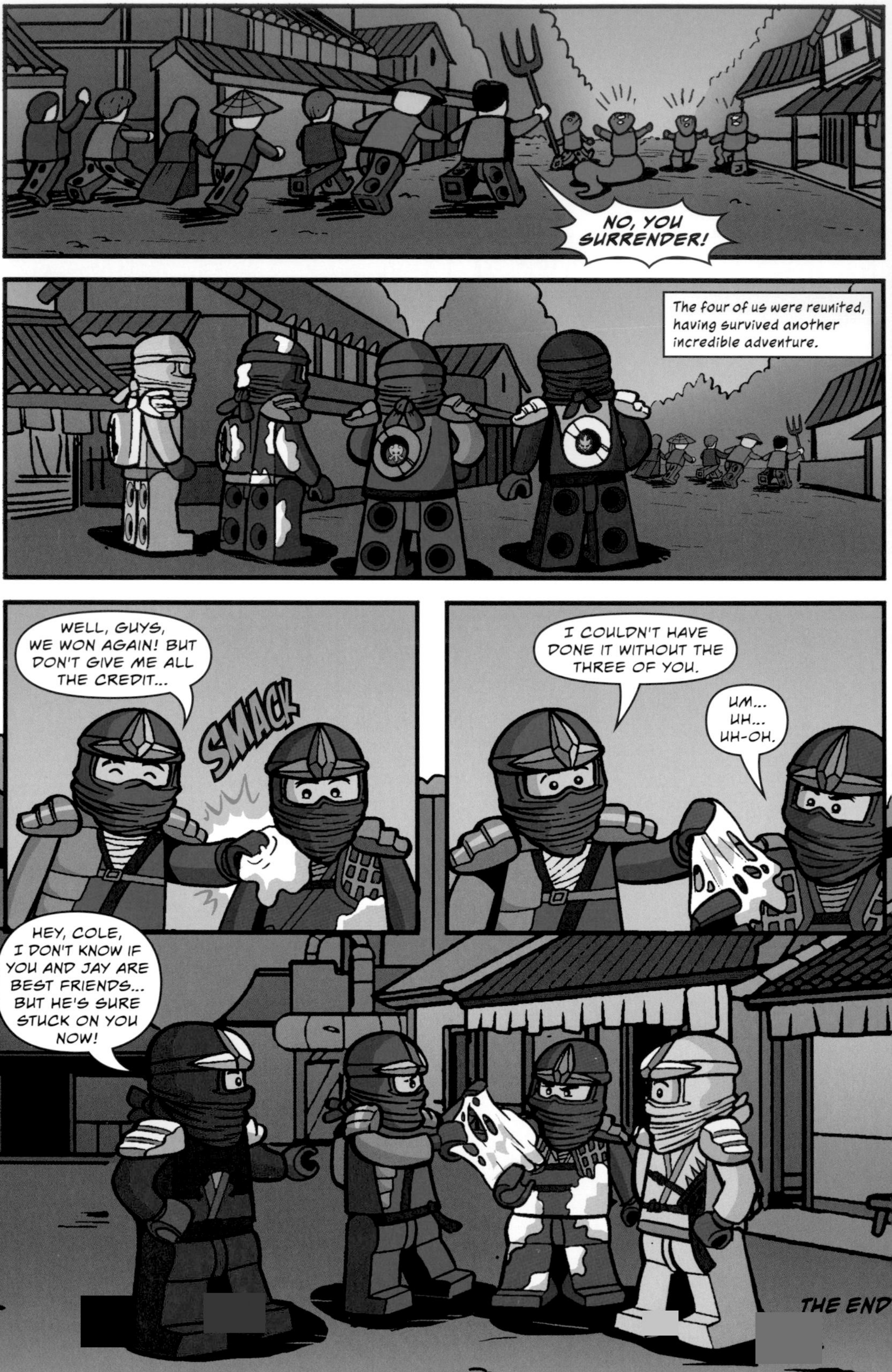
NO, YOU SURRENDER!
The four of us were reunited, having survived another incredible adventure.
WELL, GUYS, WE WON AGAIN! BUT DON'T GIVE ME ALL THE CREDIT...
SMACK
I COULDN'T HAVE DONE IT WITHOUT THE THREE OF YOU.
UM... UH... UH-OH.
HEY, COLE, I DON'T KNOW IF YOU AND JAY ARE BEST FRIENDS... BUT HE'S SURE STUCK ON YOU NOW!
THE END

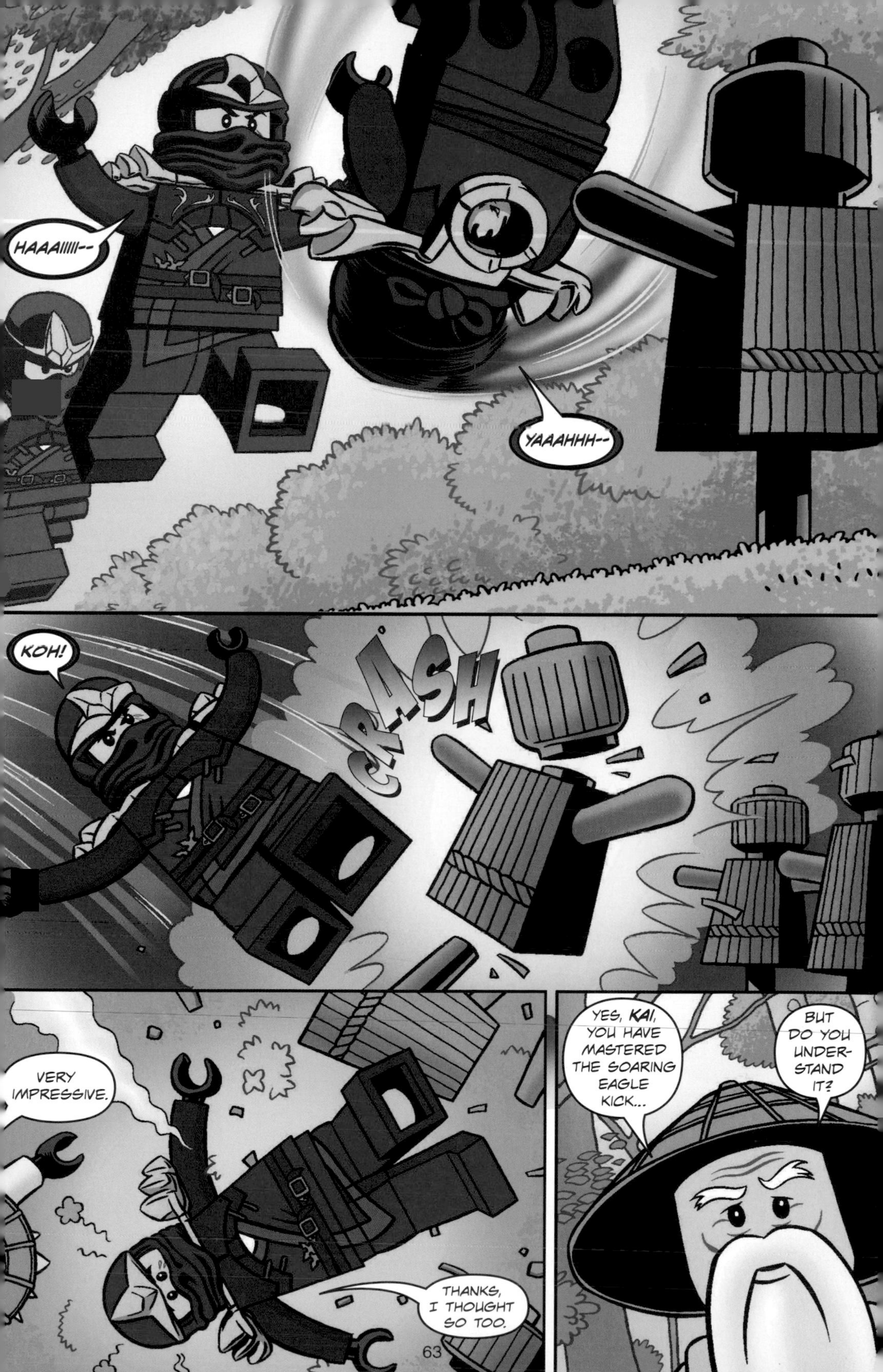
HAAAIIIII--
YAAAHHH--
KOH!
CRASH
VERY IMPRESSIVE.
THANKS, I THOUGHT SO TOO.
YES, KAI, YOU HAVE MASTERED THE SOARING EAGLE KICK...
BUT DO YOU UNDER-STAND IT?

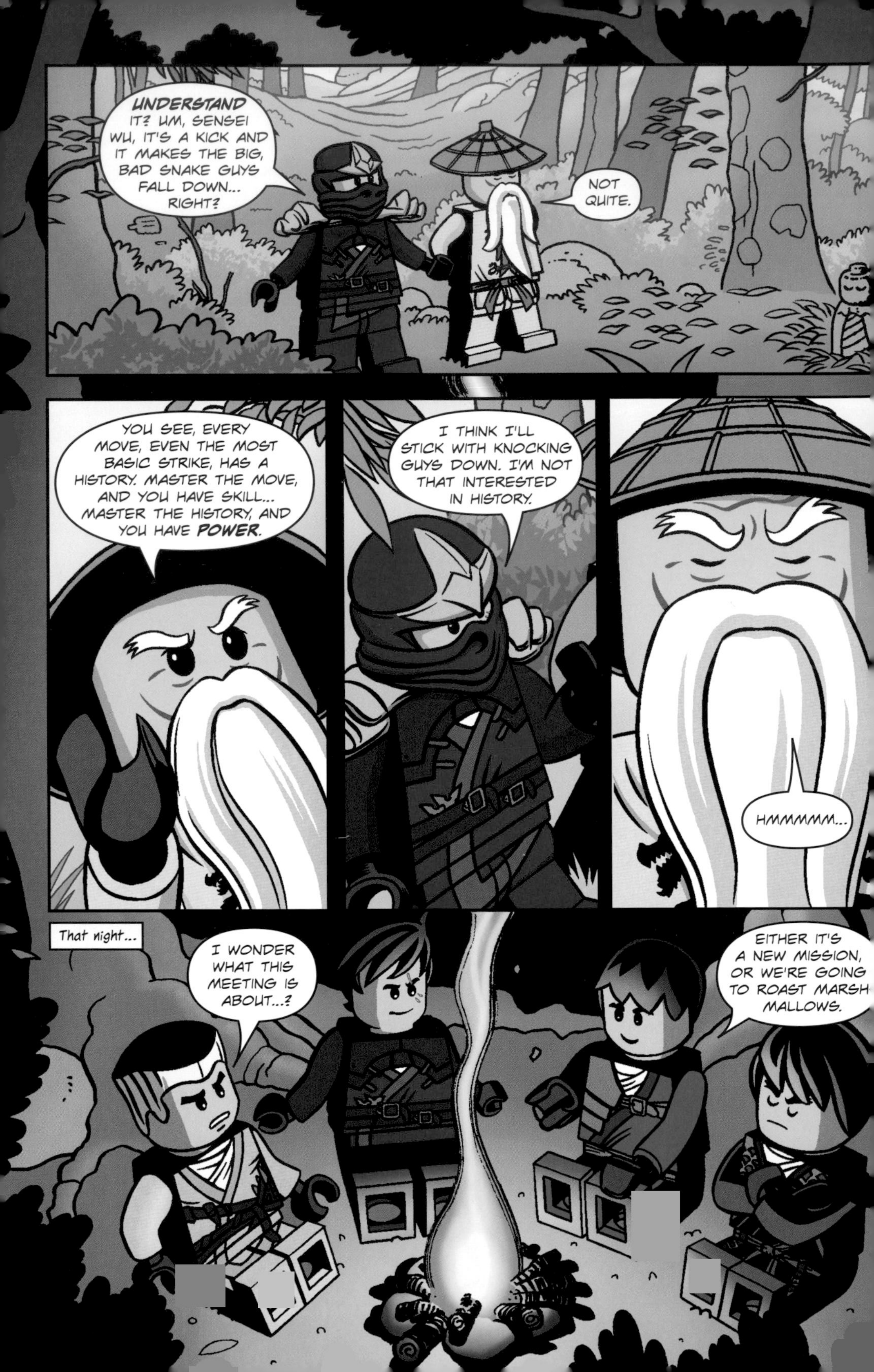
UNDERSTAND IT? UM, SENSEI WU, IT'S A KICK AND IT MAKES THE BIG, BAD SNAKE GUYS FALL DOWN... RIGHT?
NOT QUITE.
YOU SEE, EVERY MOVE, EVEN THE MOST BASIC STRIKE, HAS A HISTORY. MASTER THE MOVE, AND YOU HAVE SKILL... MASTER THE HISTORY, AND YOU HAVE POWER.
I THINK I'LL STICK WITH KNOCKING GUYS DOWN. I'M NOT THAT INTERESTED IN HISTORY.
HMMMMM...
That night...
I WONDER WHAT THIS MEETING IS ABOUT...?
EITHER IT'S A NEW MISSION, OR WE'RE GOING TO ROAST MARSH MALLOWS.

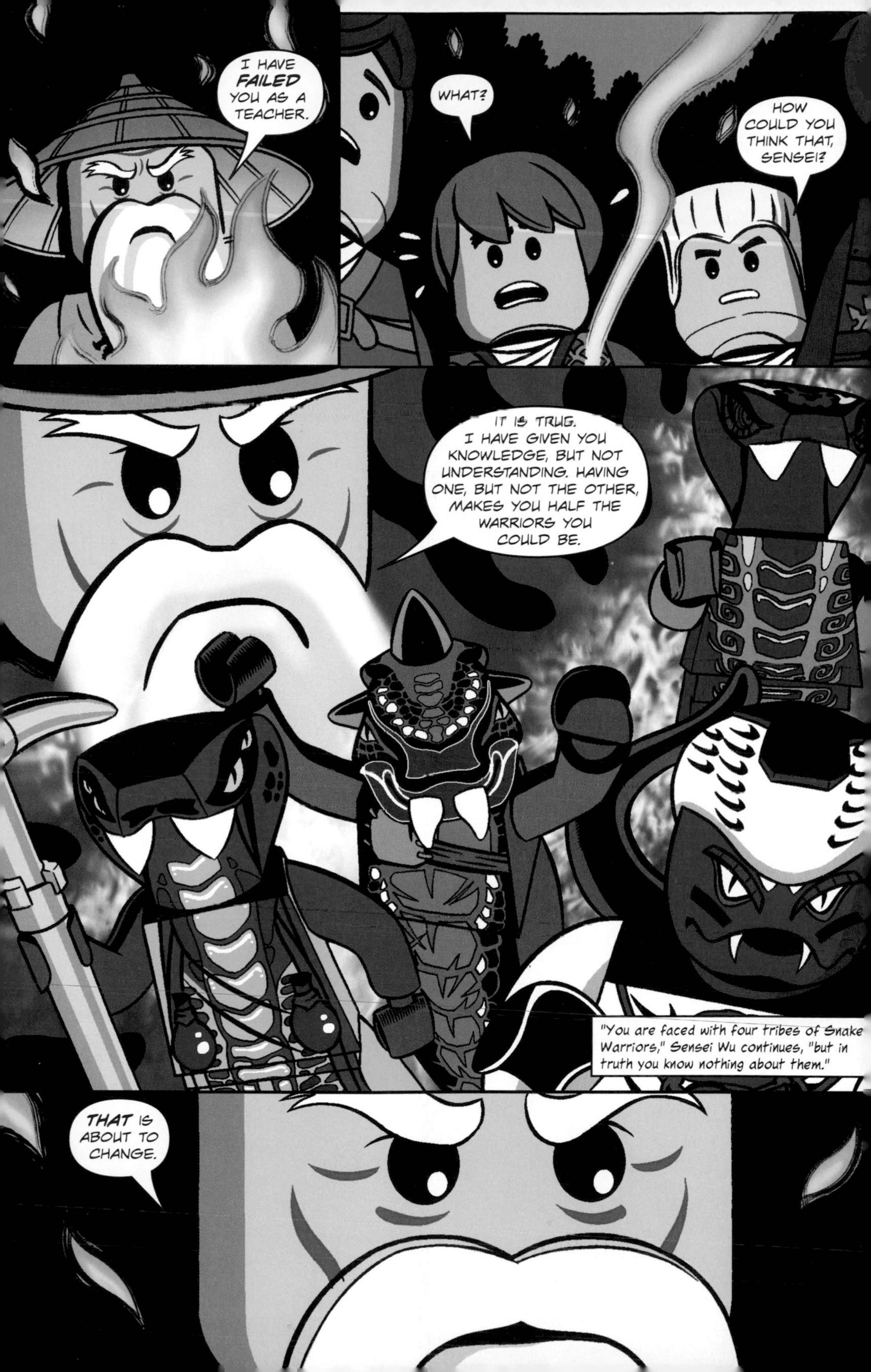
I HAVE FAILED YOU AS A TEACHER.
WHAT?
HOW COULD YOU THINK THAT, SENSEI?
IT IS TRUE. I HAVE GIVEN YOU KNOWLEDGE, BUT NOT UNDERSTANDING. HAVING ONE, BUT NOT THE OTHER, MAKES YOU HALF THE WARRIORS YOU COULD BE.
"You are faced with four tribes of Snake Warriors," Sensei Wu continues, "but in truth you know nothing about them."
THAT IS ABOUT TO CHANGE.

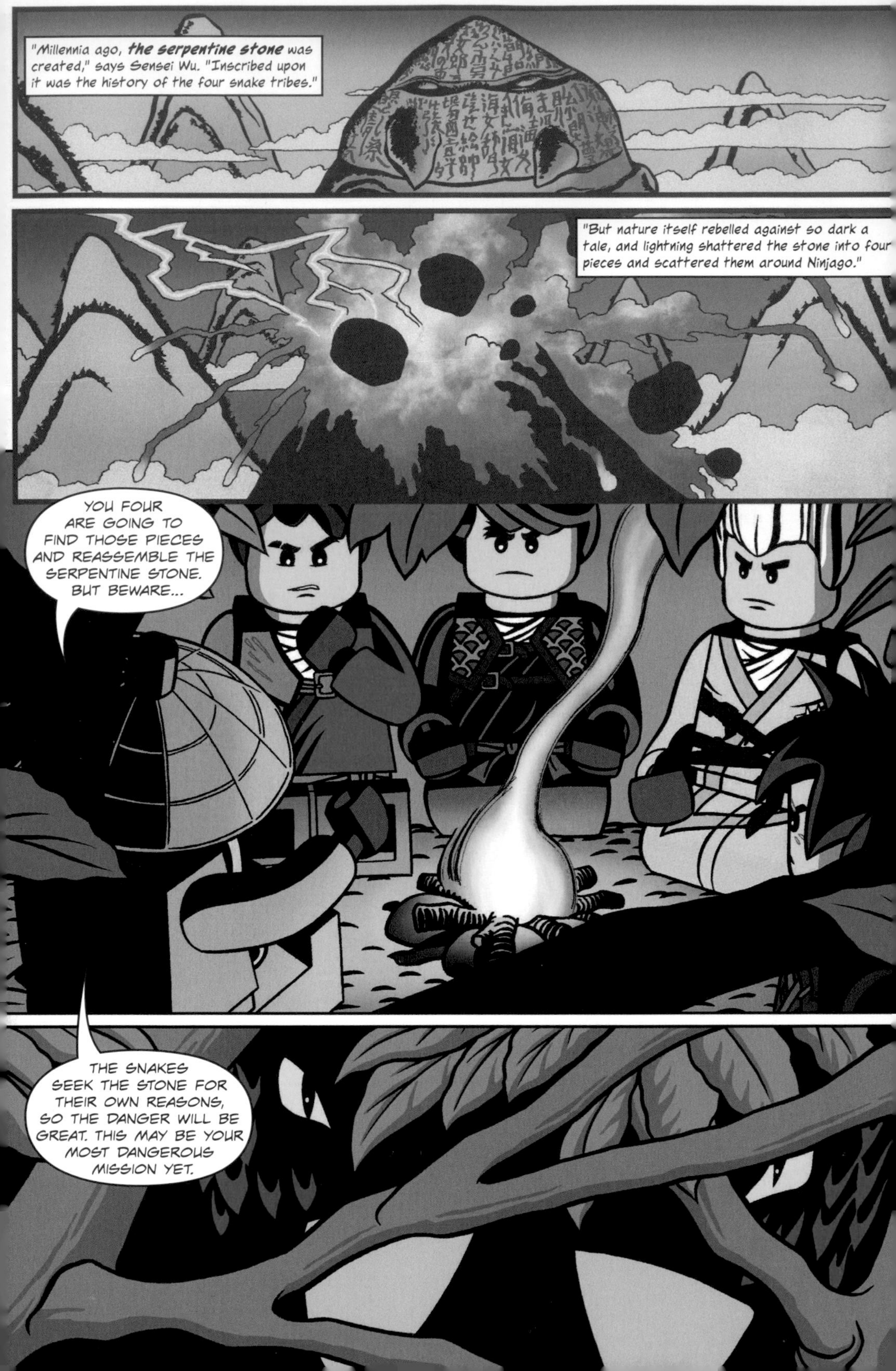
"Millennia ago, **the serpentine stone** was created," says Sensei Wu. "Inscribed upon it was the history of the four snake tribes."
"But nature itself rebelled against so dark a tale, and lightning shattered the stone into four pieces and scattered them around Ninjago."
YOU FOUR ARE GOING TO FIND THOSE PIECES AND REASSEMBLE THE SERPENTINE STONE. BUT BEWARE...
THE SNAKES SEEK THE STONE FOR THEIR OWN REASONS, SO THE DANGER WILL BE GREAT. THIS MAY BE YOUR MOST DANGEROUS MISSION YET.

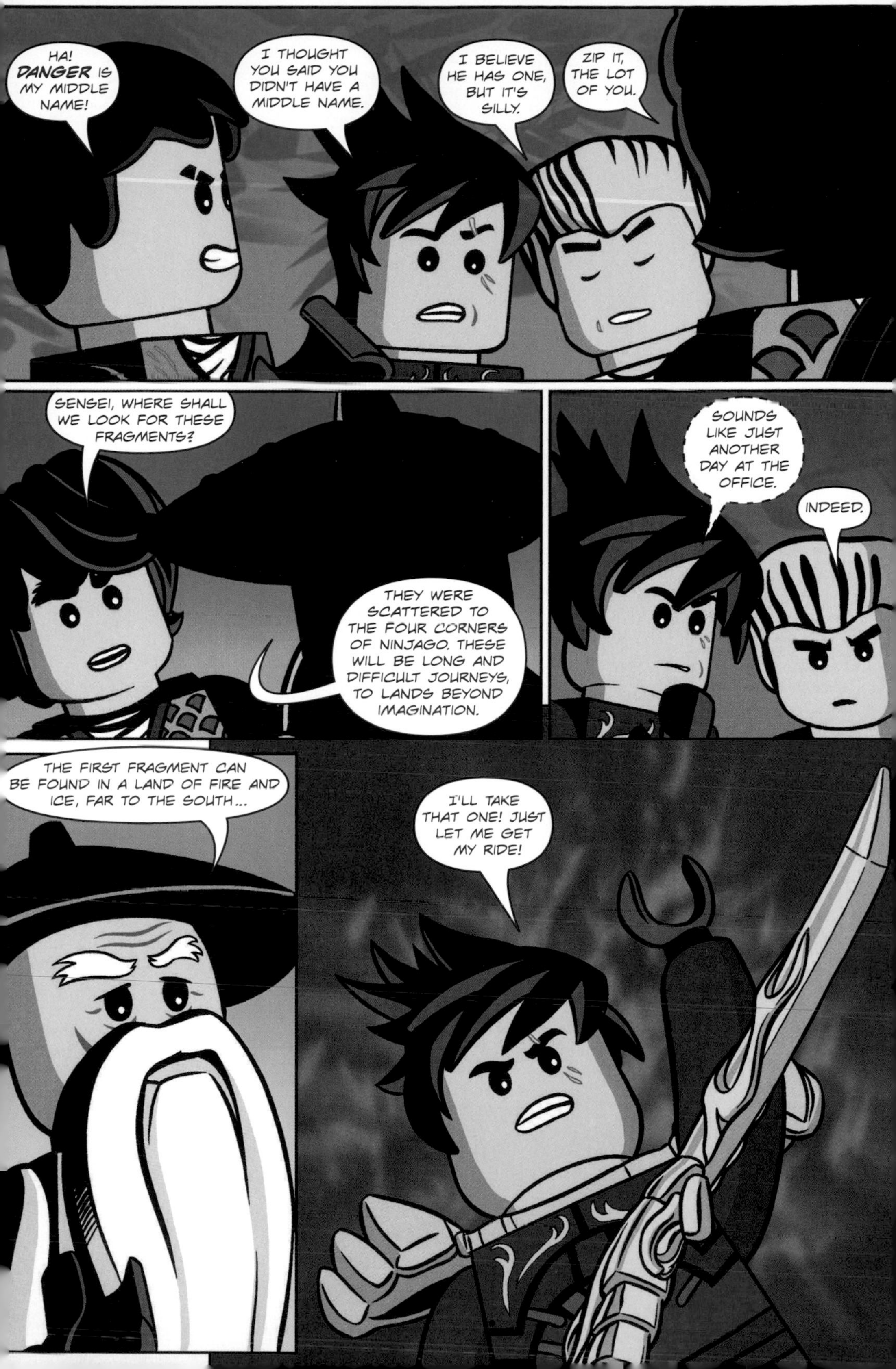
HA! DANGER IS MY MIDDLE NAME!
I THOUGHT YOU SAID YOU DIDN'T HAVE A MIDDLE NAME.
I BELIEVE HE HAS ONE, BUT IT'S SILLY.
ZIP IT, THE LOT OF YOU.
SENSEI, WHERE SHALL WE LOOK FOR THESE FRAGMENTS?
THEY WERE SCATTERED TO THE FOUR CORNERS OF NINJAGO. THESE WILL BE LONG AND DIFFICULT JOURNEYS, TO LANDS BEYOND IMAGINATION.
SOUNDS LIKE JUST ANOTHER DAY AT THE OFFICE.
INDEED.
THE FIRST FRAGMENT CAN BE FOUND IN A LAND OF FIRE AND ICE, FAR TO THE SOUTH...
I'LL TAKE THAT ONE! JUST LET ME GET MY RIDE!

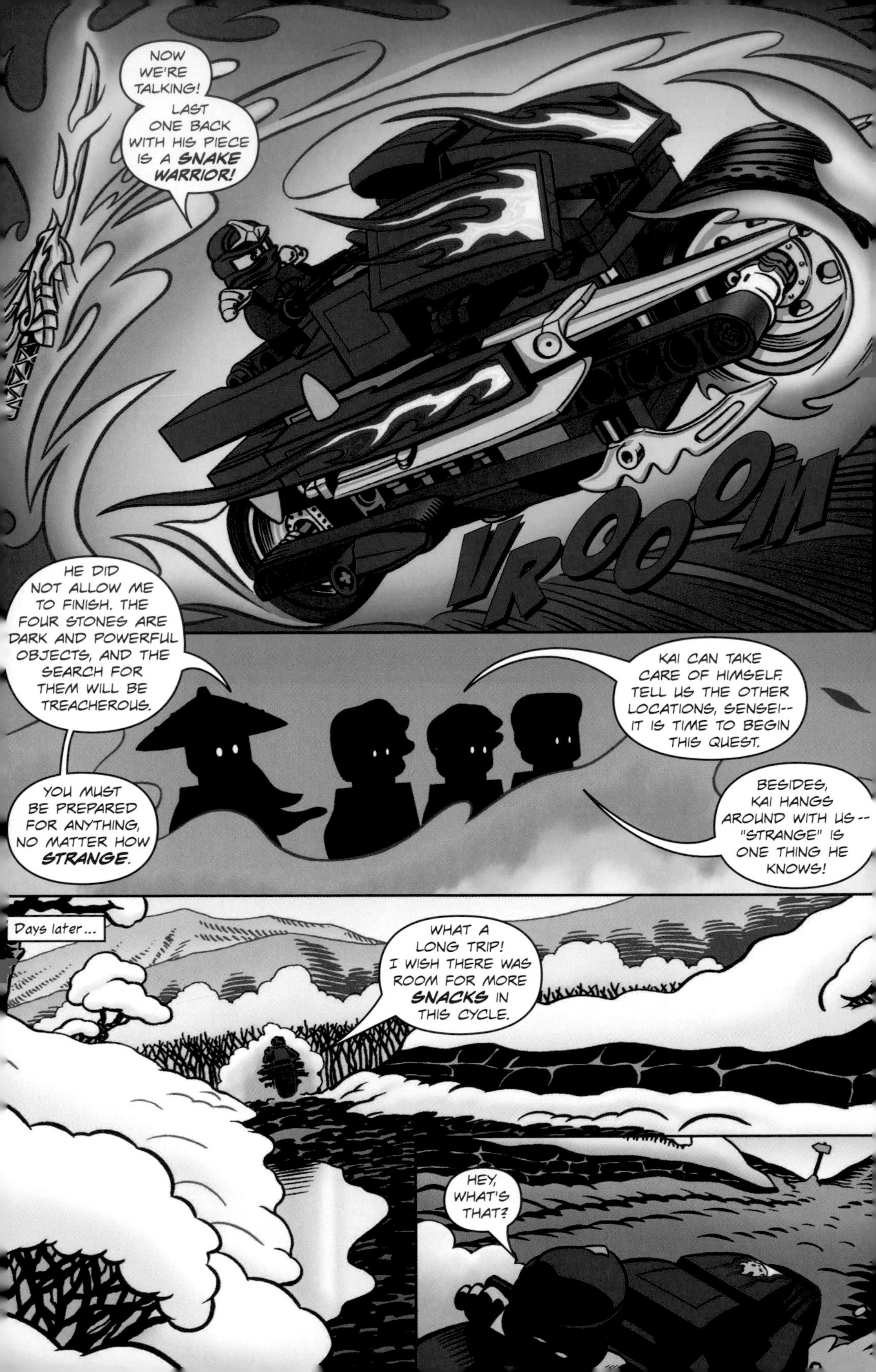
NOW WE'RE TALKING! LAST ONE BACK WITH HIS PIECE IS A SNAKE WARRIOR!
VROOOOM
HE DID NOT ALLOW ME TO FINISH. THE FOUR STONES ARE DARK AND POWERFUL OBJECTS, AND THE SEARCH FOR THEM WILL BE TREACHEROUS.
YOU MUST BE PREPARED FOR ANYTHING, NO MATTER HOW STRANGE.
KAI CAN TAKE CARE OF HIMSELF. TELL US THE OTHER LOCATIONS, SENSEI-- IT IS TIME TO BEGIN THIS QUEST.
BESIDES, KAI HANGS AROUND WITH US -- "STRANGE" IS ONE THING HE KNOWS!
Days later...
WHAT A LONG TRIP! I WISH THERE WAS ROOM FOR MORE SNACKS IN THIS CYCLE.
HEY, WHAT'S THAT?

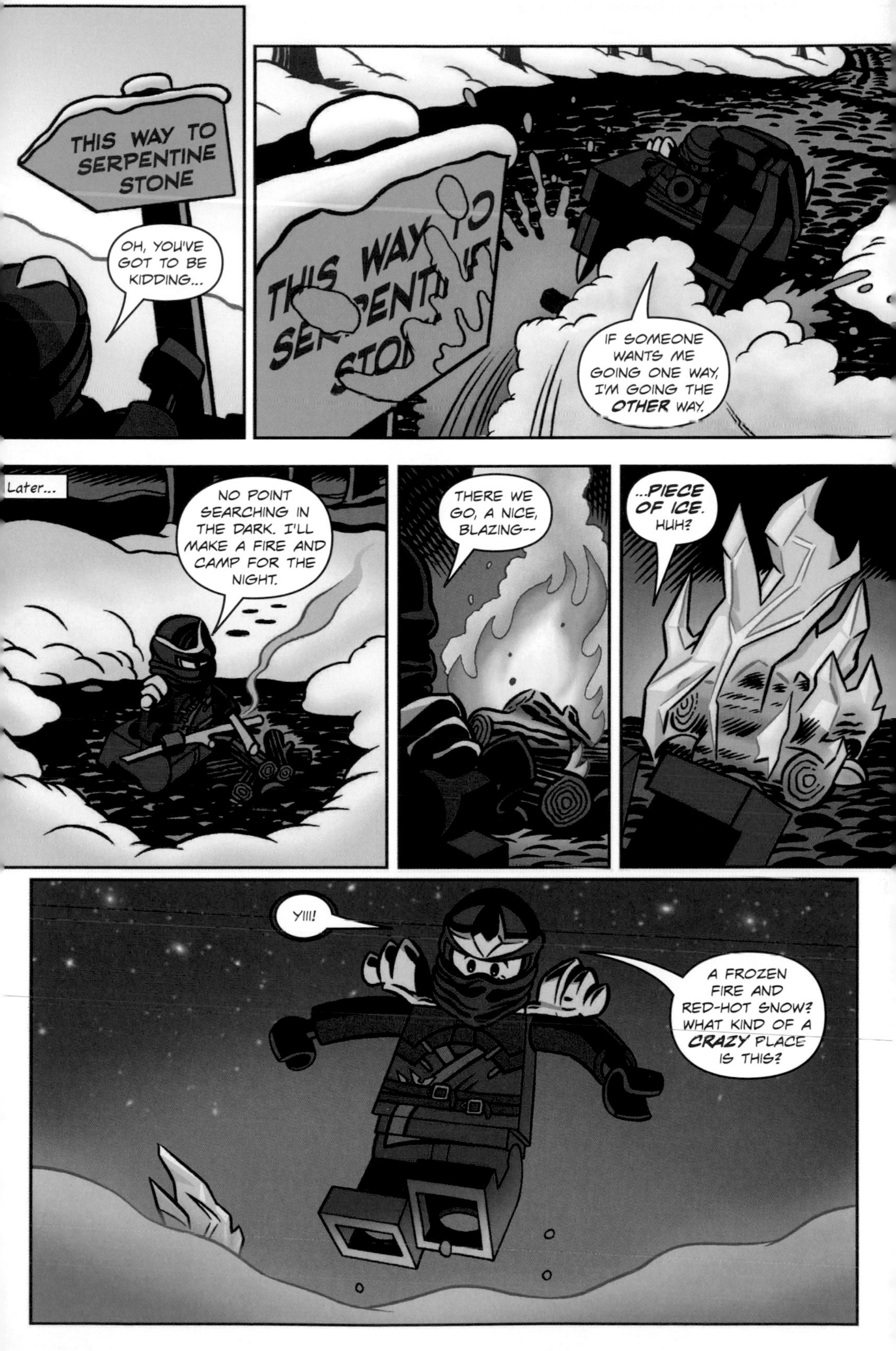
THIS WAY TO SERPENTINE STONE
OH, YOU'VE GOT TO BE KIDDING...
IF SOMEONE WANTS ME GOING ONE WAY, I'M GOING THE OTHER WAY.
Later...
NO POINT SEARCHING IN THE DARK. I'LL MAKE A FIRE AND CAMP FOR THE NIGHT.
THERE WE GO, A NICE, BLAZING--
...PIECE OF ICE. HUH?
YIII!
A FROZEN FIRE AND RED-HOT SNOW? WHAT KIND OF A CRAZY PLACE IS THIS?

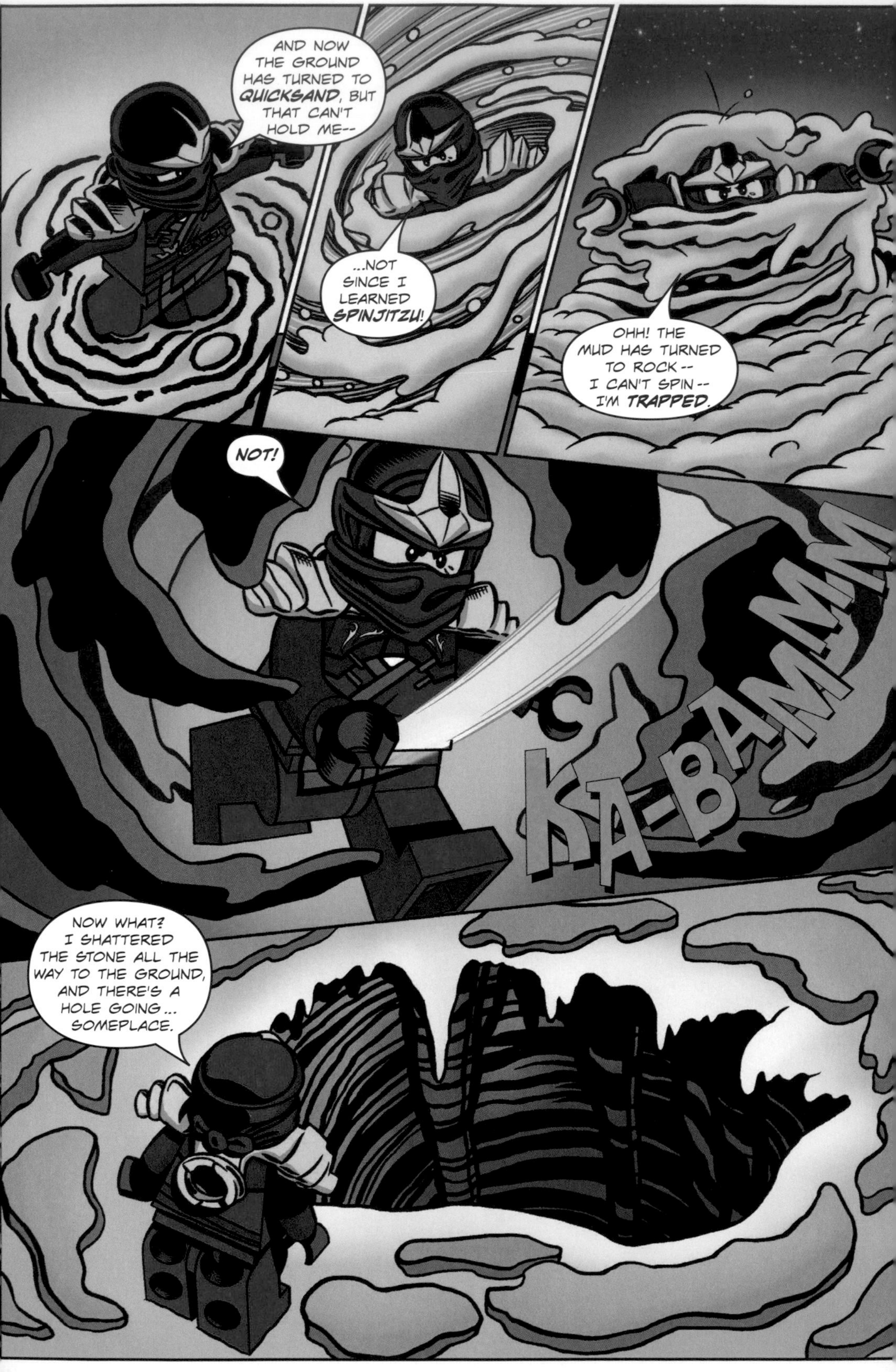
AND NOW THE GROUND HAS TURNED TO QUICKSAND, BUT THAT CAN'T HOLD ME--
...NOT SINCE I LEARNED SPINJITZU!
OHH! THE MUD HAS TURNED TO ROCK -- I CAN'T SPIN -- I'M TRAPPED.
NOT!
C KA-BAMMM
NOW WHAT? I SHATTERED THE STONE ALL THE WAY TO THE GROUND, AND THERE'S A HOLE GOING... SOMEPLACE.

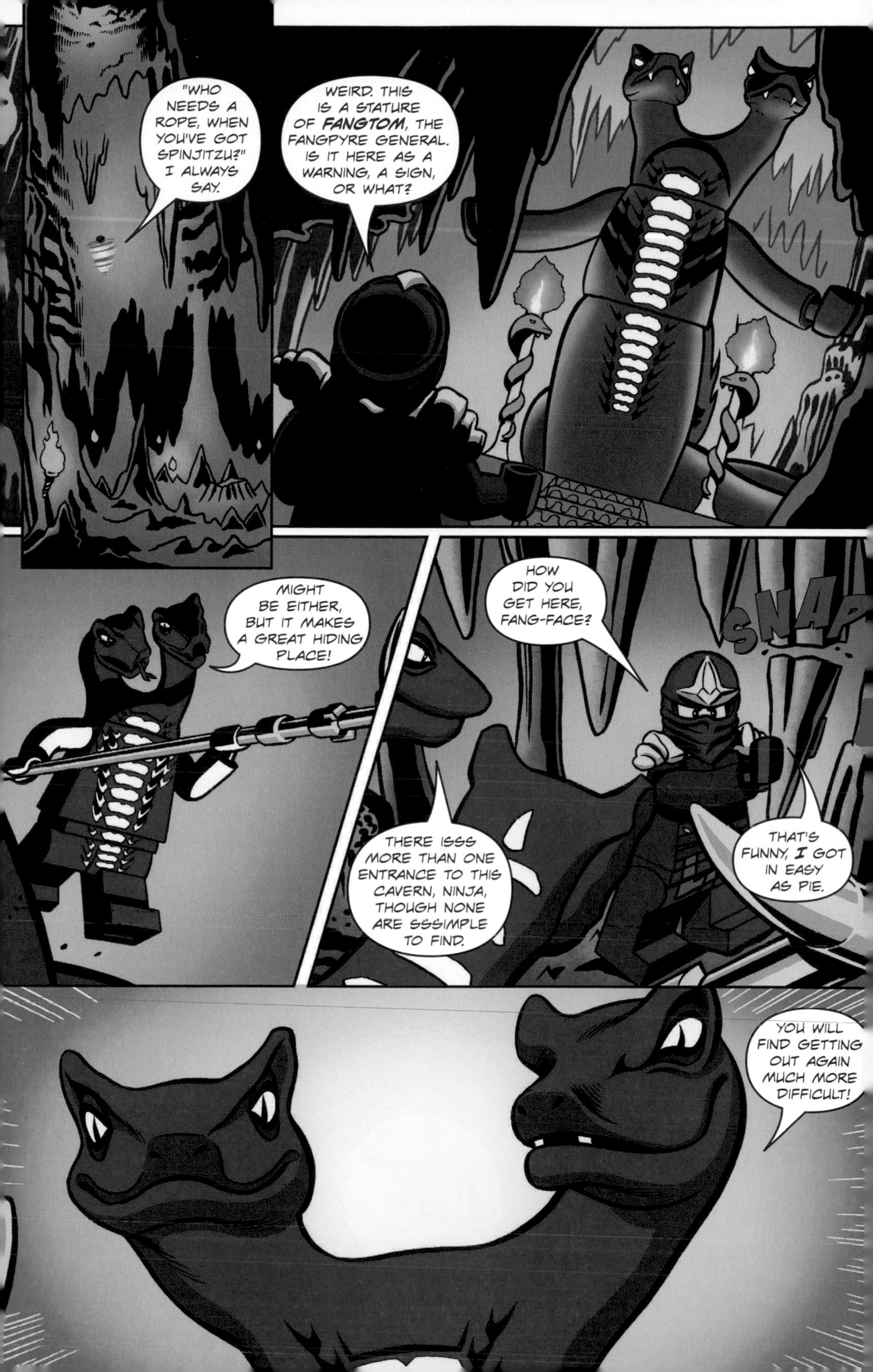
"WHO NEEDS A ROPE, WHEN YOU'VE GOT SPINJITZU?" I ALWAYS SAY.
WEIRD. THIS IS A STATURE OF **FANGTOM**, THE FANGPYRE GENERAL. IS IT HERE AS A WARNING, A SIGN, OR WHAT?
MIGHT BE EITHER, BUT IT MAKES A GREAT HIDING PLACE!
HOW DID YOU GET HERE, FANG-FACE?
SNAP
THERE ISSS MORE THAN ONE ENTRANCE TO THIS CAVERN, NINJA, THOUGH NONE ARE SSSIMPLE TO FIND.
THAT'S FUNNY, **I** GOT IN EASY AS PIE.
YOU WILL FIND GETTING OUT AGAIN MUCH MORE DIFFICULT!

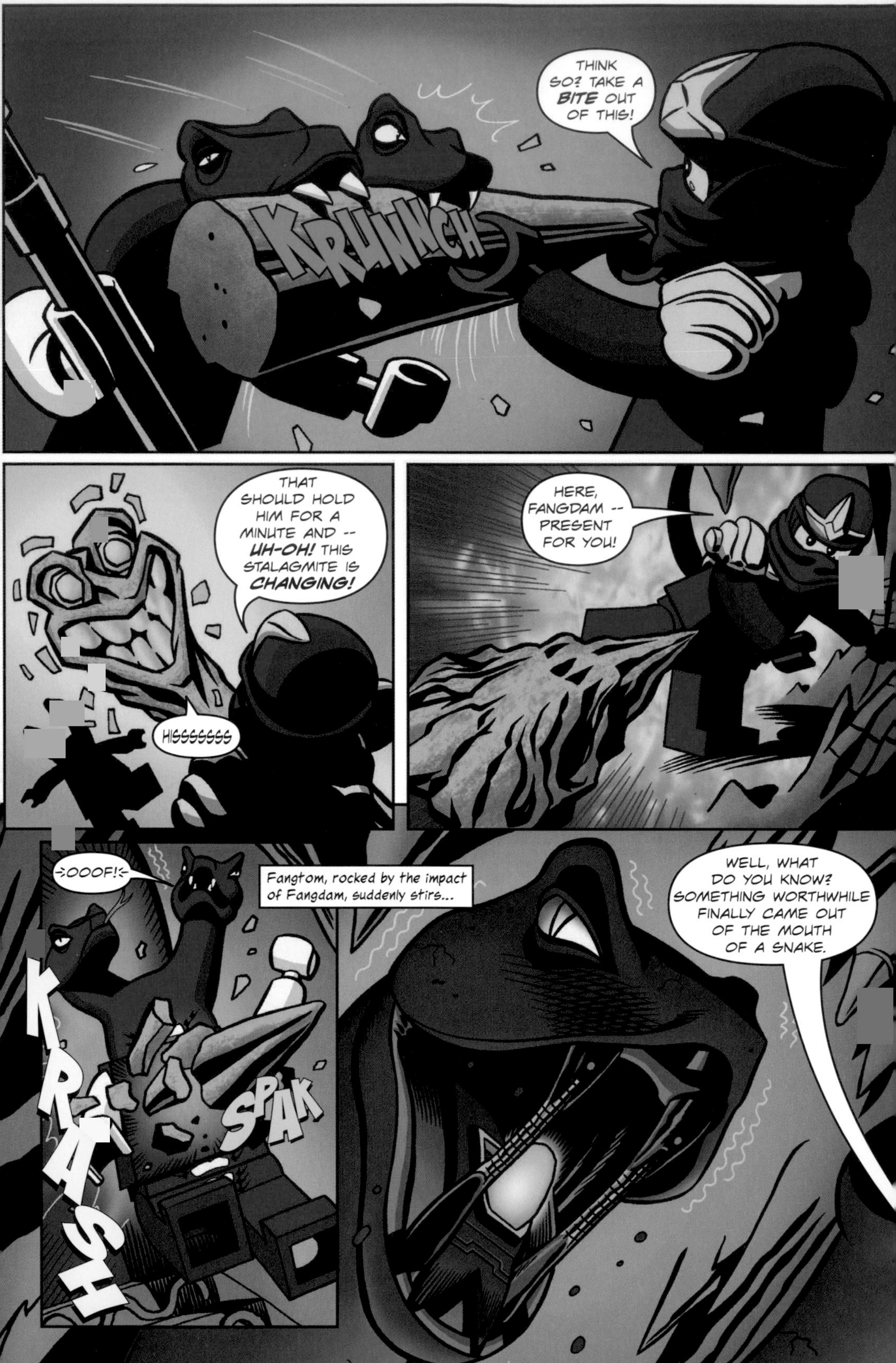
THINK SO? TAKE A BITE OUT OF THIS!
KRUNNCH
THAT SHOULD HOLD HIM FOR A MINUTE AND -- UH-OH! THIS STALAGMITE IS CHANGING!
HISSSSSSS
HERE, FANGDAM -- PRESENT FOR YOU!
OOOF!
Fangtom, rocked by the impact of Fangdam, suddenly stirs...
KRASH
SPAK
WELL, WHAT DO YOU KNOW? SOMETHING WORTHWHILE FINALLY CAME OUT OF THE MOUTH OF A SNAKE.

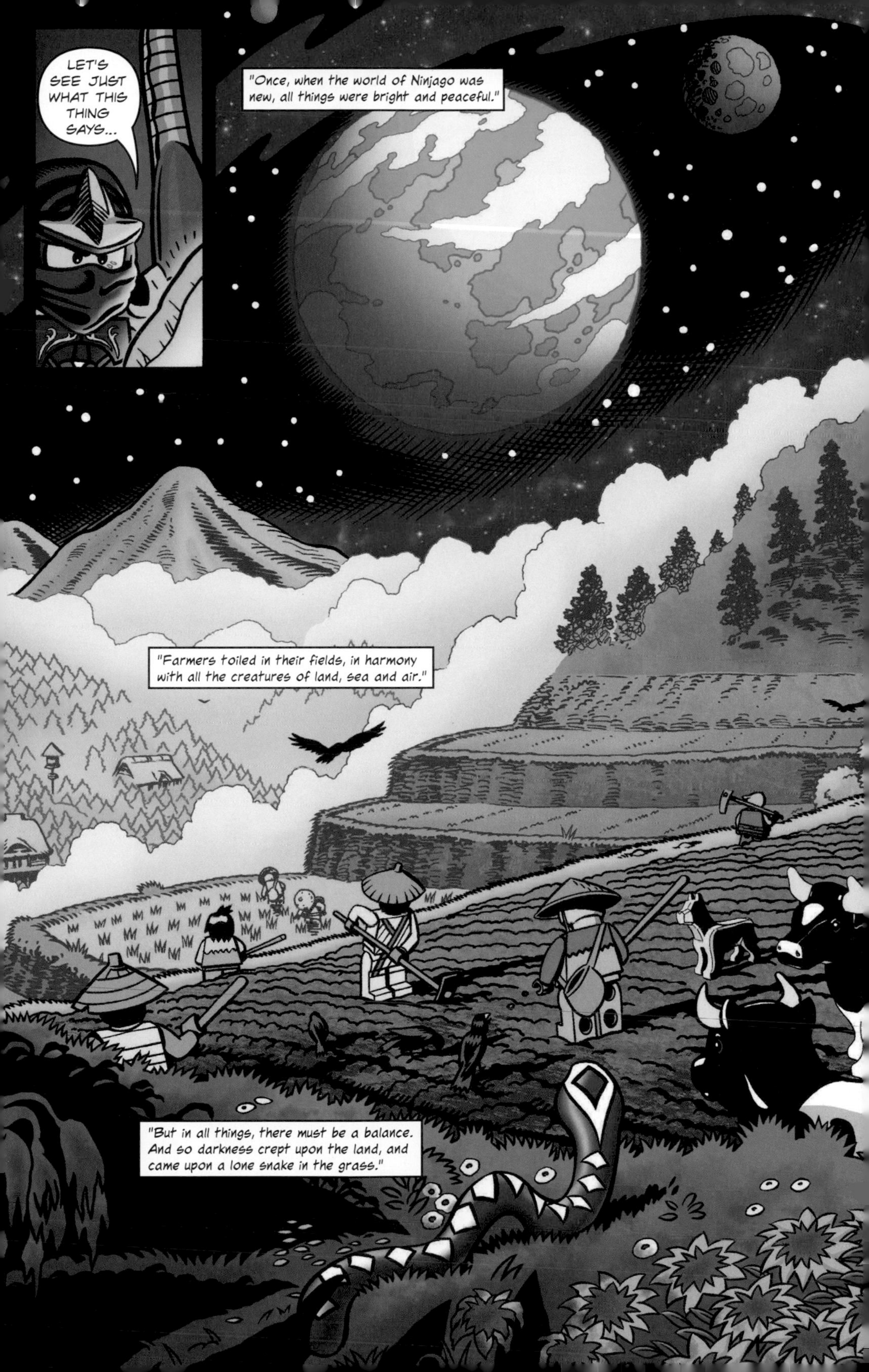
LET'S SEE JUST WHAT THIS THING SAYS...
"Once, when the world of Ninjago was new, all things were bright and peaceful."
"Farmers toiled in their fields, in harmony with all the creatures of land, sea and air."
"But in all things, there must be a balance. And so darkness crept upon the land, and came upon a lone snake in the grass."

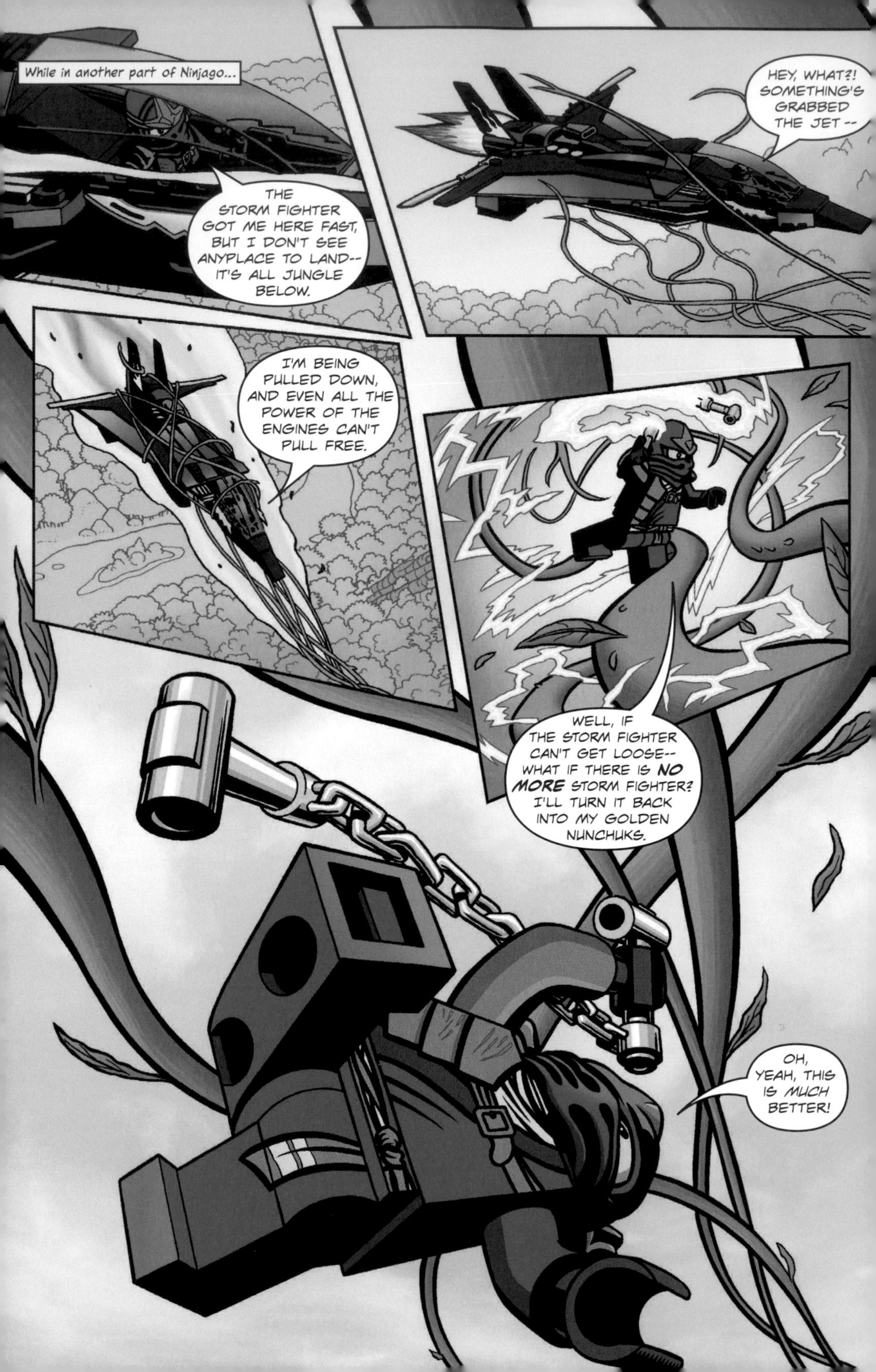
While in another part of Ninjago...
THE STORM FIGHTER GOT ME HERE FAST, BUT I DON'T SEE ANYPLACE TO LAND-- IT'S ALL JUNGLE BELOW.
HEY, WHAT?! SOMETHING'S GRABBED THE JET --
I'M BEING PULLED DOWN, AND EVEN ALL THE POWER OF THE ENGINES CAN'T PULL FREE.
WELL, IF THE STORM FIGHTER CAN'T GET LOOSE-- WHAT IF THERE IS NO MORE STORM FIGHTER? I'LL TURN IT BACK INTO MY GOLDEN NUNCHUKS.
OH, YEAH, THIS IS MUCH BETTER!

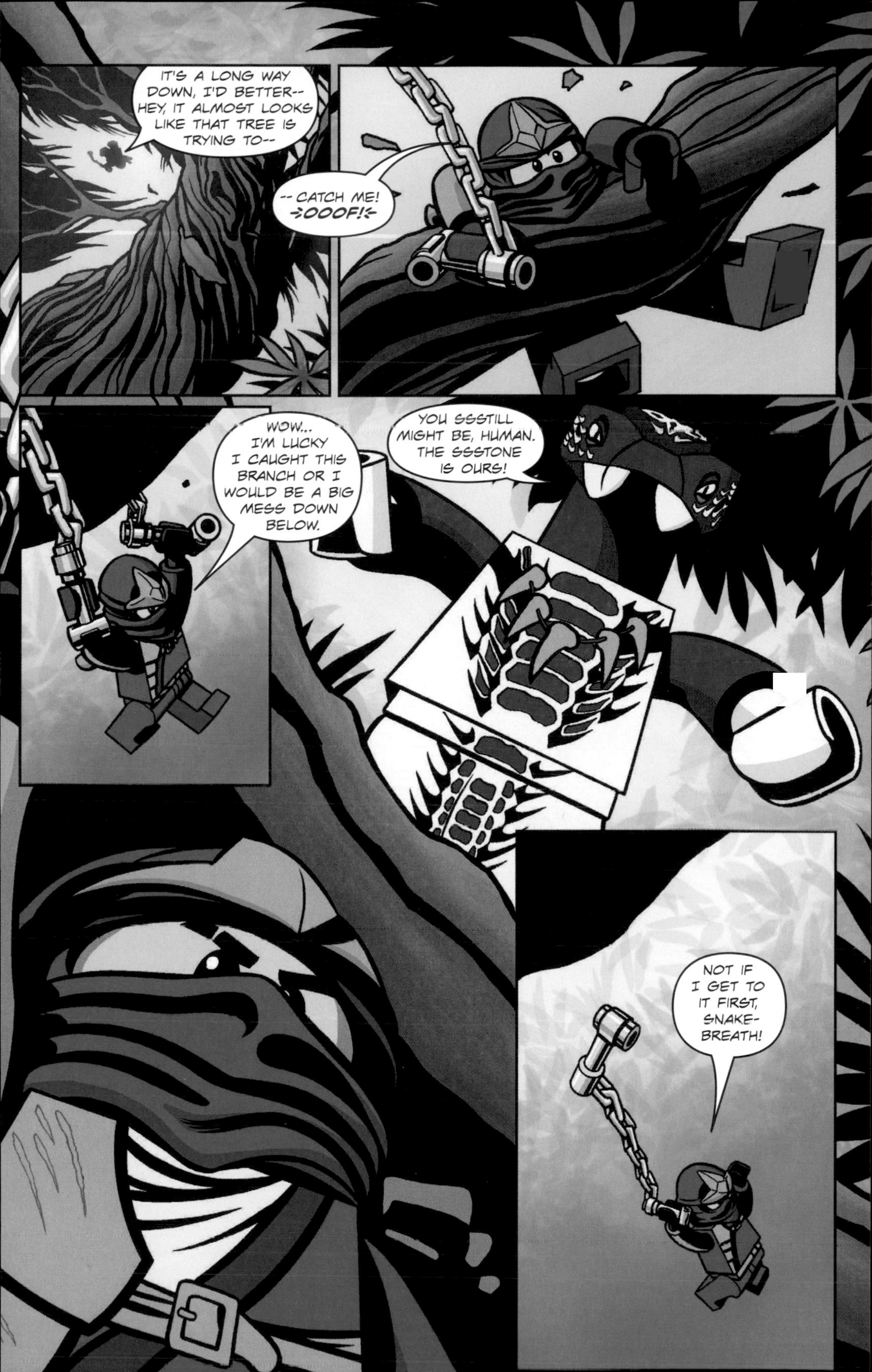
IT'S A LONG WAY DOWN, I'D BETTER-- HEY, IT ALMOST LOOKS LIKE THAT TREE IS TRYING TO--
--CATCH ME! OOOF!
WOW... I'M LUCKY I CAUGHT THIS BRANCH OR I WOULD BE A BIG MESS DOWN BELOW.
YOU SSSTILL MIGHT BE, HUMAN. THE SSSTONE IS OURS!
NOT IF I GET TO IT FIRST, SNAKE-BREATH!

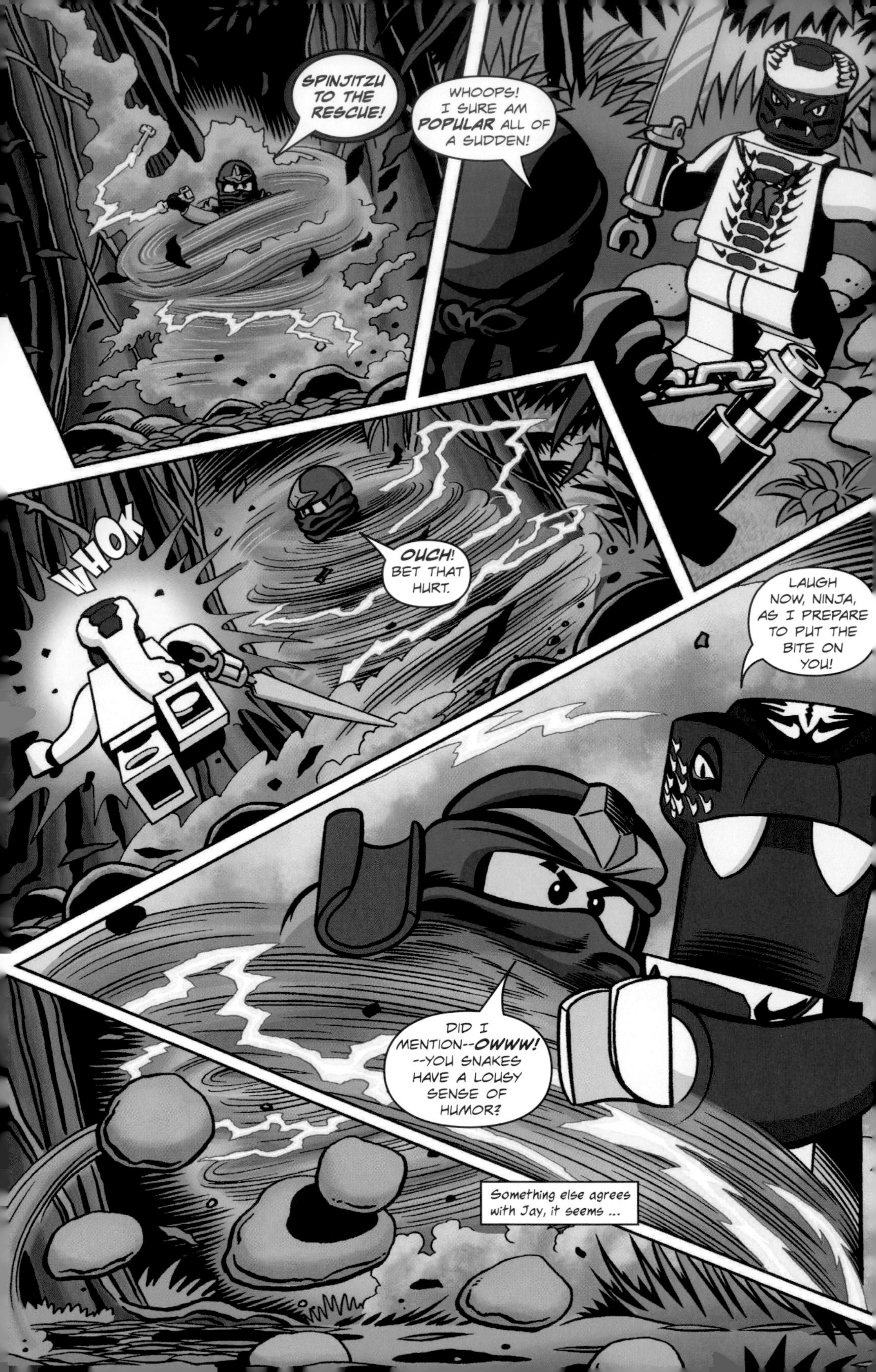
SPINJITZU TO THE RESCUE!
WHOOPS! I SURE AM POPULAR ALL OF A SUDDEN!
WHOK
OUCH! BET THAT HURT.
LAUGH NOW, NINJA, AS I PREPARE TO PUT THE BITE ON YOU!
DID I MENTION--OWWW! --YOU SNAKES HAVE A LOUSY SENSE OF HUMOR?
Something else agrees with Jay, it seems ...

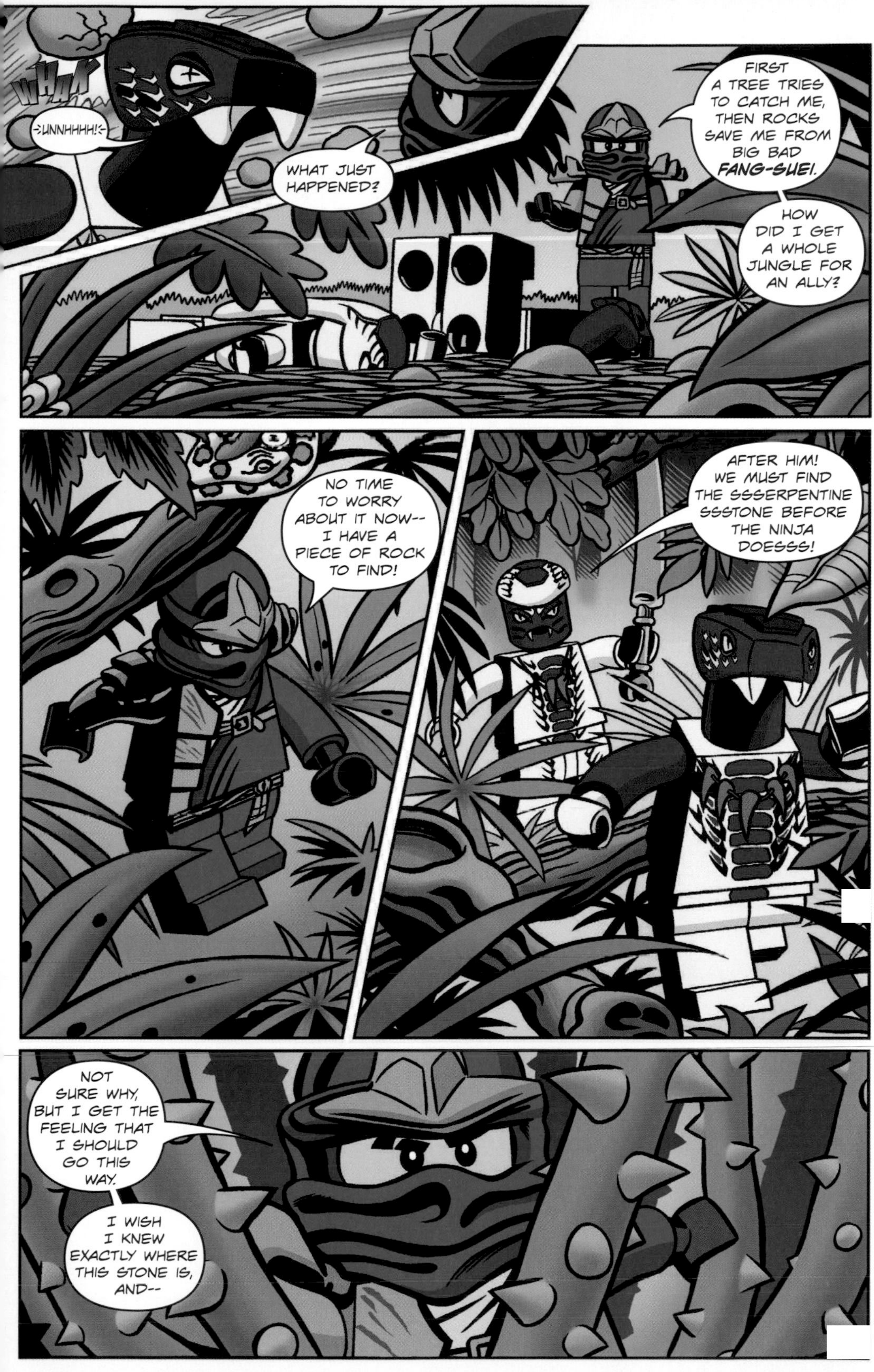
WHAK
-UNNHHHH!-
WHAT JUST HAPPENED?
FIRST A TREE TRIES TO CATCH ME, THEN ROCKS SAVE ME FROM BIG BAD FANG-SUEI.
HOW DID I GET A WHOLE JUNGLE FOR AN ALLY?
NO TIME TO WORRY ABOUT IT NOW-- I HAVE A PIECE OF ROCK TO FIND!
AFTER HIM! WE MUST FIND THE SSSERPENTINE SSSTONE BEFORE THE NINJA DOESSS!
NOT SURE WHY, BUT I GET THE FEELING THAT I SHOULD GO THIS WAY.
I WISH I KNEW EXACTLY WHERE THIS STONE IS, AND--

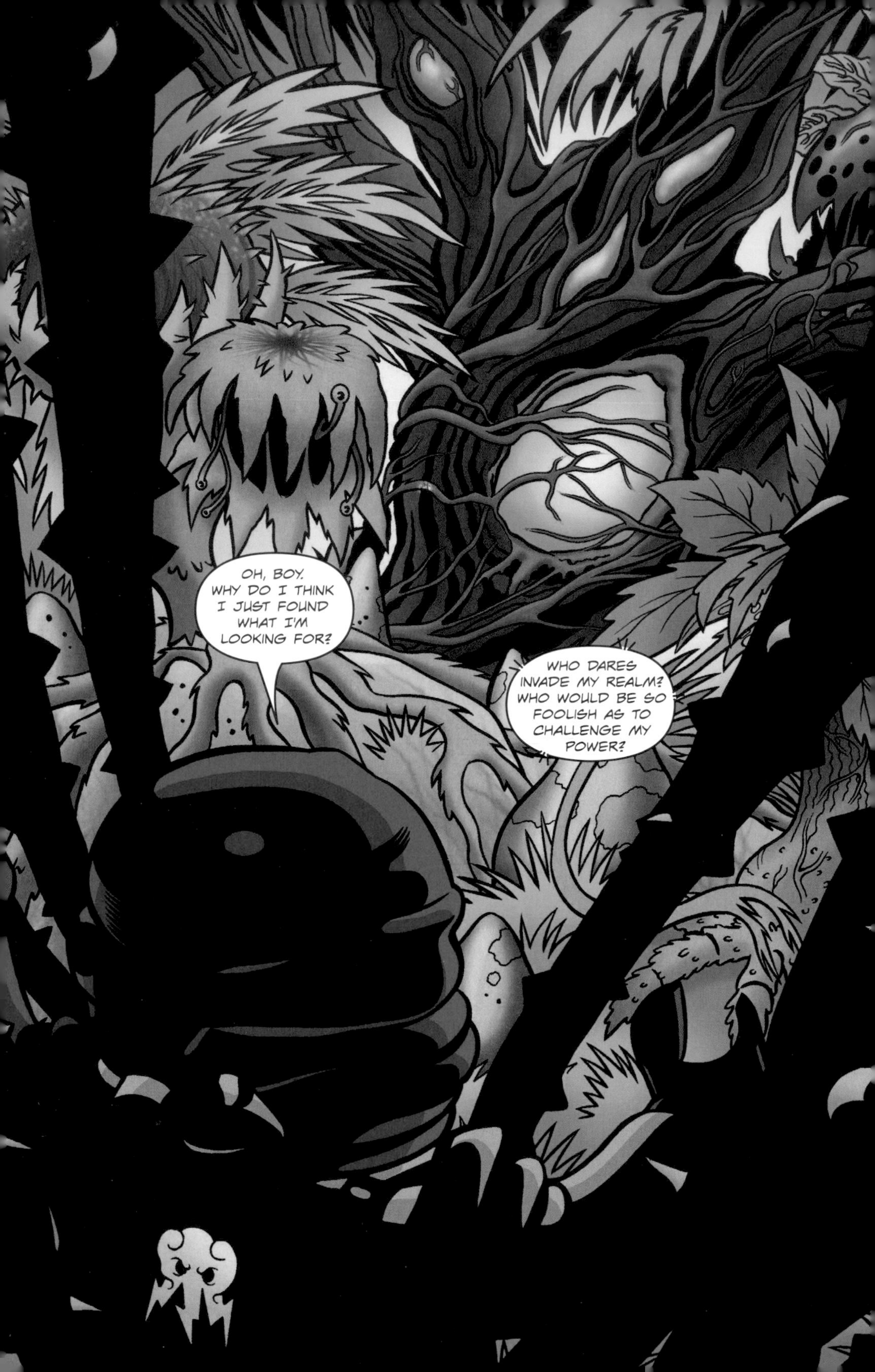
OH, BOY. WHY DO I THINK I JUST FOUND WHAT I'M LOOKING FOR?
WHO DARES INVADE MY REALM? WHO WOULD BE SO FOOLISH AS TO CHALLENGE MY POWER?

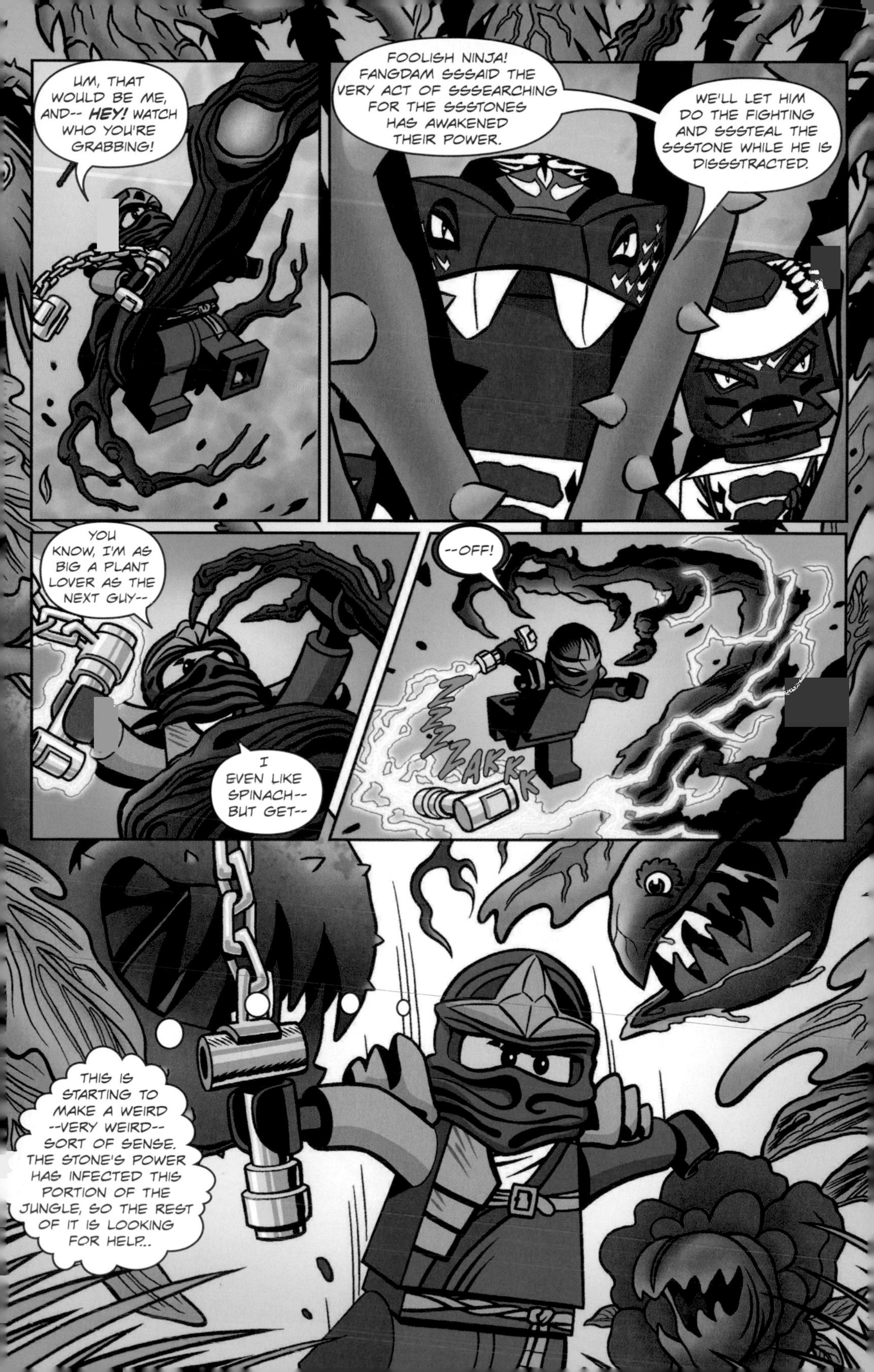
UM, THAT WOULD BE ME, AND-- HEY! WATCH WHO YOU'RE GRABBING!
FOOLISH NINJA! FANGDAM SSSAID THE VERY ACT OF SSSEARCHING FOR THE SSSTONES HAS AWAKENED THEIR POWER.
WE'LL LET HIM DO THE FIGHTING AND SSSTEAL THE SSSTONE WHILE HE IS DISSSTRACTED.
YOU KNOW, I'M AS BIG A PLANT LOVER AS THE NEXT GUY--
I EVEN LIKE SPINACH-- BUT GET--
--OFF!
ZZZZAKKKK
THIS IS STARTING TO MAKE A WEIRD --VERY WEIRD-- SORT OF SENSE. THE STONE'S POWER HAS INFECTED THIS PORTION OF THE JUNGLE, SO THE REST OF IT IS LOOKING FOR HELP..

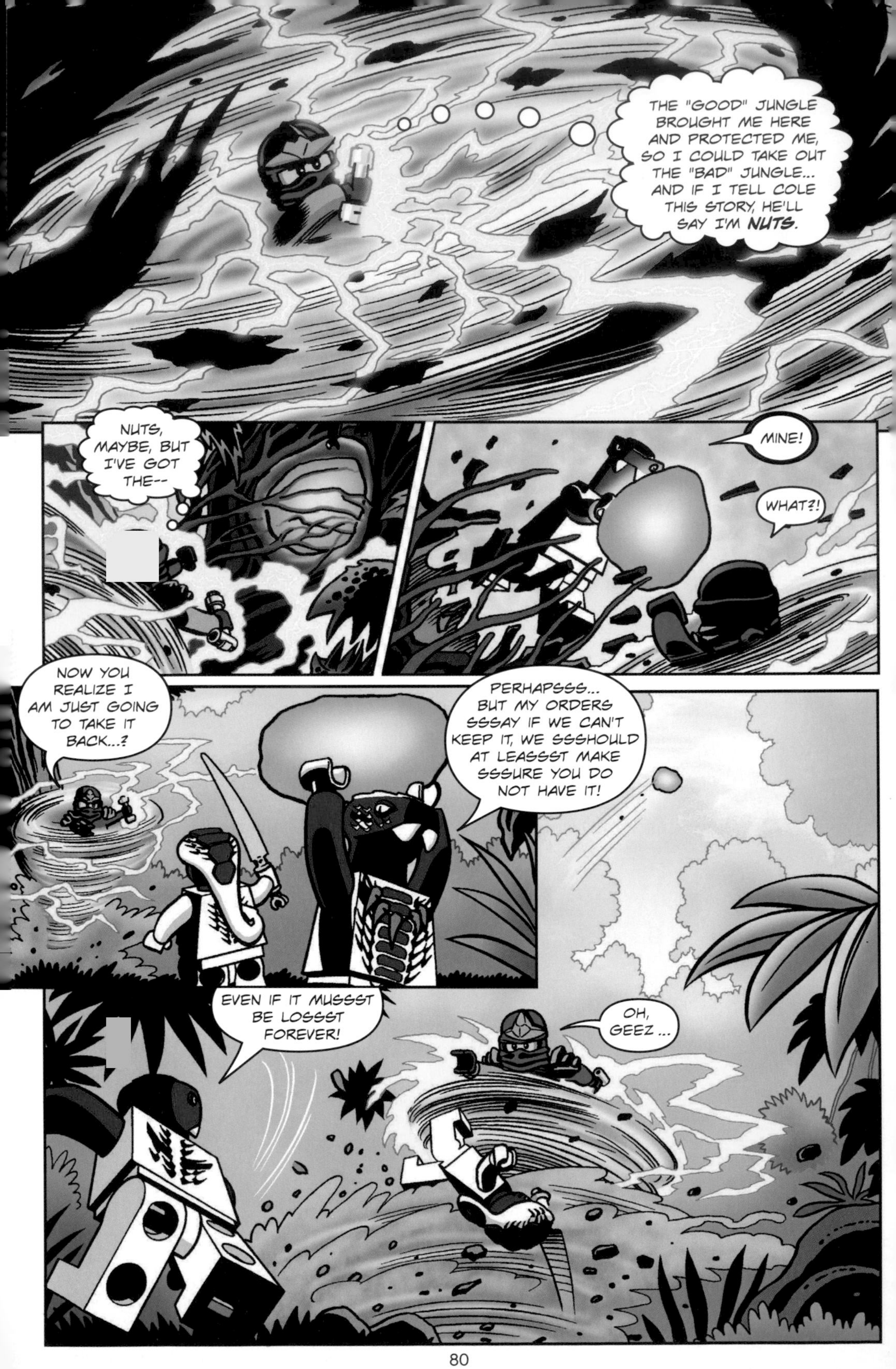
THE "GOOD" JUNGLE BROUGHT ME HERE AND PROTECTED ME, SO I COULD TAKE OUT THE "BAD" JUNGLE... AND IF I TELL COLE THIS STORY, HE'LL SAY I'M **NUTS**.
NUTS, MAYBE, BUT I'VE GOT THE--
MINE!
WHAT?!
NOW YOU REALIZE I AM JUST GOING TO TAKE IT BACK...?
PERHAPSSS... BUT MY ORDERS SSSAY IF WE CAN'T KEEP IT, WE SSSHOULD AT LEASSST MAKE SSSURE YOU DO NOT HAVE IT!
EVEN IF IT MUSSST BE LOSSST FOREVER!
OH, GEEZ ...

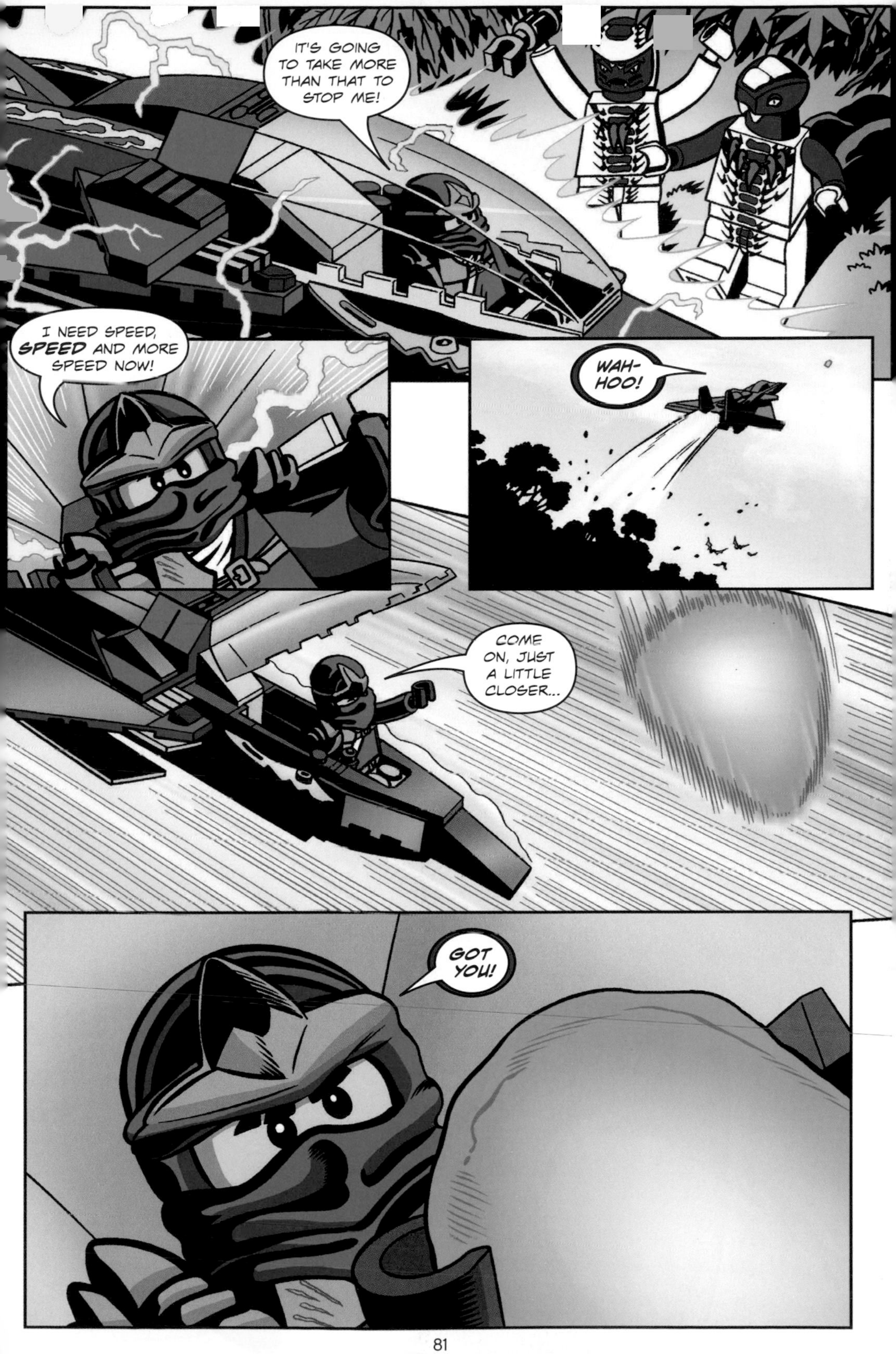
IT'S GOING TO TAKE MORE THAN THAT TO STOP ME!
I NEED SPEED, SPEED AND MORE SPEED NOW!
WAH-HOO!
COME ON, JUST A LITTLE CLOSER...
GOT YOU!

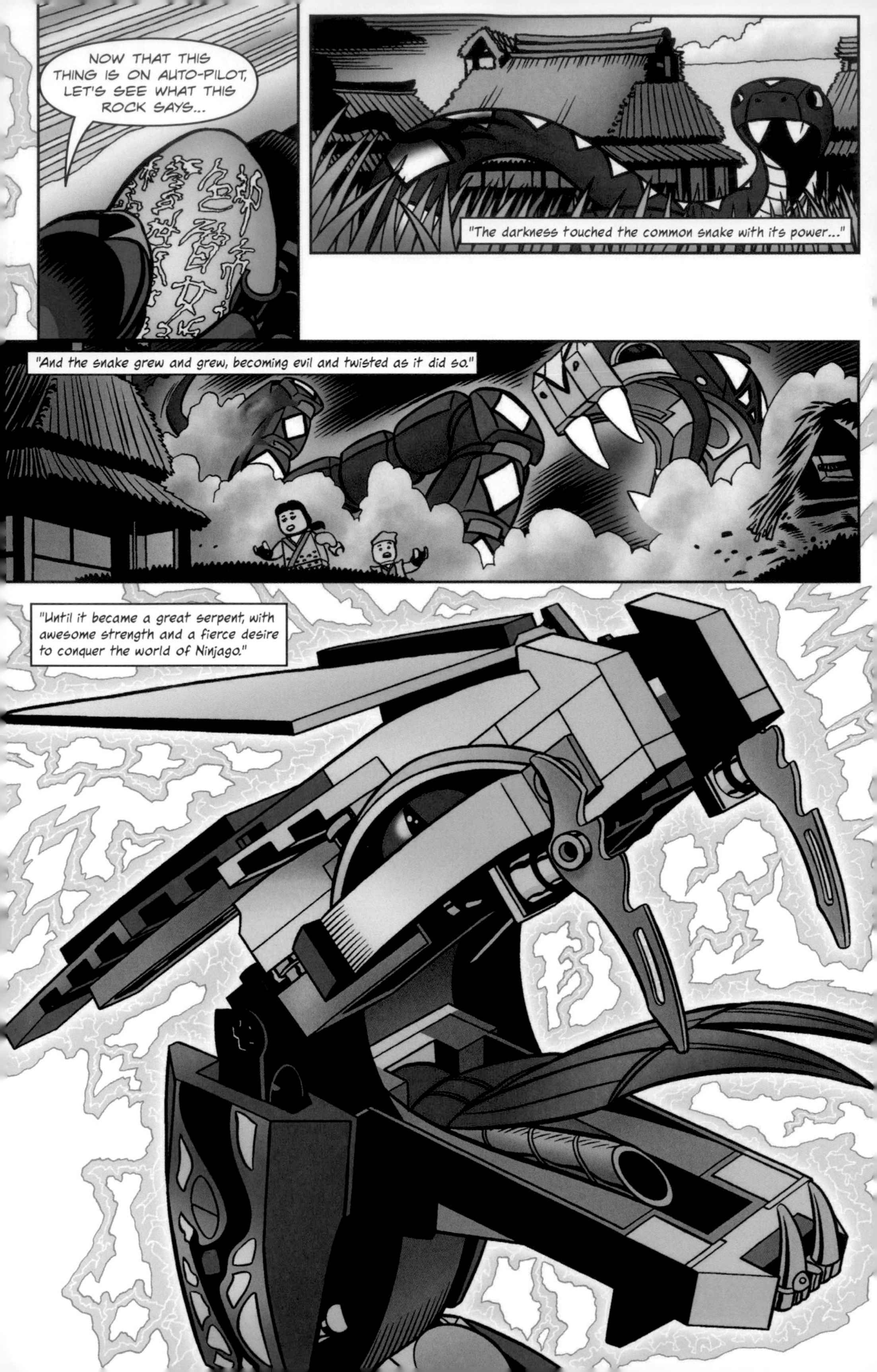
NOW THAT THIS THING IS ON AUTO-PILOT, LET'S SEE WHAT THIS ROCK SAYS...
"The darkness touched the common snake with its power..."
"And the snake grew and grew, becoming evil and twisted as it did so."
"Until it became a great serpent, with awesome strength and a fierce desire to conquer the world of Ninjago."

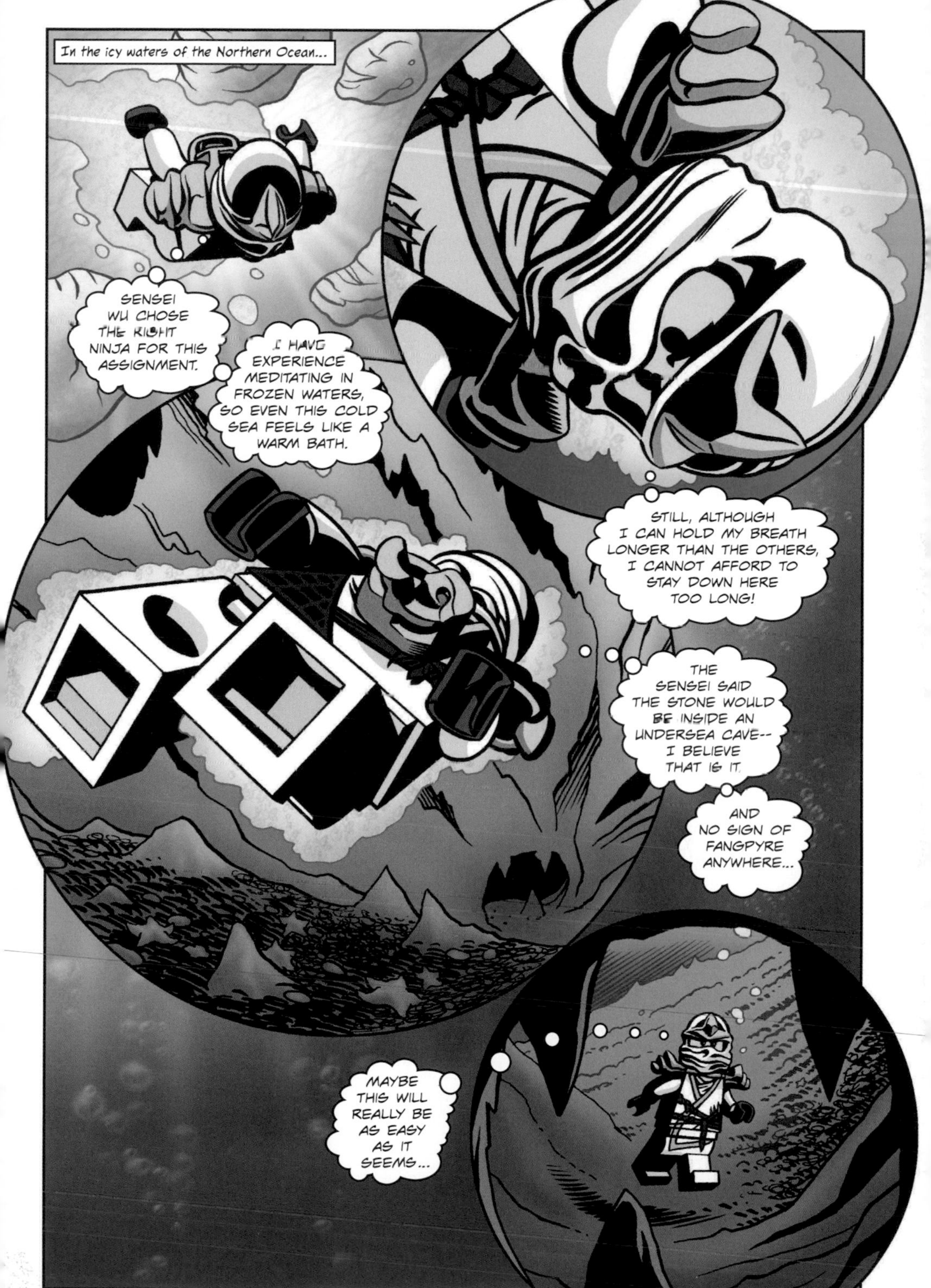
In the icy waters of the Northern Ocean...
SENSEI WU CHOSE THE RIGHT NINJA FOR THIS ASSIGNMENT.
I HAVE EXPERIENCE MEDITATING IN FROZEN WATERS, SO EVEN THIS COLD SEA FEELS LIKE A WARM BATH.
STILL, ALTHOUGH I CAN HOLD MY BREATH LONGER THAN THE OTHERS, I CANNOT AFFORD TO STAY DOWN HERE TOO LONG!
THE SENSEI SAID THE STONE WOULD BE INSIDE AN UNDERSEA CAVE-- I BELIEVE THAT IS IT.
AND NO SIGN OF FANGPYRE ANYWHERE...
MAYBE THIS WILL REALLY BE AS EASY AS IT SEEMS...

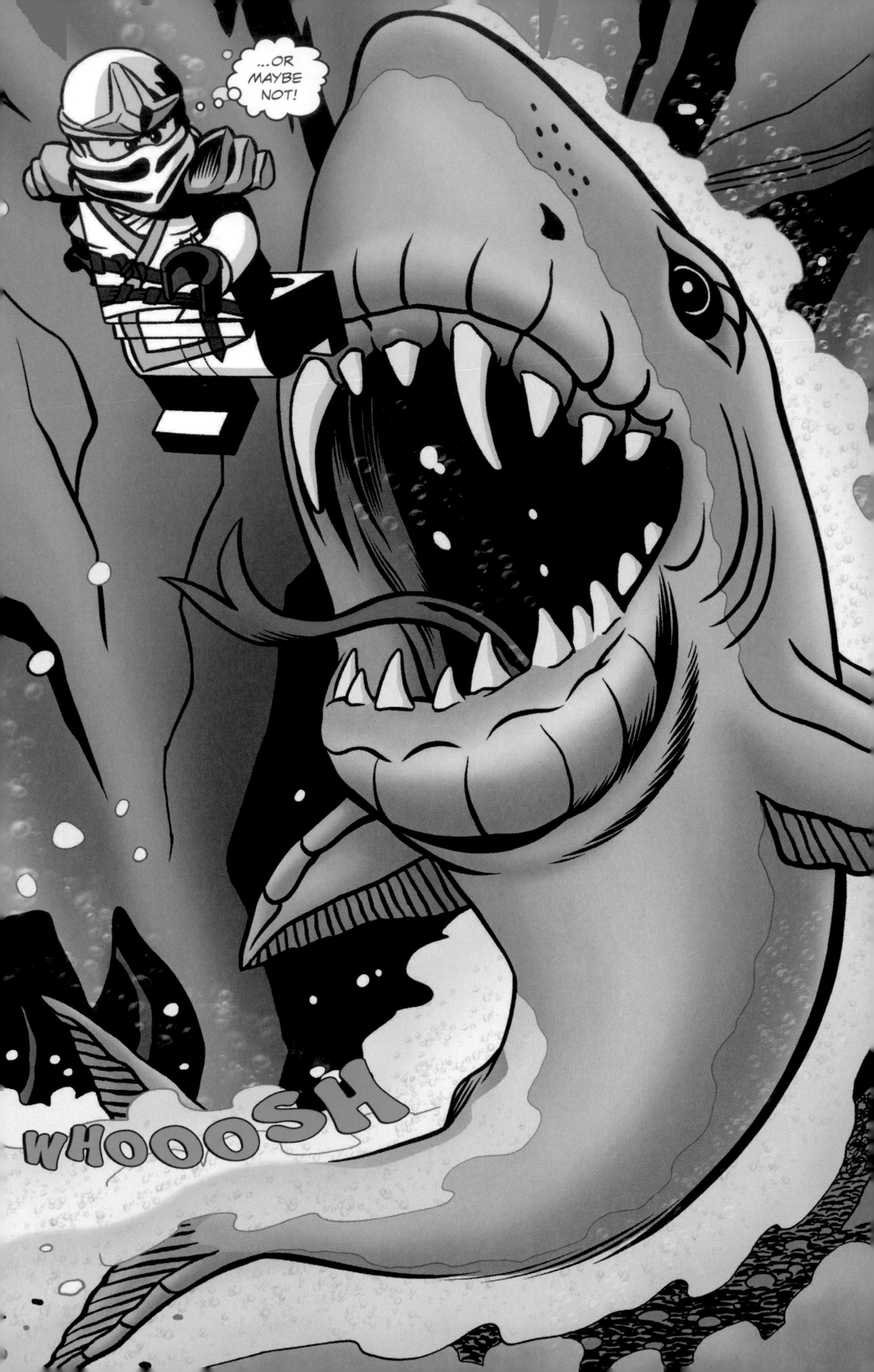
...OR MAYBE NOT!
WHOOOOSH

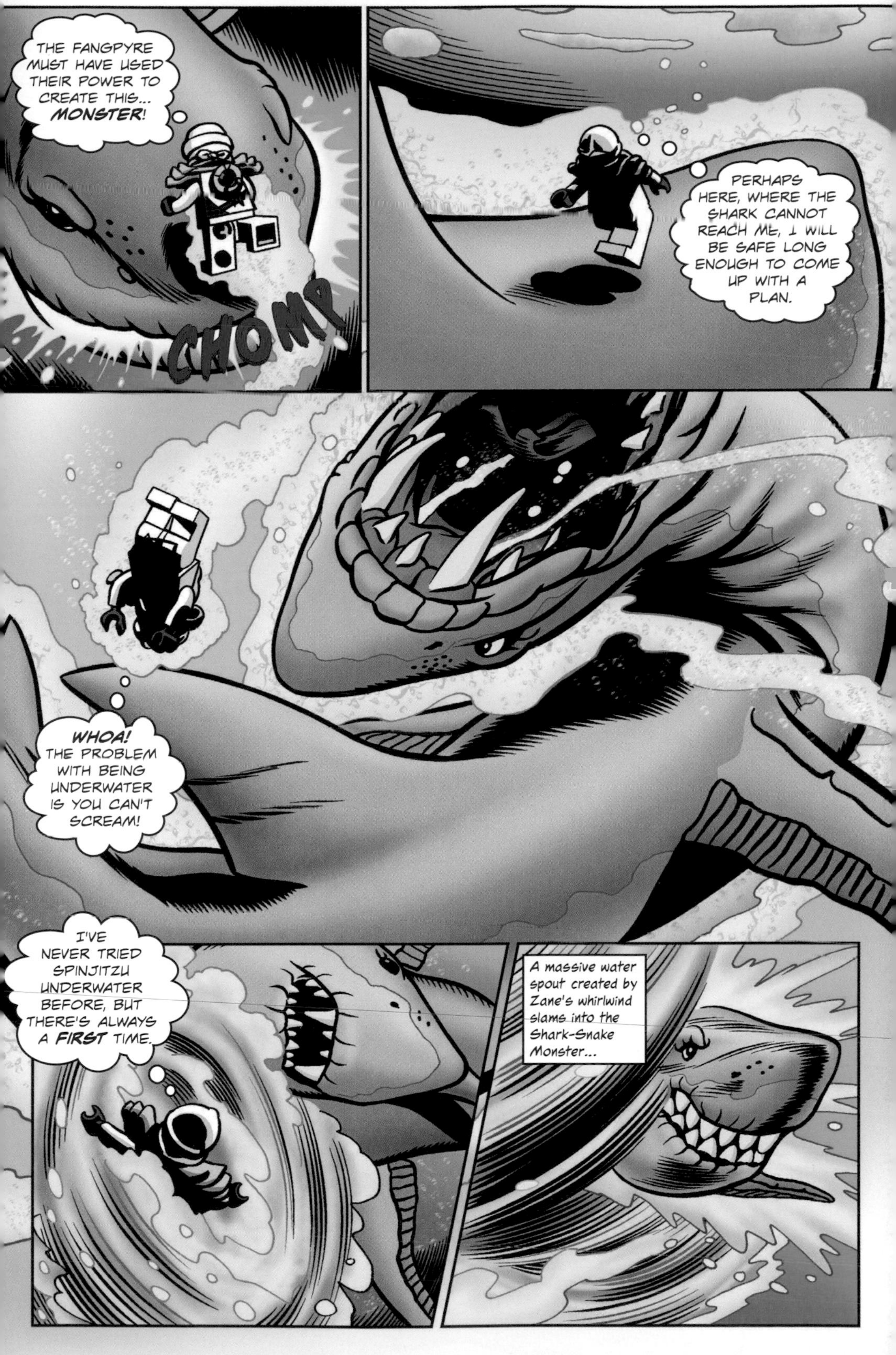
THE FANGPYRE MUST HAVE USED THEIR POWER TO CREATE THIS... MONSTER!
CHOMP
PERHAPS HERE, WHERE THE SHARK CANNOT REACH ME, I WILL BE SAFE LONG ENOUGH TO COME UP WITH A PLAN.
WHOA! THE PROBLEM WITH BEING UNDERWATER IS YOU CAN'T SCREAM!
I'VE NEVER TRIED SPINJITZU UNDERWATER BEFORE, BUT THERE'S ALWAYS A FIRST TIME.
A massive water spout created by Zane's whirlwind slams into the Shark-Snake Monster...

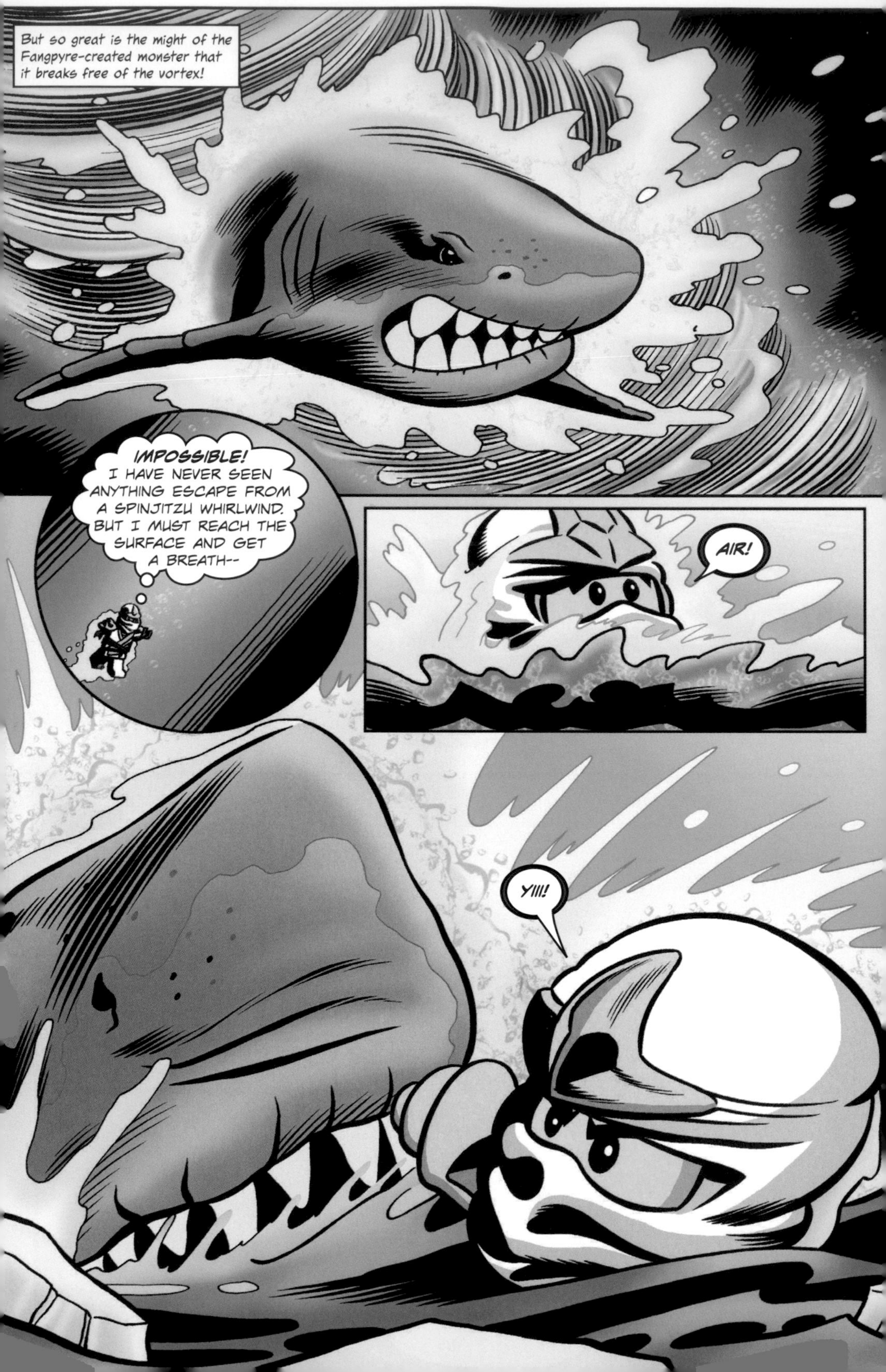
But so great is the might of the Fangpyre-created monster that it breaks free of the vortex!
IMPOSSIBLE! I HAVE NEVER SEEN ANYTHING ESCAPE FROM A SPINJITZU WHIRLWIND. BUT I MUST REACH THE SURFACE AND GET A BREATH--
AIR!
YIII!

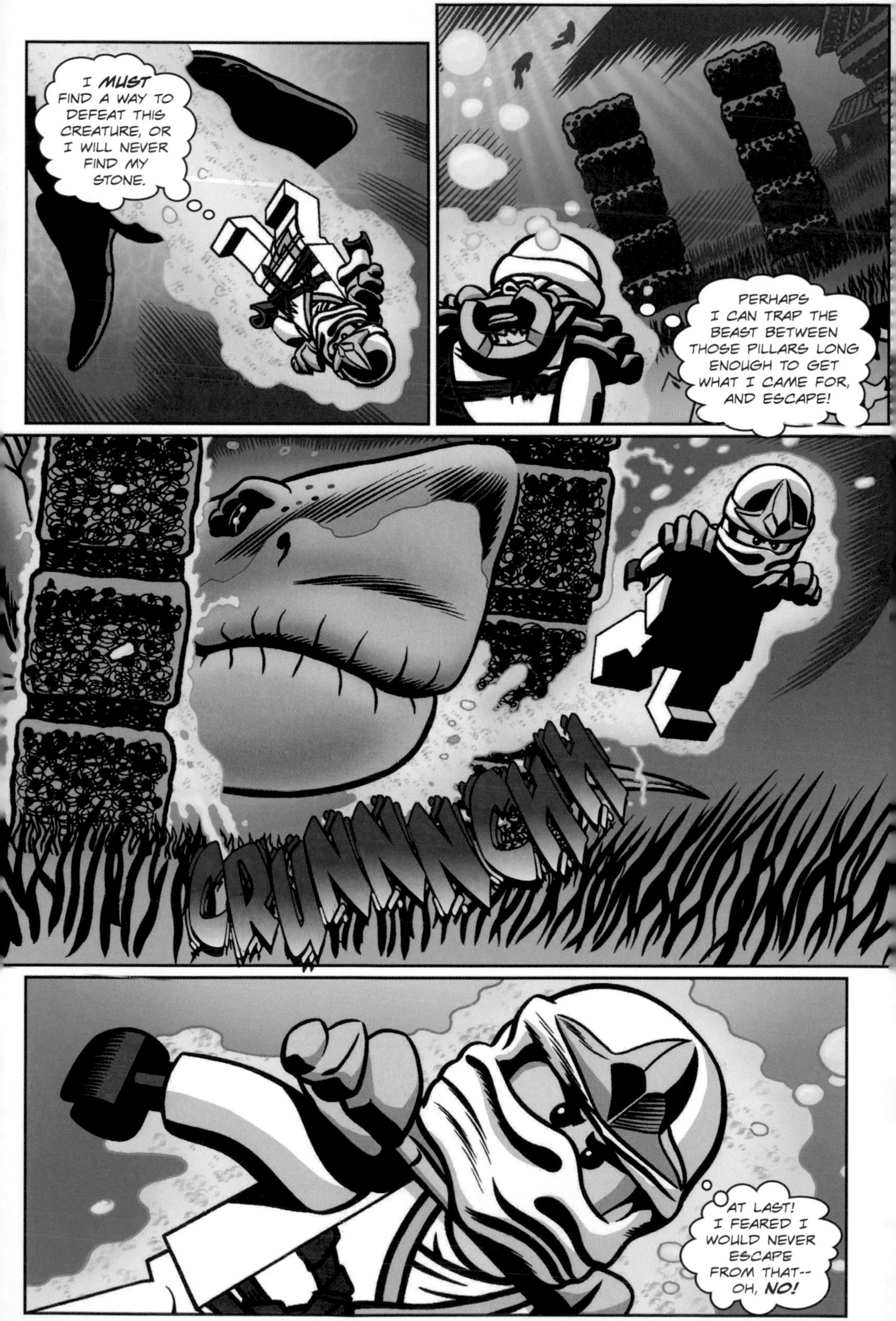
I MUST FIND A WAY TO DEFEAT THIS CREATURE, OR I WILL NEVER FIND MY STONE.
PERHAPS I CAN TRAP THE BEAST BETWEEN THOSE PILLARS LONG ENOUGH TO GET WHAT I CAME FOR, AND ESCAPE!
CRUNNNCHH
AT LAST! I FEARED I WOULD NEVER ESCAPE FROM THAT-- OH, NO!

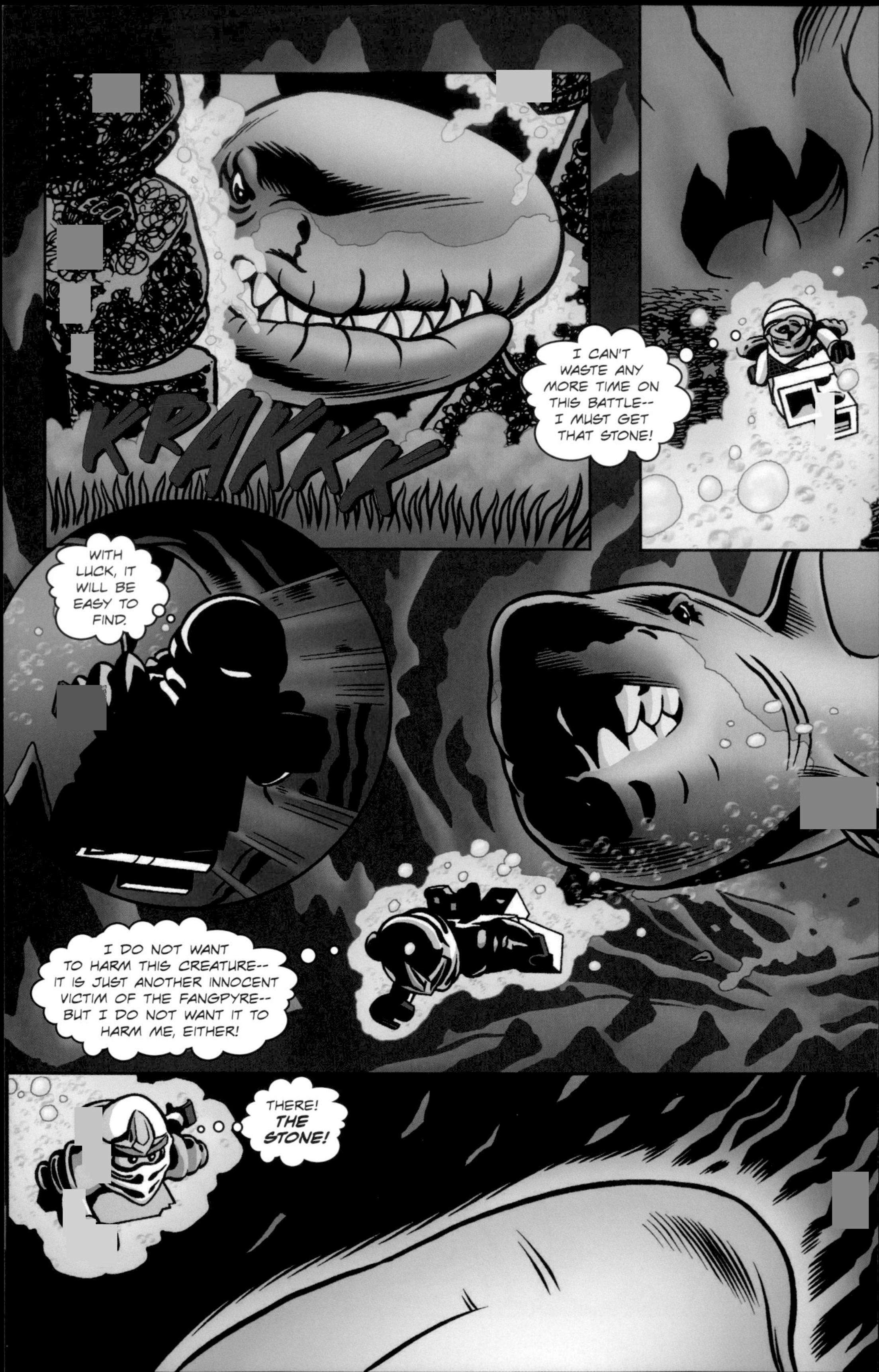
KRAKKK
I CAN'T WASTE ANY MORE TIME ON THIS BATTLE-- I MUST GET THAT STONE!
WITH LUCK, IT WILL BE EASY TO FIND.
I DO NOT WANT TO HARM THIS CREATURE-- IT IS JUST ANOTHER INNOCENT VICTIM OF THE FANGPYRE-- BUT I DO NOT WANT IT TO HARM ME, EITHER!
THERE! THE STONE!

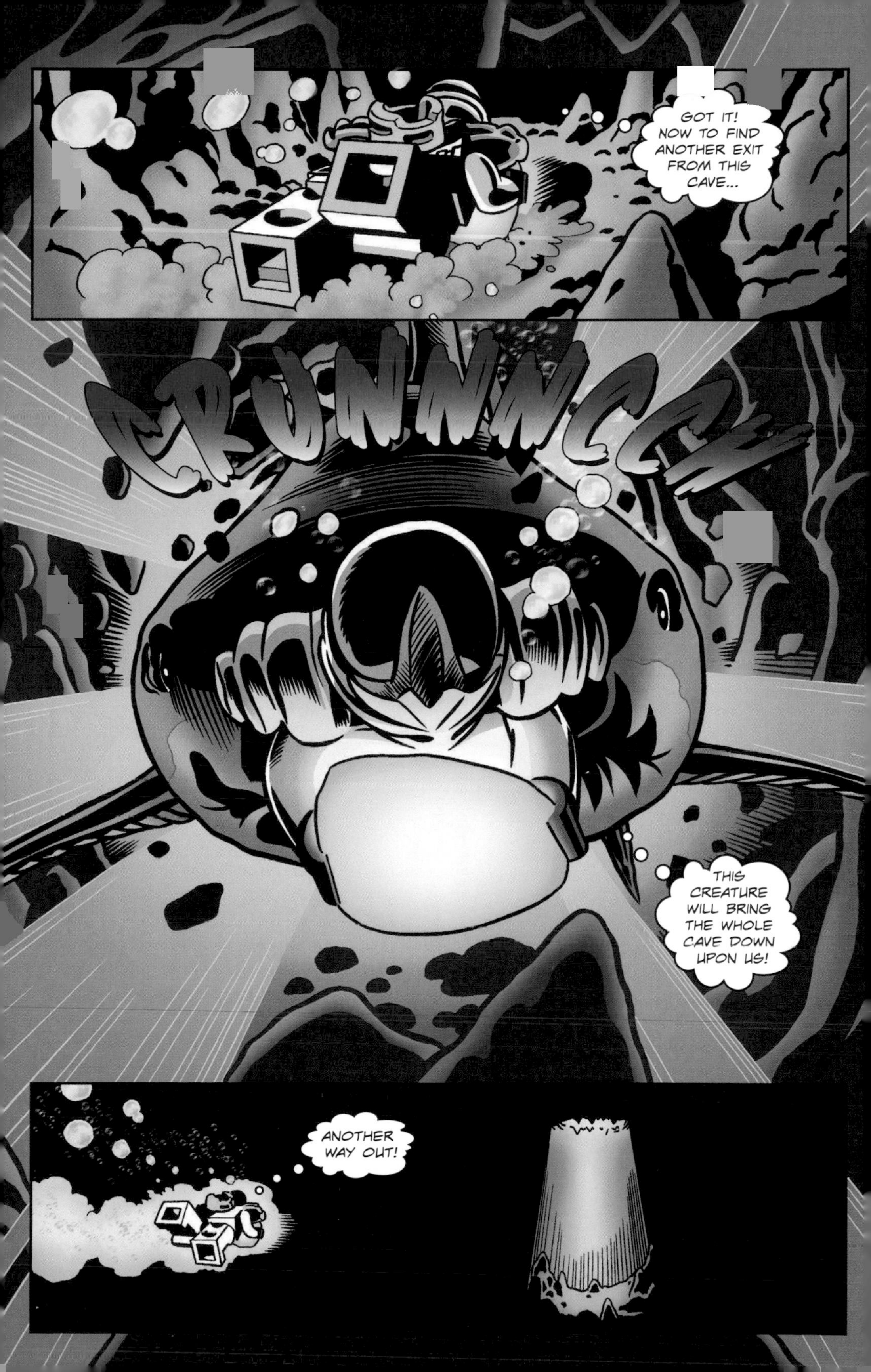
GOT IT! NOW TO FIND ANOTHER EXIT FROM THIS CAVE...
CRUNNNCCH
THIS CREATURE WILL BRING THE WHOLE CAVE DOWN UPON US!
ANOTHER WAY OUT!

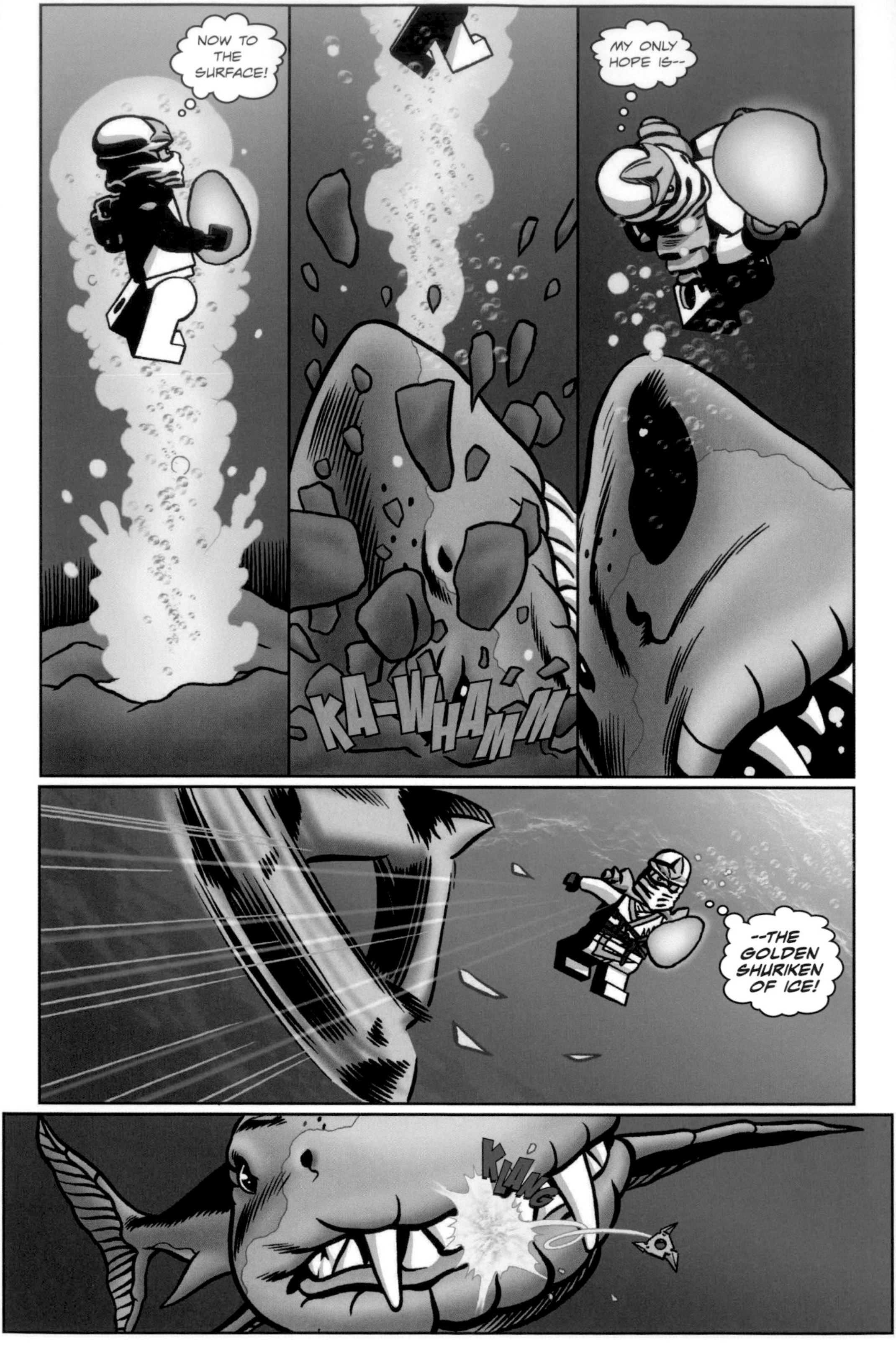
NOW TO THE SURFACE!
KA-WHAMM
MY ONLY HOPE IS--
--THE GOLDEN SHURIKEN OF ICE!
KLANG

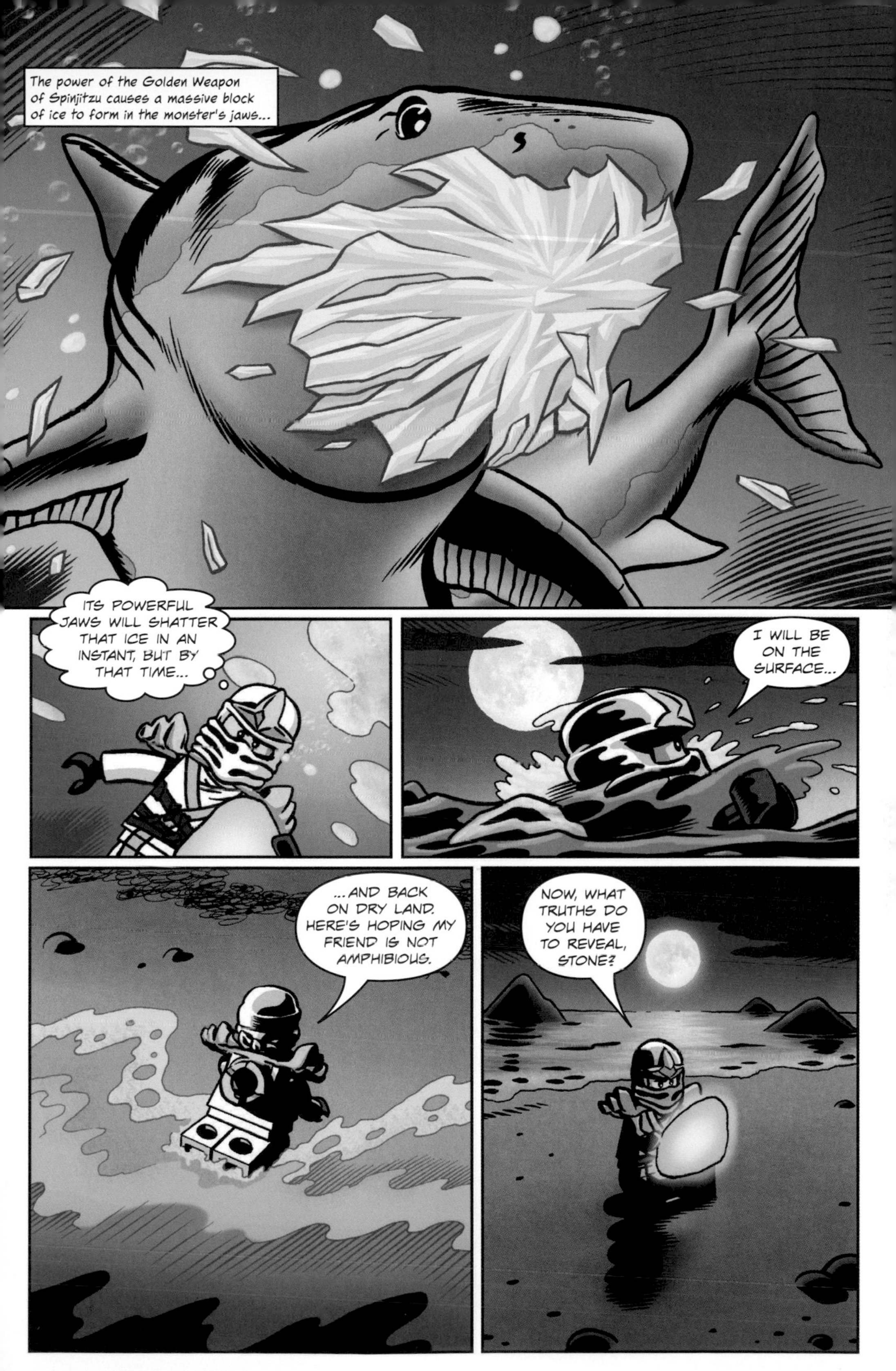
The power of the Golden Weapon of Spinjitzu causes a massive block of ice to form in the monster's jaws...
ITS POWERFUL JAWS WILL SHATTER THAT ICE IN AN INSTANT, BUT BY THAT TIME...
I WILL BE ON THE SURFACE...
...AND BACK ON DRY LAND. HERE'S HOPING MY FRIEND IS NOT AMPHIBIOUS.
NOW, WHAT TRUTHS DO YOU HAVE TO REVEAL, STONE?

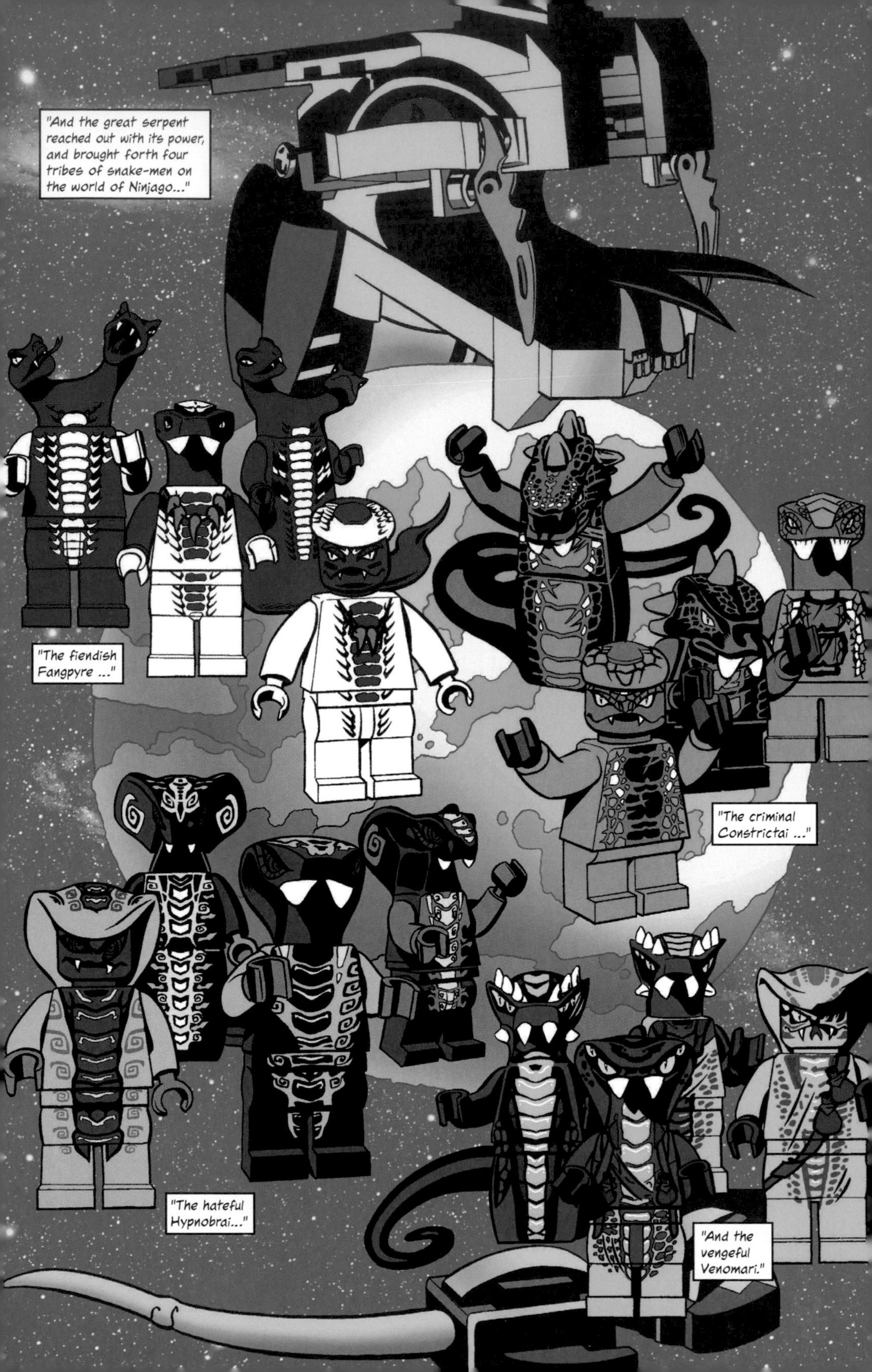
"And the great serpent reached out with its power, and brought forth four tribes of snake-men on the world of Ninjago..."
"The fiendish Fangpyre ..."
"The criminal Constrictai ..."
"The hateful Hypnobrai..."
"And the vengeful Venomari."

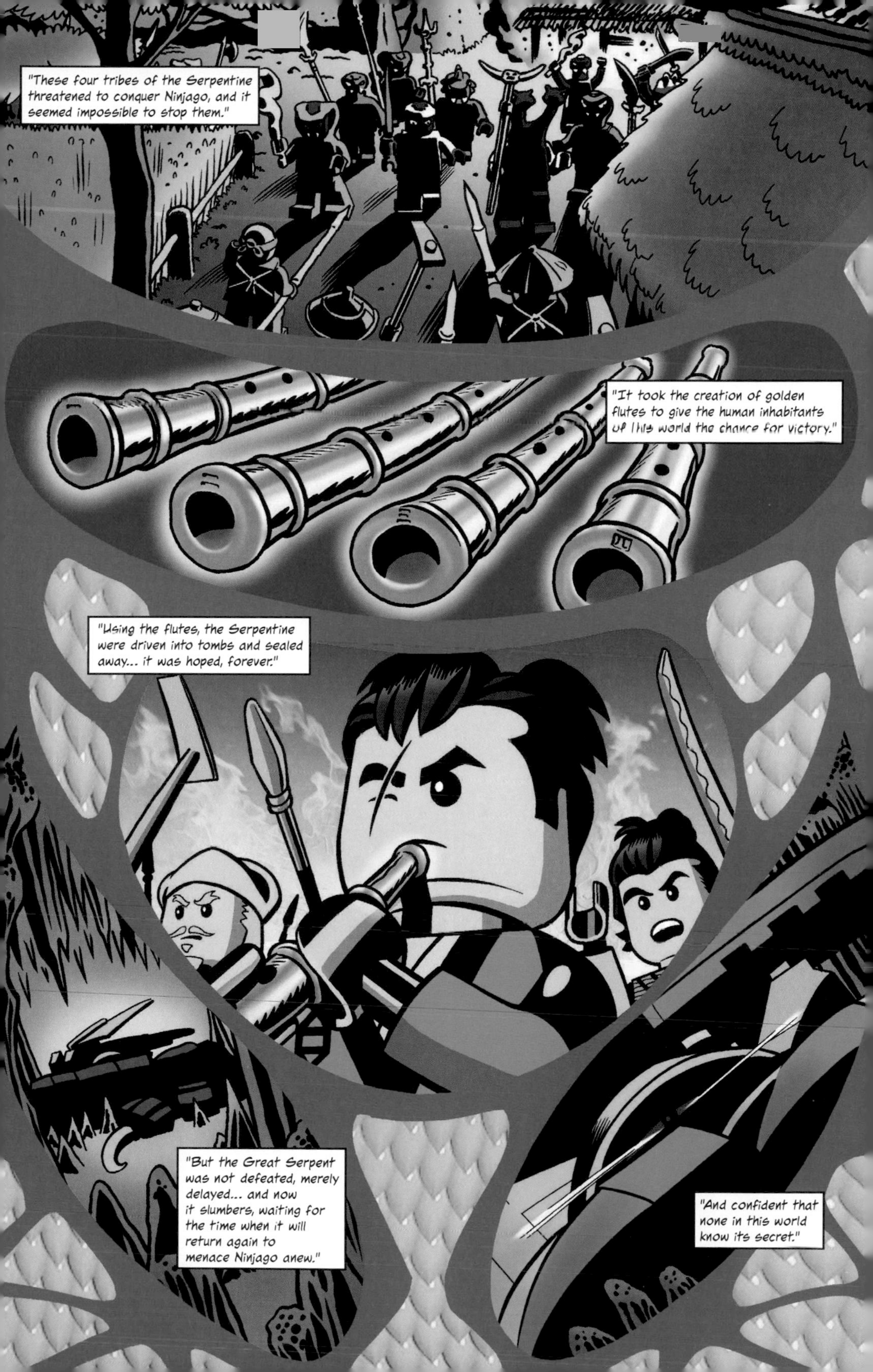
"These four tribes of the Serpentine threatened to conquer Ninjago, and it seemed impossible to stop them."
"It took the creation of golden flutes to give the human inhabitants of this world the chance for victory."
"Using the flutes, the Serpentine were driven into tombs and sealed away... it was hoped, forever."
"But the Great Serpent was not defeated, merely delayed... and now it slumbers, waiting for the time when it will return again to menace Ninjago anew."
"And confident that none in this world know its secret."

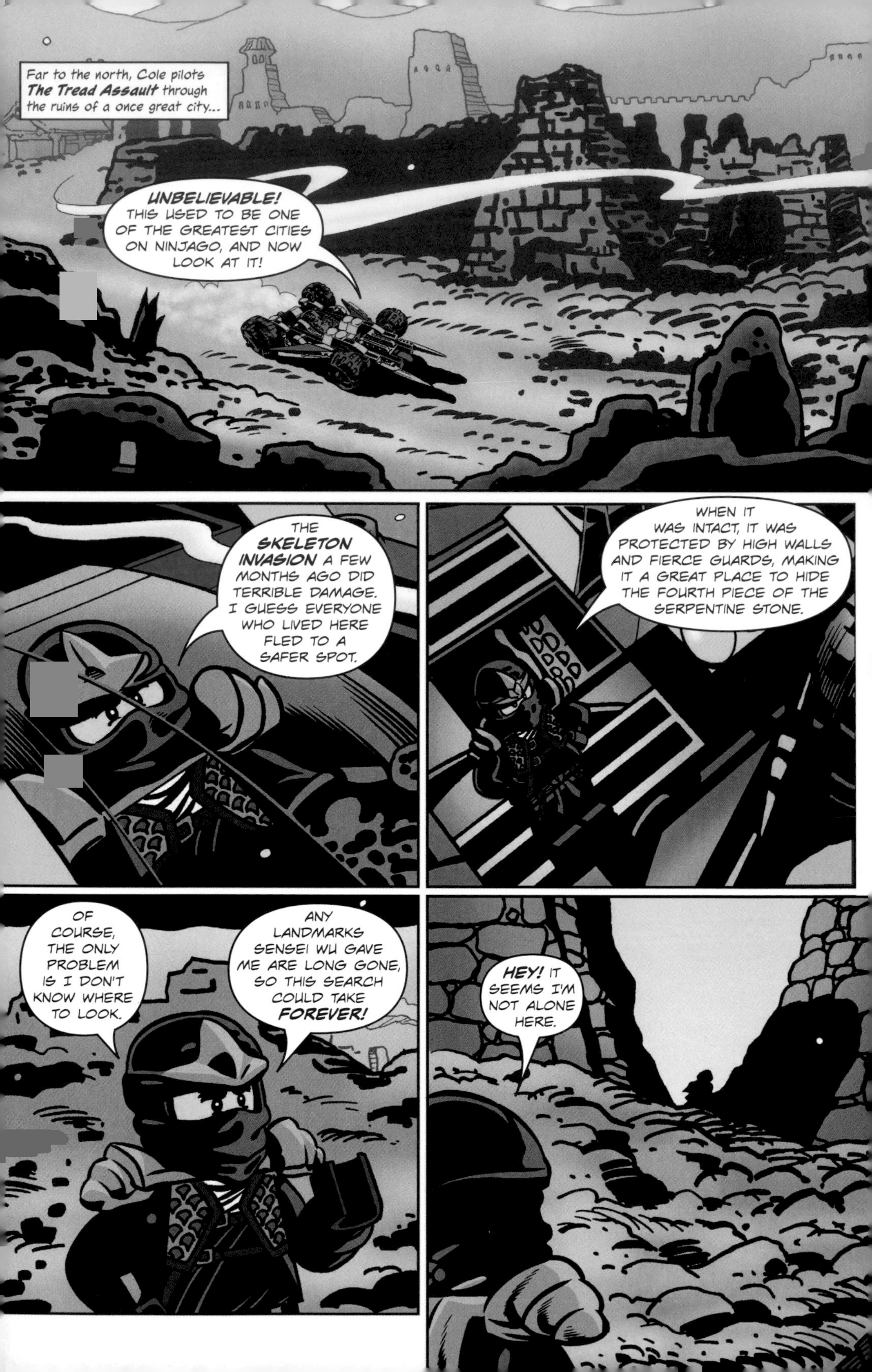
Far to the north, Cole pilots ***The Tread Assault*** through the ruins of a once great city...
UNBELIEVABLE! THIS USED TO BE ONE OF THE GREATEST CITIES ON NINJAGO, AND NOW LOOK AT IT!
THE ***SKELETON INVASION*** A FEW MONTHS AGO DID TERRIBLE DAMAGE. I GUESS EVERYONE WHO LIVED HERE FLED TO A SAFER SPOT.
WHEN IT WAS INTACT, IT WAS PROTECTED BY HIGH WALLS AND FIERCE GUARDS, MAKING IT A GREAT PLACE TO HIDE THE FOURTH PIECE OF THE SERPENTINE STONE.
OF COURSE, THE ONLY PROBLEM IS I DON'T KNOW WHERE TO LOOK.
ANY LANDMARKS SENSEI WU GAVE ME ARE LONG GONE, SO THIS SEARCH COULD TAKE ***FOREVER!***
HEY! IT SEEMS I'M NOT ALONE HERE.

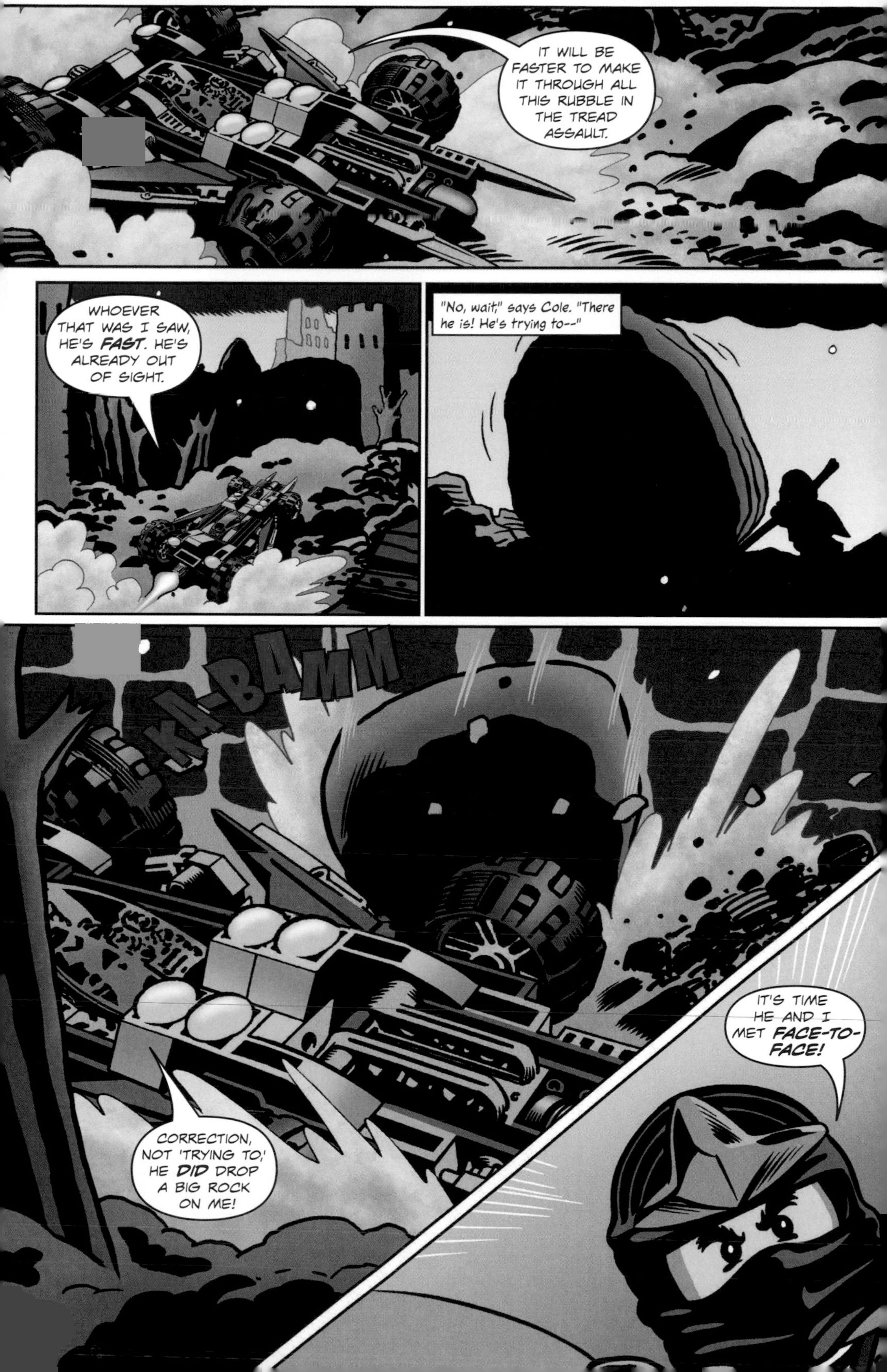
IT WILL BE FASTER TO MAKE IT THROUGH ALL THIS RUBBLE IN THE TREAD ASSAULT.
WHOEVER THAT WAS I SAW, HE'S FAST. HE'S ALREADY OUT OF SIGHT.
"No, wait," says Cole. "There he is! He's trying to--"
KA-BAMM
CORRECTION, NOT 'TRYING TO,' HE DID DROP A BIG ROCK ON ME!
IT'S TIME HE AND I MET FACE-TO-FACE!

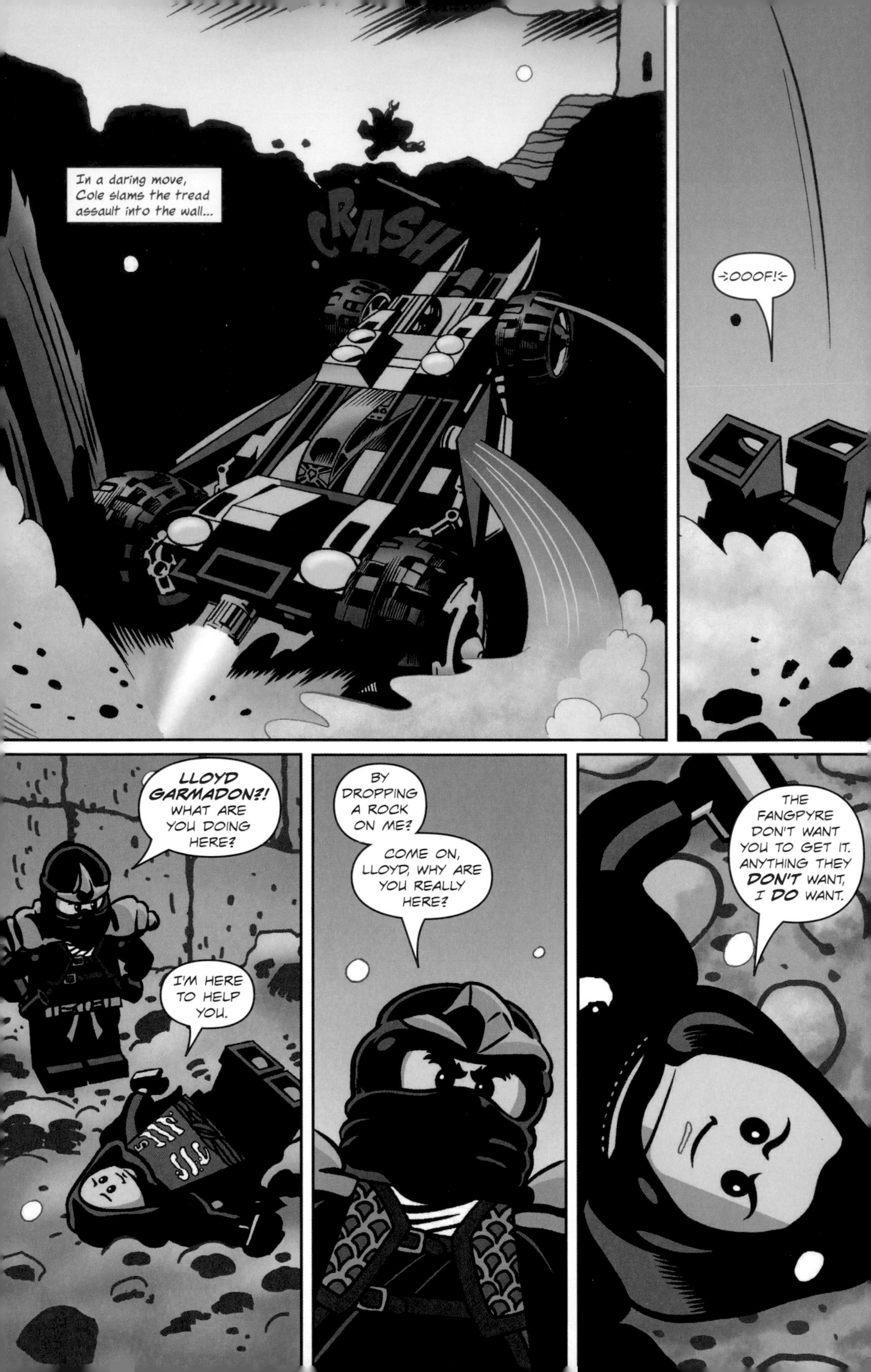

In a daring move, Cole slams the tread assault into the wall...
CRASH
OOOF!
LLOYD GARMADON?! WHAT ARE YOU DOING HERE?
I'M HERE TO HELP YOU.
BY DROPPING A ROCK ON ME?
COME ON, LLOYD, WHY ARE YOU REALLY HERE?
THE FANGPYRE DON'T WANT YOU TO GET IT. ANYTHING THEY DON'T WANT, I DO WANT.

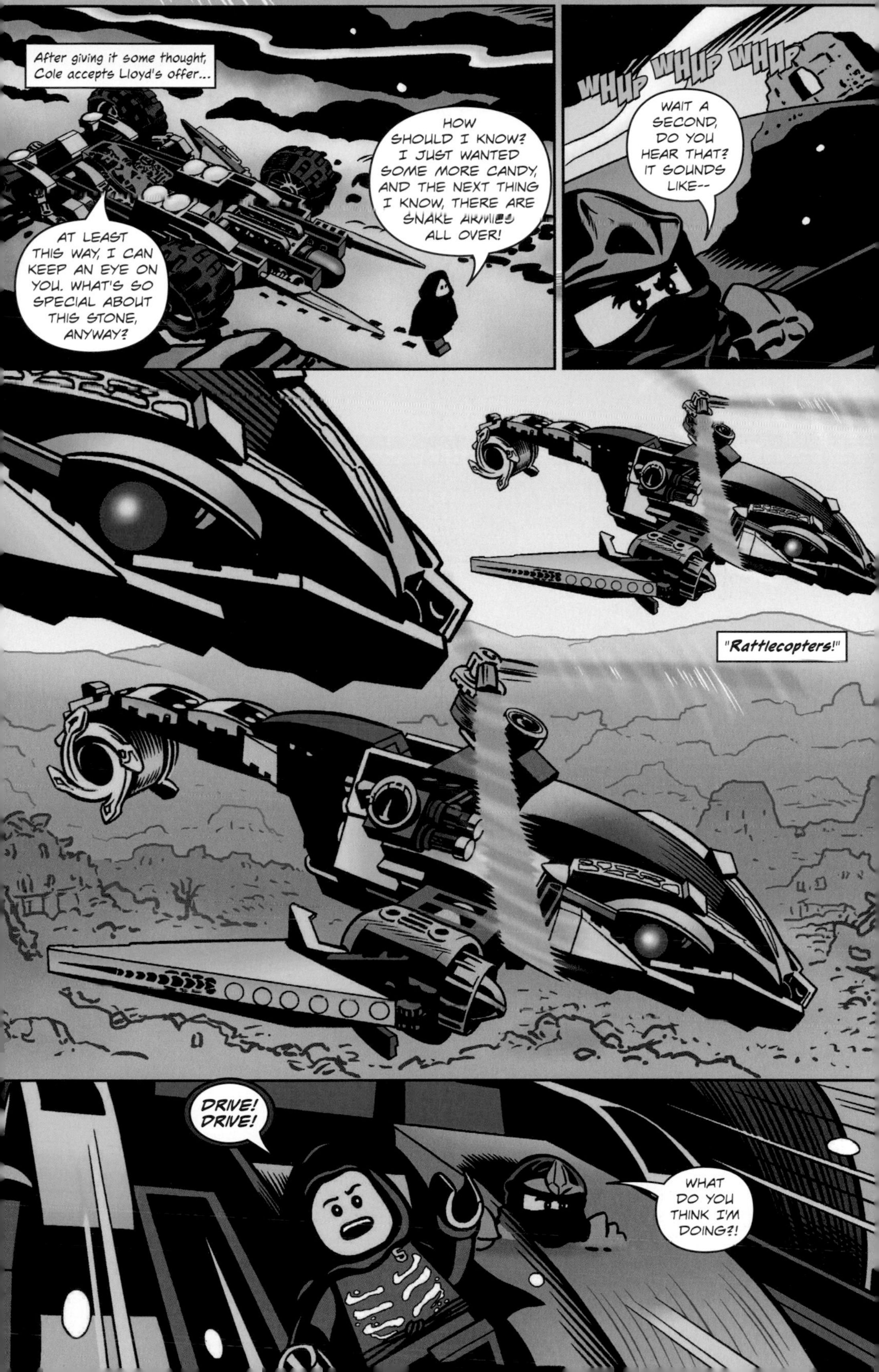
After giving it some thought, Cole accepts Lloyd's offer...
AT LEAST THIS WAY, I CAN KEEP AN EYE ON YOU. WHAT'S SO SPECIAL ABOUT THIS STONE, ANYWAY?
HOW SHOULD I KNOW? I JUST WANTED SOME MORE CANDY, AND THE NEXT THING I KNOW, THERE ARE SNAKE ARMIES ALL OVER!
WHUP WHUP WHUP
WAIT A SECOND, DO YOU HEAR THAT? IT SOUNDS LIKE--
"Rattlecopters!"
DRIVE! DRIVE!
WHAT DO YOU THINK I'M DOING?!

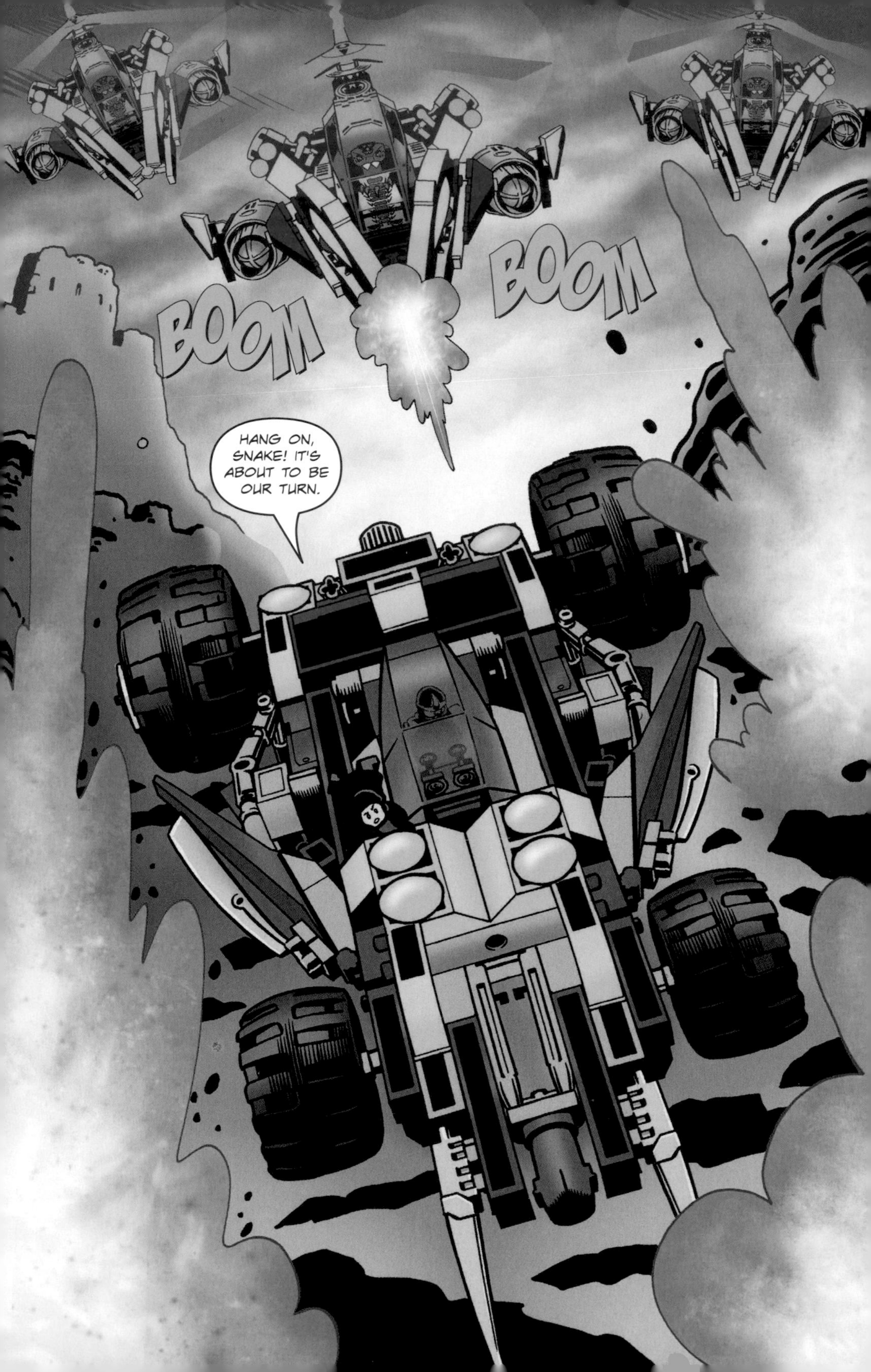
BOOM
BOOM
HANG ON, SNAKE! IT'S ABOUT TO BE OUR TURN.

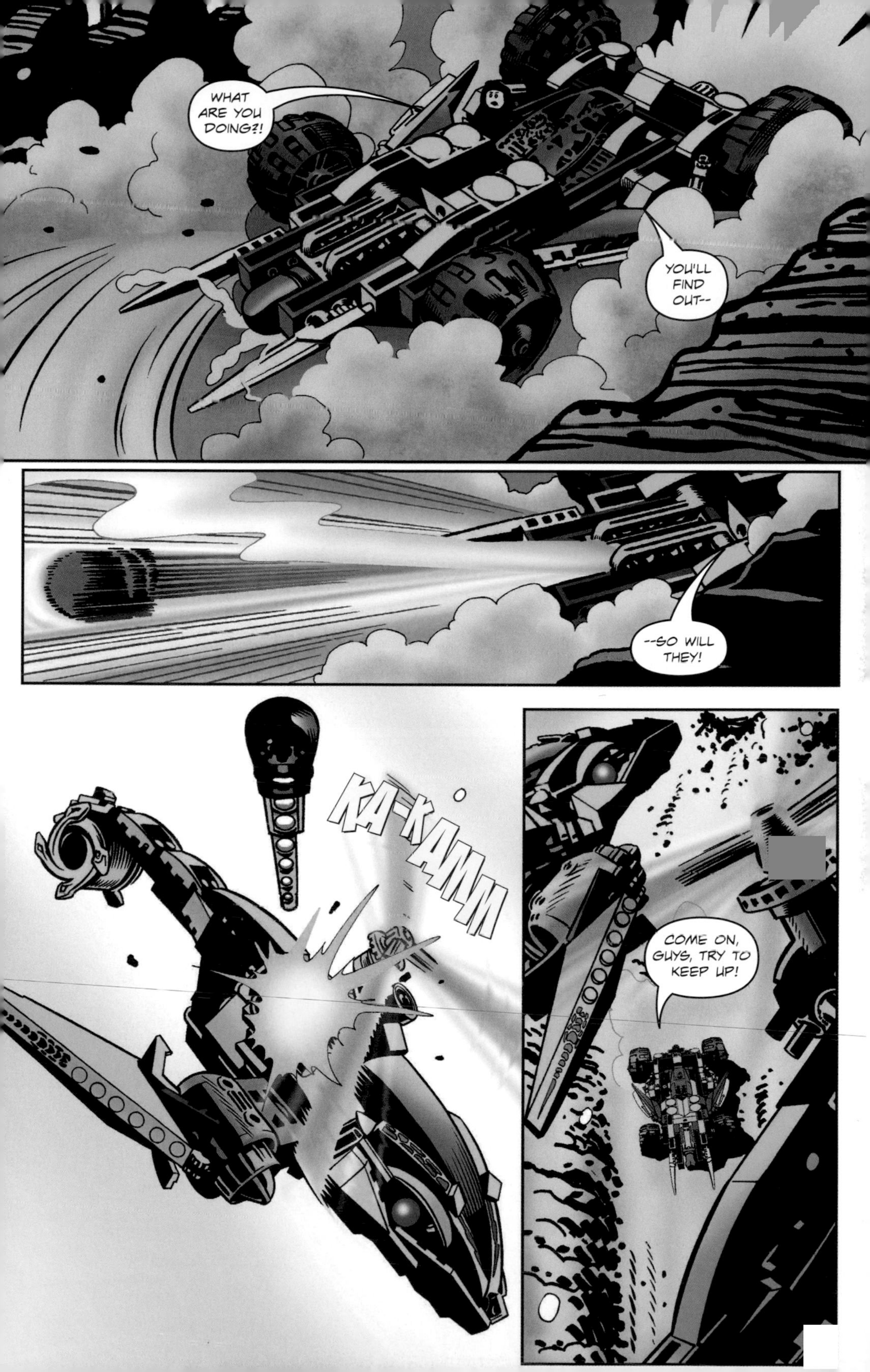
WHAT ARE YOU DOING?!
YOU'LL FIND OUT--
--SO WILL THEY!
KA-KAMM
COME ON, GUYS, TRY TO KEEP UP!

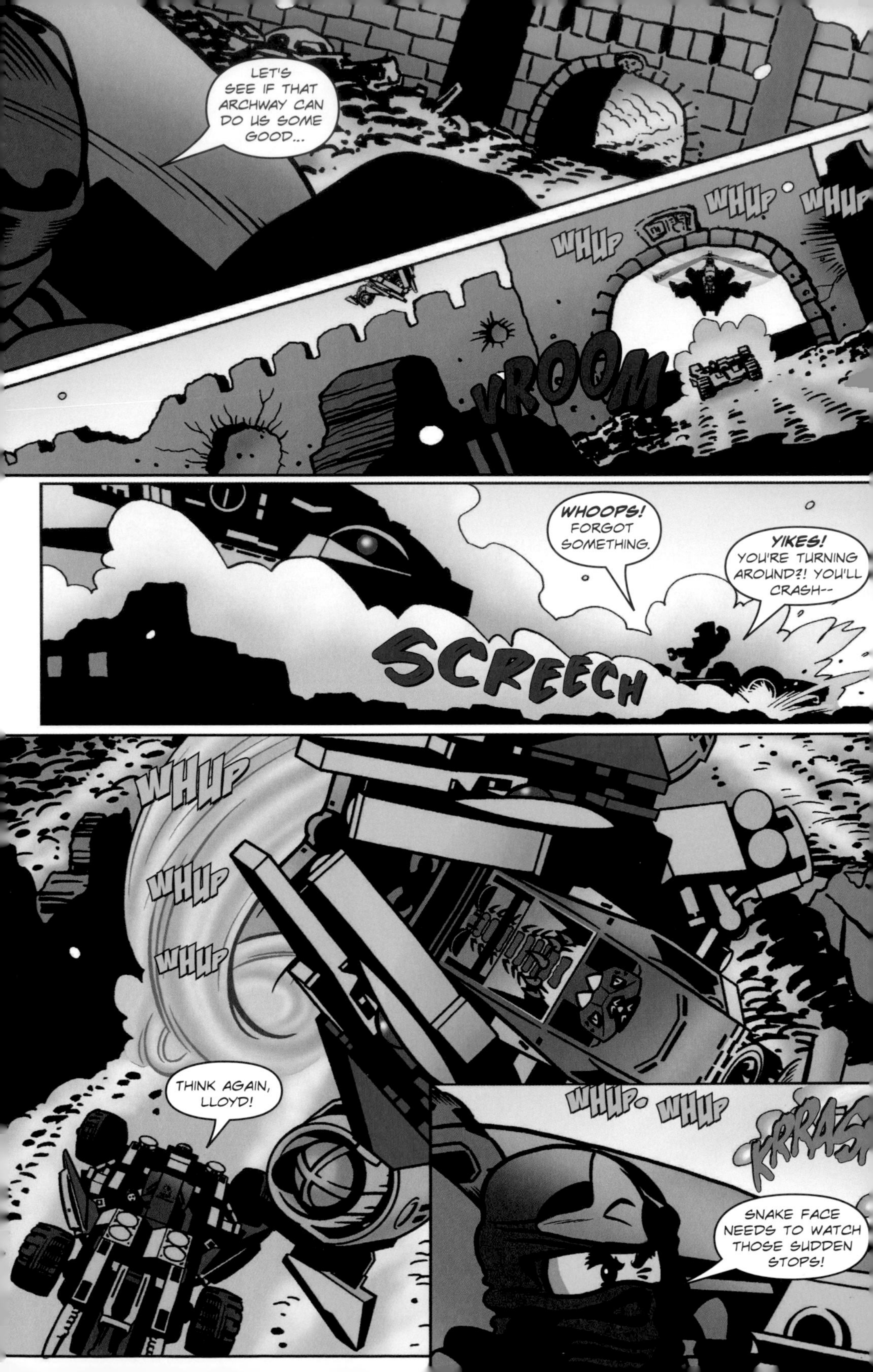
LET'S SEE IF THAT ARCHWAY CAN DO US SOME GOOD...
WHUP
WHUP
WHUP
VROOM
WHOOPS! FORGOT SOMETHING.
YIKES! YOU'RE TURNING AROUND?! YOU'LL CRASH--
SCREECH
WHUP
WHUP
WHUP
THINK AGAIN, LLOYD!
WHUP WHUP
SNAKE FACE NEEDS TO WATCH THOSE SUDDEN STOPS!

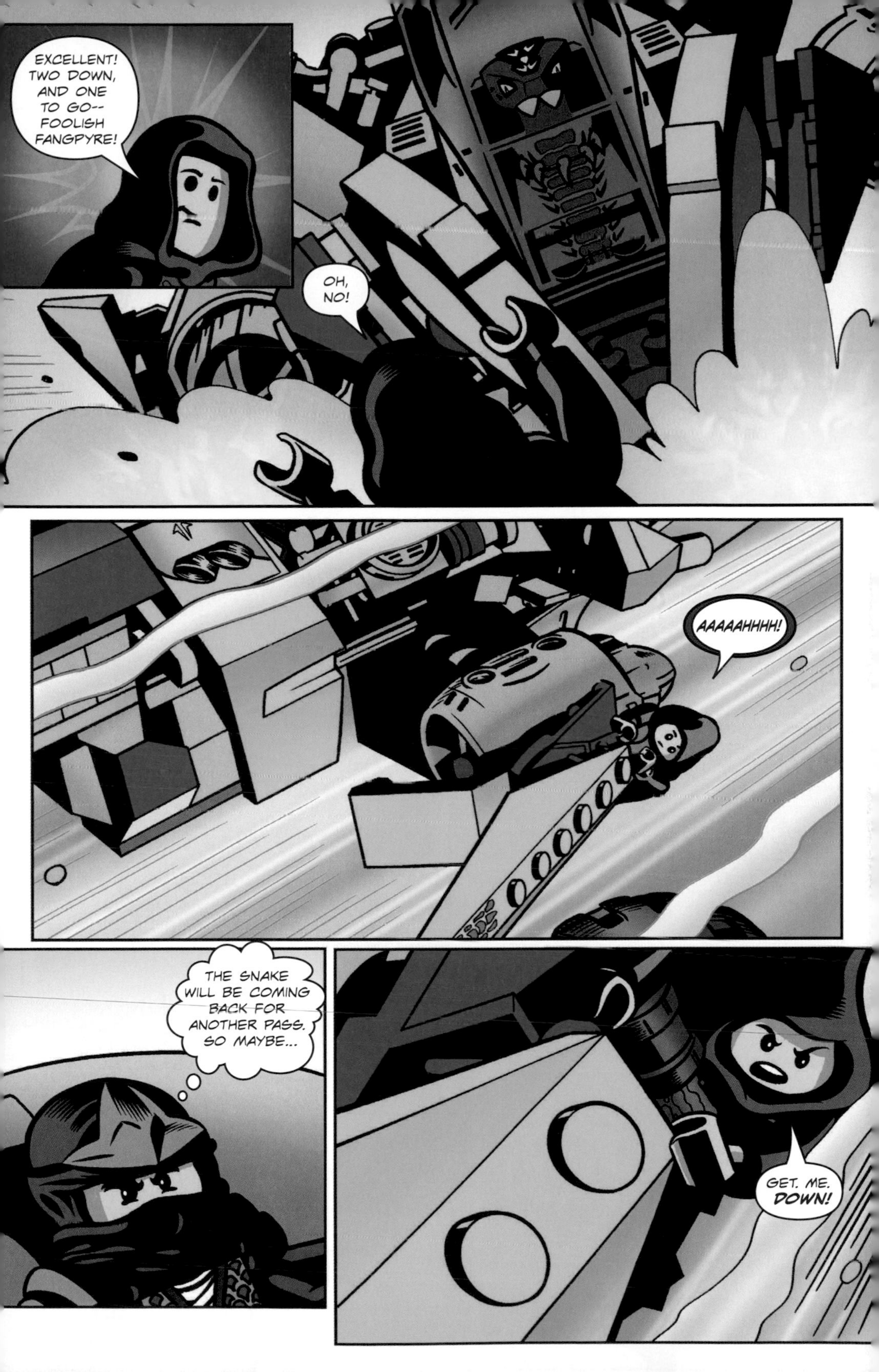
EXCELLENT! TWO DOWN, AND ONE TO GO-- FOOLISH FANGPYRE!
OH, NO!
AAAAAHHHH!
THE SNAKE WILL BE COMING BACK FOR ANOTHER PASS. SO MAYBE...
GET. ME. DOWN!

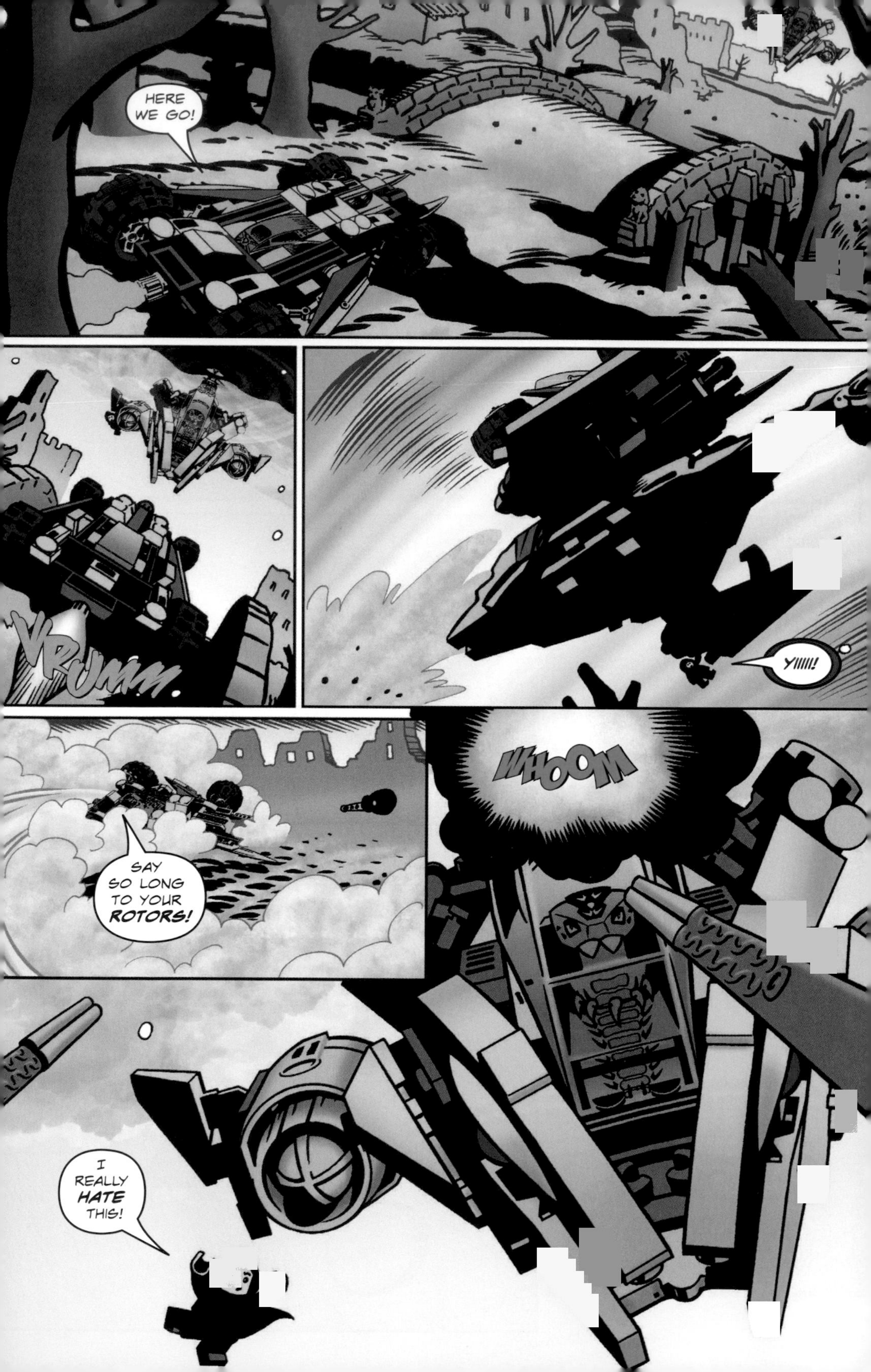
HERE WE GO!
VRUMM
YIIII!
WHOOM
SAY SO LONG TO YOUR ROTORS!
I REALLY HATE THIS!

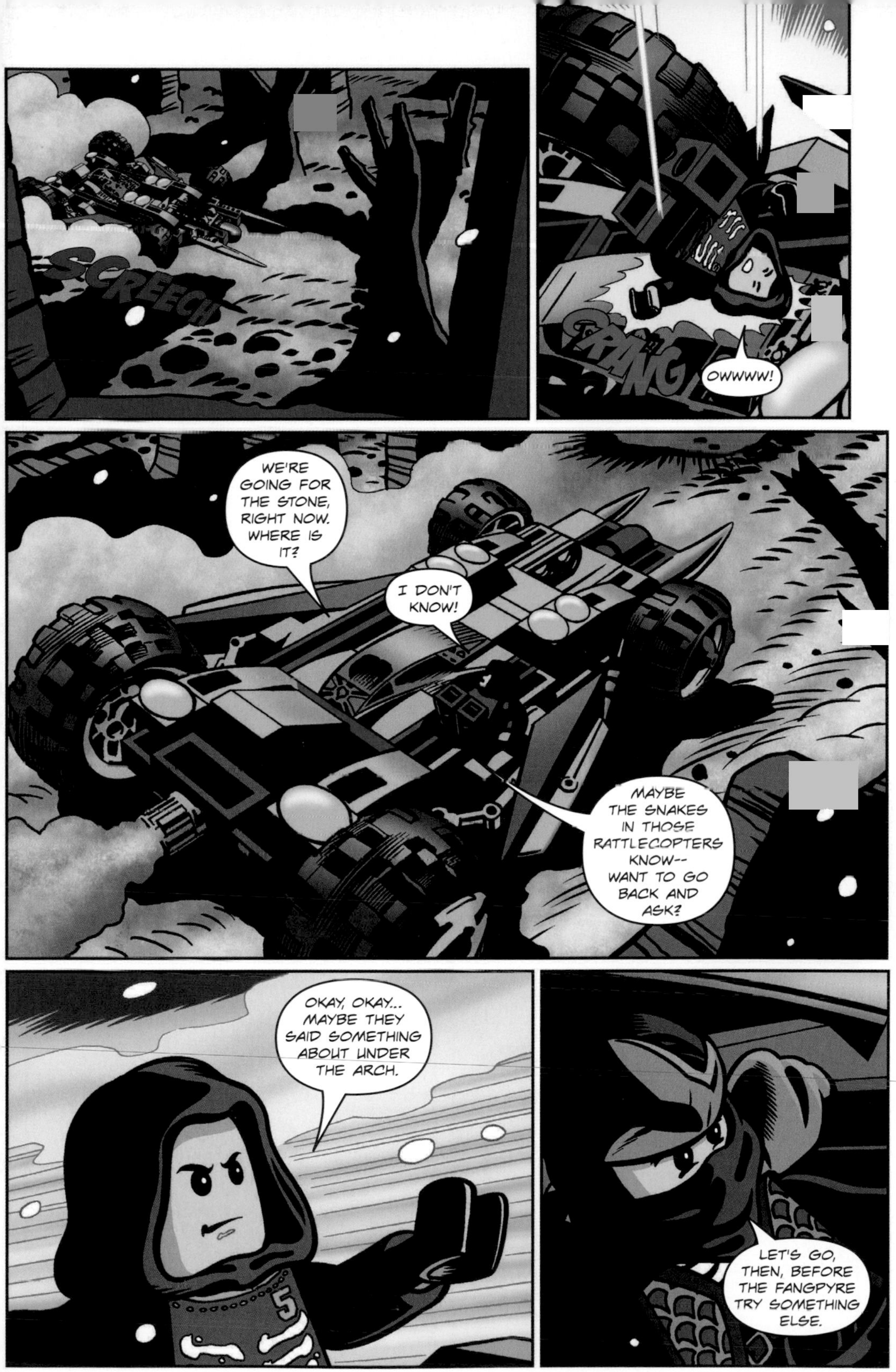
SCREECH
CRANG
OWWWW!
WE'RE GOING FOR THE STONE, RIGHT NOW. WHERE IS IT?
I DON'T KNOW!
MAYBE THE SNAKES IN THOSE RATTLECOPTERS KNOW-- WANT TO GO BACK AND ASK?
OKAY, OKAY... MAYBE THEY SAID SOMETHING ABOUT UNDER THE ARCH.
LET'S GO, THEN, BEFORE THE FANGPYRE TRY SOMETHING ELSE.

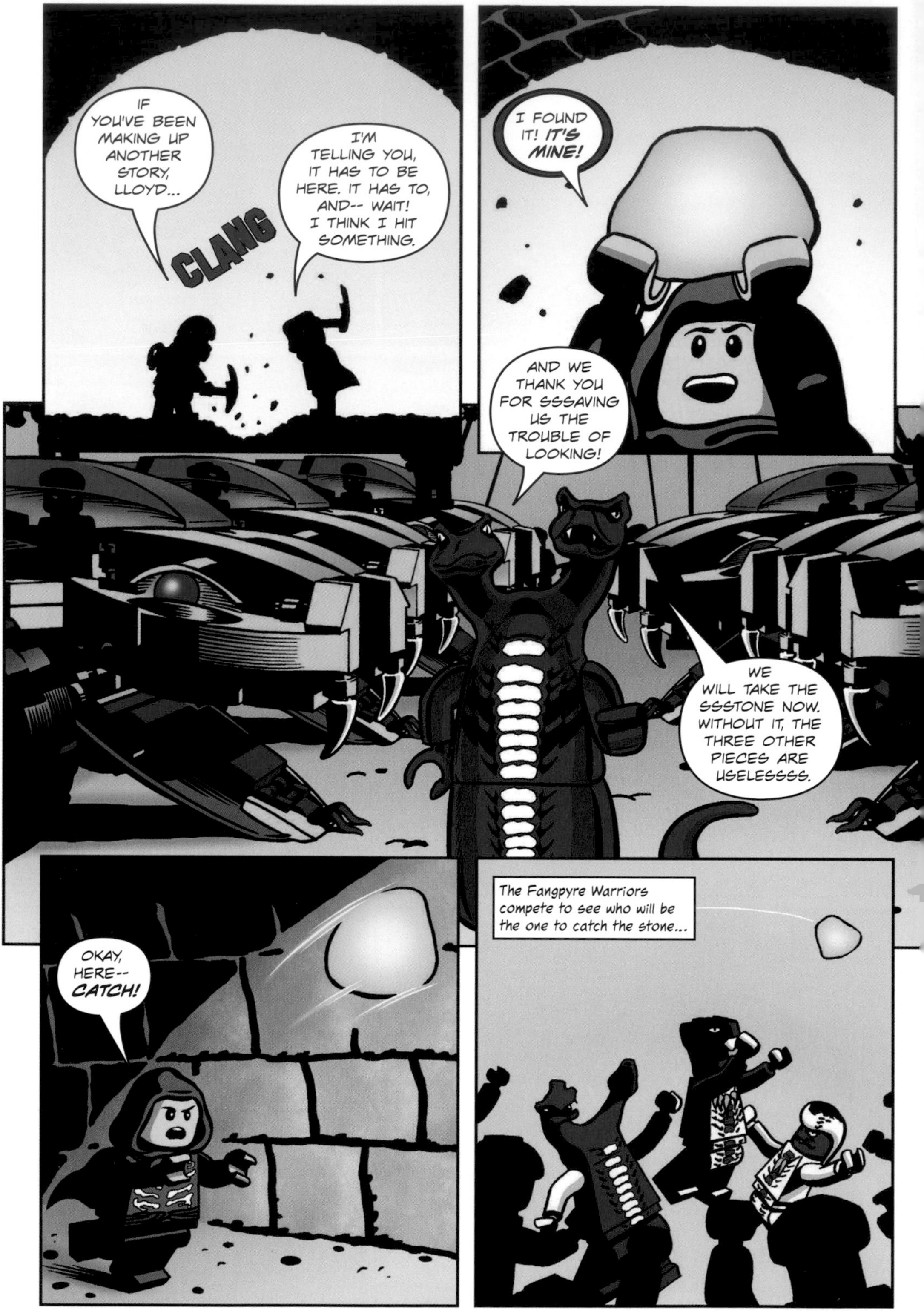
IF YOU'VE BEEN MAKING UP ANOTHER STORY, LLOYD...
CLANG
I'M TELLING YOU, IT HAS TO BE HERE. IT HAS TO, AND-- WAIT! I THINK I HIT SOMETHING.
I FOUND IT! IT'S MINE!
AND WE THANK YOU FOR SSSAVING US THE TROUBLE OF LOOKING!
WE WILL TAKE THE SSSTONE NOW. WITHOUT IT, THE THREE OTHER PIECES ARE USELESSSS.
OKAY, HERE-- CATCH!
The Fangpyre Warriors compete to see who will be the one to catch the stone...

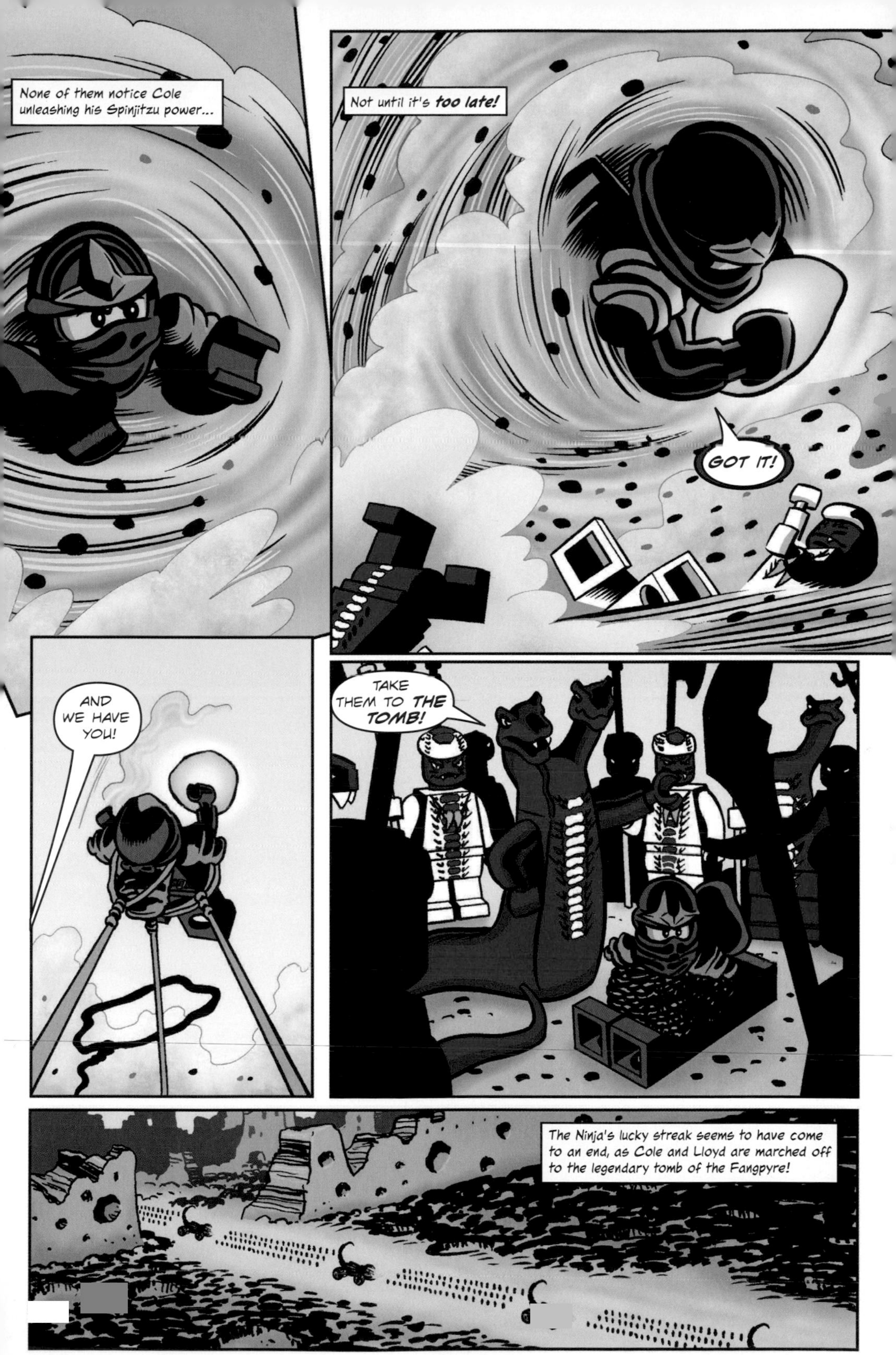
None of them notice Cole unleashing his Spinjitzu power...
Not until it's too late!
GOT IT!
AND WE HAVE YOU!
TAKE THEM TO THE TOMB!
The Ninja's lucky streak seems to have come to an end, as Cole and Lloyd are marched off to the legendary tomb of the Fangpyre!

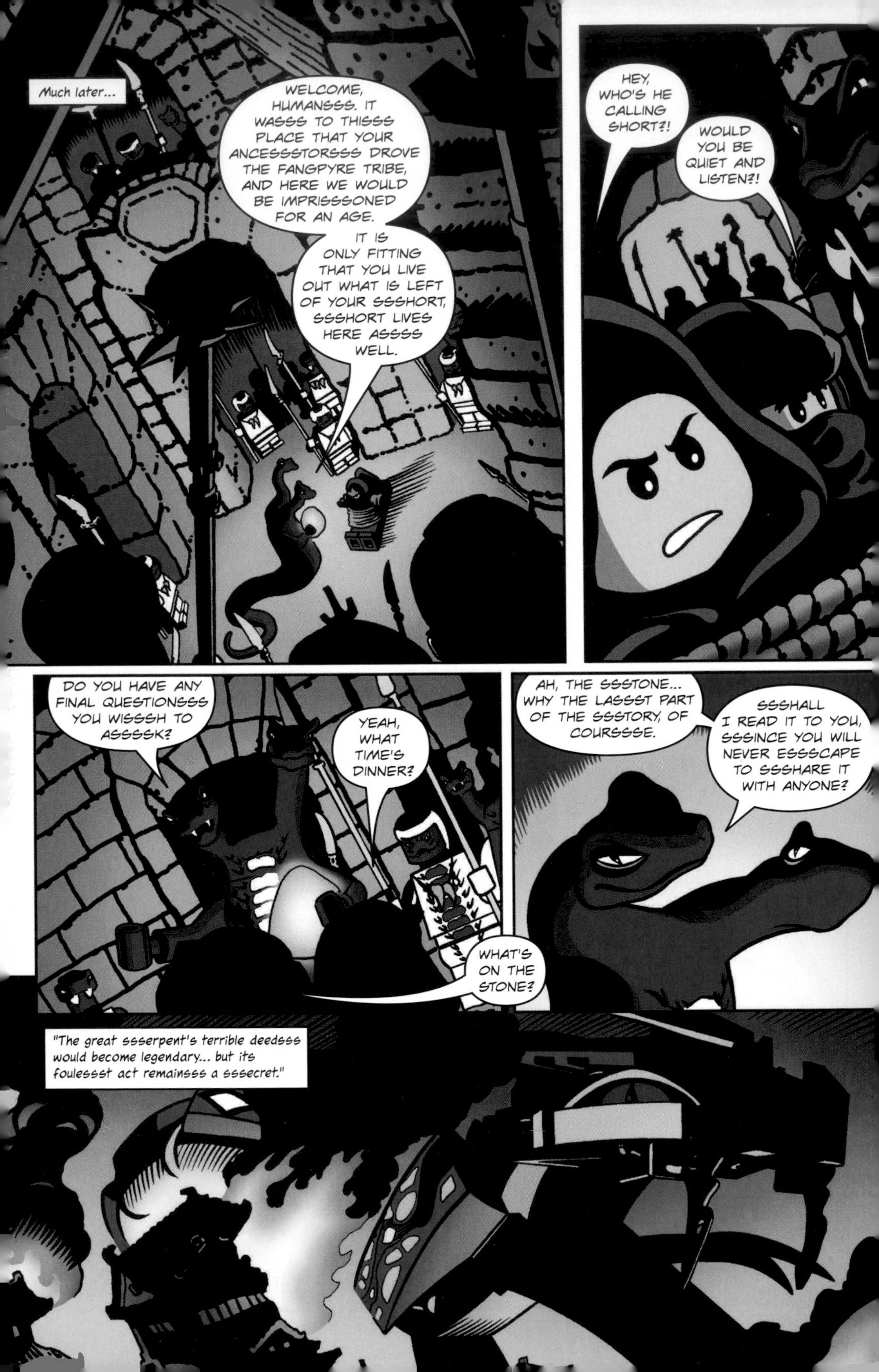
Much later...
WELCOME, HUMANSSS. IT WASSS TO THISSS PLACE THAT YOUR ANCESSSTORSSS DROVE THE FANGPYRE TRIBE, AND HERE WE WOULD BE IMPRISSSONED FOR AN AGE.
IT IS ONLY FITTING THAT YOU LIVE OUT WHAT IS LEFT OF YOUR SSSHORT, SSSHORT LIVES HERE ASSSS WELL.
HEY, WHO'S HE CALLING SHORT?!
WOULD YOU BE QUIET AND LISTEN?!
DO YOU HAVE ANY FINAL QUESTIONSSS YOU WISSSH TO ASSSSK?
YEAH, WHAT TIME'S DINNER?
WHAT'S ON THE STONE?
AH, THE SSSTONE... WHY THE LASSST PART OF THE SSSTORY, OF COURSSSE.
SSSHALL I READ IT TO YOU, SSSINCE YOU WILL NEVER ESSSCAPE TO SSSHARE IT WITH ANYONE?
"The great ssserpent's terrible deedsss would become legendary... but its foulessst act remainsss a sssecret."

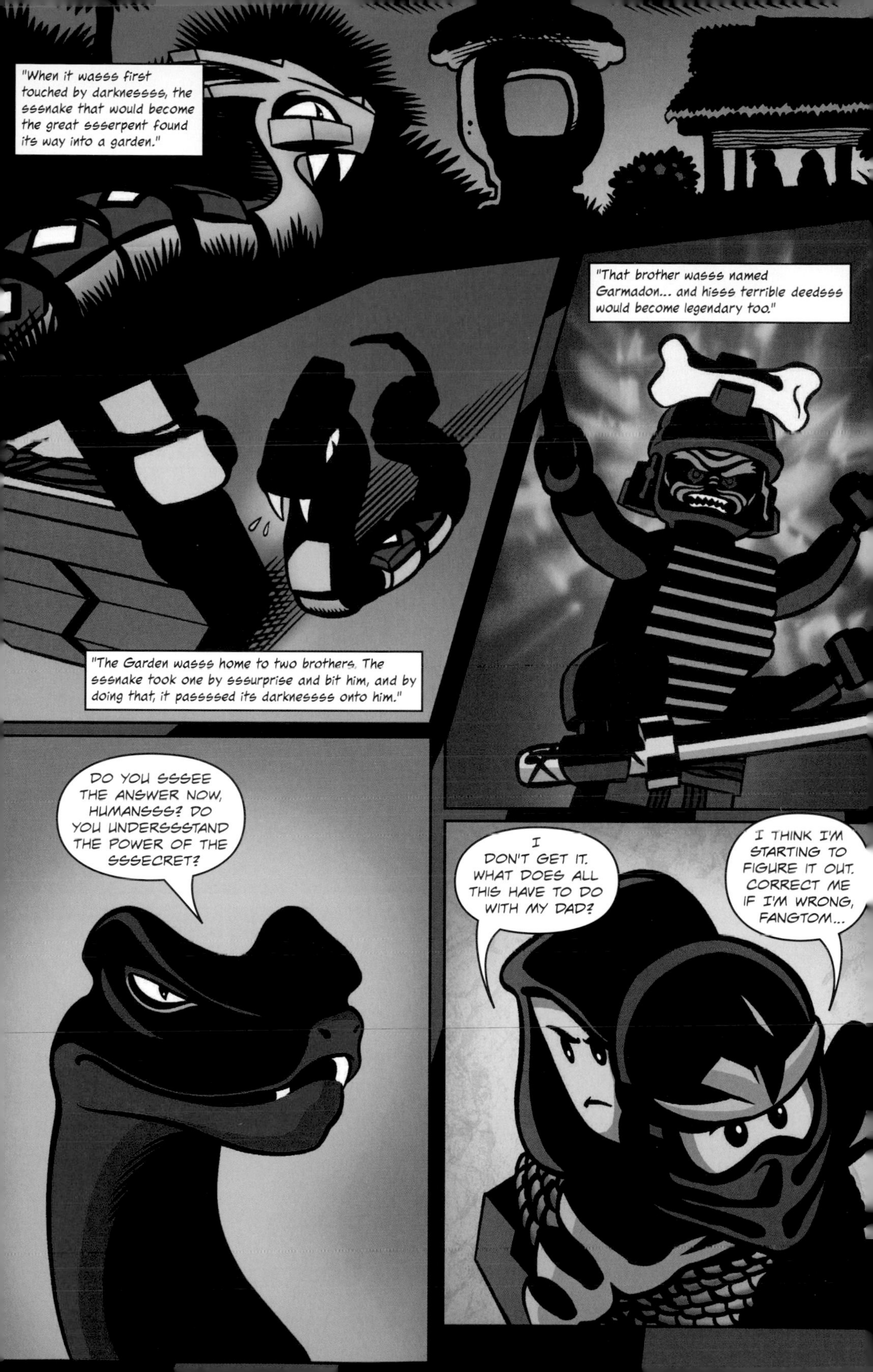
"When it wasss first touched by darknessss, the sssnake that would become the great ssserpent found its way into a garden."
"The Garden wasss home to two brothers. The sssnake took one by sssurprise and bit him, and by doing that, it passssed its darknessss onto him."
"That brother wasss named Garmadon... and hisss terrible deedsss would become legendary too."
DO YOU SSSEE THE ANSWER NOW, HUMANSSS? DO YOU UNDERSSSTAND THE POWER OF THE SSSECRET?
I DON'T GET IT. WHAT DOES ALL THIS HAVE TO DO WITH MY DAD?
I THINK I'M STARTING TO FIGURE IT OUT. CORRECT ME IF I'M WRONG, FANGTOM...

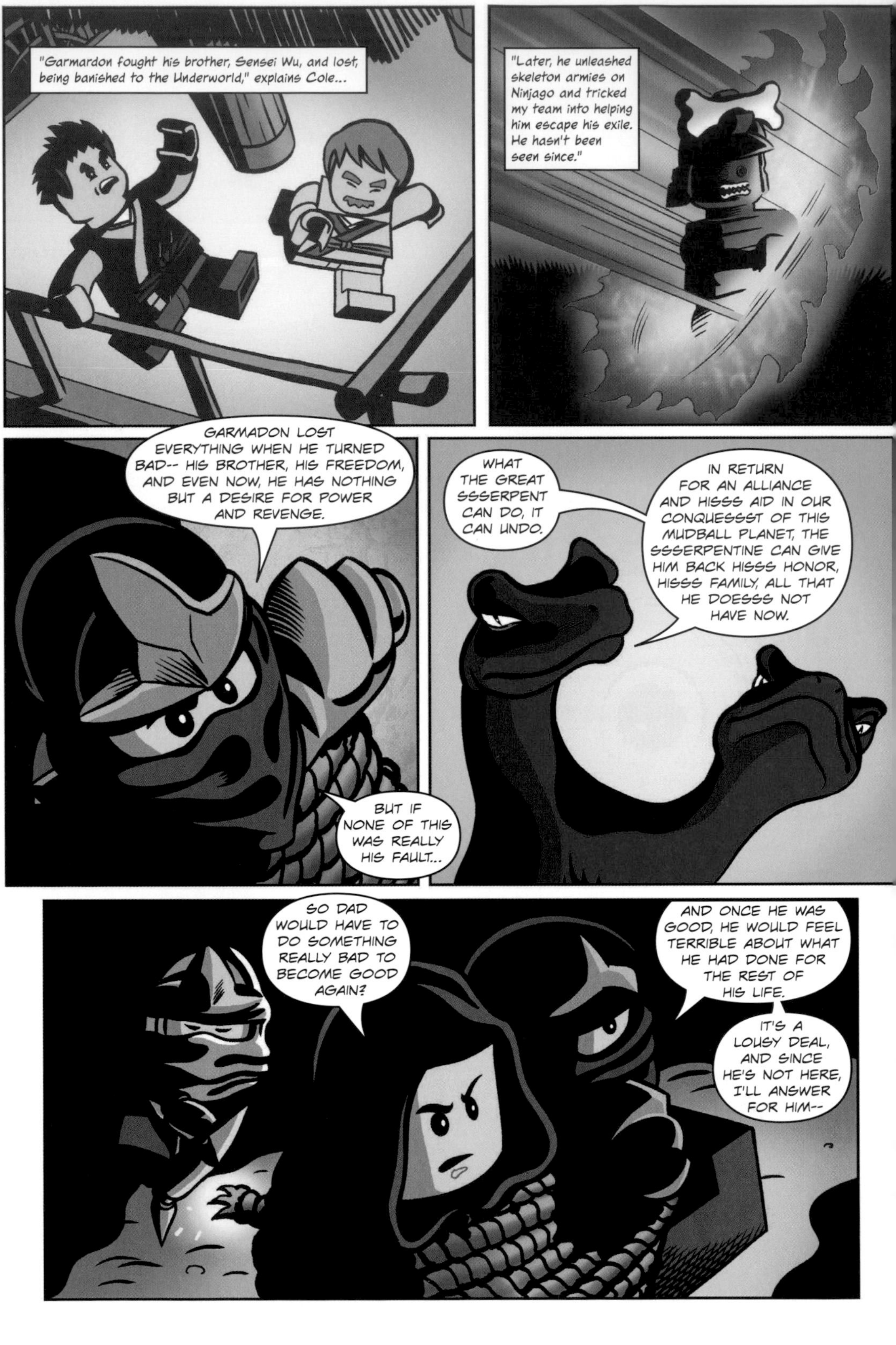
"Garmardon fought his brother, Sensei Wu, and lost, being banished to the Underworld," explains Cole...
"Later, he unleashed skeleton armies on Ninjago and tricked my team into helping him escape his exile. He hasn't been seen since."
GARMADON LOST EVERYTHING WHEN HE TURNED BAD-- HIS BROTHER, HIS FREEDOM, AND EVEN NOW, HE HAS NOTHING BUT A DESIRE FOR POWER AND REVENGE.
BUT IF NONE OF THIS WAS REALLY HIS FAULT...
WHAT THE GREAT SSSERPENT CAN DO, IT CAN UNDO.
IN RETURN FOR AN ALLIANCE AND HISSS AID IN OUR CONQUESSST OF THIS MUDBALL PLANET, THE SSSERPENTINE CAN GIVE HIM BACK HISSS HONOR, HISSS FAMILY, ALL THAT HE DOESSS NOT HAVE NOW.
SO DAD WOULD HAVE TO DO SOMETHING REALLY BAD TO BECOME GOOD AGAIN?
AND ONCE HE WAS GOOD, HE WOULD FEEL TERRIBLE ABOUT WHAT HE HAD DONE FOR THE REST OF HIS LIFE.
IT'S A LOUSY DEAL, AND SINCE HE'S NOT HERE, I'LL ANSWER FOR HIM--

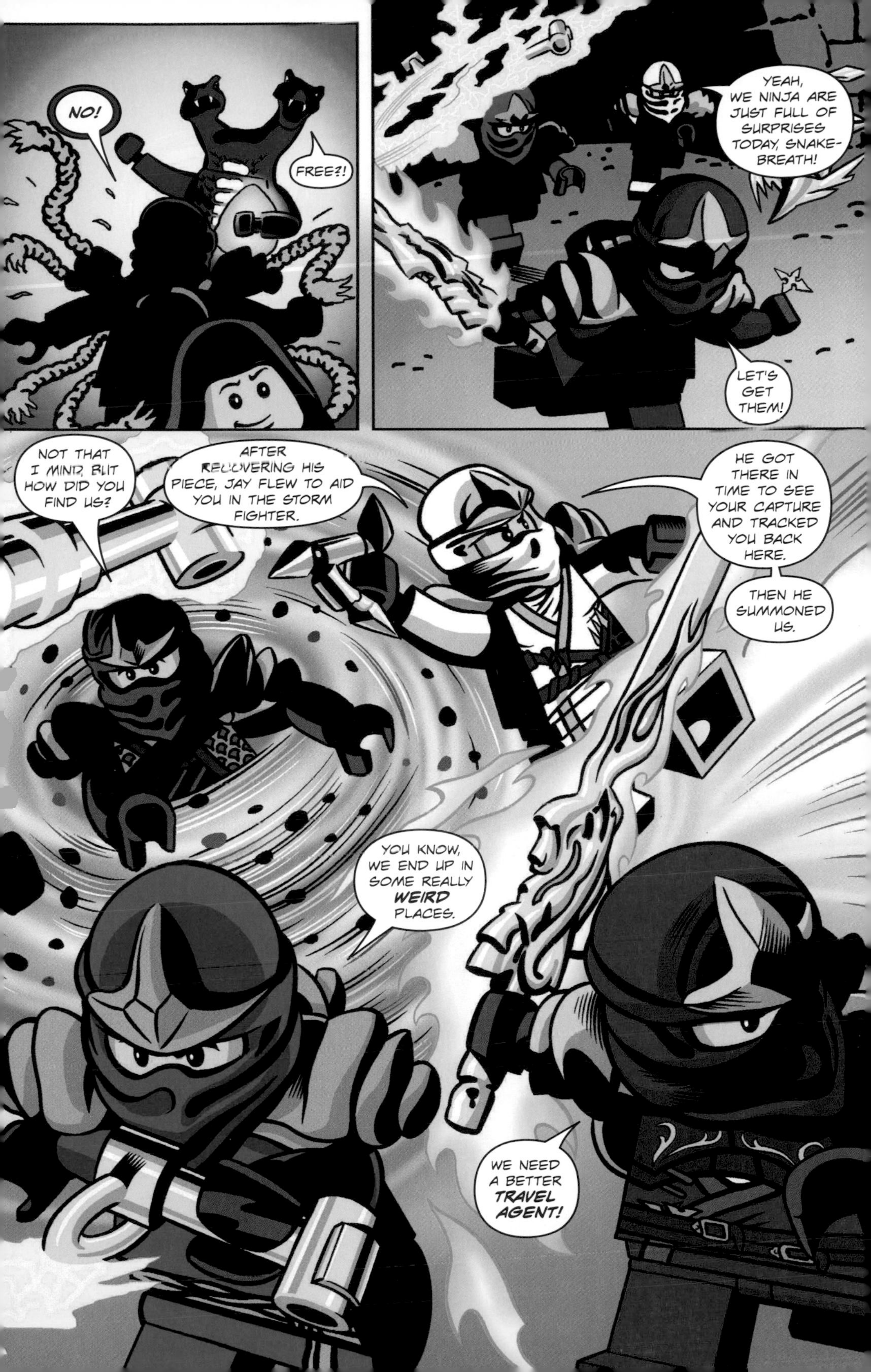

NO!
FREE?!
YEAH, WE NINJA ARE JUST FULL OF SURPRISES TODAY, SNAKE-BREATH!
LET'S GET THEM!
NOT THAT I MIND, BUT HOW DID YOU FIND US?
AFTER RECOVERING HIS PIECE, JAY FLEW TO AID YOU IN THE STORM FIGHTER.
HE GOT THERE IN TIME TO SEE YOUR CAPTURE AND TRACKED YOU BACK HERE.
THEN HE SUMMONED US.
YOU KNOW, WE END UP IN SOME REALLY WEIRD PLACES.
WE NEED A BETTER TRAVEL AGENT!

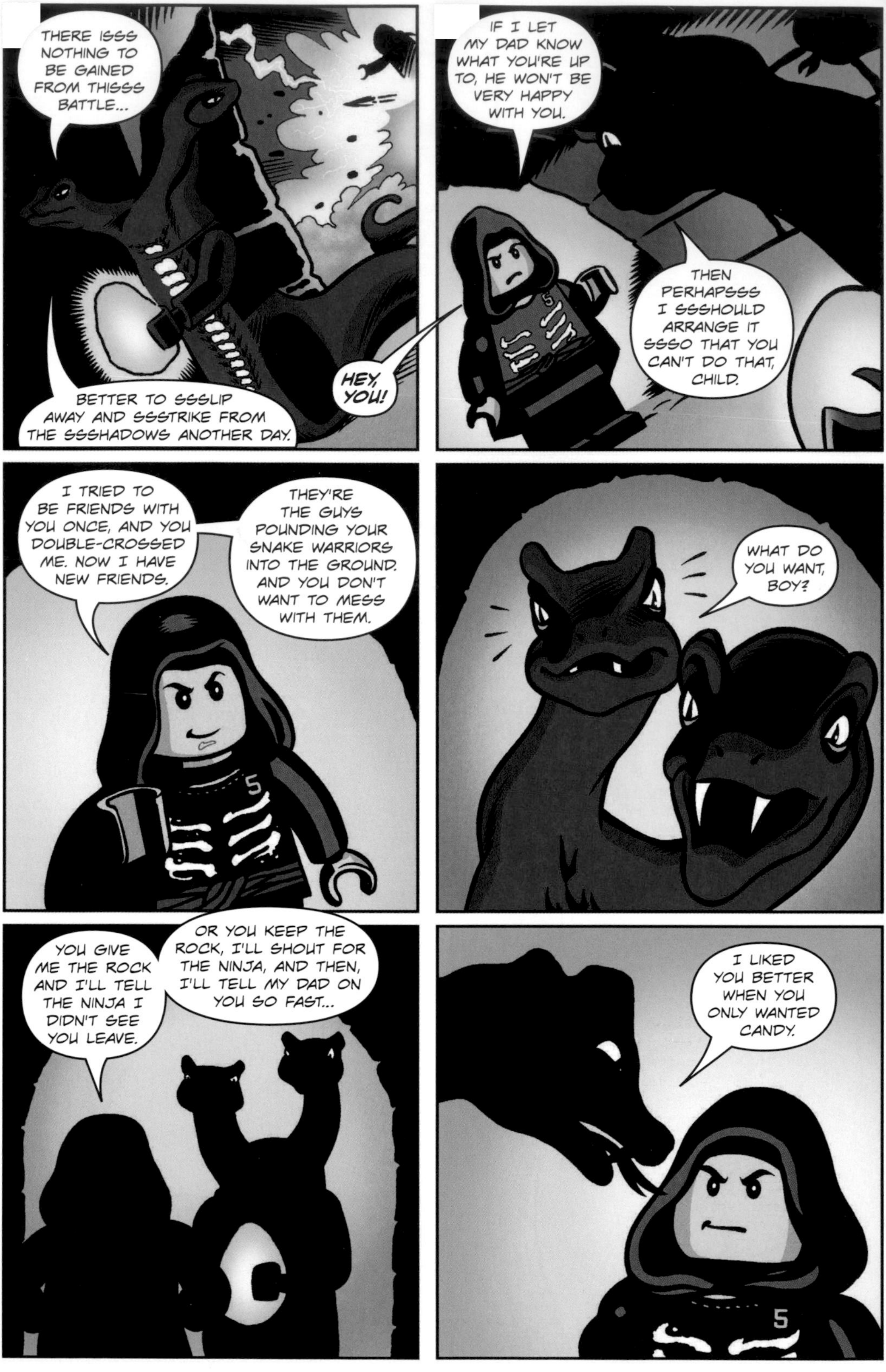
THERE ISSS NOTHING TO BE GAINED FROM THISSS BATTLE...
BETTER TO SSSLIP AWAY AND SSSTRIKE FROM THE SSSHADOWS ANOTHER DAY.
HEY, YOU!
IF I LET MY DAD KNOW WHAT YOU'RE UP TO, HE WON'T BE VERY HAPPY WITH YOU.
THEN PERHAPSSS I SSSHOULD ARRANGE IT SSSO THAT YOU CAN'T DO THAT, CHILD.
I TRIED TO BE FRIENDS WITH YOU ONCE, AND YOU DOUBLE-CROSSED ME. NOW I HAVE NEW FRIENDS.
THEY'RE THE GUYS POUNDING YOUR SNAKE WARRIORS INTO THE GROUND. AND YOU DON'T WANT TO MESS WITH THEM.
WHAT DO YOU WANT, BOY?
YOU GIVE ME THE ROCK AND I'LL TELL THE NINJA I DIDN'T SEE YOU LEAVE.
OR YOU KEEP THE ROCK, I'LL SHOUT FOR THE NINJA, AND THEN, I'LL TELL MY DAD ON YOU SO FAST...
I LIKED YOU BETTER WHEN YOU ONLY WANTED CANDY.

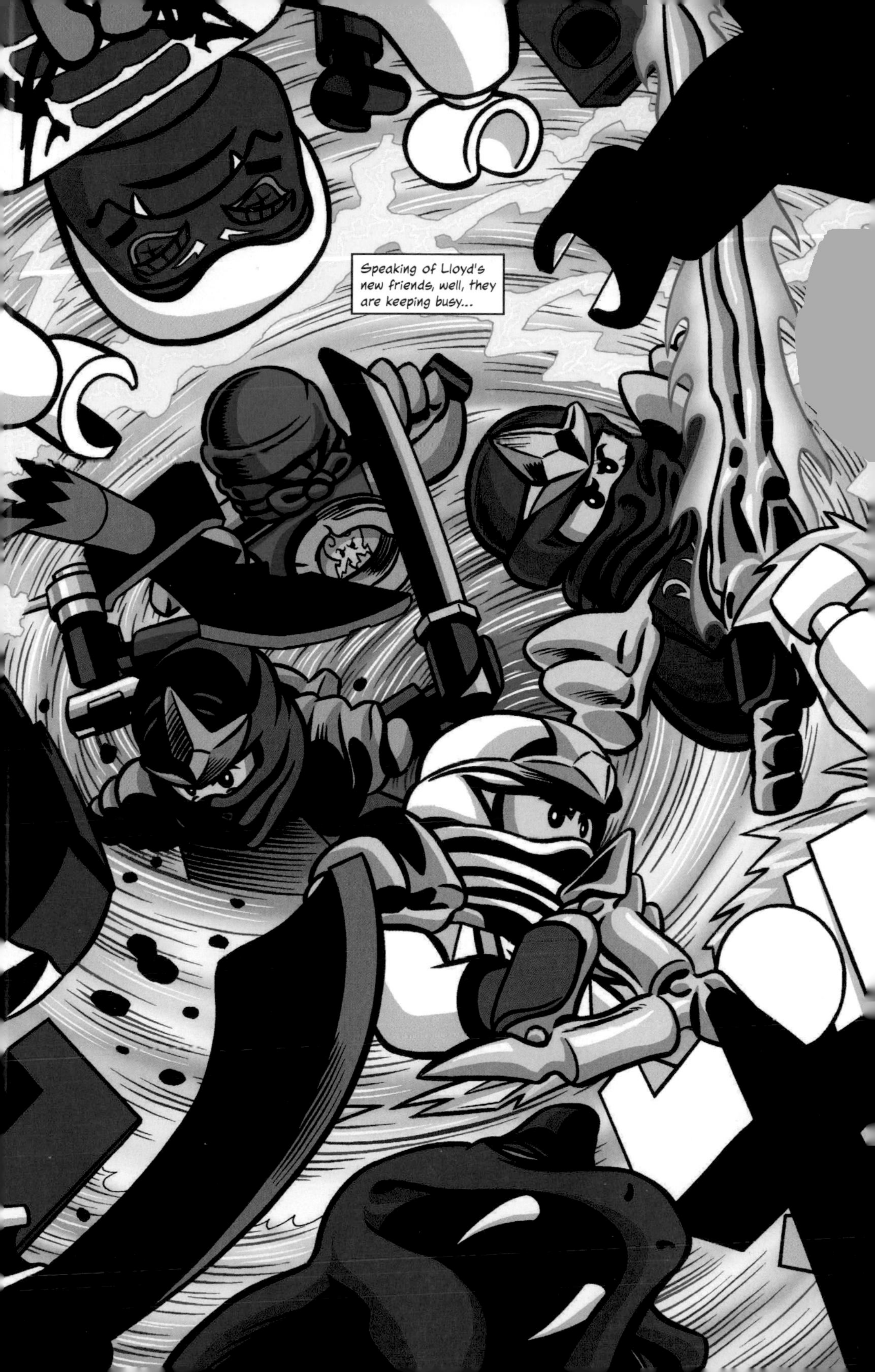
Speaking of Lloyd's new friends, well, they are keeping busy...

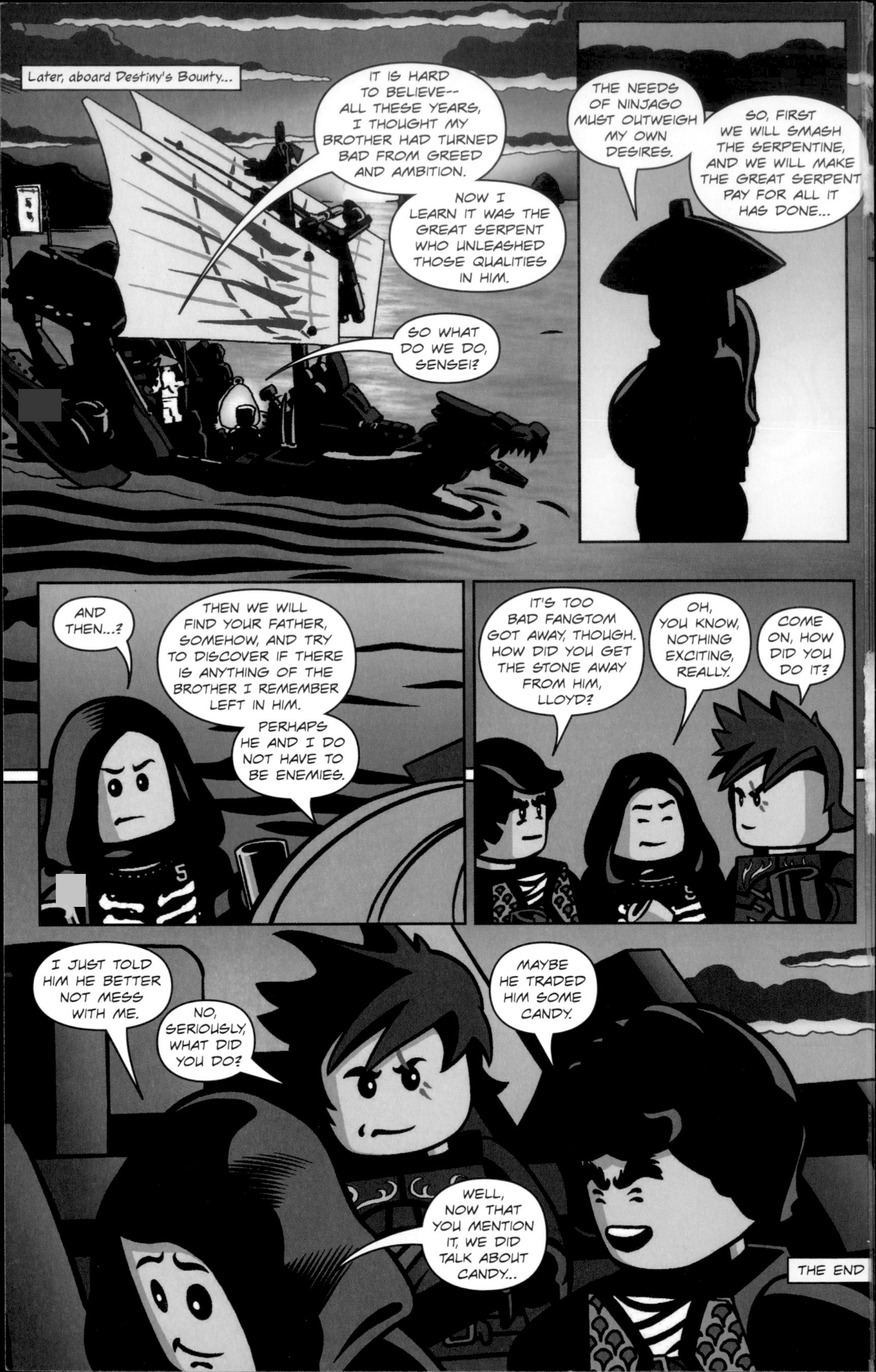

Later, aboard Destiny's Bounty...
IT IS HARD TO BELIEVE-- ALL THESE YEARS, I THOUGHT MY BROTHER HAD TURNED BAD FROM GREED AND AMBITION.
NOW I LEARN IT WAS THE GREAT SERPENT WHO UNLEASHED THOSE QUALITIES IN HIM.
SO WHAT DO WE DO, SENSEI?
THE NEEDS OF NINJAGO MUST OUTWEIGH MY OWN DESIRES.
SO, FIRST WE WILL SMASH THE SERPENTINE, AND WE WILL MAKE THE GREAT SERPENT PAY FOR ALL IT HAS DONE...
AND THEN...?
THEN WE WILL FIND YOUR FATHER, SOMEHOW, AND TRY TO DISCOVER IF THERE IS ANYTHING OF THE BROTHER I REMEMBER LEFT IN HIM.
PERHAPS HE AND I DO NOT HAVE TO BE ENEMIES.
IT'S TOO BAD FANGTOM GOT AWAY, THOUGH. HOW DID YOU GET THE STONE AWAY FROM HIM, LLOYD?
OH, YOU KNOW, NOTHING EXCITING, REALLY.
COME ON, HOW DID YOU DO IT?
I JUST TOLD HIM HE BETTER NOT MESS WITH ME.
NO, SERIOUSLY, WHAT DID YOU DO?
MAYBE HE TRADED HIM SOME CANDY.
WELL, NOW THAT YOU MENTION IT, WE DID TALK ABOUT CANDY...
THE END